D0209725

INTO THE REAL

ALSO BY Z BREWER

The Cemetery Boys

The Blood Between Us

Madness

THE CHRONICLES OF VLADIMIR TOD

Eighth Grade Bites

Ninth Grade Slays

Tenth Grade Bleeds

Eleventh Grade Burns

Twelfth Grade Kills

THE SLAYER CHRONICLES

First Kill

Second Chance

Third Strike

The Legacy of Tril: Soulbound

INTO THE REAL

Z BREWER

Quill Tree Books
An Imprint of HarperCollinsPublishers

Quill Tree Books is an imprint of HarperCollins Publishers.

Into the Real

For information address HarperCollins Children's Books, a division of HarperCollins Publishers, 195 Broadway, New York, NY 10007.
www.epicreads.com

Library of Congress Control Number: 2020937712
ISBN 978-0-06-269138-5

Typography by Carla Weise and Joel Tippie
20 21 22 23 24 PC/LSCH 10 9 8 7 6 5 4 3 2 1
❖
First Edition

For Gracie King & Griffin Schumow

INTO THE REAL

The Rippers were out again. I could tell because of a victim's screams echoing through the air. The piercing cries turned into gurgling, followed by moist chewing sounds. Teeth ripping flesh away. Lips slurping skin and muscle and hair into their hungry mouths. All because somebody had left their shelter a little too early. Rippers were nocturnal. Everyone knew that. *Stay indoors at night. Wait until day before stepping outside.* They were simple rules to follow and key to survival in Brume.

The sounds were nothing new to me. In fact, they'd become an alarm clock of sorts. A chomping, chewing, swallowing alarm clock. But that's Brume for ya. If you couldn't run or didn't hide, it would chew you up and sp—well, actually, it wouldn't spit you out at all. It would swallow you. Bite by bite. Chunk by chunk.

Good morning, Quinn. Try not to get eaten today.

I lay in place for a while, listening to the irrefutable symphony of mayhem outside, staring at a ceiling and walls that I couldn't remember, wondering where I'd slept. After some time, I withdrew the map from my bag and scanned it, looking for any clue as to where I was. It was hard to keep track of where I found rest every night, because I had to keep moving, keep changing things up, if I didn't want something terrible to happen to me. I often ended up finding shelter just in time, ducking into a house and going straight for the best hiding place. The map helped me keep my bearings. It also helped me keep my sanity. It was jarring to wake in a new place almost every morning, and it always took me a moment to shake off the fog clouding my memory.

I traced my finger around the borders of Brume. The town hadn't always been such a living nightmare. There had once been family picnics in the park and neighbors waving hello to one another. But that was before. Now those things were all but a memory. Now things were shit.

Maybe I was shit too.

Stretching and shaking my thoughts away, I sat up,

careful not to make much movement so I wouldn't attract anything lurking outside the window. The sky was a gray haze, but it was day once again. Still early, judging by the few rays of light pushing through the clouds. I'd slept the whole night through—a rarity. Despite the rotting roof and warped floorboards, the house had felt welcoming, even comforting. If I willed myself, even for a moment, I could almost imagine that it was my home. But my home was long gone burned to the ground. Not by monsters, either. No, some of the worst atrocities in Brume were committed by the other humans. Other survivors. Now home was anywhere I could find a moment's rest. Now home was me.

I stood and strapped my leather pouch to my thigh, ready to begin my morning rounds.

If I was lucky, the roaming gangs wouldn't be out for hours. They tended to party pretty late, getting drunk on whatever was left in the old liquor store or the cabinets of the houses they'd raided that day. Some of them were even brewing their own booze now. That might explain the bodies I'd found slumped out on the porch when I snuck in here last night. They'd had no cuts or bite marks that I could see. They weren't elderly and didn't look sick. They were rather young and simply . . . still. Forever still. Broken glass lay on the doormat, as if they'd dropped bottles on their way out. I hadn't thought much of it at the time. But the quiet of morning brought a clarity with it, and now I was pretty sure those two had accidentally poisoned themselves to death by drinking bathtub gin. I imagined so many of the gang members drank booze just to forget about the horrors of life in Brume, and these two wouldn't be the first to have died from it. Stupid. But then, my assumption of their stupidity was based mostly on the fact that they were members of a gang—Lloyd's, considering the X-shaped scar on each of their left cheeks. Lloyd liked his followers well marked. He reveled in the glory of being the leader of a group—even if that group was a bunch of mindless clones, intent on pleasing him enough to go on surviving. Maybe I'd never thought the gang members were all that intelligent because they were followers, and I was anything but a follower.

If you swore allegiance to Lloyd or any of the other gang leaders, you didn't have to worry so much about food or clothing or even safety. But I'd be damned before I sold my soul for an apple or a heavy jacket. The only thing that had ever tempted me was the promise of sage. It was the most valuable thing you could find or trade in Brume. The only thing known to mask human scent from the Rippers. Rumor had it that a couple of the gang leaders had bags of the stuff. But not even sage was worth selling my soul.

A woman's scream filtered in from the distance, but it wasn't followed by any chewing sounds, so I was willing to bet it was a Screamer. I'd never seen one—those who did generally didn't live to talk about the experience. But rumor had it they were large and birdlike, with bony, translucent wings. With their patchy gray coloring, they blended perfectly with the clouds as they flew above Brume. Their calls were the screams of their victims, mimicked perfectly, bait to draw other people to them. Nasty things. I hoped I'd never run into one. So far, so good.

My stomach rumbled its argument that we should find something to eat, but I pushed down the hunger. There were more important things on my plate to be dealt with first. I grabbed my bat from the floor by the dusty mattress I'd slept on. It was comforting, the sensation of that bat in my hand. The wood was worn where I gripped it. I'd had it for a long time now, and it bore the bloodstains to prove it. This bat had saved my life on several occasions. If it were human, it might have been my friend. I didn't have many of those. If I was honest, I had just the one. Lia. But she was loyal, protective, kind, and generous, which made her much more valuable than the bat.

The floorboards creaked beneath my feet as I moved to the bedroom door, pausing to listen to whatever could be on the other side of it. Ready to swing at anything that might come at me, I threw the door open, but the hall was empty, the house still. The hammering of my heart in my ears quieted until it was once again the solid, familiar thumping in my chest that reminded me on the regular that I'd survived another moment in Brume. Some days it seemed like Brume was too terrible to be real.

Moving through the house, I stayed alert but managed to keep any paranoia at bay. A steady hand and a clear head were key to staying alive in Brume—something I'd learned after facing down my first Ripper alone, when I'd pretty much failed at both. My fingers had trembled. My thoughts had been a messy jumble. It was a wonder I'd survived the encounter.

It was a wonder I was still surviving now.

Decaying floral wallpaper covered every room in the house, as if the owners had tried to bring inside the beauty of an outside world that no longer existed. Now Brume was what it was: ugly, dangerous, and primal. According to Lia, daydreaming about anything else was a waste of time and thought.

I wondered if having a worldview like that made her lonely.

The air around me carried a chill that raised goose bumps on my skin. The house creaked and groaned. My daily task stretched out before me like an endless desert—the promise-filled whisper of hope the only thing driving me forward. If I ever lost that spark of hope . . . well . . . I might as well pay the Rippers a visit and be done with it already.

Shut up, Quinn. Just shut up.

The smell of the lake filled my nose when I stepped out the front door. The familiar musty scent always stirred up memories from my past. Countless fishing trips with my dad. Swimming in its coolness with my brother. Skipping stones with my mom. But among those reflections was always *that* day. I hated thinking about it, but it lurked there, just below the surface of my recollection. The day hope became a fragile thing.

Without explanation, my dad had piled my mom, Kai, and me into a small rowboat with him, two boxes of food, and four sleeping bags. He'd paddled us as far as he could, the whole time without a word to my brother or me. But we knew what he was doing. He hadn't been able to find a way out of town on the roads or in the fields, but maybe on the other side of the water . . .

The air had grown colder the farther away from land we got, and my mom wrapped her arms around me and pulled me close to her. Maybe she did it to keep me warm. Maybe she did it to calm us both in the midst of the strange and dangerous trip. Strange, because my father had begun to wonder if all the crazy theories of the townsfolk might have weight to them, and he was running out of ideas on how to disprove them. Dangerous, because fog had rolled out over the water, and the Unseen Hands were said to lurk both in darkness and in fog.

My father's eyes had focused on the horizon, and my eyes had locked on his expression. A determined, maybe worried, crease lined his brow. He didn't speak a word. None of us did. Mom told me not to look as she wept into my hair, but I dared a peek to find what might lie beyond the lake.

We must have gotten turned around somehow, because ahead of us was the same dock we'd left. It was the fog, Dad said. We'd just gotten turned around in the fog. Gripping the paddles, he maneuvered the boat around again and headed straight for the other side of the water. The fog grew so thick that I could barely see Kai's face. When it finally thinned, I saw something ahead of us. Something familiar.

"Goddammit!" Dad had yelled, confirming my fears. We'd come around again to the dock once more. How had we gotten turned around like that twice? Was that possible? My dad might not have been a sailor, but he could certainly maneuver a boat in a single direction.

Dad ignored Mom's urging to stop, bringing the boat around again and paddling faster than he had before. Determination drove each stroke. Mom didn't seem to notice how tightly she was clutching me to her chest. Water splashed at every lunge of the paddles. Drops of it dotted my skin. The paddles hitting the water were the only sound besides my father's frustrated breathing. The boat inched forward, into the thick gloom.

After what seemed like forever, Dad's face dropped. With a shaking voice, he said that we were docking. We were going home. It was the first time I could recall hearing fear in my father's voice or seeing defeat in his eyes. It was as if the small shred of hope that he'd been clinging to had evaporated into the fog. That sound—that image—frightened me far more than any of the strange creatures that were only rumored to be lurking around town back then. Prior to that moment, my dad had clung to hope with a determination that kept the entire family certain of survival, of escape. But he was different after that. He changed forever that day. We all did.

Once more, I tucked the memory back in that part of my mind where I stored all the ugly things that I'd seen. I focused my mind on the present, where it needed to be if I wanted to survive. The fog permeating Brume was thin compared to most days, but it was still thick enough to hang over every bit of it—the mailboxes, the streetlamps, the rusting vehicles, the everything. Every day in Brume brought with it the oppressive feeling of loneliness. I missed my family. I missed my mother.

She was a wise woman, caring and tender. She'd never

questioned it when I came to her at thirteen years old and told her that I was genderqueer. Of course, I didn't know the word for it then. I just knew that I was fluid when it came to being male or female. I just knew that sometimes I was one or the other, sometimes both, sometimes neither. I just knew I was different from my family. And Mom said that made me special.

The movement of a bright orange ladybug with tiny black spots brought me back to the present. It landed on my bloodstained bat, and I watched it crawl along for three inches or so before it flew off again. Mom would have liked that.

Well. Maybe not the blood so much.

Despite the fact that the air was heavy with moisture, it wasn't raining, which meant it was a good bet that I'd find Lia outside somewhere—probably on the north end of town, since she'd stuck to the south the day before. We usually met up once a day, often spending nights together as well. But sometimes, whenever she got that look in her eye—the one that told me she was thinking about what happened to her mom—she needed to be alone, and I respected that. But together or not, we kept moving, kept changing up our routines. The Rippers had a keen sense of smell and pretty good memories. Like sage, changing locations was another tool to keep them one step behind us. We moved to avoid the gangs as well. And if we avoided darkness, we had a solid chance at dodging the Unseen Hands. As for the Screamers . . . we had no idea if moving about, using sage, or staying in the light helped keep them at bay. Defense was all just a guessing game when it came to Screamers.

I stepped off the porch and waved a quick hello to Mr. Thompson and Mr. Johnson, who were making their way down the street, eyes darting from one shadow to the next for any sign of danger. They were some of the few remaining adults. The darkness of Brume had taken the majority of the grown-ups first, but now anybody was fair game to its incessant hunger. Lia theorized that being older just slowed a person down and thereby shortened their lifespan, but I wasn't convinced. Did anyone really know why Brume had changed from a normal town to the living nightmare it was now?

I sure as hell didn't.

My footfalls were as soft as I could manage as I moved down the sidewalk, but it was impossible to be completely silent. I kept a keen eye on my surroundings, including the sky, watching for danger, ready to defend myself at a moment's notice. As I crossed to the next block, I looked at the neighborhood around me—really looked—trying to find the good that Mom had always been able to see and was quick to point out. What leaves remained on the trees were dark green and glistening with morning dew. A small vine had curled its way up the post of a mailbox ahead. If it managed to survive, it would be something to see. Flora didn't have much luck lasting in the unrelenting gloom. Such things required sunshine, and we were lucky if we got a glimpse of that big fiery ball in the sky two, maybe three times in a year. Certainly not enough to inspire hope in most of the residents here. But I had hope. I gripped it like a lifeline, holding on to my belief that Brume was either escapable or could be restored. I just had to figure out how.

I thought about the vine for the next three blocks, until I reached the eastern edge of town, where the old hardware store stood. At one point, there had been more street to follow beyond the stop sign there, more sidewalk to walk. But now both the sidewalks and street ended beneath a thick wall of fog. The fog was at its densest here—white smoky gloom that curled around my limbs as I approached the place where the pavement ended and impossible questions began. With my breath locked inside my lungs, I peered into the nothingness. I couldn't make out anything on the other side of the haze. I listened but didn't hear anything within or beyond the fog.

Breathing deep, I moved forward into the dense murk, as I'd done the day before. And the day before that. Lia called my excursions futile. Though I'd never admit it to her, I was beginning to worry that she might be right. But I couldn't stop trying. Maybe I had a bit of my dad in me. Or maybe I was picking up where he'd left off in my memory because, on some level, I blamed myself for what happened to him.

The mist kissed my skin with small droplets of moisture. The gray all around me was disorienting, but I kept my steps straight and sure, determined to escape the madness into which we'd all been plunged. The only sounds within the cloud of fog were my steps on the pavement and my breath as I inhaled and exhaled.

My heart rate picked up at the sight of something ahead of me, blanketed by the thick fume. "Please," I whispered to myself. "Please let it be something new."

A building came into view. Then another. For a moment, I felt a surge of joy. But my elation crashed down on the pavement at my feet when I recognized the houses as the ones I'd passed not two minutes before.

Free of the fog, I looked back and sighed. I refused to be defeated. Even the sturdiest of walls had weak spots. It was just a matter of finding the weak spot in this wall as well, I was certain.

With a steady hand, I marked the spot on my map with an X and tried not to focus too much on all the red dots around it that had been X-ed out. There had to be another way. There had to be something else I could try in order to ensure I was moving through the fog in a straight li—

I snapped my gaze to the hardware store. My footfalls slapped on the ground as I took off in a near sprint to the front door. My hair whipped back from my forehead. I pulled the door open, but barely noticed the heft of it in my hand. My focus was on one thing. An object, a plan, that might help me cross the gloom. Three aisles in, I found what I was looking for.

I slung the hundred-foot extension cord over my shoulder, grabbed a roll of duct tape, and hurried back to where I'd entered the wall of fog before. A stop sign marked that part of the street. On top of it were two street signs. One read Taylor Drive. The other was Oaks Avenue.

Once I'd tied one end of the cord around my waist and the other around the signpost, I wrapped each knot in several layers of duct tape, just to be sure they'd hold. The extension cord was stronger than rope, and duct tape was a pain in the ass to rip through, so the likelihood it would break was small. My only concern was that a hundred feet might not be enough to find anything beyond the thickness of the wall. But I had to try.

With a deep breath, I stepped forward into the fog, moving slow and sure. It had to work. If I kept the cord taut, I'd be certain I was still heading in the same direction. Twenty steps in, I glanced over my shoulder, but could only make out about three feet of cord. The fog was that dense. I kept moving, each step more determined than the last.

Then, my heart in my throat, I saw a shape in the distance. Shapes that became clearer with every step. Buildings. Trees. A stop sign.

A stop sign with the remnants of a broken extension cord tied and taped to its post.

A stop sign that it was impossible for me to be standing in front of.

Panic welling up inside me, I looked down at the cord around my waist and followed the taut tether with my eyes, into the gloom. Something had bitten off the end that had been tied to the sign. That same something was holding it now and could yank me into the haze at any second. My fingers flew as I ripped the duct tape off and untied the knot. I was almost free when the cord fell limply to the ground.

A scream readied itself in my lungs, but I swallowed it and released myself from the bonds of the extension cord, stumbling away from the wall of fog. This was Brume. I was still in Brume.

And Brume didn't want me to leave.

By the time I found Lia, my hands had finally stopped shaking. But only just. She was outside an old warehouse, kneeling next to a small campfire—one that she'd built the way I'd taught her, and Kai had taught me, with the sticks forming a cone and plenty of kindling tucked underneath. By the look of it, she'd only just coaxed it to life. A blond guy around our age stood next to her. I didn't recognize him—a notion that set my nerves on edge. There were maybe a thousand people left in Brume. I may not have known them all by name, but I certainly recognized their faces when I saw them. Still, it wasn't the newcomer that I was urgently concerned about. Kicking dirt onto the small flames, I stomped on the ashes, extinguishing them. "Just what the hell do you think you're doing? Christ, you're going to get us all killed!"

"Hey. I'm Caleb." New Guy stepped forward as he spoke, but I ignored him.

"Lia, you know you can't build a fire out in the open like this. What, are you *trying* to attract danger?"

"She was just helping me." His words were an attempted explanation, but he wasn't the person I wanted answers from.

Lia was still kneeling by the firepit, not looking up at me, not speaking to me.

"Well?"

Her eyes were daggers when she at last met mine. She stood, slinging her bag over her shoulder and picking up her crossbow with her free hand. Four arrows poked out of the leather quiver on her thigh. Last time I'd seen her she'd had six. "You don't know everything about survival, Quinn."

"I know that people who build fires out in the open don't survive long. Isn't that enough?" I thought she knew that too. It seemed she had yesterday. What was so different today? Had she finally given up on hope completely? Had she wanted something to kill her?

"I think we should all just calm down and start this conversation over." New Guy flashed me a smile that didn't quite reach his eyes and extended a hand. "Nice to meet you. My name's Caleb."

"Yeah, I heard you the first time." I looked at his hand and met his eyes. I didn't know him, so I didn't trust him. What if he was a spy sent from one of the gangs, or a new type of monster we'd yet to encounter? Caleb cleared his throat and dropped his hand, his fragile smile weakening. He cast an uncertain glance at Lia.

With a begrudging sigh, she took it upon herself to introduce me. "Caleb, this is Quinn."

I kept my hand at my side and looked at him, sizing him up. He was nothing special. He'd be out of our lives faster than he'd entered them, for sure. After all, he was baggage. He was deadweight. His shirt and hands were covered with dried blood. He had no supplies—not even a weapon—and there was a haunted look in his eyes that pegged him as someone who needed someone else to keep him alive. A guy like him wouldn't last a week on his own—which begged the question of where he'd been before joining Lia's side by the fire, and who'd been taking care of him. He'd have to find someone else to look after him now. Lia and I just weren't the babysitting type. Unless . . .

What if he'd come through the fog? If he had . . . if he had gotten into Brume . . . that meant we could get out. Hope welled up inside of me, but I pushed my questions down for the moment. Turning my attention back to Lia, I said, "Just tell me what you were thinking, building a fire out in the open like that."

Her breathing was louder, showing her frustration—and maybe her embarrassment, I couldn't be sure. "We were safe. I checked around, listened. There was nothing. No one. No growls, no anything. Besides, Caleb wanted to learn how."

"I'm sure Caleb would've learned just as effectively in that warehouse building or something. It was reckless, Lia. You could've died." The last word hung heavily in the air between us. I scanned the area for a good place to make camp. No way I'd risk staying inside the warehouse building nearest us now. Not with that campfire only just extinguished. But there was another not far from where we stood, on the edge of the water. "Let's get somewhere safe before something notices us."

The air felt thick, almost muggy, as we made our way—me leading, Lia taking up the rear, and Caleb nestled carefully between us. The usual chill had diminished for a moment. Maybe that meant the sun would peek its way out soon. Maybe it meant nothing. You couldn't trust anything in Brume.

Caleb double-stepped to catch up with me. His thumbs were in his front jean pockets. He wore a humble expression that irritated me for no sensible reason I could point to. "I'm sorry if I caused any problems," he said.

"It's okay. You're not the one who caused them." I threw a glance over my shoulder at Lia, who was keeping a watchful eye on the dark spaces between buildings. "I haven't seen you around before, Caleb. Where'd you come from?"

He wet his lips and lowered his eyes, his muscles tensing. I'd struck a nerve. "It's kind of a long story."

With a shrug, I said, "All I've got in this world, Caleb, are Lia, this bat, and time. If you feel like talking about it, I'm listening."

Caleb pursed his lips but didn't speak. So much for getting to know one another.

The side door to the warehouse was blocked with an old propane tank and some boards—remnants, maybe, of a past visitor's attempt at securing the place—but the big overhead door in front was clear of debris and partially open. Before I knelt, I took a look around just to be sure I was clear. Lia gave me a confident nod. She'd have my back, like always. Kneeling down, I peered inside. The space was large and open. Light sifted in through the small windows near the ceiling. Paint was peeling off the walls. At the center of the room was a pile of ashes, but it looked old, as if whoever had built that fire hadn't been back since. I dropped my bat to the ground and slid underneath the rusty door. Once I was in, I grabbed my bat, stood, and listened.

Silence.

But silent didn't mean safe.

The room appeared empty. No shadows dark enough to worry about. No indication that Rippers had ever been inside. My footfalls were quiet on the cracked cement floor as I circled the perimeter for signs of danger. The interior office door was rusted shut, and all I saw when I peered through the glass was dust-covered office furniture. From behind me, a soft creak reached my ears, sending goose bumps over my skin. I whipped around, bat in hand.

But I found nothing there to fight.

Perplexed, I held still and listened once again, my eyes sweeping over the large space. At the far end of the warehouse was another door. It stood slightly ajar and creaked as it opened an inch before closing again. The tightness in my chest released some. A breeze. It was just a breeze. I was pretty certain. But I had to make sure.

Lia and Caleb were still outside, following a system Lia and I adhered to. One of us would stand guard while the other scoped out a location. There was nothing in here but me and my bat.

The warehouse was big, but it felt like no time had passed before I reached the door. It was covered in rust. I watched it for a moment, waiting, wondering what might be lurking on the other side of it. Finally, it moved as it had before. Opening slightly. Closing again. With my left hand, I reached out to push it open, my bat clutched in my right, ready to swing. My palm pressed metal and I shoved, my heart hammering in my ears as the door swung wide.

The door led outside, where there were no monstrous creatures trying to get in. Only gray and fog and gloom. The only sound to reach my ears was that of water lapping at the shore. The handle was cool in my hand as I pulled the door shut, twisting the dead bolt until I heard the click that told me it was locked. It was a sturdy door. Odds were, it would hold. Maybe not against a Ripper, but the strength of a door was the least of our concerns if a Ripper came looking for us.

I slipped my fingers into my mouth and whistled, signaling Lia. She and Caleb slipped under the big warehouse door with ease, carrying with them some of the boards that had been outside. Lia pulled down on the door, but it was too much for her to close by herself. By the time I'd reached her side, she and Caleb had finished the job. We were safe now. Well, safer than we had been.

I nodded to the wood they'd carried in, bitterness in my tone at Lia's recklessness. "Wanna build a fire *now*?"

Lia shot me a look that I knew well. One that meant *stop*. I broke a couple of the boards into pieces, and Lia got started on the fire. The cone was solid, but she sat back with a frown. "We need kindling."

"I'll go."

Lia and I looked at Caleb, who shrugged. "It's the least I can do."

"Some free advice? Never travel anywhere without a weapon. I'll go." I'd intended my tone to be kind, but it came out sharp.

"No need. I just remembered I found this this morning." Lia pulled a cotton bandanna from her knapsack and stuffed it beneath the firewood before digging out a pack of matches as well. She removed one and struck it against the pack. The small flame burst into life, and she fed it the cloth, which soon caught the wood. In no time, we had a healthy campfire and settled around it. My bat was lying close to my side. Lia's crossbow was inches from her hand. Experience had taught us to be prepared for anything—which made me again question why the hell she'd taken the risk of building a fire outside.

The flames crackled. Small embers popped free and landed on the concrete. I watched the fire for a while, marveling at the beauty of the living element. There were so few consistently beautiful things here, but I could always count on fire. Shaking free of my thoughts, I looked at Caleb. "I'm ready to hear the long story of where you came from anytime now. So why don't you get started?"

"Jesus, Quinn, what's gotten into you today?" Lia looked annoyed and tired of my bullshit. And it was bullshit. I had to give her credit for noticing. "I already asked him about it yesterday, and he said he wasn't ready to talk about it. Give the guy a break."

I held my hands up in apology. It wasn't an authentic one and she knew it. "I'm just curious."

"You're being a jerk." She was right. I was. She must have seen the acknowledgment in my eyes, because the look in hers softened, as did her tone. For a moment, it felt like it was just us two again. "Look, just because you didn't like that I'd started a fire out in the open doesn't mean you get to be an ass all day. I know you were scared for me. But sometimes your concern shoots out of your mouth like bullets. Caleb didn't force me to do anything. So be nice, okay?"

A lump formed in my throat. I hated that I'd hurt her. I hated more that it hadn't been the first time. Nodding, I choked out, "I'll try. It's just . . . it's hard to trust someone if you don't know their story."

"It's okay, Lia. I don't mind. Really. I just have to figure out where to begin." A far-off look had begun creeping into his eyes—one that set me on edge. It might not have been so unnerving if he weren't covered in dried blood that had clearly been there for days. It made it all the more unsettling that I didn't see any wounds. Which meant it had to be someone—or something—else's blood. Blood he hadn't washed away. "My parents were . . . well . . . to put it mildly, they were really protective of our family."

I cocked an eyebrow. "And if you remove the 'mild' filter?"

"They were survivalists. Had a bunker and everything, tons of supplies. 'Just in case,' they said. I never asked, 'Just in case what?' but from the conversations I overheard growing up, it was the government they were concerned about—that and societal collapse. When the, uh, power shut off, they moved us all into the bunker to live."

He glanced at me and paused, as if waiting for me to acknowledge that that was a long time ago. I didn't. "Is the bunker in Brume?"

"Of course it is." After clearing his throat, he continued. "They had their theories as to what had happened, but they just wanted to protect us from whatever might be on the outside of that hatch. We lived down there for years. Ate, slept, bathed, exercised. You name it. Only Dad ever left the bunker. They said it just wasn't safe."

Lia was looking at him with an amount of concern I hadn't often seen in her expression. It sent a ripple of irritation up my spine. She said, "So it was just you and your parents?"

"At first. Then my sister, Kally, came along. She was a skinny little thing from birth—never really grew out of it. Cute kid too. Blond hair twisted into braids and the biggest, brightest blue eyes I'd ever seen. Mom tucked her in each night telling her fairy tales with happy endings. One night, after Mom and Dad had gone off to sleep, Kally asked me if the fairy tales were true. I told her they weren't real, but they were a nice idea." He swallowed hard. When he spoke again, his voice was a bit raspy. "Then my four-year-old sister said, 'I thought so. They sound too happy to be real.'"

My heart hurt. When I glanced at Lia, I saw the pain I was feeling for that little girl reflected in her expression as well. For a moment, there was no sound but the crackling of the flames.

"I couldn't let this sweet little girl believe that happiness was this unattainable thing. I'm her big brother. I'm supposed to take care of her. So later that night, I did the unthinkable. I opened the hatch and climbed out of the bunker." He took a deep breath. It rattled when it left his lungs. His fingers were trembling at the memory. "I just wanted to bring her a present. Like a bouquet of wildflowers, maybe, or a toy of some kind. Whatever I could find. I was willing to risk my life against whatever our parents were afraid of, for the sake of Kally's happiness. Only . . ."

"Something came after you?" I hadn't realized that I'd been sitting forward, fully immersed in his tale, until after I spoke. I didn't want to care, didn't want to feel anything but mistrust for the guy who'd just wandered his way into my and Lia's collective life—but it was difficult not to.

"No. I left just fine. Found Kally a small baby doll—a bit tattered, but the perfect gift to instill some hope in her." That far-off look in his eyes returned. "When I got back to the bunker, I couldn't figure out how the hatch door had been opened . . . or why it was so dark inside. We had lanterns with LED bulbs and an extensive supply of batteries, plus a giant crate of glow sticks. There was no reason for the darkness . . . or for the ladder to be slick as I climbed back down into the bunker. The smell . . . it was so metallic and nauseating. My hands were shaking, but I finally found a candle and a box of matches on the table to the left of the ladder. And when light spilled into the space, I saw what I had done. Their blood was everywhere, you see. No bodies. Just blood. And I . . . I . . ."

Lia wiped her eyes. Her voice was a whisper. "Oh, Caleb."

Without a conscious effort, my mind brought Kai's face

to the front of my thoughts. His kind smile. The way he threw his head back when he laughed. He was my only brother, and he was gone forever—taken by the horrors of Brume. I had to clear my throat to keep tears at bay. Caleb and I weren't so different, it seemed.

"I must not have closed the hatch right when I left. Other than the blood and my missing family, not a thing was out of place. It was . . . awful. I don't care about the supplies or the protection of the bunker . . . I'll never go back there again." His cheeks were wet. He wiped them with the palms of his shaking hands and said, "That was just four days ago."

Lia gasped. Her fingers found her lips, and she shook her head in silent horror.

I wanted to tell him I was sorry about his family. I wanted to tell him that it was possible they might still be alive. I wanted to say something . . . anything. But I couldn't find any words worth speaking. The silence stretched out until it was thin and awkward. Caleb was the one to break it.

Swallowing away his anguish for the time being, he said, "I haven't seen much of Brume, but what I have seen tells me that you girls are strong and brave as hell. It's a scary place."

The corner of my mouth twitched at his presumption of my gender. It wasn't something I'd given much thought since life in Brume had become solely about survival. Nowadays, no one cared if you were male, female, other, or nothing at all. Now all that mattered was food, shelter, weapons, and strategy.

I squeezed the handle of my bat without thought. My heart ached for the poor guy having lost his family . . . but that didn't mean I liked him. Him or his assumption.

Lia swallowed hard and found her voice once again. "Um, Caleb? Quinn's not a girl. Not a guy either, really. They're kind of both. Or neither, depending on the day. Depending on a lot of things, I guess."

"Oh." He traced me from head to toe with his eyes, confusion blending into what seemed like understanding. I hadn't seen that look in a long time. "Sorry. I just assumed—"

"I'm sure you did."

Lia threw me a glance that told me to behave and give the new guy a chance—especially considering what he'd just been through. I pushed my hood back and sighed. "So you don't know a lot about Brume."

"Not much, no."

"You don't know about the Unseen Hands? The Screamers? The Rippers?"

His eyes widened. "Are they . . . are they as bad as they sound? What are Rippers?"

"Trust me. You'll know a Ripper when you see it." I leaned closer, lowering my voice just enough that he'd have to lean in to hear me. "They feed. It's all they do."

His Adam's apple bobbed up and down as he swallowed hard. "On what?"

"On us."

Always the peacekeeper, Lia interrupted. "Quinn—"

"Y'know, a Ripper's teeth grow over a foot and a half a year. So you gotta wonder." I sat back, resting my palms on the cool cement floor, my eyes on Caleb the whole time. "Do they have to chew all the time because their teeth grow so fast . . . or do their teeth grow so fast because they're always chewing?"

Caleb's chest rose and fell in quickened breaths. His eyes darted all around us in growing panic.

Taking pity on the guy, I said, "Calm down. They're nocturnal."

"Quinn, you're scaring him." Lia flashed me a look that said she meant business.

"So what if I am? I'm also helping him." I met Caleb's gaze. "You've gotta get tough if you want to make it out of here alive."

A spark lit up in his eyes—one I recognized. "There's a way out?"

"No." The word left Lia's lips like the crack of a whip. Her eyes were locked on the fire, and as far as she was concerned, that part of the conversation was over.

But it wasn't over for me. Not just yet. "We don't know

that, Lia. There may be a way out. There . . . there has to be."

Her eyes shimmered. "Does there, though?"

The three of us sat in silence for a time, until Caleb asked, "What happened to this place? I remember what it was like before we went into the bunker. The sun came out almost every day, and people were generally happy. I mean, until the power went out."

I cleared my throat, hating that we had to bother explaining it to him, but understanding that Caleb deserved to know what had happened—at least as much as we knew. It wouldn't be fair to keep him in the dark. "Yeah, you've missed a few things being down there so long. Shortly after the fog closed in around town, people started disappearing. It took folks a while to realize there was something lurking in the darkness. It ripped people to bits, but we never saw it. Someone started calling it the Unseen Hands. The name stuck."

"The Rippers appeared shortly after that," Lia said. "When people started disappearing by the dozen, that's when everyone started to panic. I wish I could say that every death was caused by the Unseen Hands and Rippers, but people can be the worst monsters of all—especially when they're afraid." Lia's voice quieted as she spoke. I wondered if she was thinking about her mother again, but I didn't dare ask.

She was stirring something in a pan she'd placed on the fire. The smell of whatever was cooking made my stomach rumble with hunger. I said, "What's for breakfast?"

I didn't have anyone left to care about but Lia. If she needed me to drop a subject, it was dropped. If she was happy, I was happy. Well . . . the happiest a person could get in a place like this.

She finished cooking, and as she scooped servings onto three small tin plates and passed two of them to Caleb and me, she said, "By the look of the light, it's more like lunch. We've got a regular feast today. Sorry, I don't have any utensils. They must've fallen out of my bag."

Caleb dug right in, picking up small handfuls of scrambled eggs and stuffing bites into his mouth. I wondered if he'd eaten much in the past four days. I wagered not. I looked at the food Lia had cooked and couldn't help but ask, "Where'd you find eggs?"

She took her time chewing a bite and swallowed. "Does it matter?"

I could think of only one place in Brume to find nests of any kind, but there was no way she'd have gone there. Not after what had happened. Our eyes met. I did all I could to keep an accusatory tone out of my words but failed. "Lia. You didn't go to the park, did you?"

She winced and focused her attention on the food on her

plate. "It was worth the risk. For once, we get a proper meal. Besides, nothing happened."

Through a mouthful of chewed eggs, Caleb said, "We went into the school afterward. There are tons of supplies in there. Rations, blankets, tools. Medical stuff too."

He was acting like I was new to Brume, like I had no idea how to survive without hand-holding and guidance. He was acting like I was him. I knew what could be found in the school. Pretty much everyone did. We just didn't go there. Or the park. Nobody. Not unless we had very good cause. And a couple of eggs weren't worth the risk.

I couldn't help but notice that Caleb wasn't carrying any of the goods he'd mentioned. And if Lia was, they were well hidden within her bag. Maybe they had a secret stash somewhere. Something I wasn't a part of. It wasn't unusual for people to hide stashes of goods—especially gangs, who tended to booby-trap their stash locations with explosives and the like. But it would be strange for Lia to hide one from me.

My jaw felt sore. It took me a moment to realize that I'd been clenching it.

"You should be more careful. There are reasons people don't go there. You know that, Lia." The two of them exchanged a meaningful glance—a glance that made me feel like a third wheel. It was a strange sensation, to feel like I wasn't in on some secret that Lia had. We'd always shared everything with each other. "Am I missing something?"

The fire crackled as it gobbled up the wood that fueled it. Finally, Lia said, "We saw Coe."

My eyes flicked between the two of them as my heart skipped in fear. "You did not. No one sees Coe and gets away unscathed."

Lia nodded, her plate steady in her hands. "We did. His skin was scaly and black, like an oily snake. He had long, spindly arms . . . and claws."

We. The word rang through my mind like the tolling of a bell. I chewed a mouthful of food, mulling over what to say. Lia knew how dangerous it was to go to the school. Why would she risk it now for a couple of eggs and some bandages? We were hungry, but not starving. Brume had other resources for food, and any bit of fabric could be torn into a makeshift bandage. Lia knew all of that. So what had changed that made it worth the risk in her mind?

I looked at Caleb, with his sharp cheekbones and firm biceps and bright blue eyes, and I was fairly certain I had my answer. "How close did you get to Coe?"

"Twenty yards or so," Caleb replied. Tall, blond, and careless, this one.

"You're lucky you weren't seen. You're lucky you weren't killed . . . or worse." I debated not laying into Lia for doing something so stupid, but after the fire earlier, after what had happened to her mother, how could I stay silent? "You, more than anyone, know what can happen to people once Coe gets to them. How could you take a risk like that, Lia? After what Coe did to Kai? After . . . what happened to your mother?"

Despite the fire, the air around us seemed to chill as Lia snapped her eyes to mine. We never spoke about her mom.

"Look, I know you worry about me, Quinn, but I'm fine, okay? I'm a big girl. I can take care of myself. If memory serves—and it damn well does—I've saved your ass more times than either of us can count. So yeah. I'm fine, despite seeing Coe. And in case you were wondering, Caleb's fine too." Her face flushed, and her eyes grew bright with anger as she stood and kicked over the wood and stomped on the embers, extinguishing the fire. She stuffed all her supplies, minus the plate I was holding and the still-hot pan, into her bag and turned abruptly toward the warehouse door. I'd hurt her. I knew I'd hurt her. And I wasn't certain why. I only knew that I'd done it on purpose.

Way to go, Quinn.

"Lia—"

"Enjoy your meal. We're finding somewhere else to stay. Come on, Caleb." Her tone was biting. I deserved it. She flashed me a glare before turning away. "Oh, and you might wanna change your clothes, Quinn. Green doesn't look good on you."

I had no idea what she was implying. Glancing down, I noted that I was wearing what I normally did. Leather boots; gray cargo pants; a loose-fitting, faded black pullover hoodie; and a leather belt with a pouch that strapped to my right thigh. Not one thing I was wearing was green. So what in Brume was that supposed to mea—

The realization hit me hard that Lia had accused me of being jealous. Jealous of what? Caleb? With his blond hair and broad shoulders and the way Lia's eyes sparkled when he spoke?

Not even a little bit.

Lia walked away in a huff, and Caleb hurried to catch up with her. As they pulled the door open and slipped outside, he said something that made her laugh, despite her mood. Annoyance prickled its way up my spine, and I couldn't help but wonder if Caleb—someone who clearly identified as male—was exactly what Lia was looking for.

I'd filled up on guilt, so my appetite waned, but I ate the rest of the eggs that Lia had given me anyway. There was no sense in wasting food—especially food that she'd gone to such dangerous lengths to acquire.

The warehouse may have been a good place to crash, but it was tainted now by our argument, so I stepped outside.

With one last glance in the direction that Lia and Caleb had walked, I turned and headed west. There were some decent houses to be found in this direction, but nothing so upscale that I would attract any unwanted attention by crashing at one. If I was lucky, I might find some canned goods to pick through for dinner, or maybe even an actual bed to sleep on.

The streets were quiet. I hurried on my way, my head full of images of black snakeskin and spindly arms.

Coe.

Goddamn it, Lia.

Coe.

What were you thinking?

Brume had been a town at one point, but it was something else now—more like the shadow of a town. Or the disintegrating skeleton of one.

The west side was full of houses with large porches, grand entryways, and attractive details like stained-glass windows and wrought-iron fences. As with all the houses in Brume, though, the paint was peeling, the wood was rotting, and the fences were rusting.

All seemed relatively calm today, which had my nerves on edge. It was almost more unsettling not to hear screams of terror. Nothing was ever calm in Brume. Except for maybe those moments with Lia, when we'd laugh over some ridiculous memory we shared.

Time marched us all from midmorning to afternoon. As I wound my way through the streets in search of a place to crash that night, I mulled over how I'd left things with Lia. An apology was due, and damned if it wasn't due from me.

"Well, if it isn't the famous rebel, Quinn." Lloyd's razor-sharp tone cut through the growing fog, slowing my steps until I finally came to a reluctant stop and turned to face him. Shit. I'd been so distracted by my thoughts that I hadn't been paying as much attention to my surroundings as I normally did. I was lucky it was just Lloyd and his gang, and not something unearthly. Not that he was any prize.

Several of his followers were spread out in a line behind him, looking menacing and filthy in the way that stray cats sometimes did when you came into their turf. Lloyd stood in front of them, his shirt blood-spattered, a crowbar resting over his right shoulder. The X-shaped scar on his cheek was paler than the rest of his skin. He looked confident, cocky even, and just the sight of him put me on the defensive.

He'd been after me for months to join his gang. The first few times he broached the subject, he was kind about it. He made it sound like a family more than a group of thieves and thugs. I turned him down, but a guy like Lloyd can stand hearing the word no only so many times before his invitations become orders, and his orders become violent.

We'd had our arguments before, but the last time, he'd taken a swing at me. So, I'd swung back . . . with my bat.

I hadn't meant to hit him. Just to get close enough that he'd reconsider his insistence about me joining his gang. But the bat had made contact, and with that single swing, I'd bloodied him up but good. By the looks of him now, it didn't seem like Lloyd was in much of a forgiving mood. If it was just Lloyd standing in front of me, I wouldn't worry so much. It was his loyal followers that had me on edge.

"What do you want, Lloyd?"

"Want? Who says I want anything?" He eyed me with his icy gaze, waiting for a response that I damn sure wasn't going to give him. I was very aware of the bat in my right hand—the smooth wood, the worn section where I gripped it, the heft of it. When I'd hit him with it before, my chest had tightened in fear. I'd never hit a person with the bat before that—plenty of Rippers, but never a person. It had scared me. *I* had scared me.

Without waiting for my answer, he said, "Oh, but wait. I owe *you* something, don't I? A little payback for that love tap you gave me last time I saw you."

A small snort escaped me. Love tap. It was so like Lloyd to downplay the fact that I'd hit him in the face with a bat, spraying his blood over my hands. It was like him, too, to leave out the part about how he'd begged me not to hit him again before I'd walked away. The truth was, if I'd been a different sort of person, I could've killed him. Hell, a small, dark part of me had wanted to. But then I would've been no better than he was . . . and if I was anything, I was better than Lloyd.

He brought the crowbar down off his shoulder, slapping the weight of it into his free hand. The soft sound of heavy metal hitting skin seemed louder than it should have. I swore I could hear the breath enter his nose and exit his mouth, even from several yards away. Funny how your senses could be fine-tuned with an abrupt rise in tension. Suddenly, as my heart began to beat faster, I was very aware that I was on my own.

There would be no talking my way out of a fight if he wanted one, but I was damn sure going to try. I kept my voice strong and even-keeled. "So, what? You want an apology or something?"

His eyes gleamed. "For starters. But I sought you out to make you an offer."

"I'm not joining your gang, Lloyd."

Two of his thugs chuckled. One I recognized as a girl named Susan. I thought the other was a boy called Collins, but I couldn't be certain. The only thing I was certain of was their stance—poised, eager, like wild animals ready to attack. Lloyd was all that stood between them and me. At that moment, he was both my biggest threat and my temporary savior. I hated him for it.

"I'm just asking for a favor. There's a certain stash of booze that none of us are small enough to access. You go in, get the stuff, bring it out to us, and I'll forget all about our last unfortunate encounter." He cocked an eyebrow. A small smirk touched his lips. "By the way, how's Lia doing? I'd hate for anything to happen to her."

Dick move, threatening my friend, but no surprise. This was Lloyd, after all. With a sigh, I rolled my eyes. "Where's the stash?"

His smirk spread into a satisfied smile. "I knew you'd come 'round. See that house at the end of the block? The big one with the porch? There's a wine cellar beneath the kitchen. We can't access it through the basement, and there's a heavy chunk of broken marble blocking the entrance from the kitchen."

The house he was referring to was the biggest on the street. It was also the least battered by time and neglect. "I may be smaller than your goons, Lloyd, but I can't exactly teleport through walls."

His voice dripped with condescension. "A big piece of marble is covering an opening in the floor of the kitchen that leads down to the wine cellar. We can lift the marble, but only about a foot or so, and none of us can wiggle through the opening. That's where you come in. You crawl inside, hand us any full bottles you find, and we're finished here."

My need to protect Lia lurked in the back of my mind. "How do I know you'll help me get out again? How do I know you won't just leave me there?"

"The truth?" Lloyd combed his dark hair back from his forehead in a move that might have been somewhat charming if it hadn't been him. He looked at me—his eyes just as dark—and shrugged. "You don't know. But then, you never know if you can trust anyone until you give it a try. Do we have a deal or what?"

I looked up at the sky and gauged how much time I had to spare before night began, and I didn't look at Lloyd when I gave my answer. "Okay. But no matter what happens, you stay away from Lia."

"Not an easy thing to do. She's just so . . . irresistible. Wouldn't you say?" His words snapped my eyes to him. I wasn't sure if he was implying that I had feelings for Lia, or if he was threatening to hurt her in some disgusting way, but I didn't care for either. With a chuckle, he said, "I'm kidding. Naturally."

"Let's just get this over with."

Lloyd led the way down the street to the house in question. Paint was peeling from the columns out front, drawing jagged lines down them that resembled claw marks in the fading light. The porch was large, sagging some on the left side. As we moved up the steps, the boards creaked in protest. We didn't belong here, and it felt like the house knew it.

As I stepped through the door into the living room, I took note of the thick layer of dust coating every surface in the room. A sofa and two chairs, all covered in blue floral fabric, surrounded an oval coffee table, on top of which sat some coasters and a deck of cards. The lamp on the end table wore cobwebs like a woman might wear a gown. A mirror hung over the fireplace, so dirty that any images it reflected were muted.

"In here," Lloyd called from the next room. Without further examination of the front room, I entered the kitchen, which—apart from the large piece of broken marble countertop lying on the floor—looked just as untouched as the first room had. Lloyd gave me a nod. "It's under here. You ready?"

It didn't matter if I was ready or not. Before I could respond, Lloyd and two of his followers had lifted the large piece of marble with a groan. Dropping to my knees, I peered into the opening, but it was pitch-black inside. Images of blood filled my head. It was a perfect place for the Unseen Hands to appear.

Lloyd's voice was strained. "What are you waiting for,

Quinn? This isn't exactly featherweight."

"It's dark in there."

"So?"

"So, hand me a lantern or something."

"How are you going to hold a lantern *and* climb down? Get in and I'll hand you one." His patience was running thin. If I didn't hold up my end of the bargain soon, he was going to make me pay for it in one way or another.

With Lia's face locked in the forefront of my mind, I climbed through the hole and dropped to the floor below. Not an ounce of light could be found inside the cellar. I called up to Lloyd, "Okay, I'm in. Now give me a lantern."

My request was met with a lingering silence. What were they doing up there?

From behind me came a noise that I didn't recognize as anything but movement. My heart jumped to a racing pace so fast that my head swam. "Lloyd. I'm not messing around. Give me a light."

The darkness was thick. Maybe I was imagining it, but it felt harder to move. Were Unseen Hands closing in on me now? Would it be painless when they tore me to bits? Or would I feel their fingernails digging into my skin and tearing through my muscles—their hands gripping my bones and crushing them?

A tapping, scraping noise sounded to my left. Fingernails

on wood. It had to be. The Unseen Hands were coming for me. My chest tightened in panic. "Lloyd!"

The fingernails scratched across the floor toward me. They were coming. They were coming. They were co—

A small, soft body bumped into my ankle and crawled over my boot. A rat. It was just a stupid rat.

Laughter burst out above me, which made me wonder if they'd known about the rat and had planned a prank in advance. Pricks. Barely able to contain his amusement, Lloyd said, "What's the matter, Quinn?"

"Nothing," I snapped, kicking the rat away from my feet. I had to restrain myself from punting the stupid thing across the room. All that intense fear over nothing but a flea-ridden rodent. I was going soft. "Just . . . give me the damn lantern already."

Muttered words from above gave me the impression that Lloyd was handing off his share of the heavy load to one of his gang members. I had no idea who, and frankly didn't care to ask. I just wanted to be done with this little excursion and on my way to the next place to crash.

The lantern illuminated the wine cellar with a soft glow as Lloyd lowered it down to me. Three of the walls were lined with large wooden racks, mostly empty. The bottles that were there were covered in dust and cobwebs. I wondered how long wine would stay good. I imagined a long while.

After all, it was pretty much just rotten grape juice. How much rottener could it get over time?

"What's the haul look like down there?"

After doing a quick count, I said, "About ten bottles. Maybe fifteen."

"Careful handing them up. These are precious goods we're talking about."

With an eye roll, I reached for the first bottle and lifted it from its place. I think I detested Lloyd's condescension the most out of all his *endearing* traits. "Don't worry. I can manage."

It took me only a few minutes to empty the shelves, handing the bottles up to Lloyd two at a time. The rat had disappeared by then to who knows where.

I had dropped about six feet to get into the cellar. I sure as hell wasn't going to be able to make my way back out again on my own, even if I made use of the wine racks as a ladder. Once I'd handed the last dusty bottle up to Lloyd, I said, "Give me a hand, would ya? Help me up."

"Not yet." Lloyd's face appeared through the hole above me. The glow from the lantern lit up his confident smile. "You and I still have to have a little discussion first. One about loyalty."

Shit.

"A discussion about how you're going to join my friends

and me in our makeshift family."

Of course. Why had I expected a fair deal from him in the first place? Shaking my head, I said, "I'm not doing that. I told you before."

His accompanying gang members had fallen silent—either that or the majority of them had exited the house. At least three were still holding the marble up. But it was just the three of us in that cellar—me, the rat, and my utter hatred of Lloyd.

"The thing is, I could stay here and listen to your reasons—how you don't trust us, how you don't like the way we 'terrorize' people, how you think you're better off going solo for however long you have left in this world before something kills you too. Or . . ." The corners of his mouth curled into the triumphant smile of a guy who knew he'd already won. In that moment, I was glad I'd hit him in the face with my bat. "I could stand up, have them drop the marble back in place, and leave you here to starve. Or worse. It is, as you so kindly pointed out before, quite dark down there. And that lantern is running pretty low on oil."

Textbook Lloyd. "You're a real piece of shit, you know that?"

In agreement with my assessment, he offered a casual nod. "I may be. But you're smart enough to know when you're screwed. So how about you get on with agreeing to join our little family, and I help you outa that hole? It's not like it would be the worst thing you've ever experienced. You'd have protection, food, supplies . . . as much sage as you needed."

Lia's face entered my thoughts. Her hands. Her eyes. The sound of her laughter filled my head.

My tongue felt heavy in my mouth. I hated Lloyd, hated everything he stood for—no matter what he offered me. Glaring up at him, I growled, "Deal. Now get me out of this damn hole."

With a satisfied smile, he extended his hand and gripped my forearm. I pushed up with my feet, bracing myself on the cellar shelves as best as I could. Several of the smaller pieces of wood broke off under my weight. With a final hard pull from Lloyd, I was waist-high out of the hole and crawling free of it. Once I was clear, his followers dropped the marble back into place and Lloyd stood tall over me. Again, the people standing behind him reminded me of stray cats—only now I was the mouse for them to toy with. Despite my efforts to appear calm, my jaw tensed as I moved my eyes over the kitchen in search of a path of escape.

Lloyd slid his dagger free from the sheath on his thigh. The scar on his cheek was smooth and shiny. He took a step toward me, lifting his blade. His hands were steady, and his eyes gleamed with triumph. "Welcome to the family, Quinn."

Four arms pulled me to my feet and kept me captive as Lloyd approached with his blade. He put the knife to my cheek, dragging the tip of it along my skin. Not enough to break the surface. Just enough to send a frightened chill up my spine. But the cut was coming—an X on my cheek to mark me as one of their own. The physical pain I could handle. Yielding to a group of bullies and their demands—that's what soured my stomach.

A sound thundered through the house, shaking it. It was an explosion, I was sure, and not one far off. One of the gang's stash-protecting booby traps had been tripped. Lloyd eased the blade back as he looked toward the door. The hands on me relaxed, only for instant, but I jumped at my chance. Slipping free of their grip, I bolted through the kitchen and living room, out the front door. Lloyd's shouts followed me as I jumped from the porch to the ground and ran as fast as I could down the street, my footfalls slapping the pavement as I flew. It was already growing dark outside—making it darker still on the street for several blocks, under the canopy of trees. I didn't know where I was headed. I only knew that I was better off anywhere than in Lloyd's collection of mindless followers, and that wherever I was going, I had better get there fast.

Lloyd's so-called family didn't stay behind for long. Soon their approach was all I could hear. They were growing louder and louder as they closed in on me. Hunting me. Chasing me down. As if they'd anticipated an attempt at escape, several of them already had the spaces between houses ahead of me blocked. They were tunneling me in, so I had nowhere to go but forward, down the street—and I was willing to bet that I wouldn't be allowed that freedom for much longer. How long before a couple of them found their way around me, drawing near, and doing who knows what to me? I wagered they'd drag me back to Lloyd, but how was I to know?

Behind me, I heard a loud *pop*, followed by what sounded like a very brief rain shower. Screams followed, and I heard some of the chasing footfalls cease, but not all. My heart raced in fear as I pushed myself forward at a quicker pace. Another *pop*—this one closer—made me stumble. When I turned my head to glance back, I saw a mist of red hang in the air for just a moment before falling to the street. One boy was standing next to the puddle, his shocked face and shaking hands coated in it, his mouth agape, bottom lip trembling. It was the Unseen Hands. It had to be. I hadn't thought it was dark enough on the shadowed streets for them to be a real threat. But what else could it be?

I picked up my pace, my feet slapping the ground as I ran. At the end of the street, the trees broke and revealed a patch of pale sunlight. I could make it. I could—*POP!* The blood spattered the right side of my body. Before I could get even another yard down the street, another *POP* sounded to my left, covering me in gore. Pushing myself harder than I ever had, my lungs burning, I ran toward the light against a symphony of murder—nothing but screams and exploding bodies in my wake. Daring another glance back, I saw that the deaths were occurring in such quick succession now that a cloud of blood was behind me. Within it, I swore I saw . . .

No. No, it couldn't be.

The outline of hands—only visible because of the blood that surrounded them. They stretched out, reaching for me. I swore I felt fingers grip my hood. Diving forward, I stretched out my body, reaching for the light. I hit the ground with a grunt and scrambled farther, whipping my head back just to catch a confirming glimpse of what I'd sworn I saw in the blood. Only . . . there was nothing. No sign of Lloyd or any of his gang members. At least a dozen of my pursuers had been torn into liquid, specks of flesh and bone that now dotted the streets in messy crimson puddles, but otherwise, the street was empty.

A sharp pain lit up my arm, and when I looked down, my nerves were once again on edge. A rusted piece of rebar had punctured my biceps when I fell. Gripping the metal in my hand, I pulled it free. A scream tore through my throat, and my world went out of focus.

A voice—exasperated, frightened, concerned—sounded

in the distance, then moments later, in my ear. "Quinn! What happened? You're covered in blood! Jesus, look at your arm! Come on. Let us help you. It's getting dark. We've got to get you somewhere safe."

We. The word pierced my heart. Four arms lifted me to my feet and kept me balanced as we stumbled for safety. Lia's . . . and Caleb's.

22

The world was on fire and I was its kindling. I felt like I was burning up, burning alive. How long had I been like this? Hours? Days? Years? I couldn't be sure. Time didn't work right anymore. The smell of sage filled my nostrils, making me feel safe. I felt removed from the world. Maybe I was. Now there was only heat, and pain, and me.

Something cool and wet filled my mouth, and I swallowed, grateful for whatever it was and whoever had given it to me. Then there was nothing. Like sleep, I supposed, but like death too.

Just . . . nothing.

Like the edges of Brume.

Then there was the sensation of my head on something soft, my back against a hard surface. A moist cloth dabbed at my forehead. Opening my eyes took concerted effort. When I finally managed, I saw Lia kneeling beside me, wiping my fevered brow.

"Lia?" Clearing my throat, I croaked, "How long have I been out?"

Her eyes met mine, a spark of surprise lighting them. But she didn't let her surprise show in her tone. "You've been out of it for hours. At first, we couldn't get the bleeding to stop. Then the fever set in. Pretty sure it's infected."

"After only a few hours? Is that even possible?"

"You'd be surprised how fast an infection can take hold. How's your arm feel?"

"Hurts, but I'll live." She winced at my words. It was slight, but I saw it. Was she actually concerned that I wouldn't? My arm felt like a foreign object lying on my chest. Heavy. Strange. "How'd you find me?"

"It was inching toward night, and I didn't care for the way we left each other earlier, so I thought, 'If I were a giant pain in the ass named Quinn, where would I be?' The rest was just happenstance." She poured a little water from her canteen onto the rag she was holding and washed the blood from my cheeks. The cool kiss of moisture was a welcome relief.

Looking around, I could see that we were indoors, but didn't recognize the room. Moonlight poured in through a large bay window. The floor I lay on was cracked marble. Lia's jacket was rolled up and tucked under my head like a pillow. My skull felt like it was full of unstable waters, my brain sliding violently from one side to the other with the slightest movement. Images flashed through my mind of the events of the day and I muttered to an absent Lloyd, "I hope the rotten grape juice was worth it."

Lia hung the rag over the back of what had once been a chair. "What were you doing back there?"

"Nothing. Just . . . it was stupid." With my uninjured arm, I reached out and took her hand in mine. Her skin was soft, like the petals of the orchids that used to grow down by the docks. "Thank you. Not just for saving my ass from bleeding to death. For taking care of me."

She gave my hand a gentle squeeze, brushing my hair from my eyes with her free hand. "It's what we do, isn't it? Take care of each other?"

And it had been that way for as long as I could remember since the wall of fog appeared. But now Caleb was here, and I wondered if Lia might want something romantic with him. It was news to me that she might be interested in anything like that at all, as she'd never mentioned it before. I wasn't going to tell her how much it bothered me to see the way she looked at Caleb, in a way she'd never looked at me. I couldn't quite figure out why, if she *was* interested in something more than friendship, she hadn't thought of me in that way. She and I were close, compatible, balanced each other perfectly. Was it because I was genderqueer? Did she need someone who identified as male to love? A spiderweb crack spread through my heart. "Listen, Lia. About the way I acted earlier—"

"Hey, Quinn. Found this on the ground back there. Thought you might want it." Caleb had entered the room without a sound that I'd noticed, but for his voice. He was standing over me, holding out my bat. I released Lia's hand and took it from him, laying it on the floor beside me. I didn't thank him, and I didn't much care that Lia seemed to expect me to.

Lia lifted the makeshift bandage from my arm and frowned. For a moment, I felt as if we'd been in these exact positions before—as if she'd tended to my wounds a thousand times—but that wasn't true. This was the first time . . . wasn't it? "That cut's looking pretty nasty, Quinn. We should find some fresh bandages for it. Some antiseptic too, if we can."

"I'm fine." I was lying, and she knew it. So I tried another approach. The last thing I wanted was for Lia to worry about me. "It's fine."

"It's deep. And it's getting worse." One thing I had to give

Lia credit for: she didn't take bullshit lightly. "If you don't want the infection to spread, you need medical supplies, and you know what that means. I won't take long, I swear. I'll be back before you can miss me."

She had that look on her face—the one that she always got whenever she knew she was about to do something I wouldn't want her to do. She'd never listened before, but that wasn't going to stop me from trying to keep her safe. "Tell me you're not thinking about going back to the school."

She shook her head as she covered the wound once more with the bandage. "I'm not thinking about it. There's nothing to think about. This infection could kill you by morning, so waiting until then isn't an option. I'm going. I'll be back with the supplies. We need to fix you so you're nice and strong the next time you decide to do something stupid."

"I know what I said earlier about your mo—" Snapping my mouth shut, I met her eyes with an apology. "I know it was a real asshole move, but I only said it to shake some sense into you. It's dangerous there, Lia. You know that."

Her eyes shimmered a bit, but she blinked the tears away before they could fully form—tears that I had caused by bringing up her mom. Again. "Everywhere's dangerous. We're in Brume, remember?"

As if to remind us that he still existed, Caleb said, "I'll go."

"No. No one's going." I lifted my head, but immediately

laid it down again. The room wasn't spinning, exactly. It felt more like parts of it were melting and the rest of it had disappeared altogether. "I feel strange."

"It's the fever. Just rest now, okay? Everything will be all right soon. I promise. And when I get back, we can . . ." Lia's words faded as I sank back into that fiery world of darkness. I floated there for what felt like an eternity. It was less hot this time, and familiar now, so I rode it out and thought about Lloyd and the *POP*s of blood behind me as I'd run. I'd never forget that sound and the way it had grown louder as the Unseen Hands had closed in on me.

The dark heat of my fever dreams cooled before I regained full consciousness. Maybe the infection wasn't as bad as Lia thought. Maybe it was going to pass without anyone taking a chance at running into Coe.

Warmth touched the left half of my body, but it wasn't my fever and it wasn't unpleasant. When the familiar sound of crackling flames reached my ears, I opened my eyes. Across the room crouched Caleb in front of a fireplace, stoking flames within, oblivious to the fact that I'd woken. The growls of Rippers rolled in from the distance. Not distant enough for my tastes. I dragged myself to standing, feeling much more stable than I had before, and picked up my canteen. As I poured water onto the fire, extinguishing it, I shot Caleb a glare. "What are you, stupid? You can't have a fire going after dark. You might as well ring the Rippers' dinner bell. Don't you know anything?"

Caleb's face went ghost white in realization. I almost felt guilty. "I'm sorry. I just—what about the Unseen Hands? Don't they lurk in darkness? That's what Lia told me. How can we sleep knowing they could attack us while we dream?"

"You still dream?" I looked around, but as far as I could tell, Caleb and I were alone. My heart began to race. "Look, the Unseen Hands don't appear in moonlight. That's one of the reasons we sleep near windows on moonlit nights. The other is that we can see without lighting a fire, so as not to attract Rippers."

His Adam's apple bobbed as he swallowed hard. Maybe I was just hoping I saw it in his eyes, but he looked a little embarrassed at his ignorance. "And on moonless nights? What then?"

I met his gaze with a deadpan expression. "Then . . . we trade off sleep and keep watch best we can. Moonless nights are the worst."

"And the Screamers?"

"From what I've heard, we only have to worry about them during the day. Where's Lia?"

After a moment of silence, he cleared his throat, as if a lump had formed there. "How's your arm?"

I snapped, "Where is Lia?"

"She'll be back soon. She told me to keep an eye on you."

"Well, good goin', Caleb! You've barely known Lia for a day and managed to put her life in mortal peril. Way to go. Good guy. I can see why Lia seems to like you." The pain from my wound sharpened with the smallest movement. I hugged my arm to my side and picked up my bat with my free hand. There was no way I was just going to trust that Lia was safe in the school. Especially not after dark. Especially not alone.

"Where do you think you're going?" As he stood, he glanced down at my injured arm. "She seems to know what she's doing. I'm sure she'll be fine."

"No. Lia won't be fine." I met his eyes with daggers. He had no business acting like he and Lia were close, like he knew her even a little. "Has she told you what happened to her mom during your lengthy friendship?"

His jaw tensed. "No, and it's none of my business."

"You're right about that. But just so you get where you went wrong by letting Lia go to the school . . . Lia's mom went there a few years back. We're not sure why. Supplies, maybe. Curiosity. A death wish. But when she came out, she was different. Disconnected. Strange." He wore a guilty expression, but I didn't care. I got my bearings and headed out the door toward the high school. Caleb took a quick look around the room, as if debating his options, picked up a board with three nails sticking out of the end of it, and followed. I guess he'd taken my advice about carrying a weapon. "That lasted about six months. Then things got worse. Rumor has it that Coe can do many things, and I've heard more bad than good. Whatever Coe did to Lia's mom, the experience ripped out everything that made her the person she was and left her catatonic for months."

My heart raced at the memory of it all. Those hollowed eyes, sunken cheeks, mouth closed in an endless frown. The pain in my arm had added a sharpness to my tone, I was certain, but I couldn't afford to scrounge up civility while my best friend was making what could be the worst decision she'd ever made. "One day her catatonic state just ceased. And then the nightmare really began. After that, she came after Lia relentlessly, flying, her feet inches above the ground. Sometimes the tips of her toes would scrape against the gravel until they dripped with blood. But it never fazed her. Whatever it was that she had become—that Coe had turned her into—it hunted Lia for months. It tried to kill her."

Lia's screams echoed through my memory as I navigated my way to the front door. The cool night air was a pleasant welcome as I stepped outside. I scanned the area, picturing the map in my head. The high school wasn't far away. Two or three blocks and we'd be there. Hopefully in time to stop Lia from doing what I feared she meant to do.

Caleb walked alongside me in silence. As we passed a

rusted stop sign on the corner, he found some words. "That's messed up, what happened to her mom."

Understatement of the year, Caleb.

"Yeah. But the really messed-up part is that Lia was forced to kill her own mother." The image of Lia's large eyes peering out from a face coated in her own mother's blood filled my head, refusing to leave. I picked up my pace, double-time. "Or at least, the thing that her mother had become."

Caleb shook his head. He was trying to make sense of it all. I could have told him that it was useless to try. But that was his journey, not mine. I'd been down that road—the one filled with trying to rationalize what strange things occurred on the regular in Brume. It had gotten me nothing but more unanswered questions.

Caleb said, "Sounds like she had no choice. It was self-defense."

"That she didn't, and that it was. It was also the only way to put the woman out of her misery." On the corner, half hidden beneath a holly bush, was a small sage plant. It was hard to believe gang members had missed it, but I wasn't about to ignore my luck and leave it there. Slipping the knife from my boot, I collected as much as I could and tucked it into my pouch before continuing. Once it had dried, it'd make for good kindling . . . and maybe save our hides from the Rippers' jaws.

The school at last came into view. Long, dying weeds covered what had once been the schoolyard. Vines grew up the corners of the structure like wiry, too-long fingers clinging to its edges. There were boards nailed over the windows I could see, even though the windows weren't broken. It was as if someone had added the boards to keep people out . . . or to keep whatever was inside from escaping.

A thick, rusted chain and padlock held the front doors closed. There were other ways into the school, but most people knew better than to look for them. People only came to Coe's lair for two reasons. Either they were too stupid to know better, or they had a death wish of some kind. I wasn't entirely convinced that Lia meant to escape with her life intact.

A shaky breath exited my lungs. I didn't know how to save Lia. I wasn't even sure she could be saved. I just knew that I was willing to die for her.

When I spoke, it wasn't just to Caleb, but to myself—a reminder of the darkness my friend had faced. "Lia has never forgiven herself . . . or Coe. So Lia going to the school is more dangerous for her than it is for anyone. Because I think she means to take down Coe while she's here. Or die trying."

He shook his head, horrified. "I didn't know."

"No. You didn't. But you heard me tell her not to go and

you ignored me." I met his eyes with a steely gaze and gestured to him with my bat. "When we get Lia out of there, you and I are going to have words, Caleb. And if Lia doesn't survive, you'd better believe me, neither will you."

Caleb looked from my bat to me. His tone was calm and steady. "Quinn, I know you're upset. You're angry and afraid, and who wouldn't be in your situation? But I'm not Lia's keeper. I didn't force her to come here, and right now, I'm your only ally. I want to help you. I want to help her."

My fury waned. Who was I really mad at? Caleb, for not protecting her? Or Lia, for not protecting herself the way I wanted her to?

A high-pitched scream, muffled by the walls of the building, peeled out into the night. I had only heard that scream once before, but I would have recognized it no matter how muffled it might have been. It was Lia. In fear or in pain, I had no idea. I bolted for the side of the building, pulling at some of the loose boards that covered one of the windows. Before I could uncover the filthy glass panes, Caleb was at my side, yanking just as hard at the slabs of wood. When the window was clear, he said, "Come on. I'll boost you up."

The corner of my mouth twitched in insult. Dropping my bat to the ground, I jumped and gripped the ledge with my fingers before pulling myself up. Once I pushed the window open and slipped inside, I gestured for Caleb to hand me my bat. Tempted as I was to leave Caleb outside, I thrust my good arm out the window, grabbed his hand, and pulled. He climbed up and in after me, and the look on his face once he was clear of the sill was one of surprise. I smirked. "What, you didn't think someone like me could be this strong?"

His only response was dumbfounded silence.

A musty smell of age and abandonment permeated the building. A cursory glance around told me we'd entered a classroom. Dust-covered, rotting desks dotted the room. Cobwebs hung from the ceiling in wispy bunches. The tiles of the floor were filthy. Many were cracked or missing. On the wall at the front of the room hung an old, green chalkboard. Someone had carved sharp, jagged words into it that sent an unsettling feeling through me, as if I'd heard the words before.

You can't run from the monster. The monster is you.

Shaking off a sensation that I could only attribute to nerves, I pushed forward into the hall, which wasn't any more welcoming. Paint had peeled from the walls and the lockers lining either side.

Caleb turned left, clutching his weapon in his hand, but he didn't get two steps before I stopped him. "Where are you going?"

Nodding farther down the hall, he said, "The stairs are right there. I'll check the second floor. You cover this one."

When is splitting up ever a good idea? Never, Caleb. The answer is never. "We should stick together."

"From the sounds of it, we should find her fast and get out of here. Besides . . . I'm worried about her." He ran a hand through his hair, brushing it back from his face. He shifted his feet, and his skin flushed, as if he were embarrassed about something.

"We're both—" I cut my sentence short, in stark realization. The blush on his cheeks. The way he kept darting his eyes all around.

Lia had a thing for Caleb. And he returned those feelings.

I felt sick. Heartbroken and sick. In a case of boy meets girl, where did a genderqueer person like me end up?

He said, "I'll be back. If you find her, just shout, okay?"

All I could manage was a nod in response. Once Caleb was out of sight, I pushed my heartache way deep down inside of me. There would be time to hurt later. Right now, our lives were in danger just by being here. We had to find Lia and get the hell out.

Apart from the creaks and groans of the aged building, I heard no sound out of the norm. The fact that I wasn't hearing any more screams made me question whether I'd heard one in the first place. But Caleb had clearly heard it as well. So Lia had to be here somewhere. Didn't she?

It occurred to me that we could be too late. Lia might already be dead. I wasn't sure which would haunt me more—her screams, this horrible silence, or the impossible, painful lack of her.

Lia, who'd saved my life on more than one occasion. Lia, who looked at Caleb in a way she'd never look at me. Lia, who I feared might need a person who was born in a binary gender to fill her heart.

I'd never questioned our connection before. We were a team, she and I. And no one could ever come between us . . . that is, until Caleb walked into our lives.

A low chattering as soft as a whisper reached my ears. I turned my head, trying to locate its source. It sounded like words, many voices running together, but I couldn't discern anything sensible from it. The hair on the back of my neck stood on end. Lia wouldn't speak so softly if she were in trouble. But if it wasn't Lia I was hearing, then who . . . or what . . . was it?

Keeping my footfalls soft, I moved down the hall. The chattering didn't get louder or quieter no matter where I was, which might have been the most disturbing thing about it. Its rhythm was so constant, for a moment I questioned whether it was coming from somewhere in the school . . . or from inside my head.

Movement at the end of the hall startled me. I hadn't

gotten a clear view, but it looked like a person dashing to the right. Lia. It had to be. But where was she going? Resisting the urge to call out to her, I picked up my pace, hurrying as quietly as I could. It wasn't until I reached the corner that I realized the strange chattering had ceased, replaced by another eerie silence.

I didn't have time to wonder what that meant. I had to get Lia. With sure steps, I turned the corner. At once, the air locked inside my lungs. Just disappearing into one of the dilapidated classrooms were dark, spindly arms, almost too thin to carry the creature's weight, but they did so, impossibly. The body of the thing—large, black, and scaly—paused for a moment in the doorframe, without turning around to face me. Without even looking at me, it was aware of me.

Coe.

My body felt like it was frozen, but like every cell was vibrating as well. The pounding of my heart filled my head, and in my terror, I wondered if it was loud enough for Coe to hear it. My world tilted on its side as my body reminded me of the infection I was fighting. The sensation of claws digging into my brain overwhelmed me, a strange dizziness on its heels. Pinpricks covered every inch of my skin. My fever was back. There was no doubting that. I wasn't standing still in the presence of the most dangerous being in all of Brume because I wanted to be—I stood there not knowing if I *could* turn away in my current state. What's more, an engulfing sense of wrongness had glued me to the spot. But I had to break free of it all. I had to get as far away from this place as I could, no matter the cost.

Pivoting on my heel, I turned to run.

21

"I can't believe you! How can you do this to me? To us? To yourself, Quinn? It doesn't make any sense!" Lia was pacing back and forth, her footfalls causing the picture frames on my dresser to shake. Her fingers turned white as she gripped her cell phone. At the same time, the sunshine streaming through the window caught her hair just right and made it gleam. Brume had gifted us with an early summer, so I'd opened my bedroom window to let the soft breeze in. On it came the scent of my mom's rose garden. It would have been the perfect day, if I weren't causing so much chaos for everyone I'd ever loved. "I mean, it's not like you're having an operation to turn into a guy or something. You just like girls. There's nothing wrong with that!"

I sat on the bed watching her, wincing a bit at the way she referred to someone transitioning, fiddling with the beaded bracelet on my wrist—a birthday gift from my brother, Kai, last year. I knew Lia was going to be upset, but I'd been hoping that maybe she'd take the news better.

She was right. It probably was senseless. But it wasn't like I had much choice in the matter. Mom and Dad had made that crystal clear. Go get help for what they called my "condition," or they'd kick me out. At least with the camp, I'd be back in a couple weeks and could see Lia again. Being homeless would ruin everything for me. Lia's foster parents wouldn't take me in. Kai would have to go back to the dorms, and his roommate probably wouldn't want his little sister sleeping on the floor, so I couldn't stay with him. I'd have nowhere to go. Besides, there was still a lingering question in the back of my mind that I needed an answer to. Was I really a lesbian? Or was my relationship with Lia all a mixture of confusion and curiosity? "I just . . . have to give it a chance, Lia. Can't you just support me and tell me everything will be all right?"

"No, I can't." The mattress squeaked as she sat down beside me and cupped my hand in hers. Her fingers meshed so well with mine, like our hands were made to be joined.

Her skin was tan, mine pale. Her fingernails were clean, but unpolished. Mine had a fresh coat of pink. Giving her hand a squeeze, I met her gaze. I didn't think I'd ever seen her eyes so blue. "Those people, Quinn—they brainwash, they lie, they twist your heart into believing it's wrong, and you're willingly going to enter one of their stupid programs?"

She was giving voice to everything I was afraid of, which didn't help, exactly. "I'm not going totally willingly."

"I don't see you putting up much of a fight."

What did she expect me to do? To oppose my parents like I was the protagonist in some progressive movie who could defy the odds, stand against homophobia, and come out on top?

"I'm seventeen, Lia. I don't have much of a say in what I can do for another eleven months."

"I know. I'm just . . . scared for you." She'd lowered her voice—maybe in defeat, maybe in pain and disbelief. Probably all of the above.

"I have to do this."

The dam broke. Tears spilled over her cheeks. "But why?"

It was the only secret I'd kept from her, the wondering I'd hidden away since we'd started dating last year. The thought of revealing my doubts about my orientation made my stomach shrivel into a hard, solid ball. But I owed her that much. "What if my parents are right? What if I'm not gay?"

The look on her face was one of shock and heartbreak. The truth may set you free, but that doesn't mean it will do so without ripping you to bits first. "Then explore that question without doing *this*. Get a therapist. Start taking yoga. Do whatever you have to do to clear your mind so you'll know what your truth is. But I'm begging you. Please don't go there, Quinn. Please."

"Lia—"

"I'm not asking you to stay for me. I'm asking you to stay for yourself. People like that—who say that being anything but straight is evil—people like that are dangerous." Her voice cracked on the last word, and with it, my heart.

The breeze picked up, billowing the sheer white curtains. A beautiful day, indeed. But not for me. "I'm not going there to be 'cured.' I know that's what my family wants, but it's not what I'm doing. I'm going there because I just don't know anymore."

She brushed a strand of hair from my forehead and cupped my cheek in her silk-soft palm. I leaned into her touch and closed my eyes, blocking out the world for a moment I hoped could last forever.

"You're not supposed to be here." My eyes flew open at my mother's biting tone. She was standing in my bedroom doorway, eyeing Lia with more judgment and dislike than I'd ever seen.

As a reflex, I stood up and took two steps away from my bed. Away from Lia. "We were just talking."

"Alone in your bedroom? Isn't this precisely what we discussed?" She'd snapped her eyes to me but turned her attention right back to Lia, as if my girlfriend were some sort of dangerous animal that had to be watched at all times. "You need to leave her alone and let her heal."

"She can't heal." Lia stood, venom coating her every word. "Because she isn't sick."

Mom's face went red. She pointed to the door and barked, "Out."

The two women I cared about most in the world stood at odds in front of me, and I couldn't think of a single way to calm the chaos I'd created. "Mom—"

"Now. And if I ever see you with my daughter again, there will be serious consequences."

I didn't know what my mom had in mind. A restraining order, maybe? I only knew that she meant what she said. Once my parents made up their collective mind about something, nothing could change it.

Lia cast me a glance, wiping away a tear as she stormed out of the room. "Have fun at Camp Bigotry."

I whispered, "Lia—"

"We're leaving in five minutes. Are you finished packing?" For a brief moment, my mother's frosty exterior thawed. "Oh, sweetheart. One day soon you'll see this is really for the best. You're just confused. Everything will be all right. You know your dad and I only want what's best for you. Camp Redemption can help you."

"So, what if I go to Camp Redemption and get . . . get . . ." The word felt strange to say, but I had to say it. It was the only way she'd really hear my question. ". . . better? If I get better, can Lia and I still hang out?"

Her eyes betrayed her answer before she even spoke. "We'll discuss that when you get home."

If I determined at this camp that I was straight, I was going to lose Lia. But if clarity led me to confirm I was gay, my parents were still going to do all they could to remove her from my life.

Let them try.

"How long will I be there?"

"As long as it takes for you to get well." She held my gaze for a moment, as if there was more that she wanted to say but was struggling with how to say it. More than anything, I wanted her to tell me that she loved me no matter what. I wanted her to say that it didn't matter if I was gay, straight, or anything else. That all that mattered was the fact that I was her child. I waited for those words, or some like them, to leave her lips, but instead she said, "You know, you'd look so pretty if you'd grow your hair out."

It took me a moment to remove the lump from my throat. "I guess."

"Hurry up now. Your dad's got the car running." With that, she whisked herself out the door, leaving me behind with more questions than answers, more heartache than support.

"Hey, kiddo. You okay?" Kai was leaning against my doorjamb, his arms folded in front of him. His chocolate-brown hair was hanging in his eyes a bit. He needed a haircut, but I knew he wouldn't get one. The last time he'd been home from college, he said he was growing it out just to piss off Dad. Much like my parents, once Kai had set his mind on something, he did it. Even if it was just a simple act of defiance.

Releasing a heavy sigh, I said, "You've gotta ask?"

The corner of his mouth pulled a bit to the side, like he was trying to avoid frowning. "They just want the best for you."

"But do they, though? I mean, what if I'm not confused or sick or whatever? What if I really do like girls?"

He brushed his hair from his eyes and looked past me to the window. Maybe he was checking to see if Mom was outside by the car, out of earshot. It seemed like something he'd do. We'd shared and kept each other's secrets for as long as I could recall. "Are you saying you're happy being gay and just going to this place to keep the peace?"

"No. I really don't know for sure if I'm gay or not. Sometimes I think so. Some days I don't. I'm going to Camp Redemption to try to figure that out." It sounded stupid when I said it out loud, but that didn't make it any less true.

The crystal hanging in my window was reflecting beautiful, bright dots of light on the wall. Small things. But they made all the difference. Like Kai.

He said, "You just make sure you're the one answering that question, okay? Nobody but you has the right answer. Plus, you may find out you're something else altogether. Bisexual, pansexual . . ."

"What about you?"

"I'm straight."

Only my brother could make me smile in almost any given situation. "Not what I meant. How would you feel if it turned out I was into girls?"

"Honestly, I'd feel conflicted." My stomach dropped in surprise. I'd thought that if any one person would support me no matter what, it would be him. An aching loneliness crept into the corners of my heart. But then he said, "On one hand, we could check out girls together. On the other, you'd be competition."

I rolled my eyes at him and gave his shoulder a light shove. "Be serious for a minute."

Outside, Dad honked the horn in three quick bursts.

I sighed, flicking my eyes toward the window. "Do you think I could be the daughter they want and the girl Lia wants at the same time?"

"I feel like what you're asking me is a paradox."

"I'm just looking for a solution that won't make me lose Lia or our parents."

"That's the essence of a paradox—it cannot be solved. It essentially asks a question that cannot be answered." Kai's smirk melted away. He met my gaze and held it. Sometimes I forgot how pretty his eyes were.

"And if it is a paradox?"

"Putting it in the most scientific of terms . . . you'd be fucked." His tone was teasing, his smile easy. "Look, if you want answers and think this place might help you find them, then go. I'll be here waiting for you when you get home. Straight or gay."

My eyes burned with tears. I hurried so fast into his embrace that I swore I almost knocked him over. My words came out in a rattle. "I worry I'll break Lia's heart."

His breath was warm as he spoke into my hair. His arms were warm wrapped around me. All of Kai was warm. "You can't risk your heart to protect hers. If you're into guys, then you're into guys and she's gonna have to understand."

Sniffling, I pulled back from him and dried my eyes with my hands. "What if she doesn't?"

"Quinn, we're waiting!" Mom called from out front. The tone of her voice suggested that if I didn't walk out the front door right away, she and Dad were going to carry me out.

Kai picked up my backpack and carried it downstairs. We stepped out the front door onto the porch, and he handed the bag to me. I grabbed it, but he didn't let go right away. "Stop worrying so much about what other people think. It's not their life. It's yours. And you only get one. Live it out loud."

I hugged him tight, and the strange feeling that I'd never see him again—that I'd somehow lost him before—washed over me. I pushed that feeling away, attributing it to nerves. As I slid into the back seat and closed the door, Kai waved. I waved back and let my fingers rest for a moment against the glass. "There's a student council meeting in three weeks, right before school starts. Do you think I'll be able to make it?"

Mom said, "Oh, honey, I'm sure you'll be better by then. If not, I've been informed that Camp Redemption offers homeschooling as part of their program. Just in case."

I bit my bottom lip. Was she really thinking that far ahead?

We pulled out of the driveway and turned left, leaving everything but my questions behind. The drive across town was brief and quiet, and I was grateful when my dad turned on the radio. It made it easier for me to sit in wondering silence for a while. On one corner was a stop sign, with two street signs on top of it. One read Taylor Drive. The other read Oaks Avenue.

We passed tree-lined streets and kids playing in their yards, streetlamps and historic homes, postal employees delivering mail with a sun-drenched background. We passed the cave in the park where Kai and I had played when we were younger. Something about it triggered a memory I couldn't pin. I'd entered the cave once. And at the back there was . . . something. Something that had frightened me. I couldn't remember what now.

My thoughts dissolved as we passed my high school, now closed for the summer. Leaning against the building was a man I didn't know, inhaling on a cigarette as he watched our car pass by. As he drew in the smoke, the ember at the tip glowed. He wore a long, black snakeskin trench coat that seemed like it might be too warm to wear in the summer. His dark hair, wet and stringy, hung in his eyes. As I watched him, I got the unsettling impression that he was watching me back. The sight of him made goose bumps rise on my skin, despite the warm weather.

When the sidewalks ended and the rural area outside of Brume proper began, my dad slowed the car and turned us onto a small, winding road. At the end of that road was a large, white farmhouse. The grounds were filled with lush flower gardens and big trees. The porch was home to two rocking chairs and a crystal wind chime. It didn't look like a gay conversion camp. At least, not at all what I'd imagined. It looked like a place people went for convalescence. It looked nice. Picturesque. Almost too pretty to be real.

My nerves let up some as Dad brought the car to a stop in front of the house. He and Mom exited right away. I took two deep breaths before opening the door and getting out of the back seat.

A woman wearing a white cotton dress, pink gardening gloves, and a straw sun hat saw us and smiled. She stood from where she'd been tending to a bed of impatiens and removed her gloves, dropping them into a basket containing a variety of gardening tools, and approached our car. "Welcome! It's so nice to meet you, Quinn. I've heard so much about you. I'm looking forward to getting to know you. My name is Alice. I'm the liaison here at Camp Redemption."

"Nice to meet you." The screen door opened, and a girl stepped outside with a watering can. I watched as she tended to the ferns that were hanging along the porch. She was dressed in jeans and a T-shirt but was clearly too young to be staff. I'd thought, for some reason, that patients—or whatever we were called here—would be in scrubs or something. The normalcy of her attire was comforting.

"You're probably a little nervous about coming here. Don't worry. That's normal for newcomers. But it won't take long for you to view our camp as a second home. A safe space of healing and support. I'll just get one of our staff to help you to your room." Alice scanned the grounds, squinting her eyes against the sunlight. "Roderick? Could you come help—"

"I'll help her."

A guy my age appeared to my left. He kept his dark eyes focused on Alice, but I got the impression he was enjoying having an audience for this encounter. Maybe for any encounter.

The look on Alice's face said she didn't care much for him. "I'm sure Roderick can—"

"Or if you'd prefer, I can stay here and chat with her parents while you show her to her room. Choice is yours." I couldn't see the smirk that went with that, but I knew it was there. He extended his hand to me, and as I shook it, he said, "Name's Mike. Mike Oxlong. And if you get that joke, you and I are gonna be fast friends."

It took every ounce of my will not to crack up laughing. Mike Oxlong. That was fantastically dirty. Lia certainly would have been fast friends with this guy.

Alice paused, as if debating how not to make a scene. Finally, she relented. "Thank you, *Lloyd*. It would be nice of you to help our new friend get acclimated. Quinn, you'll be in room three. Lloyd will see that you find it all right. Your parents and I have a few details to discuss, but you should say your goodbyes now so we can begin your healing process."

My heart felt both heavy and hopeful, though I wasn't sure how it could feel both ways at the same time. I looked at my parents. My dad wouldn't meet my eyes. My mom looked like she could start crying any minute. "So . . . I guess I'll see you soon, then, huh?"

Dad gave me a brief hug and said, "Work hard. Get well. God loves you, Quinn."

Mom squeezed me tight and kissed my cheek. "Bless you, sweetheart. Everything will be okay."

"Ready?" Lloyd picked up my suitcase and flashed me a smile. With a nod, I slung my backpack over my shoulder and followed him up the porch steps. As he held the screen door open for me, he said, "So. The tour. Not counting staff quarters, there are ten beds here. Eight are in the main house. The other two are in the guesthouse. Only six beds are taken at the moment. Looks like you lucked out. The AC is way better in here. If you need me for whatever reason, I'm in the guesthouse by myself, for the time being."

The inside of the house was just as quaint and welcoming as the outside. Cozy-looking furniture, tasteful wall art. It was everything you'd expect a modern farmhouse straight out of Pinterest to be. "If there are open beds in the main house, why are you in the guesthouse?"

"Because I'm . . . How did Dr. Hillard put it?" He looked up, as if the answers were written on the ceiling, before snapping his fingers in recollection. "Oh yeah. A potentially harmful influence."

"Have you been here long?"

"Six months so far." He led me up a set of stairs to the second floor. The hall was long, and each door was painted a different color. Lloyd snickered. "Think they have any clue that it looks a bit like a pastel rainbow up here?"

He wasn't really asking me, so I didn't really answer him. Besides, I had a more pressing question for him. "Six months seems like a long time. The program. Is it . . . working?"

"Not for me, sweetie. But then, I'm not the one with the problem. My parents think that the best way to solve a problem is to send it away until it fixes itself. The thing is, I may be pansexual . . . but I'm sure as hell not broken. Nobody here is. It's just that so many of them fear that they might be." His words saddened me, because I was one of the "them" he was talking about. I wasn't sure I felt whole loving another girl, when I had to keep it behind closed doors. What I had with Lia didn't always feel like real love—maybe because we always had to hide it.

Lloyd interrupted my thoughts by rapping on the lavender door at the end of the hall. "Here's your room."

When I turned the glass doorknob and pushed the door open, I was greeted by a room as nice as any guest room in a real home. A hand-sewn quilt lay on the four-poster bed, atop which sat several decorative pillows. The Tiffany–style table lamp on the nightstand depicted deep-red roses and what looked like black vines. The tall dresser near the window was painted in crackled cream-colored paint. In the corner, there was a green wingback chair. The air smelled like cinnamon, but not in an overpowering potpourri way. More like someone had baked a pie in the kitchen and the delicious scent had found its way here. I nodded and set my backpack on the bed. "It's nice."

Lloyd's jaw clenched for a moment. "Not too bad for a gilded cage, right? If you like watching TV, you're shit out of luck. Secular entertainment isn't allowed or condoned here at Camp Happy Sunshine. There's a bathroom at the other end of the hall, near the stairs we just came up. Dining room is down the stairs to the right. Dinner's at six. I'll save you a seat."

"Thanks."

"Don't thank me. All I did was show you to your room at the end of the rainbow." With a wink, he exited, shutting the door behind him.

The end of the rainbow. I couldn't help but think that would have been a more fitting name for a place like this than Camp Redemption was.

The single window was framed in walnut, with white sheer curtains that reminded me of the ones that hung in my bedroom back home. Outside, the sun was shining down on a couple of gardeners, along with Alice and a man wearing a sweater vest and tie, who I could only guess was the Dr. Hillard Lloyd had referred to. My parents were pulling away from the house, and I watched their car until I couldn't see it anymore. It was strange, to be away from home and not know for how long, or even what to expect during my stay here. What if I hated it? What if I loved it? What if it changed me?

Stop it, Quinn. Focus on the basics before you move on to existential questions.

One of the gardeners was standing in the yard leaning on a rake. His hair was stringy and looked wet even from a distance. He looked so familiar to me, but it took me a minute to recognize how he very much resembled the man who'd been leaning against the wall of the high school. The sight of him made my stomach flip-flop. Not only was he strange and out of place beside all the clean-cut employees at Camp

Redemption—he was also looking right at me, with a small, knowing smile that sent a chill down my spine. He offered me a casual salute.

I drew the curtains closed and started unpacking. It was impossible not to notice that my hands were shaking as I put my clothes away.

When I'd finished, I glanced at the clock and was surprised to see that it was so close to six. With a deep breath, I opened the door and stepped into the hall. It seemed so much longer now that I was walking it alone. Maybe that was just because I didn't know exactly what lay ahead of me—both literally and figuratively. The stairs creaked under my feet as I descended, and I heard voices coming from the back of the house. Following them, and with Lloyd's directions, I found my way to the dining room, which looked just as homey and welcoming as the rest of the house. Setting the table was a boy with blond hair and blue eyes. He looked to be lost in his own world, and wherever that world was, it didn't look like a happy place. I cleared my throat so that I wouldn't startle him. "Hi there. I'm Quinn."

A fork dropped from his hand to the table, but he recovered and flashed me a small smile. "Hey. Um. Good to meet you. I'm Caleb."

"Want some help?" That lurking pain crossed his eyes again, as if I'd pulled him from wherever his mind had been only to push him right back there. Maybe what I'd asked was a loaded question here. I gestured to the table. "With the dishes, I mean."

"Oh. Yeah. That'd be cool." The darkness in his eyes evaporated once more. As we worked to set seven place settings, he said, "So, you're new here."

"Yeah. Just got here today. How about you?" He was taller than me, but a bit shorter than Lloyd. His fingers moved deftly as he folded a napkin and put it on the table.

"Two months."

And here I'd been hoping that Lloyd's life sentence was the exception, not the rule.

"What's it like? I mean—"

"Treatment? It's . . . slow." His frown was immediate and lingered on the edges of his mouth when he spoke. "Alice and Dr. Hillard are understanding and patient, though. I just . . ."

I waited for him to finish his sentence, but he didn't. "You just what?"

His blue eyes grew moist, reminding me immediately of the ocean. I'd only seen it once, but was captivated by the very sight of it. The depth and expanse and everything of it. He said, "I just wish I was recovering faster."

Recovering. The word hung in the air like the toll of a bell. "Can I ask why you came here?"

He shrugged. "Same as you, I imagine. I keep having these . . . urges. Unhealthy feelings about other guys. Sick thoughts that I shouldn't be having. I mean, I have them about girls too, and that's fine, but God hates faggots. I came here to get better."

My heart skipped a sickened beat. I wondered if he knew the etymology of the word "faggot." Maybe if more people knew that it had begun as a way to refer to a bundle of sticks—specifically those used to burn heretics—they wouldn't use it so freely. Or maybe they would anyway. Maybe even more. People could be awful.

Alice swept into the room carrying two bowls—one filled with glazed carrots and the other with mashed potatoes. Following her were four other kids, including the girl I'd seen on the porch earlier, all carrying food. Alice smiled. "Oh, Caleb, how nice. I see you've already met Quinn. I was hoping you two would get to know each other. Do you like your room, Quinn?"

I nodded and followed the others' example by taking a seat. Alice sat at the head of the table. "It's really nice. I was surprised I don't have a roommate, being new and all."

"All the rooms here are singles. I hope you like yours. I thought it best to put you in the main house." Without waiting for me to respond, she continued. "Far from any bad influence."

"Talking about me again, I see, Alice. Can't say I blame you. I am rather inspiring." Lloyd swept into the room with the confidence of a guy who knew he drew attention wherever he went, and, good or bad, enjoyed every moment of it. He took a seat across from me. "Sorry I'm late, Quinn. I meant to save you a seat, but instead I spent the past hour being told that my soul is salvageable, if only I go against everything that I know to be true about myself. Fun stuff, actually."

"Can I count on you to behave yourself during dinner, Lloyd, or will you be dining with Dr. Hillard again tonight?" Alice's tone was quiet and calm, but firm. A threat lingered in her eyes.

"In honor of our new guest, I'll be on my best behavior. Unlike Caleb on the pool table last night." Lloyd blew a kiss Caleb's way. Caleb sank down in his seat, looking more than a little mortified. I had a feeling nothing had happened between them. I also had a feeling that Lloyd reveled in making people squirm. As he winked at Caleb, he said, "Talk about hitting it in the corner pocket. You naughty boy."

One of the other kids said, "You have a dirty mind, Lloyd."

Without missing a beat, Lloyd shot back, "Filthy as charged."

Alice slapped the tabletop hard with her palm, making everyone jump. Everyone, that is, but Lloyd. I wondered if there were any more surprises left for him to find here after six months. "This will be your first and last warning, Lloyd. One more disgusting outburst—"

Lloyd put up his hands in mock surrender. "Okay. I'll behave. Promise."

The same man I'd seen outside from my bedroom window, the one with the sweater vest and tie, entered the room, bringing with him an air of comfort that I welcomed. With a confident step, he approached me and shook my hand. His skin was warm and soft. "You must be Quinn. I'm Dr. Hillard, the administrator here at Camp Redemption. I apologize for not being available to greet you when you arrived. Normally I would have, but I had an emergency session at the last minute."

Behind his spectacles were hazel eyes that reminded me of my grandfather. It made talking to him feel easy. "That's okay. It's nice to meet you."

Lloyd coughed, and the moment Alice shot him a reprimanding look, he sipped some water and cleared his throat. "Sorry. Must be coming down with something."

The air in the room changed, and at first, I couldn't discern why. But then Dr. Hillard met Lloyd's eyes, and I knew that the others feared him in one way or another. Whether it was the fear of disappointing him or the fear of angering him, I didn't know. "I look forward to our session tomorrow, Lloyd."

Lloyd's face went slack with fear, too. It was only for a

moment, but it seemed so out of character for him that a flash of worry tore through me.

Then the air lightened again and Dr. Hillard's pleasant smile returned as he addressed me. "I look forward to speaking to you more as well, young lady. Bless you all. Good night."

I should have known, I supposed, that we hadn't set an eighth plate, but it seemed off to me. Where was he going? My voice came out softer than I'd intended when I said, "Dr. Hillard doesn't eat with everyone else?"

The girl next to me muttered, "The king? Dine with the peasants? Never."

Either Alice hadn't heard the snide remark or else she'd chosen to ignore it. "Now that we're all here, I think introductions are needed. You've already met Lloyd, Caleb, and me. Shall we go around the table?"

The girl beside me had shoulder-length auburn hair. Like me, she had tiny freckles dotting her nose and cheeks. When she smiled, her eyes sparkled. She said, "Hey there. I'm Susan."

Next came the boy who'd called out Lloyd's dirty mind. He was thin and had the clearest skin I'd ever seen on a teenager. "My name's David, but most people just call me by my last name, Collins."

Across from Collins sat a girl who had clearly not been

anatomically female at birth but was working to fix that. Her facial features had softened, her curves had been defined. I wondered if her parents had anything to do with her getting and using hormones, or if she had found another way. I couldn't imagine them helping her only to send her to a place in order to change her, so I was betting it was the latter.

Susan might have been cute, but this girl was gorgeous. She smiled at me, but it didn't quite reach her eyes. She looked almost angry, but I was about to learn that it wasn't anger—it was defiance. "I'm Valerie."

"Jeffrey, we've talked about this. Your name is not Valerie. God made you a male in his image, and this delusion is dangerous and wrong. Stop it at once or—" As if realizing that her voice had risen to near shouting, Alice took a couple deep breaths and calmed herself before speaking again. Her skin was flushed pink. I didn't know if it was because she was pissed off or embarrassed at the way she'd lashed out. Either way, she'd managed to silence everyone in the room. "Jeffrey, I hope you realize that this incident will require a firmer approach to your treatment. After dinner, you'll come with me so that we can address it properly."

Fear passed through Valerie's eyes, and on its heels, sadness.

Keeping order, Alice said, "Now, Randall, would you please introduce yourself?"

The guy sitting next to Valerie looked caught off guard, but then, we all had been. "I'm . . . Randall?"

When Alice spoke again, she was back to her cheery, pleasant self. "Now that introductions have been made, you should be aware of the fact that we have a very precise schedule here that you should put to memory, Quinn. We expect promptness. I put a copy of the schedule as well as the rules on your nightstand. Breakfast is at seven o'clock each morning. We expect you to be present, clean, and dressed. After breakfast is what we call our morning constitutional. It's a time for peaceful reflection on the sins you've committed, your progress or lack of progress, and how you can do better moving forward. Therapy sessions rotate throughout the day, with breaks for lunch, which is at noon, and dinner, which is at six. You will be in the house with lights out at nine and will not be permitted to leave campus. There are security measures in place for your protection."

My head was spinning from the litany of information she'd just thrown at me, but not so much that I didn't notice the words "security measures." "So, we're not allowed to leave campus at all?"

"I'm afraid not. It would interfere with your progress. Now, who would like to say grace?" Lloyd shot his hand into the air, which sparked Alice to choose someone else immediately. "Randall, why don't you do the honors?"

Randall and the others bowed their heads—all but Lloyd, who smiled at me and rolled his eyes when Randall began to pray. My parents were big on prayer—on church as a whole—but that dedication to faith hadn't fully filtered down to Kai and me. After he went off to college, his views changed even more, which made me really question what the preacher was saying up there behind his pulpit. I went to service on Sundays and bowed my head when it was time for prayer, but I wasn't convinced that God required any of those things. Nevertheless, I folded my fingers together and bowed my head as Randall recited his prayer. "Dear Lord, bless this food to our bodies. May it give us the strength to endure the trials that lie before us, the wisdom to know right from wrong, and the fortitude to stand up for those beliefs. Bless all those seated at this table to your will and your grace. In Jesus's name. Amen."

Alice passed a basket of still-steaming biscuits to me and said, "Your mom told me a few things about why she and your dad thought coming here would be good for you, but I want to hear from you. What are you hoping to accomplish while you're with us, Quinn?"

"I'm just . . ." I could feel every set of eyes in the room on me. Her tone had been so casual, like she was asking me what I'd had for breakfast that morning. Why was she asking me in front of everyone? Wasn't that something I was supposed to explore in therapy alone? "I guess I'm maybe just confused about some things."

Alice leaned forward, her eyes full of sympathy for my plight. "Like God's plan for you?"

God's plan. What might a liaison at Camp Redemption know about an all-knowing deity's plan for me? I kind of doubted she had his number on speed dial. "I guess. My parents say I'm sick and I want to figure out if they're right. Or if I'm really in love with Lia."

"Lia?"

"My girlfriend."

The air in the room felt heavier. The rest of the kids were eating in silence. I couldn't help but notice that Lloyd was watching our interaction with great interest.

Alice swallowed the food in her mouth, but it looked like the bite went down hard, as if she were forcing herself to eat something revolting. "Ahh. The root of your temptation to sin. Well, I look forward to talking about this further with you during your stay here. Aside from our regularly scheduled sessions, you should be aware that I'm always available whenever Dr. Hillard isn't."

"Thanks." I didn't know what to say other than that. Was Lia a temptation for me? Oh yes. Especially when she wore her hair up and I could see the nape of her neck. Or when she placed her hand on the small of my back. Or when she . . .

Stop it, Quinn. Just . . . stop it.

"Don't worry. We'll dig that root out and restore your purity." Alice placed her hand on mine and gave it a squeeze, as if I needed comforting. Maybe I did. "If you'd like, the others normally gather in the rec room for some wholesome fun before lights-out. But if you'd rather be alone your first night, everyone will understand. There's always a bit of an adjustment period."

Most of the others had finished eating. I looked down at my plate and realized that I hadn't taken a single bite. Hunger eluded me. Maybe it was nerves. Maybe it was something else. All I knew was that a wave of guilt and sadness had washed over me the moment I started thinking about Lia, and how much I missed her already. "I think I'll just go to my room and read."

"That's fine. I put some acceptable reading materials on your dresser. I'm sure you understand that we had to confiscate any potentially harmful items."

"You went through my things?" My mind started scrolling through a list of everything I'd brought with me. My cell phone, a few books, clothing, toiletries—nothing dangerous. But I'd also brought a picture of Lia. Had they taken that too?

"We find that the treatment process goes smoother without any distractions from the secular world. It's important that your confusion isn't aggravated by any influence from outside the camp." Without waiting for my response, she stood up and clapped her hands together, as if we'd all just enjoyed a family dinner and a nice chat together, rather than . . . whatever that had been. "If you decide to join the others, Quinn, the rec room is downstairs. Susan, please clear the table. Randall, you're on dishes tonight. Jeffrey, you're coming with me. Good night, everyone. Remember, lights out at nine, but say your prayers first."

I returned to my room feeling heavier than I had before dinner. Upon inspection, I noticed my phone was missing, as well as my books and picture of Lia. A sick feeling washed over me, but I pushed it away. If Camp Redemption had helped people before me, maybe they knew what they were doing and I just had to trust the process. It wouldn't be easy, I was certain, but if I had my answers in the end, it would be worth it. Wouldn't it?

I'd planned on putting on pajamas and slipping into bed early, but as I pulled a pair from my suitcase, I noticed the pamphlets sitting on my nightstand. I picked up the one on top and read. "Choosing to engage in homosexual conduct is sinful in the eyes of God, and those who do so without redemption shall burn forever in the fires of hell."

The next one took a gentler approach. It said, "Doing nothing to correct the confusion within you regarding sexuality only allows you to sink deeper into a lifestyle that God warns against."

The third pamphlet stated that the bad feelings I was likely experiencing would go away if I just pushed them down deep enough and released my compulsion to lust. My stomach flip-flopped.

I sat on the edge of the bed and thought about my reasons for coming here. Was I an abomination? Was I sick? Was I confused? Or was I just running away from something in order to please my parents?

I looked at the alarm clock and realized that I'd been sitting there for almost an hour. A knock on the door startled me from my thoughts, and when I opened it, I was surprised to find Lloyd standing there. "Come."

He turned around and started toward the stairs, as if he knew I'd follow him. He was right.

Without hesitation, I closed the door behind me and quickened my steps so that we were walking side by side. "Where?"

"With me."

"Why?"

"Orgy in the rec room." He said it so casually. I didn't even feel my jaw drop, just realized it had when he looked at me and started laughing. "Oh my glob, you are too easy. I refuse to let you spend your first night in hell reading pamphlets on how every same-sex encounter leads to HIV and AIDS. Now get your ass downstairs so I might have even the slightest chance for competition at the poker table."

We made our way down the stairs, turned left, and passed through a door that led to more stairs. At the bottom was a large room with orange shag carpeting and fluorescent velvet posters on the walls. In the far left corner was a Ping-Pong table. It was as if someone had decorated the room thinking that they knew what "kids these days" were into. Only no one had bothered to tell them that it was no longer 1975.

In the center of the room stood a huge wooden spool that acted as a table. Susan, Collins, and Randall were perched on stools around it. Caleb was sitting on one of the beanbags on the floor near it. The look on his face suggested he was sulking.

"Hey, Quinn." Collins smiled at me and slid a deck of cards across the table to Randall. "Your deal, dude."

I took a seat on one of the empty stools. Lloyd sat down next to me. "What are we betting with exactly?"

Randall shuffled the cards over and over again. "Anything of value, really, but if you've got cash, that's the best way to go."

"Just don't tell Alice or 'Doctor' Hillard about our poker games." Lloyd made quotation marks in the air with his fingers when he said 'doctor,' which made me wonder what exactly Dr. Hillard was a doctor of, if he was really a doctor at all. "Poker is on their list of no-no's, because apparently, God frowns on capitalism in any form. Guess Camp Redemption didn't get the memo on that one before they cashed my parents' check."

I thought I heard a grumble coming from Caleb but couldn't be certain. Maybe I was too distracted by what Lloyd had just said. "Wait. Our parents paid for us to come here?"

"Yeah, they did. And as long as the checks clear, they can keep us here until we're legally old enough to say otherwise. In two months, I'll be eighteen. If I last that long, I'm gone." Lloyd's jaw tightened in justified anger. "So, I guess it's a pay-to-pray-away-the-gay kind of situation. I'm amazed they don't have a gift shop selling snake oil."

My parents had left me with the impression that this was some charitable ministry that just wanted to help people like me. The notion that my parents had paid real money in hopes that I'd come home straight soured my stomach. "Aren't there laws about us missing too much school or something?"

Susan shrugged. "Who's gonna report it? The parents that drop kids here are instructed to tell our schools that we're being homeschooled. I wonder if our parents believe it."

There was a hole at the center of me. My parents hadn't lied. Not exactly. But they'd withheld the truth, which was just as bad. "That's crazy."

Lloyd picked up his cards and said, "Not to be a hypocrite

or anything . . . but amen, sister."

We played a couple hands. I didn't do too bad at first, but then Lloyd put on his bluffing face and everything went south as far as my pockets were concerned. Dropping my cards on the table, I sighed. "That's it for me. I'm out."

"Hey, me too!" Lloyd's laughter was infectious. It spread around the table but stopped short of affecting Caleb, who still seemed to be in a sullen mood.

After a beat, Susan said, "So, earlier today, Dr. Hillard told me that God wants me to be normal. Like, what even is normal, anyway? Who gets to decide that? It was insulting."

"'Doctor' Hillard's concept of God is insulting." Air quotes from Lloyd again, only this time, they were accompanied by a tone of absolute anger. "Any god who'd hurt people for being the way he made them is a hate-filled prick."

"God wants us to be normal because he loves us. Because God *is* love." No one had been expecting Caleb to speak. In fact, I'd been wondering why he'd stayed in the room if the company wasn't making his evening any better.

Under her breath, Susan said, "Normal?"

Lloyd's chest rose and fell in quick breaths. It might not have been on purpose, but Caleb was testing his temper. "Oh, really, Caleb? 'Cuz I'll tell ya something. If God is love, he sure as hell isn't here."

Caleb shook his head, as if he realized he was beginning

to fight an uphill battle but was too stubborn to back down. "You just need to have faith."

Lloyd rolled his eyes. He pressed his lips together before he spoke. "Oh, you're right. Because up against logic, it's the only thing you've got."

I'd seen boys disagree before, watched disagreements turn into arguments, witnessed arguments turn into fistfights. I didn't want that to happen, so I interjected, "Why are you so angry, Lloyd?"

"You wanna know why? You really wanna know?" He was almost shouting, and I wondered if any of the staff would hear him and come downstairs. If they did, we were in trouble. The cards and money were still sitting on the table.

Susan said, "Lloyd, don't. You'll scare her."

"Good. She should be scared." As he stood, Lloyd lifted his T-shirt and pulled it off over his head, revealing tan skin and lean muscles. His stomach was firm. His chest was defined. And Caleb noticed every inch. The look of longing in his eyes as he traced Lloyd's half-naked body was almost sad to see, because it was so swiftly replaced by suffocating guilt. Lloyd stood and turned around, revealing his back, which was marred with scars and cuts. Some were old. A few were fresh. "This, Quinn, is what happens when you refuse to follow their rules here. This is what happens when you hold on to the fact that you're queer no matter how many times they hurt you. It happens over and over again. And our parents pay them to do it. They're monsters, all of them."

You can't run from the monster. The monster is you.

The words whispered through the back of my mind like a vague memory of a bad dream. Was that what I was? What we all were? Monsters? Maybe I was the only one here fighting my demons—or at least trying to understand them—but I doubted it. I couldn't be the only one questioning the feelings I had for someone of the same gender. So if I was a monster, I could only take comfort in knowing that I was surrounded by other monsters, and in the lingering hope that, one day, we might all be free of whatever it was that plagued us.

My chest grew tight as I took in the image of Lloyd's back. Without thinking to ask if he'd mind, I reached out and ran a finger along one of the healed scars. It was smooth. A curved line like a sliver of the moon. Goose bumps appeared on his skin and I pulled my hand back with a nervous jerk. I wasn't sure why I'd touched him—especially without his permission, which left a sick feeling in the pit of my stomach. It wasn't like I was attracted to him. I mean, I found him attractive—who in their right mind wouldn't? But I wasn't attracted *to* him. Caleb, however, absolutely was. And I could tell he was beating himself up about it. I could tell because I recognized the feeling. I said, "You okay, Caleb?"

"Yeah. I just . . ." Caleb studied Lloyd's scars, disbelief

coating his expression. But there was something else there. Worry, maybe. Worry that he'd been misled. Worry that he'd been wrong. "You're lying, Lloyd. They don't whip anybody here."

Lloyd turned back around to face us all. His voice was calm, but it was only just covering a layer of understandable anger. "Oh yeah? You've been here two months and are buying into their bullshit, Caleb. Just imagine if it was six months and you refused to bow down to their homophobic doctrine. What might your back look like then?"

"But why? Why would anyone resort to"—Caleb gestured to Lloyd's back with a nod—"that?"

"The first time was after 'Doctor' Hillard referred to guys who had sex with guys as fags. I suggested that if he was so focused on men screwing other men, maybe he should go fuck himself." A smile touched Lloyd's lips, but the bitterness he felt for Dr. Hillard weakened it. "It was worth every lick."

"How many times?" I knew—I think we all knew—that Caleb was asking how many times Lloyd had been whipped. It was like he couldn't bring himself to say the word "whipped." Maybe he was still clinging a little to his apparent delusion that all was kind and understanding here in Camp Redemption.

"Six."

Caleb was quiet for a long time, as if he were processing all that he'd seen and heard. He shook his head, his words close to a whisper. "I'm sorry. I . . . I didn't know."

"I know it may seem like I'm an asshole sometimes, Caleb. But it's not like I don't have reason to be." Their eyes locked. The argument between them had been forgotten, or at least put aside for the time being, replaced by something else. Something indefinable. And beautiful.

Lloyd took his time sliding his shirt back on and Caleb's lingering gaze said that he noticed . . . and that he liked what he saw. Their eyes met and a silent conversation passed quickly between them. Lloyd's voice sounded softer, kinder, than it had since I'd first heard him speak. "You all right?"

Caleb's face flushed pink. "I'm fine. I'm just . . . tired."

Lloyd held his gaze, and I realized that I was holding my breath. No one else in the room was speaking, so I knew they were as intrigued by the current developments as I was. We were all watching in utter fascination—a silent audience to what felt like an intimate beginning of something real. "Maybe you should go to bed. I was thinking of turning in for the night too. Want some company on the way upstairs?"

"Yes." A look of genuine surprise appeared on Caleb's face, like someone else was doing the talking for him. But he meant what he said, and not just to walking upstairs with Lloyd at his side—that much was obvious. He was saying yes to the feelings he had for Lloyd. He was saying yes to the sins he very much wanted to commit. And for the moment, he was saying yes to the possibility that the staff at Camp Redemption could be wrong.

In that moment, it would have been hard to argue with him.

20

The next morning, Lloyd and Caleb were late to breakfast, and when they arrived, both were quiet. But it wasn't an awkward sort of quiet. It was comfortable. And whatever it was that passed between them when their eyes met made me ache to see Lia again, to hear her voice, to lace my fingers with hers, to tell her about Lloyd's scars. How had I been here only a day? It felt like weeks at least. But then, every moment away from Lia felt—

"Quinn, Dr. Hillard is waiting for you in his office for your first session."

I'd just finished rinsing my plate. Everyone else was

seated around the kitchen table eating breakfast. Everyone but Valerie. And Dr. Hillard, of course.

"Oh. Thank you." I set my plate in the sink before waving at the others and making my way to the set of large mahogany doors at the end of the hall. I knocked three times, and when the door opened, I was greeted by Dr. Hillard's warm smile. Images of Lloyd's back flashed through my mind.

Dr. Hillard shook my hand as if we were old business acquaintances. "Good morning. Can I interest you in a cup of tea?"

He gestured to a small table to the left of the door that held a teapot, along with two cups and saucers and a bowl of sugar cubes.

"No, thank you."

"Are you sure? I've found it helps to calm the nerves. And I know from experience how emotional young girls can get." The chuckle he emitted after sounded friendly enough, but his words made my jaw clench.

"I'm good, thanks."

He poured himself a cup of tea and dropped two sugar cubes in. When he turned back to me, his warm smile had returned. "How are you enjoying Camp Redemption, Quinn?"

The inside of his office looked like something Ernest Hemingway would have called home. It was colored in rich, dark tones, full of heavy wood furniture, with bookshelves, a globe, and the decapitated head of a deer hanging over the fireplace. Because nothing said healing like having a dead thing looming over you while you revealed your most intimate secrets.

In front of the large mahogany desk at the center of the room were two chairs. As he walked around to the other side of the desk, he gestured to one of the chairs and I took a seat. The leather felt new, and not cheap. "It's okay so far, I guess. The people are nice. But I am curious about therapy. Like, do I lie on a couch and tell you my life story, or . . . ?"

"Nothing like that." He waved his hand in the air, as if erasing my ridiculous question. "I'm not what you'd call a traditional therapist. I specialize in afflictions of the soul and treat those afflictions accordingly."

I bit my bottom lip before saying, "But how exactly?"

He sat back in his chair and folded his hands together on his chest, relaxed and calm as could be. "It depends on the case, but as a few examples, through talk therapy I help those afflicted come to terms with whatever sexual abuse led them to believe they are homosexual. I, along with the rest of the staff here, work hard to recondition patients through various means. If all else fails, we offer Deliverance."

"Deliverance?" The word rang out into the room like a shot. It sounded so noble, so freeing. So sinister.

"When a soul becomes tarnished by demons of lust, that soul can only be purified by driving the demons out. Deliverance offers that."

My crazy alarm was going off like . . . well . . . crazy. "You mean . . . like an exorcism?"

"Only as a last resort. When other methods aren't effective, we have to attack the problem in a direct, firm manner." He met my eyes and chuckled, as if he knew what I was thinking. "It's nothing like the movies, I promise. No spinning heads or vomiting pea soup."

How could exorcism still be a thing? Hadn't people died undergoing exorcisms? There was no way that could be legal. "What happens if it turns out that I am actually into girls and not sick?"

"We have a very high success rate." Another vague response that didn't answer my question. Before I could press further, he opened up his notebook and picked up a pen. "Why don't we get started? Your parents tell me that you've been involved in a lesbian relationship with a girl called Lia. Why do you think you were first attracted to Lia?"

Lia's smile filled my memory. It had been the first thing I'd noticed about her that day in school. "Well, she's really pretty, funny, smart—"

"That's not what I mean." He leaned forward and rested his elbows on his desk, his clasped hands under his chin. "I want you to reach back to your first memories as a child. Can you recall any inappropriate sexual contact when you were young?"

My stomach tensed at the accusation. I could feel my breakfast threatening to reverse gears. "What? No!"

He nodded. "It's common to repress memories of abuse. I know it can't be easy to hear, but Quinn, if you believe yourself to be homosexual, I can assure you that you were most certainly sexually abused as a child. In your case, most likely by a female adult. Perhaps a babysitter or a friend of the family. Can you think of anyone who fits that description?"

I glanced out the window, half expecting to see gray skies, but the sun was still shining. "That's disgusting. No."

"Perhaps a family member, then. Maybe even a sibling. Do you have any sisters or brothers?" There was a knowing look in his eye. I would have bet anything he already knew about Kai.

My face flushed white hot at the presumption that Kai would ever do anything like that to anyone—especially me. Dr. Hillard was walking on razor-thin ice. "I wasn't molested as a child, and I don't think I have feelings for Lia because I was abused."

"Because you were what?"

"I was abused."

A look of gratification washed over his expression. After a brief pause, he scribbled something in his notebook and said, "How did it feel to say those words?"

It took me a moment to see what he'd done, and I wondered if he actually believed that tricking me into saying those words would make me believe them to be true. "I . . . I don't understand what you're trying to do here. I only came here to figure out if I'm sick or if I really am gay."

"If you weren't sick, we wouldn't have admitted you." He flipped to the next page of his notebook and scanned it before readying his pen and meeting my eyes. "Tell me about your relationship with Lia. Is it sexual in nature?"

My pervert alarm sounded, drowning out the crazy bells. "That's none of your business."

"Do you want to get well?" His eyes bore into me. I was awash in guilt but couldn't pinpoint what I'd done wrong. As if by reflex, I nodded. Mostly because I didn't know what to say. I wanted to be healthy. I just needed to determine what that meant exactly. Tightening the grip on his pen, he said, "Then answer the question."

My throat felt dry. I coughed into my hand. My face felt warm, and I knew I was probably blushing. I'd never talked to anyone but Lia about our sex life before. "We've been intimate, yeah. But our relationship is more than that. We're very close. We talk about everything."

"I see. Did you discuss your stay at Camp Redemption with her before you left home?" He glanced up from the page he was writing on and acknowledged my nod with one of his own. "And how did she react?"

Lia's words rang through my mind. *I can't believe you! How can you do this to me? To us? To yourself, Quinn? It doesn't make any sense!*

"She was angry."

"Even though you were coming here to ease your confusion?" He clucked his tongue. "That doesn't sound very supportive."

"She was just upset because she doesn't want me to—"

"She doesn't want you to go home believing that you are heterosexual."

I tried to imagine what it would be like if I returned home and told Lia that it was over between us, that I was actually straight and had just been confused this whole time. She'd be heartbroken. "I . . . I guess, yeah. Maybe. I don't know."

The warmth that had been in his expression before returned. "That sounds a bit controlling, doesn't it? Like she'll only support you if you continue to give in to your sinful urges with her?"

I shook my head. "It's not like that. She just doesn't want me to leave her."

"Do you attend church?"

Happy to put the subject of Lia and me to rest for the time being, I shrugged and relaxed back into my chair. "On holidays mostly. The big ones. Easter. Christmas. Or whenever Mom and Dad insist. I just don't feel like it's all that important to go. If God is everywhere, he's in our living room too. Y'know?"

He seemed to perk up at my mention of the G-word. "So you do believe in God?"

I shrugged. "Yeah. I mean. I guess."

"Does Lia?"

I wasn't sure what Lia's beliefs had to do with whether or not I was gay, but I put my questions aside and said, "Lia's an atheist."

The air in the room grew thick again, as if the A-word were capable of summoning the devil himself. Dr. Hillard set his pen down and leaned forward on his desk. "I find it interesting that the girl you're in a lesbian relationship with seems to want to control you and has an aversion to accepting God into her life. Those are very demonic qualities."

I almost laughed. "Are you saying that Lia is a demon?"

His tone warmed, and when he spoke, it sounded like he was trying hard to be supportive. "I'm saying that she is very likely afflicted herself. Demons want to infest as many souls as they can so the souls are tainted enough with sin to claim them for their master, Satan."

"This is all sounding a bit . . . well . . ." Images of the many movies and TV shows I'd seen filled my head. Inhuman entities with black eyes. Horns growing out of heads. Priests fighting against the forces of evil for the greater good. The very idea that something like that could be affecting my life was almost laughable. Almost. Unless, somehow, it was true. "I'm sorry, Dr. Hillard, but it sounds ludicrous."

I'd expected him to look insulted, but he didn't. He looked more like he'd been expecting my reaction. He'd probably heard it several times before, from multiple patients. "Let me put it this way. Before they are taking the right medication for their condition, do you think schizophrenic people believe that they are ill?"

"Most likely not."

"Prior to receiving treatment, possessed souls also believe themselves to be healthy. But based on our conversation today, I can assure you that you *are* ill, Quinn." His words dripped with concern, which reminded me so much of my parents' reaction upon hearing that Lia and I were dating. They were worried. Dr. Hillard sounded worried too. "It may be a long, arduous journey, but I am going to help you become pure once again. Let's talk again tomorrow. Same time."

I left Dr. Hillard's office with an overwhelming need to be alone for a while. Partly because I needed to think about the things he'd said and my reasons for being here, and partly because I didn't want to think about anything at all. I soon found myself in the rose garden out front inhaling the sweet scent of the blooms and basking in the warmth of the afternoon sun on my skin. It was a great place to lose myself, with no one around to tell me what was wrong with me or ask me why I thought anything was wrong at all. Sometimes a little bit of nothing made a whole lot of something more bearable.

A shadow blocked the sun for a moment. Brushing my hair from my eyes, I looked up to see the gardener who'd saluted me through the window yesterday. Up close, his hair was even oilier, and his skin looked sticky with sweat. I wondered when he'd last showered. I couldn't help but notice he was wearing black snakeskin boots. What a strange thing to wear for groundskeeping. But then, he was a stranger.

The Stranger, I thought. It seemed a fitting nickname for him. A lit cigarette clung to his bottom lip. He held an open pack out to me with his nicotine-stained fingers.

I shook my head. "No thanks. I don't smoke."

"Oh, that's right. Not here you don't." He slipped the pack inside the front pocket of his overalls and stood there, watching me like he was waiting for me to do something interesting.

"Quinn, why don't you help me put these away?" Alice

was standing near the van in the driveway with two large paper sacks in her arms, stuffed full of groceries.

When I turned back to the gardener to give him a polite goodbye, he was gone.

The grass tickled my ankles as I crossed the lush green lawn over to Alice and took one of the bags from her. It was heavier than it looked. As we stepped onto the porch, I swore I heard someone crying out. Pausing, I looked at Alice, who'd moved ahead of me and opened the screen door. "Did you hear that? It sounds like someone might be hurt."

Alice held the door for me and gestured for me to go inside. She didn't look fazed at all by the wailing that continued in the distance. "Sometimes the sounds of healing can seem like cries of pain. Don't worry. You're in good hands here. How did your first session with Dr. Hillard go?"

"Fine, I guess." The moment the door shut behind us, I couldn't hear the weeping anymore, but it lingered in my mind. "I was thinking about calling my brother today. Is that okay?"

"Certainly. Calls to family are allowed, so long as they're supervised."

We entered the kitchen, and I set the bag I'd been carrying down on the counter harder than I'd meant to. "Why can't I have privacy? I mean, what's my brother going to say that will harm my progress here?"

"It's for your safety."

What the hell was she implying? There were a lot of things somebody could poke at in my life, but when it came to my brother, I had a strict hands-off rule. "There is nothing on this planet safer for me than Kai."

"I understand that this is upsetting for you, but I'm afraid that's one of the rules, and we expect you to follow the rules with respect and without question." She picked up the cordless phone on the counter and held it out to me with a pointed look. "You can call your brother now if you'd like."

It took me almost a full minute to remember Kai's phone number. It was so much easier to tap his name on a screen. It rang twice, and when my brother's voice came through, my heart felt full. It was funny how quickly you could get homesick. "Talk to me, caller."

"Hey, Kai."

"Quinn? How's it going, kiddo? Everything okay?"

"I'm not sure." Alice was putting groceries away, but it was apparent that she had her ears perked for anything she deemed harmful. "How's everything at home?"

"Fine. But . . . what do you mean you're not sure?" His tone had shifted from happy-to-hear-from-me to concerned. Sometimes it felt like we shared a brain.

Right after Kai had moved out of the house and into the dorms, we'd come up with a code phrase that we'd use to let the other know that one or both of our parents were in the room. If I didn't use the code, we could talk about the parties he went to and what college life was really like, without Mom or Dad worrying about Kai or how he might be influencing his little sister. After I got my cell phone in the middle of his freshman year, we stopped using the code, because I could call him from anywhere I wanted. I was just hoping Kai recalled the code and didn't think I was losing my mind. "Did you forget to eat again?"

Without missing a beat, he said, "Somebody is listening in on our conversation, aren't they?"

"Yeah."

"Got it. Do they keep a tight watch on you there?"

"Yeah."

"I wish you . . . never mind. It's not important and it's too late anyway." I could hear the frustration and disappointment in his voice. He didn't want to make me feel stupid for having come here, but it was clear he hadn't wanted me to leave home. "I saw Lia this morning, when I stopped to get gas. She wanted me to tell you she misses you already. What's it like there?"

Alice opened the pantry next to me and put away several cans of food. She sure was taking her time with the groceries. "It's all right so far."

"Translation: this place sucks donkey balls. Am I close?"

"Definitely." *More than I can even say.* "Hey, could you tell Mom that I miss her too? I've been thinking a lot about her."

He paused for a beat and then said, "I assume that's a message for Lia. Anything else you want me to tell her next time I see her?"

I wet my lips, pressing the receiver closer to my mouth. "Yeah. Tell her I love her."

"Quinn . . ." He sounded worried. I wondered if he had good reason to be. "Are you safe?"

"I don't know, Kai. I don't think so." Alice met my eyes and tapped her wrist, indicating that my time was up. "I'll talk to you more later, okay?"

"You'd better. Be safe, kiddo."

As I hung up, an intense feeling of loneliness washed over me. More and more, it was clear that this wasn't the right place for me, but I was surer than ever that I wouldn't be welcome back at home. My parents were *paying* to keep me here. At least until I was whatever they considered to be well.

Alice was back to her smiling self. "I hope everything's okay at home."

"It is. Thank you. It was nice to talk to my brother. We're really close."

"Well, I'm sure you'll be reunited soon enough." She glanced up at the clock on the wall. "The morning seems to have gotten away from me. It's time for Reckoning."

"Reckoning?" The word felt heavy on my tongue.

"It's a time of sharing. I think it'll be good for you. Half the group meets after lunch, but I think this prelunch group would be a better fit." She led me down the hall to the right and through a set of French doors. The walls were painted soft blue with white trim, and the floor was covered with soft gray carpeting. Seated in a half circle on the floor were Susan, Collins, and Caleb. Several fluffy pillows lay all around. The room felt comforting. Welcoming.

Not at all like the kind of place where the sounds of healing imitated cries of pain.

Alice knelt on one of the pillows and eased herself onto the floor. After I'd followed her lead, she said, "Caleb, why don't you begin?"

"Okay. Umm . . ." Caleb fiddled with the ring he was wearing on his right hand—a silver cross. His fingers were trembling. "Since my last Reckoning, I've had . . . impure thoughts . . . about another guy."

The intense self-loathing that I'd seen in his eyes before he and Lloyd had walked up the basement stairs together the night before was gone—replaced by a glint of curiosity. It made my heart feel lighter to see it.

Alice said, "How did you feel afterward?"

Caleb took a moment to really examine his thoughts

before speaking them aloud. "I thought I'd feel sick. I thought I'd feel shame. But I didn't. I just felt . . . reflective."

There was a long silence before Alice spoke again. When she did, her tone was dripping with judgment. "Did you give in to temptation in any way?"

"Um . . ." Again, he seemed to mull over her question some before responding. I would've bet just about anything he was thinking impure thoughts about Lloyd right now, and whatever had happened after they'd left the basement. The corner of his mouth lifted very briefly, but he seemed to catch it and went back to fiddling with his ring. "Not really, no. But I'm still . . . tempted."

"Admitting that is very brave, Caleb. Choosing to engage in homosexual conduct is a sin, but with dedication to treatment, your sins can still be forgiven. Don't lose faith. Don't stray from God's path. Your soul can still be saved from the fires of eternal damnation." She reached out and gave his hand a squeeze. His fingers stopped shaking, and his eyes were awash with shame once again. Alice patted his hand and sat back on her pillow. "Susan?"

Susan crossed her arms in front of her, her lips a thin, defiant line.

Alice said, "You know what the repercussion is for refusing to participate."

"What repercussion?" I thought again of the cry I'd

heard and the scars on Lloyd's back.

Alice flashed me a dark glance. "It's Susan's turn, Quinn. Please respect her time. Now, Susan, you were saying?"

Susan sat up straight and stared Alice down. "To be honest, since my last Reckoning, I've decided I don't care what you're going to do to me. Despite what you may think, it's normal to be asexual, and I wouldn't change that part of me even if I could. I like being me. God made me how I am. And I refuse to ask for God's forgiveness when I'm not the least bit sorry."

She and Alice locked eyes for a long time in silent conversation. Whatever was being said in that span of quiet, Susan wasn't about to back down. Finally, Alice moved her attention to Collins. "Collins, why don't we hear from you now?"

Collins cleared his throat. "Well, since my last Reckoning, I haven't had any impure thoughts or actions. I think I'm getting better."

"Wonderful progress! Thank you for sharing." Her eyes had lit up at his admission but dimmed some when she turned them on me. It was as if she knew she'd be disappointed in my progress before I uttered a word. But how could I have made any progress in the day that I'd been here? That would be asking for . . . well . . . a miracle. "Quinn?"

I felt like everyone was staring at me, even though I could see that they weren't. Nerves are a strange thing. Still,

I couldn't shake that sensation of being watched. "Umm . . . this is my first Reckoning. I'm not sure I—"

"This is the time to share any sinful deeds you may have done in the past twenty-four hours. Just be open, honest, and forthright. After all, if you aren't, God will know." Looking up to meet her stare, I noticed a cross hanging on the far wall. It was intricate in design, with curved metal around tiny gems. I wondered how God would feel about someone bedazzling an effigy of the place where his son had died.

"I don't think I've sinned. I mean, if I have, I haven't noticed."

"You need to take this seriously, Quinn." She was looking at me like I was being defiant. I really wasn't. Clueless maybe. But defiant? Not even a little.

I said, "I am. I just can't think of anything I've done since yesterday that feels sinful."

Beside me, Susan snorted, garnering a glare from Alice, who said, "All have sinned and fall short of the glory of God. Romans 3:23."

Lloyd cracked open the door long enough to poke his head in and say, "I'd rather laugh with the sinners than cry with the saints. The sinners are much more fun. Joel, 1977. See? I can throw out arbitrary quotes too."

Alice barked, "Out!"

With a smirk, Lloyd left.

"What's your sin?" I said. I hadn't noticed the crease in her forehead before, or the way she drew her eyebrows in when she thought she was being challenged. But I noticed them now.

"Excuse me?"

I said, "If everybody has sinned, then why aren't you sharing yours?"

It took me a moment to recognize the look in her eyes. It seemed so familiar. Then it hit me. She looked at me now the way she usually looked at Lloyd. Which meant she apparently didn't like me very much. Not at the moment, anyway. "You're new here, so I'm going to give you a pass for speaking out and not participating, but it will be the first and last time. The next time you behave in this manner, there will be repercussions."

The room had grown quiet. Even Susan seemed to sink within herself. This felt more like a cage of fear than a place of redemption. I didn't break eye contact with Alice. She owed us all an answer if she expected the same from us.

Regaining her composure, Alice plastered a smile on her face. "Thank you all for joining together in Reckoning. Caleb and Collins, you'll share in kitchen duties this evening. Susan, once we're finished here, you'll come with me for additional treatment. And Quinn . . ."

I was still watching her. Still waiting for an answer that she would never give.

As she stood, she said, "You'll retire to your room after dinner and call it an early night."

"Am I being punished for not having anything to say?" I didn't think that was it, exactly. It seemed to me that I was being admonished for not digging deep to identify any of my actions as sins, even if they weren't.

"You're being encouraged to adhere to the rules." Her smile spread to her eyes. She was in charge of the narrative once again, which was right where her comfort zone lay. "Enjoy your lunch, everyone. I'll see you all at dinnertime. Susan will see you in the morning. Now get to lunch and don't forget to say the blessing."

The room emptied, and I took a breath before stepping through the door. I could hear voices chatting on the front porch, so I followed them.

Lloyd was sitting on the top step, holding court. "I'm just saying, if 'Doctor' Hillard and Alice got laid more often, maybe they'd be in better moods."

"You're disgusting." Randall could barely contain his laughter. His skin had flushed pink, as if he were embarrassed at how much he agreed with Lloyd.

"And proud. Don't forget proud." Valerie let out a chuckle. It put a grin on Lloyd's face and sent Randall over the edge in a fit of laughter.

Lloyd looked up at me, his grin never wavering. "Hey, Quinn."

“Hey.” As I took a seat on the step beside him, Collins exited the house and sat on one of the rocking chairs on the porch. There was no sign of Caleb.

From her place beside Randall on the bottom step, Valerie said, “Sorry I couldn’t join the game last night. I heard Lloyd cleaned you guys out. Little tip? He has a tell. Any time he’s lying, the corner of his mouth twitches.”

“Hey, now. Don’t you be giving away all my dirty little secrets.” He nudged her shoulder with his toe, which she playfully slapped away. When he met my eyes, I was struck again by how handsome he was. No wonder Caleb had a thing for him. “So, what’s your story, Quinn?”

“What do you mean?”

Lloyd’s smile was genuine and kind. His mind was as open as it was dirty. “Which letter in the LGBTQIA-plus spectrum suits you best? Or are there multiples?”

Valerie gave his leg a light smack. “Lloyd! You’re so nosy. It’s none of our business.”

I hadn’t noticed I’d been fidgeting with my bracelet until that moment. “Well . . . I wonder if I’m gay or not. I mean, I have a girlfriend—”

Randall interjected, “There’s your first clue.”

“—but I’m just not sure.”

Lloyd watched me for a moment, as if taking in my every word and examining each with precision and care. His tone was warm when he spoke again. "You don't have to be sure about anything or to defend your truth to any of us, Quinn. To anyone. But especially not us. We're on the same side."

My heart felt full at that moment. I'd never been surrounded by people who were so accepting, so supportive. My friends back home were great, but I never felt okay sharing my deepest secret with any of them. That I'd found this group of friends in a place like this astounded me, but I felt safe with them. Accepted. Understood.

"There's another thing. But I've never talked about it before." No one—not even Kai—knew about the feelings I'd had, more and more lately, that something about me was different. And I wasn't sure what anyone would say if I told them that sometimes I wondered if maybe my body didn't quite fit my mind.

Randall shook his head. "It's okay. You don't have to."

Everyone fell silent for a bit, until, finally, Lloyd cleared his throat and offered me an apologetic look. "Let's start over. What've you been up to since breakfast? Seeing the sights? Riding the rides?"

"I talked to Dr. Hillard for a while. Then I went to Reckoning. They're . . ." I glanced behind me to be certain no staff were within earshot. "They're really religious here, aren't they?"

Any semblance of a smile left Valerie's slender face.

"This place isn't run by religious people. It's run by people who use religion to control, influence, bully, and abuse people with traits they don't agree with. I mean, think about it. If you're questioning certain things about yourself, that's fine. It's normal to question things. What's not normal is to expect to find the answers you're looking for in a place where questions are forbidden."

From his place on the porch, Collins decided to chime in. "You shouldn't talk that way, Jeffrey. They're just trying to help us."

Lloyd snapped, "Bullshit they are. And fuck you for deadnaming Valerie."

The edges of Collins's tone burned with resentment. "You should ask for forgiveness, Lloyd."

"From who?"

"From God!"

Lloyd stood so fast, I thought he was going to seriously hurt Collins. I jumped up between them. Lloyd tried to get past me, but I placed my hands on his chest and pushed back as hard as I could. It didn't knock him back, but at least it held him still while he growled at Collins. "I don't believe in God! That pisses some people off, but it's true. If you believe in a deity, that's fine. But don't force your views on me, and don't tell me that the assholes in this fascist prison camp for wayward queers are capable of anything except trying to pray the gay away!"

"Lloyd, that is enough!" Alice stepped out the front door, one of the larger male staff members at her side. A second man appeared at the bottom of the steps, as if he'd heard the commotion and had come to intervene.

Lloyd clenched his jaw and turned his fiery eyes on Alice. "If you can't handle me and my opinions, then send me home."

Alice seemed unfazed. "You're not going anywhere yet. We're invested in helping you heal."

Lloyd's eyes were daggers. Words spilled from his lips so fast, it was as if they'd been held in by a dam that had finally broken. "You're only invested in the generous donation my parents gave you to twist the queer out of me. What gives you the right to decide who I love? Who I want? Not a damn check, that's for sure."

"Clearly you need some time to consider your words and actions." With a nod to the two staff members, she said, "Daniel, Marcus, please escort Lloyd to the Serenity Hut. We'll see how he's feeling about treatment in two days."

Lloyd's shoulders dropped. He looked afraid, like he had squaring off against Dr. Hillard at dinner last night, except worse. Lloyd was terrified.

In a blur, the two men grabbed Lloyd by the arms and pulled him down the steps. He kicked and fought, but they carried him off toward the easternmost part of the camp. His shouted obscenities quieted as they disappeared into the woods.

My heart was hammering inside my chest. "What's going to happen to him?"

"He'll be locked in the dark with no food, water, or human interaction for two days." Randall ran a shaking hand through his hair. "It's not as bad as Deliverance, but it's close."

My mouth had gone dry. "They can't do that."

"Yeah, they can. If our parents signed the waivers to get us in here, they can do pretty much whatever they want." Valerie's eyes welled with tears. She found my hand without looking and squeezed it.

Behind us, Alice spoke with conviction. Her words were tinged with triumph. "Take notice, children. Some souls cannot be cleansed. Some people are irredeemable."

19

When the next bomb blew, the wall behind me bowed, but didn't crumble. It settled uneasily, as if it were uncertain about its place in this war-torn world. It couldn't take another hit like that. I wasn't sure my team could either. Lloyd, Miranda, Collins, Stephens, Simmons, Jack, Thompson, McIntyre—they were good soldiers. If I didn't get them out of here soon, they'd be dead soldiers too. Just like Johnson.

"Sir, your orders?" A familiar voice shouted over the sounds of war. "Quinn!"

Johnson. Shit. How was I supposed to tell Millie and

their girls that he wasn't coming home? Never mind erasing from my mind the image of shrapnel blowing a hole through his chest. I'd *chosen* to carry the bloody burdens of this damned war. His wife and children had been thrust into it by proxy. They deserved better than to have their whole world turned upside down, all because I'd convinced Johnson that this would be the last run for him—one last outpost before he could go home to his girls for good.

Only now he wasn't going home. Maybe none of us were. This operation may have all been for nothing. What the hell would I tell them then?

"QUINN!" A firm hand gripped my shoulder and shook me from my thoughts.

I snapped my eyes to Lloyd, who was crouched beside me, clutching his gun to his chest with his free hand. I didn't have to ask him what he wanted. Like any good second-in-command, like any best friend, he was giving me what I needed—a good, hard slap back into reality. Bullets and bombs were still flying. Our team was in danger. They needed a leader. Mourning and guilt had to be put on hold. Time to "man up," as my father would have said. A phrase that I truly hated, but it fit the current situation.

Our mission came first. Storm the Allegiance's headquarters and take their leader, Caleb, hostage. He wouldn't be in Brume for long—maybe a week, maybe two—before he'd return to William Spencer's mansion, their national headquarters five hundred miles away. We had to grab him now or our chance would slip through our hands. There was no more time to find a way to end this war. We'd used the last of the supplies getting here, and there were thousands of people counting on us.

People like Johnson's family.

Eight outposts in total surrounded headquarters. They were small two-story buildings that formed a defensive circle. Each sported a banner that matched those outside Allegiance HQ. Red and black, with their creed: "As God Intended."

A knot formed in my stomach every time I saw those words. The Allegiance wasn't exactly accepting of those who didn't adhere to their doctrine. As far as they saw it, if you were anything but white, straight, cisgender, and hard-core conservative Christian, you didn't exist.

I wondered what their God would think of that.

Four soldiers were stationed at each outpost—two upstairs and two down. Rotating shifts every four hours ensured that they were alert at all times. No less than a dozen more soldiers circled the perimeter around all the outposts.

Twenty more had been dispatched once our presence had been detected, but we'd taken out most of them already.

Allegiance soldiers were exceptionally trained and well

armed. There was no doubt their bellies were full and their uniforms clean. Their wounds were tended to with the best of care and their nights off-duty were full of quiet rest. The Allegiance took care of its own. All you had to do to join them was sell your soul to the devil himself. Namely, Caleb.

I hadn't known Caleb before the war. But when the Allegiance had rolled into Brume, I saw him standing on top of a tank with his father, the General, at his side. The tank had come to a stop and Caleb addressed the crowd. "Greetings, citizens of Brume. Today my father and I bring you good tidings for the future of our country. Under the protection of the Allegiance, we're going to make our country better again. The best in the entire world. As God intended!"

My heart hammering nervously in my chest drowned out the polite applause. I'd expected every person there to hate him on sight, but to my horror, several gazed up at him in awe, as if they had been drowning and their savior had at last arrived. In a moment I'd never forget, Caleb met my eyes and flashed a smile so charismatic that I almost forgot for a moment that he was in charge of one of the most well-organized, well-funded hate-mongering groups to ever exist. He was handsome, and the look in his eyes was sincere. The moment was brief and probably meaningless, but it shook me to my core. This man was dangerous—maybe even more dangerous than his father.

That night invitations to a dinner hosted by Caleb were sent out to a handful of people, myself included. My gut said not to go, so I didn't. Good thing too. Once his guests were seated, Caleb gave the go-ahead for his men to open fire. He'd killed everyone in the room that wasn't part of the Allegiance, all to send a message to everyone else in Brume. The message was clear. He was in charge now, and all who opposed him and his mighty Allegiance would suffer.

Our plan was solid. If we could take out four of the outposts, we'd cause enough chaos that Collins, Thompson, and I should be able to slip inside, grab Caleb, and get the hell out of there. I wasn't worried about getting out—by then, we'd have the biggest bargaining chip possible in our possession.

Once we had Caleb, we could negotiate peace between the Allegiance and the Resistance. He was going to listen to reason if I had to smack that smug look off his face and make him listen. My people were dying . . . but so were his. The Allegiance had a way of projecting the image that every one of them was living a life of luxury, despite the war. But I knew different. Headquarter soldiers and staff seemed to have that life. The rest of them were struggling—not as much as members of the Resistance by far, but enough.

Peace. All I wanted was peace.

Both within and without.

I'd been distracted lately. Not by the war or lack of supplies or anything like that—no more than usual, anyway. But by something churning within me. This undeniable feeling of being Other. I wondered if Lloyd had noticed.

But I had to focus. The mission came first. It had to.

"Lloyd, I want you to grab Miranda, McIntyre, and Stephens and circle around the western side. Draw their fire and take out as many of those bastards as you can on your way to the next outpost." The word *bastards* had come out as a growl. Too many of my men had been lost fighting in Caleb's war—and it was *his* war. Not ours. We hadn't asked for the bloodshed. We hadn't started the fighting. Like anyone with the grit to stand against tyranny, we'd merely resisted. "Miranda and Stephens can handle that one. You and McIntyre continue on to number four."

Behind Lloyd, Collins was slipping the gun free from Johnson's corpse. Every weapon was a valuable commodity. We couldn't afford to leave one behind—even if it was covered in our fallen comrade's blood. Tearing my gaze away, I told myself to stay focused. There would be time for pain, time for reflection, later. Right now, there was only time for action. Lloyd nodded in acknowledgment of my orders. He said, "What about you?"

"Collins, Thompson, and I will work our way to number one while Jack and Simmons cover us from here, before we proceed east to number two. Don't stop until the job's done. No matter what happens, we need to take out all four outposts, and we need to do so at the same time. After the detonators are hit, Collins, Thompson, and I will head inside, locate the leader of the Allegiance, and haul balls out of there. We'll regroup at the old windmill we passed two clicks back and return to base together." My jaw was clenched in determination. "Now let's blow it all to hell, grab that asshole, and go home, soldier."

"For Johnson." A spark of sorrow and fury flashed in Lloyd's eyes. I recognized it for what it was—a yearning for vengeance. I'd seen it in my reflection countless times since this madness had begun four years ago. He pursed his lips and added, "For Millie and the twins."

Gripping his hand in mine, locking our thumbs together, I held his gaze. "For freedom."

This fight was bigger than one family. It was bigger than one battle, bigger than every life taken. If we surrendered . . . if we failed . . . all hope was lost. Freethinking would become a memory. Conformation would become expected. Silence would become the norm. No greater horror threatened us—all of us, those under Caleb's rule as well—than total, complete submission to one madman's dream.

No one knew that better than I did. First my parents, and then Kai, had chosen to go over to the side of the Allegiance, tempted by their promise of a safer America, with stronger borders, even before it was clear that when it came to the Allegiance, there was no real choice. It was join or die. Conform or perish.

I was thirteen when the war began four years ago, but I didn't feel seventeen now. I felt like I was in my forties. War ages you. It rots you from the inside out.

Before the war had begun, my life had been simple. Happy, even. I had friends, family, and the understanding that no matter what I felt, thought, believed, my loved ones would support me. Just days before the fighting began, before everyone over the age of ten was pulled out of school and handed a weapon, I'd decided to tell my mother that I understood that I was different, that the gender assigned to me at birth wasn't quite right. But then the Allegiance ripped that moment away from me before I could utter a word. The same way it had ripped my family from me.

Stop it, Quinn. Just stop it. Shake off the self-pity, get your shit together, *man up*, and take the outpost down, no matter the cost. People are counting on you.

Lloyd gathered his team and led them west. He was a good man. A good friend. So why was it that a sickened, angry feeling bubbled up within me as I watched him dart from cover to cover? For a moment, I felt wronged by him, bullied by him. The sensation passed, but it shook me. I'd never questioned Lloyd's loyalty before—not once. He was the guy who'd walked me through how to disassemble, clean, and reassemble rifles and pistols countless times, until I got it right. For three years, he'd been my best friend and number one. If anyone was loyal and trustworthy, it was him.

Jack and Simmons each had their eyes on their scopes, taking inventory of any trouble ahead. This outpost, number one, was the newest, and therefore the most solid. It'd be the toughest to take down, I was certain—which is why I wanted to oversee the infiltration of this one.

Simmons squeezed his trigger and took a shot, sending a bullet whizzing past my right ear. Instead of the predicted return fire, only silence followed, which put me on edge. Caleb's men had stopped shooting altogether, stopped sending ordnance our way. Why? Experience had taught me that there was always a method to one's madness, and always a motive behind one's method.

Jack shifted his attention to me just long enough to give a nod. Our path was clear. It was time to move.

I hand-signaled to Thompson and Collins before taking point and advancing north, winding my way around trees with care. Every ten yards or so, I'd gesture to pause under cover. The silence was deafening. I doubted Caleb's men had retreated. They had a reputation for do or die. But if they were still in the outpost, what the hell were they doing?

They had to know we'd expect an ambush. Did they honestly think they could surprise us?

Thompson mouthed the words "I can't see them." Just twenty yards from the outpost, the tree line broke, leaving nothing but forest floor between the three of us and our unseen enemies.

Unseen. A strange shiver slid up my spine. The word itself invoked a sense of fear in me, but I wasn't certain why. Shaking it off, I examined the outpost's doors and windows for any sign of life. Finding none, I braced myself and moved forward, keeping low. Behind me were the soft footfalls of boots on the ground—there was a reason I chose these two. Both knew how to move in silence and had excellent instincts when shit went sideways. And when it came to fighting, shit almost always went sideways in one manner or another.

Especially lately. My mind had been all over the place and it was starting to affect the missions, but I wasn't sure what to do about it. If things quieted down for a while, maybe I could discuss it with Lloyd. He'd understand. He always understood.

An arm locked tight around my neck from behind. A blade pressed into the seams of my vest. My ribs ached from the pressure. Whoever had me knew the weak spots of my uniform. Kevlar lined my chest and back, but along my sides was only cloth. By the pressure of his weapon, I knew he meant business. I gripped my attacker's wrist and twisted hard but couldn't break free. My back grew warm, and it was only when their grip relaxed and I turned around that I realized I was covered in blood.

But not my blood.

My assailant fell to the ground with a gurgle. Thompson stood over the body, his bowie knife in hand—its polished blade gleaming red. It wasn't the first time he'd saved my life, and I was certain it wouldn't be the last. I looked at the face of my would-be assassin and cursed under my breath.

Collins. Of all people. One of my most reliable. One I never would've expected of betrayal.

No wonder the shots had ceased. Caleb's men must have received word that their man on the inside was in place and ready to take me out. They didn't need to waste time and bullets on killing me. They'd handed that task off to someone I thought was on my side.

An intense heat spread over my body as my fury rose. Caleb's cancer had spread into my team, the people I'd handpicked. You had a man's back in battle. You counted on your team. And you never turned on your own.

How could Collins betray us like that? How could he betray me? Had the Allegiance's doctrine gotten to him on some level? What was it that made a man shift loyalties in such a violent way?

Days before the mission we'd been drowning our

sorrows in whiskey and gin. I don't think I'd ever been so drunk before. My words were slurring. It was a miracle he could understand me. "I have a secret, Collins, but you can't tell anybody, okay?"

"Sir, yessir." He grinned, his eyes glazed by the effects of alcohol.

I leaned closer and whispered, but looking back, I probably spoke louder than I'd intended. "Nobody knows I'm queer, Collins. Nobody but you, and nobody but me."

The next morning I awoke with the worst hangover of my life and the terror of knowing that I'd confessed my deepest secret. Collins never said a word about that night, other than a comment about how much we'd had to drink. Had he remembered what I'd said and decided that I wasn't As God Intended? That I had to die?

I kicked his corpse hard, my boot slamming into the meaty remains with a thud. "You son of a bitch! Why? Why?!"

I was so full of anger that I barely noticed when Thompson put a hand on my shoulder and said, "Sir?"

"What?" I snapped—I knew I'd snapped—and immediately felt bad for having done so. It wasn't his fault one of our own had changed loyalties.

"The mission."

"Right." My heart was hammering so hard inside my chest that it pounded in my ears. I searched my memory for any sign that Collins might have been an Allegiance sympathizer, but came up empty. He'd been a model soldier.

Taking point, I kept low and hurried across the forest floor to the two-story building. I could just barely hear Thompson moving up behind me. He had my six—unlike that bastard Collins. I trusted Thompson. Of course . . . I had trusted Collins too.

Maybe I was a fool to think I knew them, that I understood them. After all, can you really know and understand anyone but yourself? No. Which drove home a lesson I'd learned over and over again. In the end, you're the only person you can rely on.

Slinging my rifle over my shoulder, its strap across my chest, I withdrew my pistol. The suppressor was already on, because nothing says amateur like being unprepared for the unexpected. When I looked back at Thompson, I saw he'd done the same. I signaled him to cover me as I made my way up to the wall of the outpost, and after receiving his nod, I took a breath, held it, and kicked open the door.

The lock busted and the door swung open. I gave the room a quick look. As far as I could tell, it was empty. But I kept my pistol drawn, just in case. The absolute wrongness of the situation was chewing away at the back of my brain. I'd just dared a step inside when I heard the familiar crack of an assault rifle . . . only it was coming from behind me. I dived inside and whipped my head around. Thompson had darted inside after me and was now crouched to the right of the still-open door, holstering his pistol and readying his rifle for action with steady hands.

I scanned the room but saw nothing we could bar the door with. Shoving it closed, I couldn't help but wonder if it was Caleb's men doing the shooting . . . or one of mine. That's the thing about betrayal. Once you experience it the first time, you spend the rest of your days on high alert, knowing that what had seemed impossible could actually happen.

With a calm voice, Thompson said, "I'm hit, sir. It's not bad. Hurts like a mother, but the Kevlar stopped the bullet from killing me."

Damn. My team was already down a man. I couldn't afford to lose Thompson as well. I said, "How limited is your movement?"

"That remains to be seen, sir."

It had always impressed me that Thompson never failed to follow my orders without question. He was twice my age, with three times my experience. But Thompson respected rank and trusted me. "Are you sure you're okay?"

"Okay enough to take this outpost down despite the pansy-ass queers shooting at us." He furrowed his brow at the expression on my face. "What is it, sir?"

I stumbled over my response, taken aback by the insult that had left his lips so effortlessly. I shouldn't have felt surprised—words like that were relatively common among the soldiers I knew, and as far as I could tell, no one but I knew about my recent admission to Collins. But the feeling his words had stirred within me shook me to my core. Pulling myself together, I said, "If even half the guys on my team were as tough as you, we'd have taken Allegiance headquarters months ago, Thompson."

His mouth stretched into a grin. "Can't argue with that. What's our next move?"

"Be on guard. After I clear the top floor, I'm going to rig the C-4 and take out as many of our new friends as I can from upstairs. Once we have a window, we're making a break for it, and blowing this damn thing all to hell."

Even in the semidarkness, I could see his smirk. "Roger that, sir."

At the back of the small building was a built-in ladder with access to the next floor. As I climbed it, I listened, but heard no one. To my relief—and surprise—the room was empty.

My pack was full but not as heavy as it had been in the past. I wasn't carrying the usual medical supplies or rations, but something far more important, far more valuable.

Eight blocks of C-4, a hundred yards of detonator cord,

and one detonator. Everything I needed to reduce the outpost to rubble. With steady hands, I adhered a block to each wall and connected the cord between them. It was easy, like a kid sticking really dangerous Silly Putty to the wall. We had more than a few former military members in the Resistance, and when several of them had pushed for obtaining explosives from the Allegiance, I knew to listen. We'd lucked out on locating a stash of C-4, but we'd lost three people in the process.

There was too much death in my life. I feared I was becoming numb to it.

The crack of Thompson's gunshot ripped through the air. All we needed was to keep the soldiers outside at bay long enough to blow this damn thing, and then get to cover so we could advance unseen.

I carried my pack back down the ladder and rigged the last four blocks, connecting the detonator cord so that it would all blow at once the moment I hit the button on my walkie. Channel thirteen. It was a band that neither the Allegiance nor the Resistance used, so I'd set that channel as the trigger. One click, and the walkie would send a signal that would end the existence of outpost one. I was relieved that Caleb's people were outside. I may have become numb to death, but I hated killing.

With every kill, I lost a bit of my humanity. What would

I be when there was nothing left of me to lose? What was I now?

"Take point and head out, Thompson. Keep them off us but try to leave them alive."

He cast me a rare questioning look. "Sir?"

"Just do it. We're out in three . . . two . . . one."

Thompson pulled the door open again and did a quick check for enemies. Clouds had moved in overhead, blanketing the stars. Darkness had devoured every bit of light in the world around us. It was a painful metaphor to swallow.

He nodded to me before moving outside, with me on his six. My rifle was in my hands, ready for action. My walkie was clipped to my vest. I wanted it ready to go the moment we were clear—or if we were captured, I'd make sure to do some damage and blow the outpost before they managed to kill me.

A bullet whizzed past my head, exploding into the wood behind me. As if in reflex, Thompson aimed and fired a return shot. Muzzle fire lit up the night as Allegiance soldiers sprayed the area with bullets. Thompson and I made a break for it, keeping low as we advanced.

We ran into a grove thick with bushes, trees, and undergrowth. Dropping to our stomachs, we lay very still and waited for the sound of boots on the ground closing in, but it soon seemed that we were clear. I unclipped the walkie and thought about every life that Caleb's orders had taken. My hands were shaking—not with fear, but with anger.

I hit the trigger, and seconds later, a fiery cloud burst into life where outpost one had been. A blast wave hit me and Thompson both. My chest felt like someone had body-slammed into me, but the feeling soon passed. One after another, outposts two through four exploded. With a small smile, I pressed the button on the comm in my ear and spoke using our agreed-upon code for the mission. "The orchard has been entered, gentlemen. See you at the rendezvous point after we shake the tree, with apricot acquired. Drinks on me tonight."

Combined laughter came through on the comm. Lloyd followed it up with "You're so full of shit, sir."

He was right. It was a running gag between us. Each of them knew I wasn't much of a drinker. I didn't often partake, but I could remember my very first drink vividly.

As a movement, the Allegiance had gotten its start in small towns, with whispers, then shouts. It was when they overthrew the North Carolina state government and set up an HQ in the Raleigh capitol building that the rest of America realized they were a major threat.

By then, it was too late. The Allegiance was already sweeping through the South and over the East Coast as if there was no one there to stand against them. Some of the major cities, like New York and Chicago, held out for a while. But eventually, even they fell under the Allegiance flag.

Our country cried when hundreds were killed; protested when it was thousands; but when the number of dead reached millions, our voices fell silent in horror—what voices remained standing against the Allegiance, that is. By that time, the majority of people had sided with them.

Not everyone gave up hope, though.

Resistance groups were popping up all over the country, and by the time the Allegiance reached us in Brume, the majority of the residents here had banded together, ready to stop them before they could occupy us too. Anyone over the age of ten became a soldier. Veterans trained us how to fight. Nurses showed us how to treat battle wounds. But no one taught us how to deal with the trauma of war. No one could.

I was just thirteen when I had my first alcoholic drink. A group of us had been on the eastern side of town, doing all we could to defend ourselves in a hardware store, where many of our supplies were being kept. The shooting and the smoke had grown so intense you could barely see, until, finally, one of our men had set off a well-placed stun grenade. The Allegiance had backed off—things could've turned out much worse if they hadn't. Afterward, I'd found myself in the park, my hands shaking, tears running down my cheeks. At the height of the cross fire, I'd seen a man's head get blown in half two yards in front of me. Gore had splattered my face, sticking my hair to my forehead. If I thought about it now, I could still feel that warm, slick sensation on my skin. His blood smelled metallic, like pennies. It tasted like death.

I was still crying when my brother, Kai, had found me. He'd offered me a bottle of whiskey, and when I'd looked at him in confusion, he'd said, "Sometimes a man needs a drink, Quinn. And you are definitely a man now." For the next few hours, we sat outside the small cave in the park and shared swigs from the bottle. It was nasty shit, but it served its numbing purpose. We didn't talk. I still don't know what he was thinking in that moment, but I was mulling over what he'd said. Was I a man? What made me so? Hadn't I been one before I'd experienced the horrors of war? Or was that really what it took?

If so, maybe I didn't want to be a man at all.

That wasn't just the first time I had a drink, or the first time I started to wonder if maybe being a man wasn't all it was cracked up to be. That was also the last time my brother and I had a quiet moment together. Before he switched sides. Before he betrayed all that our family had stood for and pledged his loyalty to the Allegiance.

Damn him.

Now, silent as smoke, Thompson and I moved toward Allegiance headquarters. At one point, this building had been city hall, but no longer. Now it was draped on all sides by the "As God Intended" banners.

Our intel said that after nightfall, Caleb would be in the northwest corner of the main building, inside his quarters. Our people on the inside had confirmed it, and Lloyd and I had worked as fast as we could to organize a plan to take him into custody.

Thompson and I kept low, moving in on our target like fog. Intel said that a single guard stood watch outside the room's only window, and as we rounded the corner, I saw the soldier standing there with his assault rifle in hand. The sounds of gunfire at the outpost didn't seem to have rattled his nerves. Maybe it was the arrogance of the Allegiance filling his head, telling him that headquarters was safe. Withdrawing my pistol, I took aim, ready to prove that notion wrong. I know I said I was tired of killing, but sometimes you had no choice but to take one life in order to save thousands of others.

Before I could squeeze the trigger, Thompson placed his hand on my shoulder, drawing my attention. I followed his eyes to a man and a woman walking nearby. They were the picture of the Allegiance—both white, him with broad, masculine shoulders, her wearing a simple gold cross on a thin chain around her neck, their hands clasped together. If one of them saw us, we were dead.

I wondered if either of them had ever questioned whether being on the side of the Allegiance was wrong. Did they wonder if maybe they'd rather be holding hands with someone of a different gender? Did they keep secrets . . . the way I was keeping a secret about my gender identity?

I held my breath, as did Thompson, but in moments, the couple was gone. It was time to capture Caleb and end this war.

"Freeze!" The window guard had his rifle pointed right at us, though I couldn't be certain if it was me or Thompson in his sights. We'd been caught.

Thompson aimed at the guard and fired, but missed. The guard fired back, just grazing Thompson's shoulder. Armed guards snapped their attention to us. My heart raced inside my chest. The mission had failed. Now the best we could do was survive. "Thompson, go!"

I grabbed the grenade from my web belt and pulled the pin, tossing it toward the approaching soldiers before taking off as fast as I could after Thompson. It bounced twice and then exploded into a cloud of shrapnel. My left calf stung from a small hit, but I could still run. Chaos erupted in the courtyard. The grenade had distorted everyone's hearing and clouded the area with the dirt and debris it had thrown into the air, limiting their sight.

It was a miracle we didn't get shot.

It took Thompson and me some time, but we hoofed it to the rendezvous point. The old windmill stood sentinel as we approached. From the shadows came the rest of my team, each looking satisfied with their endeavors. One by one, I saw the realization form in their eyes that Thompson and I had failed. The supplies we'd used up taking out the outposts, the detailed planning we'd labored on, the risk of life and limb . . . they were all for nothing.

After a head count—everyone we'd started with, minus Johnson and Collins—we hoofed it back to base, shoulders slumped in defeat. My thoughts should have been on our next move, but they weren't. I could think only of Caleb, safe in his room, and me not being there to erase that smug smile from his face. Had the distraction I'd been plagued with lately affected this mission too? The thought ate at me. It consumed me all the way back to our base, all the way inside the double doors and into the main floor hall.

Since the beginning of Brume's Resistance, our HQ had been in the basement of the old high school. It had made sense at the time. It was the sturdiest building in town, at Brume's center, with room for a few hundred people to operate from. All our strategies were planned there. All the major medical tasks were performed upstairs in the makeshift hospital before moving patients to some of the homes in the surrounding area for convalescence. It was important, they said—and I still believed—that the pain and death caused by this war shouldn't be kept hidden from those planning actions in it. If we were sending people to fight and perhaps die, we'd better be able to look our wounded and dying in the face before doing so.

We'd taken great pains to hide our HQ from the Allegiance. The medical facility was located on the main and top floors of the school, with HQ tucked carefully beneath it. The interior entrance to both the basement and boiler room had been walled in, so the only access point was a heavy metal door on the back of the school, hidden by a slope of grass. A sniper was assigned to the rooftop and an armed guard just behind the slope at all times. Their sole job was to protect the base entrance. As far as anyone who wasn't involved in classified Resistance maneuvers knew, there was nothing down there but the boiler and old gym equipment.

A few of my team members lined up for medical attention. I wasn't really wounded—no more than my pride, anyway—so I only entered the hospital for one reason. To find Lia.

I moved down the hall, past countless hurt, helpless people. More than once, I noticed eyes lighting up in recognition when they looked at me—the person who'd been labeled the face of the Brume Resistance. The admiration in their eyes as I passed by filled me with an uncomfortable twinge. They owed me no gratitude. All I had done in the last four years was stand up to tyranny—the way anyone with a conscience would. The way anyone whose freedom has been threatened should.

The truth was, I was realizing more and more that I didn't *want* to be the face of our Resistance. How could I be the guiding symbol for a group that, for all its talk of standing up to the Allegiance, was hardly proving much better at making room for people who were different? At least in Brume. The men on my team had made it clear they wouldn't accept female soldiers, and the way they talked about queer people, it was obvious they didn't want them joining the ranks either. I didn't share or support those prejudices. But here I was, fighting for the cause, because it was better than the alternative. I hated hypocrites. And now I was one in more ways than I'd ever feared.

Lia hurried up the hall toward me, dressed in scrubs that had once been white, but were now stained with blood, old and new. I was about to tell her that we'd failed—that I had failed—but then she threw her arms around my neck and pressed her mouth to mine before I could speak. Her lips were soft, and as we kissed, she melted into me, holding me close like she was afraid I might disappear. When we parted, she said, "I'm so glad you're back. How'd it go?"

"Not so good. We lost Johnson and Collins. Thompson and

I were so close to grabbing that bastard Caleb but couldn't." I didn't mention Collins's betrayal. Lia didn't need to know about that. Nobody did, as far as I was concerned. Let his family think he died a hero. It was the least I could do for them.

A man dressed all in black passed by us in the hall. His hair was stringy and wet. He didn't look like any of the Resistance members I knew, and his snakeskin trench coat certainly looked out of place next to everyone's tech vests. He was a stranger to me. Probably visiting one of the wounded. I couldn't know every face in Brume and certainly didn't know his. But he looked familiar all the same.

Lia lowered her voice. "I'm sorry. We'll get by. We always do."

"Lia, we're out of food. How are we supposed to get by without that?" My tone was sharper than it probably should've been. It wasn't her fault we'd failed. It was mine.

"We'll find a way. You always think of something." She must have seen the protest in my eyes, because she changed gears. "I'm glad you're okay. I couldn't stand the idea of you getting hurt again . . . or worse."

"It comes with the job, Lia. You know that."

"I do. But I also know that you take on too much responsibility around here. And I know you dream of a peaceful end to this war, but what if the Allegiance won't listen, even if you're holding their leader hostage? What if killing Caleb is the only way to end this?" Her eyes shimmered with concern. She placed her hand on my chest, as if feeling my heart beat. Her touch sent a shiver of want through me. "I know it may not be what you'd like to hear, but taking a shot at him from afar or planting a bomb may be the only route to peace. Have you thought of that?"

"Sir?" Lloyd's timing couldn't have been better.

I planted a kiss on her forehead and said, "I've gotta go."

We moved out the front doors and took a wide berth around the building, checking carefully to be sure we weren't being followed to the basement door. The guard on duty gave us a nod in greeting. "Evening, sirs."

"Evening, Madison," I said as I unlocked the door and held it open for Lloyd. Only twenty-five people knew the entry code to the base entrance, and we kept that code well protected, changing it once a week. The door unlocked both ways. You used the code to get in and that same code to get out again. "I thought Fitzsimmons was on duty tonight."

Madison shifted awkwardly, forgetting his bearing for the moment. "Fitzsimmons took off. If he knows better, he'll stay gone."

A dull throb was working its way from the base of my skull to my temples. "What are you talking about?"

"He hit on Conrad last night. It was a total misunderstanding. They were pretty drunk. But today a couple of the guys made sure he knew that kinda thing wasn't welcome here. Matter of fact, they drove that point home with a bloody nose." The look on his face suggested he hadn't agreed with their action, but he was apprehensive about giving voice to his dissent.

I could feel my eyebrow twitching, my face heating with anger. I'd suspected for a long time that Fitzsimmons was gay—Madison too—or at least on the spectrum, but I never said anything. That was their business. And telling anyone my suspicion about Madison would land him in the same proverbial boat as Fitzsimmons. I didn't want that. He was a good soldier. So what if he preferred the company of men? Who gave a shit?

Too many people, I thought.

The way Madison looked at me now made me wonder if he was assuming things about me the same way I was assuming things about him. A silent understanding passed between us. I offered him a nod and followed Lloyd inside.

The musty smell of the basement filled my nose as I entered. Shaking off my irritation, I said, "What is it, Lloyd?"

His shoulders looked tense. All of him did. "Five of our people are dead."

"Shit," I cursed under my breath.

The basement had been divided into four sections. Central command was in the front. To the right was munitions storage. To the left was the supplies storeroom. We walked through the set of double doors at the end and entered the fourth room—my office. Maps of the town and surrounding areas hung on the walls, next to layout sketches of Allegiance headquarters, photos of their command structure, and an ongoing list of names of every Brume citizen who'd switched over to the Allegiance, as far as we knew. As Lloyd closed the doors behind us, I placed my hand on my large, mahogany desk at the center of the room. My palm was warm against the wood, and the moment I made contact, I felt a strange craving for a cup of tea.

Strange, because I hadn't had tea in two years. Stranger still, because I'd never cared much for it.

My desk was covered with the usual stacks of notes—reminders of all that remained to be accomplished. There were too many things for my heart to handle. A heavy sigh escaped me. "Spit it out."

"Apparently, while we were on our mission, some of the guys went on a rogue supply run to the warehouse on the north end of town." Lloyd paused for a beat, letting his words sink in some. "Caleb's men were expecting them. We don't know how."

"Collins told him." My words were matter-of-fact.

Snapping his eyes to me in surprise, Lloyd said, "Sir, Collins wouldn't—"

"He tried to kill me, Lloyd." I held his gaze. "Snuck up behind me like a coward while we were making our way to outpost one."

After a moment's consideration, he furrowed his brow. "He could've told the Allegiance about our plans to attack headquarters. But if he did that, then why didn't they stop us from destroying the outposts?"

"I don't know. Maybe they thought I'd lead the team inside HQ. Maybe they were willing to do a little postbattle reconstruction if it meant killing me. We all know I'm not Caleb's favorite person in Brume." The corner of my mouth twitched. "Or Kai's."

My brother and I had been as close as siblings could get. He was my mentor, my best friend, the one person I could trust without question . . . until he wasn't. Losing him would've been easier if he was dead. At least then the mourning period would end. Instead, every day carried with it reminders of the pain I'd felt when I learned that my brother wasn't the person I'd always thought he was.

"So he sacrificed some of his own men and four of his outposts just to lure you to headquarters?" Lloyd's words dripped with disgust. His hand found the butt of the gun at his hip in an unconscious manner, as if just the mention of Caleb had stirred up something violent within him. With a sigh, he took a seat. "I guess that makes sense. You're the face of the Resistance here in Brume. If he kills you, he kills all our hope of taking the Allegiance down."

"Don't give me that crap. I'm not the face of anything. The Resistance would go on without me."

He rubbed his brow, as if in an attempt to stave off a headache. "For a while, yeah. But not for long. We need you, Quinn. You're our inspiration to go on fighting."

"Really? Because I thought the inspiration for this stupid fight was all of us, standing up to the racist, immoral, and just plain wrong bullshit that the Allegiance was forcing down our throats. Just because my family chose the wrong side and I made a hard decision to stand with my morals—something anyone could do—doesn't make me an inspiration. It just makes me a person trying to do what they can for the side of good." As I sank into my chair, I raked my hair back from my face. "Sometimes, Lloyd . . . sometimes I wonder if I'm helping people . . . or damning them. There are dozens of soldiers in Brume that are older than me and more experienced. Why follow me? I'm just getting people killed."

He slapped a hand on the top of my desk, as if trying to wake me from some pitiful dream. "We've had this conversation, Quinn. More times than I can count. I told you, I'm through convincing you that you're doing good here. What are we going to do about our mission failure? News of it will spread like wildfire. People are going to panic."

"Maybe they should. What am I even doing here, Lloyd?"

"From what I can see, you're losing your grip. Now get your shit together and grow a pair, because like it or not, you are in charge. You are the one who's going to lead us to removing Caleb from power or die trying. So sack up."

Barely able to contain my laughter, I cocked an eyebrow at him. "Sack up?"

Lloyd chuckled. "It sounded cooler in my head."

Leave it to Lloyd to lighten my mood.

I didn't know what to do about the failed attack, or the lack of supplies, or the growing sense that I was fighting for a cause that wasn't really fighting for me. I only knew that I wanted a smoke. Possibly several smokes.

As I grabbed a pack from my desk drawer, a memory came to me. Familiar, softly spoken words like cobwebs on my brain.

"No thanks. I don't smoke."

"Oh, that's right. Not here you don't."

"Quinn?" Lloyd's voice broke in.

"Yeah?"

"You okay? Your face went kinda white for a second there."

"I'm fine." Get it together, Quinn. Get it there and keep it there. You've got a rebellion to run. "Any other news to report?"

For a moment, Lloyd looked like he had something more to say about the way my face had apparently paled, but he quickly shifted gears back to the business at hand.

"The medics have taken to washing and reusing bandages." Not good. Used bandages meant infection. Infection meant death. "Intel tells us that the Allegiance has stores of goods—both food and medical supplies—in an old shipping yard on the north side of town. If we can break in there and take out any guards, it could buy us another month, maybe even two."

"No."

A sliver of concern in Lloyd's expression widened into a chasm. "It'll be a challenge, but we can handle it. Preparations need to be made before we can—"

"I said no. People are dying, Lloyd." My voice cracked on the last two syllables. I could feel my eyes moistening with guilty tears, but I blinked them away before Lloyd could see. Crying meant being soft, being soft meant being weak, and a leader of the Resistance was anything but that. He couldn't be. I was supposed to "man up" and keep my shit together. That's what my dad had taught me. That's what society had reiterated to me over and over again.

Sometimes I questioned what the hell society was thinking, dictating what a person could or couldn't be.

"People are always dying." His tone was matter-of-fact. He wasn't saying it to be cruel. He was just telling me what I needed to be reminded of. "You can't save them all, Quinn. And what pain, suffering, and death has occurred doesn't fall on your shoulders alone. You've done so much good, risen the Resistance here in Brume to levels we never had a chance of achieving without you. Because of you, we're going to show those Allegiance bastards that they don't own us, they don't own Brume. But you've got to get it together. Get it there and keep it there."

Inside my troubled mind, I pictured families going without food because I'd failed to do what I'd set out to. Soldiers dying on the table from infection because I hadn't ensured their well-being. Then I saw Johnson's face, contorted in pain as he died. His wife. His girls. "It's too risky. Too dangerous."

"Quinn, people need our help, and if supplies are out there for the taking, we should be taking them. If we just—"

"Find another way!" I'd raised my voice without intending to, but was glad that I did, because Lloyd left the room right then, with purpose in his steps.

Sighing wearily, I scanned the bookcases and then the large map of Brume hanging on the wall. I glanced down to my desk, where I'd laid out a file folder, my brass knuckles, a pack of cigarettes, and a handkerchief embroidered with a cursive letter *L*. I picked up the latter and pressed it to my nose, inhaling the subtle scent of rose water. It had been a gift from Lia—one that I'd carried with me on every mission but this last one. I'd simply forgotten it. It was supposed to be good luck, a reminder that she believed in me and the cause, and I'd just left it behind.

I left *her* behind.

"Sir, can I speak with you?" Susan, one of the many soldiers who guarded our base, stood in my doorway looking anxious. Since the day I'd met her, she'd been a straight shooter, not an ounce of bullshit in sight. I liked that about her.

I returned the handkerchief to my desktop and met Susan's eyes. I already knew what she was going to ask. She'd asked many times before. When would she get that the answer was no? "What's on your mind?"

"I was hoping I could assist on the next maneuver." Her voice carried with it the strength and assertiveness that I'd come to expect from all Resistance soldiers. Which made it all the more difficult to let her down.

"You *can* assist—by staying here and guarding the base."

The corner of her mouth twitched. "But sir, I'm more than qualified."

Susan had spent thirteen years as a cop before the Allegiance had become an imminent threat to America's freedom. I still recalled the way she'd worn her hair in a tight bun—a far cry from the pixie cut she donned now. I remembered her uniform, crisp and neat. And the way she'd spoken with such authority on the day we'd met, seven years ago. Kai had been caught shoplifting some candy from the gas station and Susan had been dispatched to put a healthy amount of fear in him. As she'd talked to him about how a small action, a single poor decision, could lead to a life of crime, I'd marveled at the shiny handcuffs on her belt and wondered what it would be like to wear them. To me, her message went largely unheard. I was ten, doing things that a ten-year-old was supposed to do. Not fighting in some shitty war. Not like the ten-year-olds now.

I sat back in my chair, meeting her eyes. "We've had this conversation, Susan. The men wouldn't trust your abilities or follow your directions out there."

"Because I'm a woman?" I didn't have to speak. She saw the yes written all over my face. I wished it weren't the truth, that the Resistance was more open-minded about gender roles—better, in that way, than the Allegiance—but we both knew they weren't. A look of pure disgust flashed in her eyes. "Excuse me, sir, but that's such bullshit."

She was right, but that didn't change anything. "I wish it were different, but it's not. If it were up to me—"

"No offense, sir, but it *is* up to you. This part, anyway." Anger lit up her eyes, and I didn't blame her for feeling it. "Permission to speak freely?"

"Granted."

Her face was flushed, but she kept her tone just this side of furious. "You don't know how it feels to serve side by side with men, to work equally as hard in defense of a cause, only to be dismissed simply because of someone else's idea of how a person's gender affects the way they fit in the world. It's not fair."

She was right. It wasn't fair. It wasn't fair that she was held to a different standard than her male counterparts. And maybe it wasn't fair that I kept my feeling of Otherness to myself for fear of the repercussions. Repercussions that I'd be treated less-than . . . the same way she'd been treated. "I'm just as trapped in this patriarchal world as you are, soldier."

"No. You aren't. Men are revered in any military structure. Respected. If you're not a man, it doesn't matter how hard you work, you'll never be looked at the way they are. You can never understand that, sir. Because you're one of them."

I wanted to tell her that I did understand, at least to a point, and that my comprehension was precisely what kept my mouth shut. But in the end, my secrets were mine to bear. She was right, though. I couldn't really understand. Not fully. By keeping my mouth shut, I avoided much of that prejudice. That was an option that she didn't have. "What would you have me do? Change the entirety of society?"

“No. Just help the change begin. Send me on the supply mission. I’m more than capable.”

“I can’t.”

“Then you’re part of the problem.”

My heartbeat thumped inside my chest, reverberating up through my skull—the accompanying drumbeat to a song of my hypocrisy. I kept my tone firm. “As I was saying before, if it were up to me, gender wouldn’t be a determining factor in what we are expected or allowed to do. But I can’t change the way the world works, soldier. Not on my own. And not by sending you into battle when it could lead to infighting in the ranks.”

“But sir, if—”

“You know the rules. Women can’t serve at the front. You *know* that. You want to enlist? Fine. You want to help us fight? Great. Your past skill set is invaluable. But you help from *here*. You fight behind the scenes by guarding headquarters and no more. That’s just how it is. You’re not going on any missions. And I don’t want to have this conversation again. Am I clear?” I’d risen my voice and meant to this time.

She dropped her gaze to the floor between us. I was surprised not to see frustrated tears welling in her eyes. If our roles had been reversed, mine certainly would have been. “Yes, sir.”

“Then we’re done here. Dismissed.” As she exited the

room, my chest felt hollow and empty.

You're a hypocrite, Quinn, I thought. *You've been questioning your gender identity and couldn't even reach past the limitations of the Resistance you're supposed to be the face of long enough to begin bringing about a sliver of change. She's right. You* are *part of the problem.*

Shaking off my thoughts, I flipped open the file nearest me and jotted down the details of our failed abduction attempt. Failed, because I hadn't kept my eyes on that damn window guard. Failed, because I wasn't good enough, and now people were going to die because of my failings. With a loud curse, I whipped the pen across the room. It hit the door with a whack and fell to the ground. It was too much, this war. And I wasn't certain I could help the Resistance any more than I already had. I was running out of ideas. I was running out of steam. I was running out of hope.

I snatched my pack of cigarettes from my desk and slipped it inside my vest. I walked out of my office, trying my best not to look at the door to the supply storeroom as I passed by. Seeing the empty shelves would do me no good at the moment. I knew we were out of food, out of everything we needed to live. I wouldn't find the answers there. The answers lay somewhere inside my mind—or at least that's what my soldiers kept telling me.

After entering the pass code on the door, I stepped

outside and locked it behind me again. Shift change had happened while I was inside. Madison had been replaced by Carlton. I offered him a nod, which he returned.

With as much care as I could, I made my way to the front doors of the school unseen. Through the doors, I was greeted by the scent of sanitizer, medicines, bleach . . . and blood. Blood that was the result of my actions in one way or another.

Lia was helping a girl about three years old drink from a cup in the old nurse's office that now acted as the children's ward. With a glance at me, she straightened, and her expression fell. She folded her arms in front of her, as if she was trying to sink inside herself or maybe wrap herself in the only comfort she could count on without fail. She should be able to count on me. And I was a shit for hurting her. Even unintentionally. A sigh escaped her as I stepped closer. "You're going out there again, aren't you?"

I nodded. "Once we can find a way to safely acquire some supplies. Lloyd's gathering intel now so we can act soon."

Lia blinked, as if to blink away tears, but there were no tears. Her frustration had swallowed them. "You want to end this? Take Caleb out. It's the only way, Quinn."

"You may be right." All around us, despite the injuries and stress, eyes were lit up in hope—something we hadn't had an ounce of just a year before. "Killing Caleb is one of those ways. But before we resort to that, I have to try to find a peaceful way to end this."

"I know that. I just . . ." She sighed again, meeting my gaze. "I worry."

"Me too." About so much more than she was even aware.

Her edges softened in concern. "What's the face of the Resistance worried about today?"

"Well, for one, Lloyd told me about the bandages."

"We're doing all we can."

"That's why I have to go. Because if I don't, more people will die." There was a moment of silence in which she closed her eyes in search of something to say that would change my mind. But there was no way of changing it. I had no choice. People were counting on me.

"You've brought Brume to the brink of freedom, Quinn. That's why we all follow you, why we trust you."

A bitter feeling shot through my core—one for which I had an immediate dislike. "And Caleb? Why do his people follow him?"

"Apart from the fact that his father was the leader before he died?" She reached out and smoothed the front of my vest with her hands, keeping her palms on my chest as she replied. I wondered if she noticed the pack of cigarettes I'd tucked there. Her voice was calm and confident, with undertones of anger—but none of it toward me. "They follow him because he talks pretty, tells them what they want to hear, pretends to deliver, and makes the Resistance out to be the bad guys. Some people, no matter how much evidence they're presented, simply want to follow blindly. It's easier than searching for the truth."

In that moment, I fell in love with her all over again. Brushing a strand of hair from her eyes, I said, "When did you get so smart?"

"I've always been smart." A smile danced on her lips.

I kissed the tip of her nose and said, "I'm gonna step outside for a few. Do you wanna join me?"

Shaking her head, she said, "No way. I hate that you smoke."

"Then I'll quit."

"You always say that and you never do." She reached up and cradled my scruffy cheeks in her hands for a moment. We were okay. Better than okay. We were good. She nodded toward the door at the end of the hall. "Enjoy your so-called last cigarette."

Again, a voice whispered inside my head—like a dream I'd had and forgotten.

"No thanks. I don't smoke."

"Oh, that's right. Not here you don't."

As I pulled a cigarette from my pack and placed it between my lips, I tried to recall where I'd heard those words before, but nothing came to mind. Maybe I'd overheard the conversation somewhere. Maybe it really was just the remnants of some forgotten dream.

But if either of those things were true, then why did the words send a chill through me that I couldn't shake?

18

I stepped outside and tried to ignore the sounds of gunfire in the distance. It sounded too small to be a skirmish. Probably a training exercise. I couldn't escape reminders of the war, but I could tune them out for five minutes. Doing so used to make me feel selfish, but I quickly learned that five minutes here and there of forgetting the horrors of the world was enough to preserve my sanity. At least for the time being.

The park across the street was overgrown, but at least it was green. It was at the center of Resistance territory, which stretched six blocks in every direction. The outskirts were as well guarded as we could manage, while appearing just like any other part of town, so as not to let on where our base was located. Off to the right of my view of the park, about ten yards in, was the entrance to a small cave. Lia and I had shared our first kiss in that cave about a year before. Her lips had been softer than I'd imagined. Mine trembled. And when we really sank into the kiss, suddenly the rightness of the world came into sharp focus. Sometimes, when things felt unbearable, I'd close my eyes and take myself back to that perfect moment—when I'd fallen so hard for Lia that nothing else mattered. Guns, wounds, food, the enemy—all of it had disappeared during that first kiss.

Nothing I could ever do would pay her back for the peace, the joy, she'd instilled in me in that instant. But I'd keep trying. And, God willing, she'd keep kissing me.

The sun was setting, and if I blocked out the screams coming from the makeshift operating room Lia and the others had assembled in the gymnasium of the school, I could immerse myself in the beauty of the world, the way my mother had always encouraged me to do. It was brief, but another necessary escape. Lia wanted to know why I didn't quit smoking. That was why. It was an escape. It was something I could give myself over to without planning or rationing or fighting. It was a terrible habit, but a vice I allowed myself on occasion. I wasn't a full-time smoker. But when I returned from a mission, I needed something to erase from my mind the things I saw, the horrors I was part of.

"Got a light?"

Leaning against the school was the stranger in the trench coat I'd seen inside earlier.

The Stranger, a voice at the back of my mind whispered.

His hair parted like stringy, wet curtains to reveal a thin face and dark, sunken eyes. I hesitated for a moment before pulling the lighter from my pocket and handing it to him. He lit a cigarette and gave it back. My entire body tensed when his fingertips touched my hand. His skin was *sticky*, and it triggered a memory I couldn't place. "Do I know you?"

"You may." He sucked in a lungful of nicotine, tar, and a hundred other things that neither one of us should be inhaling, and eyed the cave in the park. "Beautiful view. But as is the case with everything, true beauty lies inside."

Weirdo. "What the hell are you talking about?"

"Its frame really is lovely. Inspired, even. Don't you think?"

His words gave me pause. I never told anyone about what I'd seen the last time I was in the cave—not even Lia or Lloyd. I'd been trying to forget about it. Because it had to be a hallucination. There was no other way to explain it. And I wasn't ready to think about what else it might mean if I was having hallucinations.

It had been dark, so I'd taken a flashlight with me. Something had compelled me to enter, but I couldn't recall what. At the far end of the cave I'd found the impossible. An enormous mirror hanging in midair. No strings, no hooks, no wires. It was just . . . there.

The frame was black and twisted, with sharp points sticking out here and there, reminding me of snakes. My reflection had stared back at me, and when I'd reached out to touch the glass, my fingertips passed through the surface like it was fog.

If this stranger had seen it too, maybe it wasn't a hallucination after all . . .

"Are you talking about the . . . mirror?"

He paused before answering, and I started to feel like maybe I was the weird one here. But then he said, "Perhaps."

My throat felt somewhat drier than it had just seconds before. "Do you know what it is, exactly?"

"Everything. Nothing. It all depends." He shrugged, holding the half-smoked cigarette just inches from his mouth with his yellow-stained fingers.

"On what?"

He turned to face me. "On you."

I couldn't stop looking at his fingers, his hands. The skin had a slight sheen, as if it had been wet recently and had never really dried. His fingers looked older than a man his age would normally have. The thought that perhaps he worked as a mechanic or a farmer passed through my thoughts and then out again. The sight of his hands was so familiar to me. If I could just grasp the wispy threads of familiarity and tie them together, maybe I could figure out—

My words grew hushed in sudden realization. "I remember you. We spoke before."

"Perhaps we did."

He'd been standing outside in the sunshine. Sweet-smelling roses had all but surrounded us. The sun had been bright, the grass green. It was here, but it wasn't here. Not exactly. Where the hell was it? "You were . . . somewhere else. And so was I."

The corner of his mouth lifted in a smirk. "Perhaps we were."

My jaw tensed in frustration. This man was testing the limits of my ability to keep my temper in check, for sure. "I'm not interested in riddles. I don't have time for this."

"That's true." A knowing smile stretched across his face.

I drew my shoulders back, ready for a fight. Narrowing my eyes, I growled, "Is that a warning?"

"Yes." He lingered on the word. It came out sounding more like a hiss.

Bile rose up in my throat, but I choked it back down again. "Who are you?"

“The real question here is, who are you?” Tapping the ashes from his cigarette, he spoke without meeting my gaze. “Two down.”

Confusion filled me. Was this another riddle? He was going to give me answers if I had to beat them out of him. My subconscious whispered the words *with my bat*, but I shook them off. “Two down? What does that mean? I don’t under—”

“Two down!” A voice came over the comm in my ear with an air of urgency. “I repeat, we have two down! Request medics for immediate evac. Location Zulu Bravo.”

My chest tightened with the realization that the shots I’d heard hadn’t just been some training exercise. Guilt filled me. I hadn’t realized it was enemy fire. I should have. People were counting on me to keep them safe. I recognized the location by the assigned phonetic code. They were at the post office near the center of town, not three blocks from where I stood. Speaking into my comm, I said, “Zulu Bravo team, do you require an assist?”

The voice crackled over the comm in broken bits. “Nega . . . in hand . . . returning . . . wounded . . . ready.”

Furrowing my brow, I said, “Zulu Bravo team, you’re breaking up. Repeat message, please. Advise if you require an assist.”

Only static came through. I turned back to the Stranger, but no one was there. No cigarette butt on the ground. No shoe prints in the earth. It was as if he hadn't been there in the first place. So maybe the mirror was a hallucination after all. Maybe the Stranger was too.

Hours later, the smell of tobacco hung in my office like a cloud. Until that moment, I'd made it a point to keep my smoking outdoors. But my nerves were beyond frayed—and not just because Zulu Bravo team had suffered injuries. That man, that Stranger, had really gotten to me. Hallucination or no, I *had* seen him before. But where? Here . . . but not here. Doing what I could to keep my shit together, I took another drag and blew it out with my words. "An ambush. A goddamn ambush."

Lloyd sat in the chair across from my desk, favoring his left wrist. "There was no way of knowing. It should've been a milk run."

"It should've been reported to me before they even left." I was pissed, and by the look on his face, he knew it. Not just because my men had made a really stupid move without clearing it with me first, but because the Allegiance had known more about their movements than I had. Lloyd dropped his eyes to the floor for a moment. He should have told me they'd been planning a supply run. If I'd been told, I'd have informed them that there wasn't anything at the post office left to grab. "How did the Allegiance know the location?"

Lloyd frowned. "Maybe they have someone else on the inside."

My head began to throb with the beginnings of a migraine.

"Christ. That's all we need." With no ashtray in sight, I stabbed my cigarette out on the desktop and slumped forward, running my hands through my hair. I was letting a lot of people down if I didn't get some supplies . . . and fast. I drew air into my lungs and blew it out in a heavy sigh. Then, reluctantly, I said, "We're going to the shipping yard at twenty-hundred hours. Tell no one but the team we took to Allegiance HQ."

Forgetting all about his wrist for the moment, Lloyd sat forward. He looked as if he wanted to question what had changed my mind, but instead he said, "I'll inform the team immediately."

I sat back in my chair in contemplation. "If you were Caleb, would you think the Resistance would be stupid enough to try to hit the shipping yard head-on?"

He paused before looking at me pointedly. "Not a chance."

It was an insane mission, and could easily be our last, if things didn't go our way. Part of me wanted to talk to Lloyd about the feelings I'd been having about being Other, while I still could. Because, odds were, we weren't all going to make it out of there alive. Maybe none of us. But the fear of anyone knowing was just so strong. If Lloyd didn't react well, I could face a different kind of violence than the kind I was used to. War was scary, but somehow it didn't make the idea of being faced with bigotry and rejection from your friends any less scary. But if I could tell anyone that I was questioning what gender I identified with, it was Lloyd. He'd have some supportive advice. He always did. "Lloyd, can I ask you something that might seem a bit . . . strange?"

"Never stopped you before."

He was right. It never had. So why was this subject so damn difficult to discuss with him? We'd always shared everything. Why did this feel like something I had to keep secret, even from my best friend? The man had saved my life countless times. He had my back in a way that no one ever had. I took in a breath and readied my resolve. "Does it bother you that the Resistance shares certain prejudices with the Allegiance? Like, maybe the Resistance's version of freedom isn't entirely equal to everyone across the board?"

"What are you getting at, Quinn?" His brow had creased in curiosity. From outside the door came the sounds of soldiers performing an ammunition count. We weren't as alone as I'd hoped. For fear someone might overhear, the conversation would have to wait.

"Nothing. Never mind." Gesturing to his wrist with a

nod, I said, "What happened to you?"

"When I heard the call, I hurried over to Zulu Bravo to assist. Damn Allegiance soldier hit me with the butt of his gun while he was turning tail. No big deal. I've had worse." He shrugged. His expression shifted to a concerned look that I knew well. "Do you plan to tell Lia about the shipping yard?"

"I'll tell her after we get back. I don't want her to worry." Though it was subdued by fear and dread, the prickle of anticipation that I felt before any mission crackled up my spine, quieting my mind about the Stranger, the mirror, and all the things I wasn't telling Lloyd or Lia, at least for the time being. "Get the maps. We have to be precise. Hit 'em hard and fast so they won't know what's going on till we're on our way out."

He grabbed two of the rolled maps from the shelf in the corner, and as he handed them to me, he said, "Lia is going to kill you when she finds out."

I unrolled one of the maps on my desktop and scanned it. "Let's give the Allegiance a shot at it first."

17

We'd waited as long as we could that night, hoping for the cover of darkness, but the moon and the clouds had refused to cooperate. As we hoofed it across town, moving toward the rendezvous point, we watched the stars twinkling above, as if they were mocking us. We passed a stop sign before turning and heading into the overgrown grass that led to the hills outside of town. On top of the sign were two street signs I knew well. One read Taylor Drive. The other was Oaks Avenue.

It was still pretty bright out when we reached our destination—the grove of trees just two clicks from the shipping yard's southernmost point—and after waiting for what felt like ages, my team and I had decided that it didn't matter—this couldn't wait.

Lloyd lowered his binoculars and sighed. "Ten guards surrounding, and looks like maybe forty more inside."

Fifty men against my ten. It sure would keep things interesting. "How confident are you in that count?"

"Very, sir."

A couple of members of my team were having a quiet conversation. I didn't catch most of it, but for the tail end of Jack saying, "—bunch of fags anyway, so who cares?"

I care, I thought. *Why don't you?* Suddenly I didn't feel like the person in charge of the mission. I felt ostracized. I felt discounted.

Bullshit. It was all bullshit.

But then, what I was doing was bullshit too. We were about to embark on a dangerous mission, where the odds we'd all get out alive were thin, and I hadn't had the balls to share my deepest secret with my best friend or my girlfriend. I owed them that at least, and now . . . now it was too late.

With a heavy heart, I held up my fist to signal silence and stillness to my troops, waiting for Lloyd to get himself and his team ready to go. The night was cool. Fireflies blinked on and off, and the stars mirrored them above, their constant cousins. Any other time, in any other place, it would have been a lovely night. But shit was about to go down, and I was going to unleash hell.

I made eye contact with Lloyd. He had his people in place. My heart hammered in my chest, my muscles tensed, ready for action. But my thoughts were scattered. I was losing focus again.

With one last glance at the stars all around me, I dropped my fist, signaling both teams to advance. We moved in fast, our feet almost silent as we approached the shipping containers. A quick count told me there were about thirty of them. Considering how many supplies each could hold, I was sure the Allegiance could spare a few boxes of bandages and a couple of crates of food.

Leading my team through the long grass, darting around trees and underbrush, I brought them to a halt beside a container on the southwestern edge of the facility. We pressed our backs against the cool metal—shadows among shadows. Lloyd and his team disappeared between two of the shipping containers on the eastern side, unlit Molotov cocktails in hand.

Moments later, I heard panicked voices in the distance.

Just as we'd strategized, members of Lloyd's team had tossed the Molotov cocktails into a couple of full, open containers as a distraction. While they were keeping the guards busy, my team and I would sweep in, grab supplies, and disappear into the night, rejoining Lloyd and his team at the designated rendezvous point. It was a solid plan.

So why were my hands trembling?

I scanned the area, but there was no longer any sign of Lloyd or his team—which was good. If I couldn't pick them out in the myriad of containers, neither could the enemy. I could, however, spot the two guards standing nearest the opening we'd planned to enter through.

Two pops tore through the silence and the guards dropped like stones. My eyes shot to Davies and Randall in a glare. If we survived this, they were going to get an earful. I'd made it a point to stress to the men that they were to take no lives during this mission unless their lives depended on it. And now, against my orders, two people were dead. Pushing down my anger, I waited and watched, but the shots hadn't alerted anyone. We were in the clear. For now, anyway.

Steadying my shaking hands, I signaled, and the rest of my team sprang into action, moving forward and spreading out, navigating the maze of shipping containers. If God was looking down on us, at least one of the containers would be unlocked. If not, we'd have to go with ever-reliable bolt cutters. I didn't have a plan C.

Focus, Quinn. Focus on the mission. There's no time for worrying about anything other than the present.

Jack made sure we were clear, then pointed two fingers to his eyes and then to a large, yellow container about twenty yards away. He, Marley, Henderson, and I moved in. Thompson covered us, his finger on the trigger, his eyes sharp.

I grabbed the handle on the door and pulled. It swung open with ease. God was with us after all. Inside were more supply boxes than the Resistance in Brume had ever had in our stores at one time. A strange mixture of awe and anger filled me. Everyone knew the Allegiance was well fed, well cared for, but seeing the proof, when we in the Resistance were hungry and tending to our wounds with filthy bandages, made my blood boil.

I barked at Randall and Davies, "Move your ass, soldiers!"

From the other side of the yard came shouts as the fire spread and chaos erupted. Several Allegiance soldiers were attempting to douse the flames with buckets filled with water from the lake. Even from this distance, peering out of the container, I could see the fear on their faces. Something was wrong.

From my comm came Lloyd's frantic voice. "Get clear! It's gonna—"

An immense BOOM ripped through the air, shaking the container we were in, its blast pushing me back. My chest ached, as if it'd been kicked hard. The sound of the explosion made my ears ring. My heart pounded within me—almost loud enough to block out everything else for a moment. My mouth tasted metallic.

Steadying myself, I looked out at the shipping yard and assessed the situation. My throat grew dry when I added up the details amid the carnage. Our distraction had become their destruction. One of the containers Lloyd and his team had set aflame had exploded. Whatever had been inside was volatile. Much that was left of the container's metal walls had curled back. People were screaming. Bodies—and parts of bodies—were strewn all around the area.

Davies and Randall strapped their bags closed and slung them onto their backs before booking it out of our container, heading south toward our rendezvous point. I remained frozen to the spot, taking in the horror. There must have been welding tanks in the now-nonexistent container. What else could explode that way? I had no idea. I'd wanted to get in and out without taking any lives. Failure consumed me. This mission had been my idea. I knew it was dangerous, and I took the risk anyway. I closed my eyes, trying not to imagine the families of the fallen and how broken they would be to hear the news of their loss. Slipping my pack on, I moved out of the container with the last part of our plan in my trembling right hand.

In the glow of the still-burning fire, I spied a familiar

face on the other side of the supply yard. The man had just climbed out of a Jeep. As if my hatred had reached out like a hand and turned his head, Caleb stared right at me. I thought I saw the flames reflected in his eyes, and wondered if he saw the same thing reflected in mine. I was briefly relieved to see him here, because it meant that he was still alive.

What the hell was that about?

Regaining my composure, I lit the Molotov in my hand and tossed it into the supply container behind me. Rationally, I knew that these were supplies we might find ourselves needing one day. But I wasn't being rational right then. I wanted to make the Allegiance suffer. I wanted what was theirs to burn.

As the bottle burst into a cloud of flames within the container behind me, I gave Caleb a sarcastic salute.

There were those who said there was no negotiating with Caleb—that killing him would be the only way to stop him. Lia was in that camp. Maybe my hesitancy to do so was what would get me in the end. Or maybe, as farfetched as it seemed, I could make Caleb see the error of his ways. Or at least get him to leave us the hell alone.

The smell of burnt flesh and hair filled my nostrils, and I had to fight to not retch at the stink of it. I trudged forward, my pack feeling heavier with every step. I couldn't block out the agonized screams of Caleb's men. Some because they'd been injured. Some because my decision to come here had murdered their friends, their family members. Shit had gone sideways in the worst way imaginable.

Shut up, Quinn. Shit always goes sideways, and you know it.

I felt my conscience twist and squirm. In a way, I was no better than Caleb. He was a monster, but I was a monster, too.

You can't run from the monster. The monster is you.

The words entered my mind so softly that I almost missed them. Hadn't I heard them before? My lips were dry as I ran my tongue over them. Had Lia said that to me when I'd told her I was going out for a smoke? No, Lia would never go that far, even when she was mad at me. Though maybe if she'd seen the massacre I'd just caused . . .

Suddenly, I was glad that I'd forgotten her handkerchief again. Maybe it was the reason for our bad luck back there, but I was relieved that Lia hadn't been any part of it.

A shuffling to my right drew my attention, and I raised my rifle instinctively, but not fast enough. Sharp pain shot through my hand as someone slammed the butt of a gun down on my wrist. I released my weapon with a curse, and it fell to the ground, quickly lost in the long grass. Before I could reach for it, they hit me again—this time in the skull. I fell into the black abyss of what-the-hell-just-happened.

* * *

My head was pounding when I woke later. I was still in the clearing, and it was still dark, so I couldn't have been out for long. I could make out shapes in the darkness—it looked like every member of my team from the shipyard, including Lloyd and his men. Their faces were drawn and showed their fear. Several looked at me, as if pleading for me to save them, to save us all. Wasn't that what the face of the Resistance was supposed to do? Rescue them all with a gun in one hand and a flask in the other, like a real man? Seeing their desperate, silent pleas for help ripped my insides to shreds. What if I couldn't save any of us? What if this clearing was where the Resistance in Brume came to an end?

Standing all around them, around me, were soldiers. Well-armed, well-dressed, well-fed soldiers. We were surrounded. Which meant that we were screwed.

In front of me stood Caleb, his shoulders back, his eyes lit up with pride.

"You're slipping, Quinn. I told Kai you'd never fall for an ambush like this, no matter how desperate you and your people were. And yet . . . here you are." He put emphasis on each of the last three words, like he was relishing them. Behind him stood my brother, Caleb's number one. Our family had been ripped apart by the tyranny of the Allegiance. The real question was, who had betrayed who?

Kai said nothing. He only met my eyes for a moment

before staring straight ahead like a good little soldier. A well-trained pet. Caleb said, "Did you really think you could get away with stealing from me, killing innocent people, and destroying the property of the Allegiance? You must think a lot of yourself, Quinn. Hasn't anyone ever told you that conceit is weakness?"

His words sent a wave of anger over me. If anyone was conceited, it was him. Parading around in a uniform sporting medals that he hadn't earned, from wars that had never happened. I clenched my jaw and fought to keep my cool. "Set my men free."

The corner of his mouth tugged upward in glee. "I'll take that under consideration."

"Do what you will with me. But send them home to their families." I looked pointedly at my brother, who still avoided my gaze, and wondered if the chasm between us was insurmountable. "You must have one ounce of decency in you somewhere, Caleb."

Caleb paused for a moment, as if considering. Maybe his soul was still salvageable.

Then, with a nod, he addressed Kai with the casual tone of someone who was asking to be passed the salt at dinnertime. "Kill them. All but one. Set the weakest among them free, so that the rest of the so-called Resistance will know what happened. A cautionary tale."

Kai unsnapped the holster on his hip and moved toward the others without a moment's hesitation. The sight of his unquestioning loyalty turned my stomach. I hated him. In that moment, I couldn't imagine ever repairing the rift between us. He was Caleb's lapdog and no brother of mine.

My chest tightened as Kai positioned himself behind Jeremy—a younger guy who'd only just started coming on missions, who'd spoken at length of his parents and how supportive they were, who'd said that one day he was going to propose to his girlfriend and they'd be married under a blossoming cherry tree. He was just a boy. Just a kid. Shaking my head, I pleaded with both my brother and his leader. "Don't do this. Please."

One member of my team let out a soft whimper and another broke down in tears. They were losing faith in my ability to save them. How I wished I could say they were the only ones.

Kai's steps never slowed. I took another breath to beg him to stop, but before I could utter a word, he withdrew his pistol and discharged it into the back of Jeremy's skull.

BANG.

He was no longer Jeremy, no longer a boy, no longer a kid. His parents would mourn him forever. His girlfriend would weep for him beneath that blossoming cherry tree.

My entire team fell silent, their tongues frozen in shock.

With barely an intake of breath, Kai moved to Thompson next and squeezed the trigger again. Panic engulfed me as the shot fired, echoing out into the world. Thompson's lifeless body collapsed to the ground. It was clear that nothing I said would deter my brother from following his orders. "Stop it, Caleb. Don't do this!"

"It's already done." Caleb smiled. He'd just ordered the execution of people who wanted nothing more than to live free, and that fucker smiled. "I must say, I take great pleasure in knowing that your faction's resolve will crumble upon learning of your demise."

He was arrogant to think that a revolution relied on one person's continued existence. But then, arrogance was Caleb's forte. As Kai fired off another shot, I cringed, steeling myself for the next. "My people aren't that weak. They don't need me to win this war. Killing me won't stop the Resistance."

Gripping me by my tactical vest, Caleb pulled me to standing. The corner of his mouth twitched. I'd gotten to him. My words had picked at a scab just enough to make him bleed. He was standing so close that I could feel the heat of his breath on my skin, but I couldn't get a read on what he was planning to do next. He released his grip, slapping a hand on my shoulder, shaking it some as if we were old friends. The smile blooming on his lips filled me with unease. He said, "Perhaps you're right. Maybe killing you won't stop the Resistance. But it will give me enormous pleasure to watch you die."

I took a hard swing at him, but his arm shot forward, blocking my hit. His fist made contact with my stomach and I bent at the waist in pain. It was a hard punch, but one I probably deserved. Maybe it would be enough to distract Kai from his task. Maybe a member of my team could get free and . . .

When I looked down, I saw a bowie knife in Caleb's hand. Blood poured from my gut onto the grass. The asshole had stabbed me. I stumbled forward in shock, falling into him, hoping that what I'd said to Caleb had been the truth. The Resistance would go on without me. It had to.

Because I was dying.

Falling forward, I was surprised when Caleb caught me, and I had to stifle a scream. He'd been nowhere near me when I'd laid eyes on Coe disappearing through a door just a moment ago. Hadn't he been upstairs searching for Lia on the second floor?

"Quinn! Are you okay?" The nailed board he'd been carrying as a weapon clattered to the floor when he caught me.

Of course I wasn't fucking okay. I was in the decaying ruins of the school. Lia was nowhere to be found. And I'd just laid eyes on the most terrifying monster in Brume. The image of those long, spindly arms dragging that scaled body through the doorway haunted me. I was about as far from okay as a person could get. Shoving him away from me, I scrambled to stand on my own.

For some reason, my stomach ached.

Caleb's voice shook in concern. "I thought you were passing out on me there. You all right? Is your arm okay? Maybe we should head back."

"No. No, I'm fine." Even I didn't believe my own words, but I put them out there anyway. I wasn't sure why. To comfort Caleb, maybe? Between the two of us, I was pretty sure I was the one who needed some comforting, but I wasn't going to tell him that. I hadn't needed his damn help to climb in the window, and I didn't need him to protect me now.

My blood had soaked through the bandage on my arm, but I paid it no attention. Health concerns aside, I had bigger problems. If we had any hope of surviving this little excursion, we had to find Lia as fast as we could and get out.

But where the hell was she?

Caleb grabbed my shoulder and gave it a firm squeeze as if to shake me from my thoughts. "Quinn."

My panic and confusion began to subside, and as I looked at him, a strange sense of familiarity washed over me. It was as if I'd known Caleb for a long time. Liked him, even. Hated him. Shaking off the weird feeling of déjà vu, I said, "Any signs of Lia upstairs?"

He shook his head and said, "No, but I heard something in the cafeteria. You good to check it out?"

My jaw felt tight. "I said I'm fine."

We moved down the hall to a pair of double doors that had once been painted blue, but were now mostly rust-colored, each of them propped open by rubble. Standing to one side, my back against the wall, I took a breath and leaned forward just enough to take a glance inside the cafeteria. Caleb stood to my left, following my lead without needing to be told.

The room was filled with long tables, but there was no sign of Lia. From the far end came the sound of metal clanking, as if someone or something was banging pots and pans around in the kitchen. Caleb and I exchanged nods—an unspoken understanding that we were going in there no matter who or what we might be facing.

Gripping my bat, I stepped forward, one foot on a tile at a time. My footsteps were soundless and slow. I wasn't exactly in a hurry to face whatever monster or thug might be waiting for me, but I was cool with going first. It wasn't like Caleb was taking any initiative to lead. Plus, if I was being honest with myself, it felt nice to let him know who was running things here. Lia and I were the group. He was just a temporary addition.

I hoped.

Outside, the wind had picked up, as if a storm was approaching. It was hard not to feel like that was a bad sign. Maybe this was the day I'd lose out to the horrors of Brume. Maybe this would be the day that I died.

My feet moved silently over the cracked tile, but Caleb might as well have been an animal on the loose, with his boots clomping on the porcelain. My eyebrow twitched, and I flashed him a glare. But he just looked at me like he had no idea what I was irritated about.

Something heavy hit the floor in the kitchen, and my heart shot into my throat. My chest rose and fell in quick breaths as adrenaline flowed through me. Carefully, I reached for the handle and cracked the door open just enough to get a good look at what we were dealing with. Caleb leaned in so close behind me, I could feel his breath on my hair.

A Ripper was facing away from the door, nosing through piles of pots and pans, and I wondered if it had smelled a rat or something. It had to be pretty hungry to go after something so small, which wasn't good news for us if it noticed us. The thing was over six feet tall on all four of its long, thin legs. Its feet—if they could be called that—looked more like clawed human hands. Translucent skin revealed every muscle, every vein.

Caleb's face went white. Scanning the room, I saw a long

pipe propped up in the corner nearest the door. The metal was cool in my hand when I plucked it from where it stood. My plan was simple—trap the thing inside the kitchen long enough for us to find Lia and get the hell out. Hopefully before it noticed our presence.

Reluctant as I was to do so, I handed my bat to Caleb. But only because I couldn't maneuver the bar through the door handles to barricade the monster inside and swing my bat at the same time, should it come down to that.

Abruptly, the beast looked back over one of its hulking shoulders at Caleb and me with its dead, lidless eyes.

"Shit!" Slamming the door closed, I held the door fast and scrambled to slide the pipe through the handles. The Ripper heaved its body against the door, nudging it open a couple of inches. The pipe fell from my hands to the ground in a loud clank. I braced my body against the door, but the Ripper pressed its skull against the seam and kept pressing until its snout was free enough to snap at me. "Caleb!"

Breaking free from his frozen terror, Caleb swung my bat hard and hit the beast on the end of its nose. It snarled and backed off enough for me to get the door closed again—just long enough for me to grab the pipe and slide it through the handles, locking the creature inside. The thing rammed the door again and again. I didn't know if the barricade would hold. I just knew we didn't want to be there if the creature got out. Grabbing Caleb by the sleeve, we took off running, following the maze of hallways. We skidded to a stop and rested our backs against the wall beside a set of lockers, our chests rising and falling as we gasped for breath. I could still hear the Ripper hitting the door, but its attacks slowed, as if it were growing tired, growing weak. It must not have eaten in a good long while.

Out of the corner of my eye, I saw a light and turned to investigate. With a chuckle, I said, "Well, would you look at that?"

The door to one of the lockers was halfway open and emitting a green glow. I yanked it open with a squeak of metal on metal to reveal a cardboard box full of glow sticks. One of them had broken and acted as a beacon. On the top shelf sat a box of bandages, ointment, and a bottle of aspirin. It must have been someone's stash. Or maybe it had been here since before the wall of fog had closed in on Brume. I didn't know and didn't care. It was mine now.

As I shoved the supplies inside my pouch, Caleb cocked his head to the side. "Do you hear that? It sounds like . . . kids singing."

"Kids singing? What are you—" My chest tightened in fear. "Caleb, wait."

Before I could stop him, he disappeared around the corner. I darted after him. He hadn't gone too far. He was standing at an open classroom door, staring inside with a look of wonder on his face. As he crouched down, he spoke to the empty room. "Kally? You're okay? What are you doing here?"

I double-checked, but the room was empty. Bits of trash covered the floor, and several rusty, rotting desks lay all around, but no one was inside. He was either going crazy, or—"Who are you talking to, Caleb?"

Ignoring me, or maybe just not hearing me, he furrowed his brow in concern and continued to speak to whoever or whatever he was convinced he saw. "You shouldn't be here. It's not safe. Where are Mom and Dad?"

Grabbing him by the shoulders, I pulled him to standing and made him face me, my words curt. "Listen to me. That room is empty. There's nobody there."

He turned his head back to the room with a doubtful glint in his eye and gestured to the space with a jab of his chin. "What are you talking about? My sister's standing right here! And there are kids playing in there. Just look."

I kept my voice even and calm, even though I was anything but. "Tell me what you see and hear right now."

Caleb sighed. "There are six kids, all under the age of five, all dressed in white. Two of them are playing a board game. Three are drawing on the floor with chalk. Kally is right here . . . and I hear a music box."

He was having a conversation with his dead sister. And it all seemed so normal to him. That could mean only one thing. Shit. "No, you don't. Because it doesn't exist. None of it exists. Think about it. We're in a school that's been abandoned long enough for the lockers to rust. This isn't real, Caleb. What you're experiencing in that room—Kally, the kids, the music—none of it's real. But it is dangerous."

He swept his arm toward his hallucination. "How could this be dangerous?"

Part of me hated to tell him the truth, hated to rip that hope away from him, rip his sister from him a second time. But I had to. Reality—even harsh reality—was better than a lie. It may not be pleasant, but at least it was real. "Because it means that Coe is aware of us. He's playing with your mind. Don't believe it."

"Quinn?"

I knew that voice. It took everything in me to turn my eyes to see something that looked very much like my brother standing in the hall next to me. My heart shot into my throat, almost choking me. In a near whisper, I spoke to myself. "It's not real. None of it is real."

"*I'm* real." He was standing so close that I could feel his breath on my skin. But it wasn't Kai. It couldn't be. Kai was dead. The thing that looked like Kai tilted its head, a soft smile on its lips. "So are Mom and Dad. It's your fault they're gone, you know. It's all your fault."

"That's not Kai. It's just Coe fucking with me." I had to keep reminding myself that this wasn't my dead brother. This was just some twisted vision conjured up by Coe. If I started to believe in the things that I saw here, I'd lose my mind . . . just like Lia's mom.

"What's the matter, Quinn? Didn't you miss me? Come here. Give your brother a hug." The Kai-thing stretched out its arms. It was about to wrap them around me when brown spots began appearing all over its skin, as if it were decaying. The spots sunk in as its flesh rotted away, falling to the floor in chunks. Slime slid down its skeleton frame. I watched in silent horror as its bones collapsed to the floor in a pile of dust.

My bottom lip shook. *Fuck you, Coe*, I thought. *Fuck you.*

Caleb's eyes were locked on the room with the invisible children. His face turned white. His lips trembled. I wondered what horrors he was being subjected to but didn't ask. Some nightmares—most nightmares—were private.

I placed my hand on his shoulder. "Maybe we should get out of here, Caleb."

As if waking from a bad dream, he looked from the room back to me. His eyes shimmered with tears that didn't fall. "Yeah. Maybe we should."

After snagging from the locker all the supplies that we

could carry and retrieving Caleb's weapon, we navigated back through the halls, listening carefully for sounds of the Ripper we'd trapped. But the thing must have lost interest or energy or a combination of both, because the school was silent as we made our exit. It bothered me that we were leaving without Lia, but I couldn't stay in the school while Coe tortured me . . . or Caleb. Besides, it was possible that she had come and gone. If I didn't see her on our way to a safe place to rest, I'd look for her first thing in the morning. And I'd find her. I always did.

Caleb dropped from the window to the ground below with ease. Once I'd landed beside him, he looked at me with lost, frightened eyes. "Where should we go?"

I threw a glance back at the school and hoped that, wherever Lia was, she was safe. But all I could do now was to ensure that we were. "We need shelter. Let's head south. Maybe we'll get lucky."

The walk was quiet—a bit too quiet for my taste. I'd expected to hear a Ripper or two. I hadn't expected the eerie silence. Four blocks down, I spied the old coffee shop where I'd crashed one night a few months before. The sign that read Common Grounds was hanging half off the front of the building, swaying back and forth with the light breeze. Most of the bulbs that had lit up the patio years before had broken. Claw marks lined the closed front door—a curve of four lines scratched into the metal, each at least three feet long. A Ripper had been here, but the marks were old. I wondered what . . . who . . . it had been hunting. There was a reason not many animals were present in Brume. Tasty snacks for the Rippers, even if the Rippers preferred humans. That was the thing about Rippers—they chewed on your meat, but they fed on your fear.

Caleb said, "What do you think? Is it safe?"

Only a few of the windows were broken, and the place looked like it hadn't been used for any identifiable purpose in quite some time—maybe since I'd been here last. With a scrutinizing glance at the area surrounding the building, I said, "I think this'll work."

It took both of us to get the door open intact, but we managed to do so without attracting the attention of anything nasty lurking in the night—gang members included. With the door closed behind us and barricaded with one of the tables inside, we made our way to the back and settled in the walk-in, where we wouldn't have to worry about windows. I snapped a glow stick and shook it, illuminating the space with a soft green light. I was pretty sure we were safe. Safe enough to relax for a while—maybe even safe enough to use the place for a few nights.

After I'd burned some of the sage I'd grabbed near the school to clear the area of our scent, I cleaned the gash in my arm with water from my canteen. I dabbed it dry, applied the ointment we'd found, and wrapped it in a clean bandage. Popping two aspirin in my mouth, I swallowed, hoping that would keep the fever under control. Maybe it was the adrenaline left over from our excursion into the school, but I was feeling much better than I had been. Not well enough to face a Ripper head-on, but not terrible.

We scraped together a dinner of beef jerky from my pouch and washed it down with swigs of water. As we ate, I voiced a question that had been rolling around in my brain ever since Caleb had caught me, stopping my fall back at the school. "Hey, Caleb. When we were in the school, how long were you and I separated before you found me? Before we heard the Ripper in the kitchen, I mean."

He thought it over for a moment before shrugging. "Maybe a minute or two. Not long. I'd just started heading upstairs when I thought about how stupid it was to split up, so I came back down to find you passing out or something."

"Huh." My fever was making me question everything. Even this beef jerky—the taste was strange, like tobacco or something, and it was reminding me of something I couldn't place . . . but I liked it. The sensation passed, but I took a drink of water to wash it away regardless. "Do you ever get a feeling like maybe you've known a person before? Like . . . like in a different life or something? In different ways?"

"You mean déjà vu? Totally. Why do you ask?"

"It's just that I have this weird feeling, this impression like maybe I've met you before. It's strange."

Caleb didn't seem to have anything to say to that. Finally, he shifted to a more comfortable sitting position, gestured to my bandaged arm, and said, "So why were those guys chasing you before, anyway?"

It was a fair question, and a nice distraction from my thoughts. "There are several gangs around Brume. Most of them won't call themselves that, but a gang is a gang. They steal and hoard food and supplies, each operating like its own little society."

Caleb raised his left shoulder in a half shrug. "Sounds . . . I dunno . . . kinda comforting. I mean, people are safer in groups, right? It must be nice to know somebody has your back."

"People are sheep. They huddle together in fear, thinking it makes them stronger, but it doesn't. That goes for the gangs. That goes for just about everybody. People in general fall into two categories: sheep and shepherds. That's not comforting, Caleb. It's suffocating." I hadn't meant to raise my voice at all. Hearing it took us both aback. It was enough to shake the bitterness from my tone. "The biggest gang is led by this guy Lloyd. For months, he's been after me to join, and I guess he's fed up with my repeated refusals. He wants to be king of the mountain at any cost, and damn anyone who refuses to bow before him. He likes to surround himself with survivors. I guess that makes me valuable to him, but I keep saying no. And that pisses him off.

"To be honest, part of the reason I don't join," I added with a smirk on my lips, "is because he's a total dick."

We both burst into laughter. Once it died down, Caleb gathered the canteens and his weapon and headed for the door. "We passed a well just down the block on our way here. Do you know if it has any water left in it?"

I nodded.

"Great. Then I'm going to go refill these."

I shook my head. "Wait until morning."

Caleb shrugged. "That jerky made me really thirsty. I'll be right back. Don't worry."

Truth be told, I almost let him go. Not because it might endanger his life and remove him from the picture, but to help him. How else would he learn how to take care of himself in Brume? He was a big boy. He could probably cross the street by himself. Mulling this over, I shook my head and said, "That's the thing. I'm worried enough about Lia. I'd rather not have to worry about you too. Tomorrow you only have to worry about Screamers and the Unseen Hands. We can only be careful about running into them. There's no defense against them. But Rippers? You're not ready to face one of those alone."

He paused by the door, weighing his options, and finally nodded, dropping the canteens to the floor before sitting down again.

Sealing the bag of jerky, I rolled it up and tucked it inside my leg pouch. The room looked eerie, lit up green from the glow stick, but it felt like a safe spot to rest. Settling back against the wall, I let myself relax a bit and tried not to think about what might have happened to Lia for long enough to get some much-needed sleep.

A piercing growl cut through the air, through the walls. It was loud, and it was close. I didn't remember having dozed off, but I jolted fully awake the moment I heard the sound. I glanced around, but Caleb was gone. I stood and threw open the door. I didn't realize I'd grabbed my bat until I'd stepped out of the coffee shop and into the coolness of evening. But once I was outside, I saw the worst possible scenario unfolding before me. Caleb was standing across the street, his limbs frozen in fear, his weapon nowhere to be found.

A Ripper stood between Caleb and me, its eyes locked on him. When it exhaled out of its long, thin snout, its breath became smoke in the night air. I wondered if it could be the same one we'd encountered in the school. If it had tracked us here. The trail of scent we'd left while walking here had likely depleted quickly, and even if it had tracked us here, it would've lost our scent due to the sage I'd burned, then moved on. But it was here. Which meant that we were in trouble.

A low, guttural growl rose from the depths of its core, the sound of it draining all color from Caleb's face. He was dead, and he knew it. The Ripper had locked its hunter's gaze on Caleb and marked him for death.

I wasn't all that certain that I could change its mind.

The creature lashed forward, snapping its jaws at Caleb. A thin strand of drool flung from its mouth and stuck to Caleb's shoulder. Caleb yelped and jumped back, throwing his hands in front of him. The canteens flew into the air. One bounced off the top of the Ripper's snout and the beast snapped at the other as it fell. I couldn't be certain if Caleb was thinking quick or just reacting in a moment of panic, but he ducked and ran behind a dumpster to his right. Maybe he thought he could hide. He was underestimating the killing machine.

The hulking beast sniffed the air, moving its head back and forth, as if scanning for Caleb in the darkness.

Slipping the knife from inside my boot, I pulled back my arm and flung the blade through the air. It stuck deep in the Ripper's shoulder, and the creature howled and snarled, whipping its head around to face me. White foam bubbled from the corner of its grotesque mouth. The drool stretched toward its shoulder. But it didn't care about me or my feeble attack. It had its sights set on Caleb, and Caleb only . . . for the moment.

I moved as fast as I could. If I could just get between the Ripper and Caleb, I could maybe save him. I could maybe stop another horrible thing from happening in this town, this reality, this life of mine.

I was scared shitless of the Ripper, but my hands weren't shaking. After Kai died, I didn't let fear stand in my way of survival. After Kai died, I'd changed. I'd had to. It was the only way to ensure that I would keep on living.

Sprinting up beside the Ripper, I took a hard swing and tagged the beast across its bottom jaw with my bat. Hitting it was like hitting a tree. It was solid; its surface had hardly any give. I swung my bat up and over, bringing it down on the Ripper's head. It dazed the thing for a moment, but only just. It gnashed its teeth and snapped at me. I jumped back, but the gravel under my feet was looser than I'd thought. My feet slid forward and I almost fell. It would have been my death sentence. As I recovered, the beast snapped again, this time catching part of my hoodie in its teeth. It tore the fabric away in a mouthful of victory. When it realized it was eating fabric and not flesh, it hulked its shoulders and dropped its head, moving toward me. Its snorted breaths came out in eager gray puffs. Forget Caleb. I'd pissed it off.

And from its stance and the look in its strange, dead eyes, I was going to be dinner.

Bite by bite. Chunk by chunk.

Good evening, Quinn. You're going to die today.

Something small flew over the Ripper's shoulder, almost tagging me in the chest. It wasn't until a second one followed, bouncing off the Ripper's back, that I realized what was happening. Caleb was standing behind the beast, whipping rocks at it as hard as he could. His efforts were admirable, but I knew from the way my bat had felt when I hit the creature that rocks weren't going to stop it. If there was any hope of killing it, it was going to take beating, stabbing, ripping, or stomping through its skull. And the only person who had easy access to its head was me.

Digging the balls of my feet into the gravel, I pushed off and aimed straight for the monster. It lunged, but I brought my bat down hard on its skull with an audible crack, stunning it. To my surprise, Caleb ran around the thing, retrieving my blade from its shoulder with a tug. Rich crimson poured from the wound, and the beast howled in pain. As Caleb lifted the knife and plunged it into the Ripper's eye, I felt a surge of pride. There he was, covered in blood and sweat, and standing tall. Caleb had never looked cooler to me.

The Ripper howled and swiped at Caleb with its right

front claw, knocking him to the ground. As he fell, Caleb gripped the knife, dragging it back through the flesh on the beast's head. He hit the ground, and the thing pounced. It was going to kill him. It was going to kill us both.

Time seemed to slow as I brought my bat up and moved closer. Everything sounded far away. I swung my weapon into the Ripper's skull, cracking it and cracking it, again and again. The monster growled and squealed, but I didn't stop. It was us or this thing. It was this thing . . . or death.

The Ripper staggered, barely able to stand. Both eyes had been damaged beyond sight—one stabbed out by Caleb, the other swollen from my blows. It snarled, and I offered a nod of respect to Caleb, who'd come to stand beside me.

Caleb slapped the knife into my palm, staring the Ripper down as it shuffled toward us.

For a moment, I looked down at myself, at the blood and spittle all over my clothes. I glanced back at Caleb, his face no longer white. I looked at him, really looked, and realized in that moment, against my will, that I was no longer in a friendship of two . . . but of three.

Grabbing one of the Ripper's ears, I pressed the knife hard against its throat and slit it open. Blood poured out on the ground, filling the air with a metallic smell. The beast stumbled, then fell. Its last breaths were released in a gurgling sound. Standing over its corpse, I should have felt triumphant. I should have felt relieved. I should have felt glad. But I didn't feel any of those things. Instead, a surprising sadness washed over me.

The Ripper had been alive, and I'd, for whatever reason, extinguished that life. It had just been doing what a Ripper does—hunting so it might feed. So what did that say about me? Had I been doing what I must do—kill living things? My chest ached. Tears welled in my eyes, but I blinked them away. I felt Caleb's hand on my shoulder, but shook it away and picked up the canteens. "Come on. We'd better get going. They hunt in twos. One attacks, and if the attacker dies, the other is ready to go in for the kill on the weakened prey."

Caleb nodded and looked like he wanted to say something more, but I pulled my attention away. There was no time for talking. We needed to get somewhere safe.

15

The streets on the edge of town were empty and quiet. We'd chosen to leave the café behind for fear another Ripper might follow us there. We were too tired to fight anymore. Exhausted, both mentally and physically. It didn't take us long to find a place to call it a night—a big, dilapidated Victorian with a rusted truck on the front lawn. It looked like the driver had lost control and crashed into the large oak out front. Apparently, he'd been a mechanic or something, because rusted hammers, screwdrivers, and wrenches dotted the lawn, making it look like a toolbox's graveyard. As we walked, I pulled a bit of sage from my leg pouch and rubbed it on my skin to mask my scent. I handed some to Caleb so he could do the same. Hopefully it was enough.

We agreed to sleep in shifts, just in case the Ripper's friend came looking for us. After burning more sage, I took first watch. I was supposed to wake Caleb after an hour or two, but I wasn't tired in the slightest, so I let him sleep and watched the night out the window for any sign of trouble. I wasn't sure I could kill another Ripper—not tonight. Every time I took one down, a piece of me died. My soul was withering away with every drop of blood spilled. You'd think ridding the world of monsters would feel triumphant and just, but the truth was, it was harder to do every time.

I wasn't a killer. I wasn't hard or unbreakable. I wanted to survive, and that meant pushing my feelings down. But the feelings were still there.

The sky outside brightened, and I realized I'd been up all night, staring out the window at nothing. It was dangerous to let my mind wander like this—to imagine a world where it wasn't kill-or-be-killed. Every moment I spent imagining a world like that was a moment I wasn't doing what I needed to do to survive in the real world.

I massaged my hands together to warm them. The room we were in had a fireplace, so I slipped outside and gathered some wood and kindling. My arms full, I returned to find

Caleb rubbing his eyes into wakefulness. "I could've helped with that," he said.

"It's no big deal. I was up anyway." Crouching by the fireplace, I dropped the pieces of wood inside. Caleb joined me in arranging them. Some kindling and a match later, the fire we'd built crackled to life. Retrieving the jerky from my pouch, I opened the bag and held it out to Caleb, who nodded in gratitude and took out a couple pieces.

Caleb fixed his gaze on the dancing flames. After picking up a stick and poking at a few of the coals, he said, "I feel pretty useless."

"Are you talking about last night, with the Ripper? Because you were anything but useless. That thing would still be alive without you." I sank my teeth into a piece of jerky and ripped a bite off, chewing. The sage I'd gathered should last a little while yet, but we were going to need more food soon.

"We wouldn't have been in trouble in the first place if I hadn't ignored you and gone out to fill the canteens."

He was right, but it wasn't like I'd never taken a senseless risk before. "Everybody screws up, Caleb."

He shrugged. "Maybe. But not everybody needs someone to look after them. To feed them, keep them warm and safe. You saved my life last night. Lia saved it the other day. I feel like I'm incapable of taking care of myself."

"Lia saved your life?"

"Oh. Yeah." He tossed the stick he was holding into the fire. We both watched it burn as he gathered his thoughts. "She found me at the docks."

I remembered the last time I'd been down near the docks. My parents, Kai, and I had been searching some of the crates stacked on the pier for supplies. My dad had headed to the boathouse. It was so dark inside. My mom had run up to him, to beg him not to go in. It was the perfect lurking ground for the Unseen Hands. As they stood there arguing, Kai and I exchanged looks, but neither of us spoke. Maybe we were too afraid to step into an argument between our parents. Maybe we knew that something terrible was about to happen. Whatevcr it was, something terrible did happen. One moment, Mom and Dad were arguing in the doorframe of the boathouse. The next, they exploded into a cloud of blood—ripped into bits by the Unseen Hands. It took just a second for Kai and me to become orphans. I imagined it would take a lifetime to forget that moment . . . if I ever did.

Swallowing the lump in my throat, I said, "Were you trying to leave Brume?"

Caleb shrugged. His voice quieted some. "I guess you could say I was trying to leave. After losing my family like that, I didn't want to live anymore. She stopped me from jumping. I was cold and alone, and ready to end it all after finding nothing in that bunker but a horror show of blood."

A heavy silence fell between us. One that Caleb broke when he said, "I'd lost everything, Quinn. It felt like my whole world had shattered. It still does. But I wanted the fear and sadness and confusion to end, and I only saw one way to end it. I know that's cowardly, but—"

"No, it's not." He met my eyes with surprise in his. My heart hurt for him, but I understood. Too many residents of Brume understood how he'd been feeling. "You were scared. Losing your family the way you did was traumatic. You're not a coward, Caleb. You're human."

An ember popped from the crackling fire, extinguishing on its own before I could put it out.

"Seeing Lia through the haze . . . she looked like an angel. For a moment, I thought I *had* died. Like maybe I'd already jumped and couldn't remember." He swallowed hard. When he continued, his voice cracked, as if he were holding back tears. "Then she introduced herself, talked to me, built a fire, and gave me some bread to eat. She showed me kindness just when I was convinced that the world was devoid of it. I owe her. She didn't have to do any of that."

He was right. She didn't. But it wasn't like Lia to leave somebody in harm's way. Even when she was little, she'd find stray cats and dogs and bring them home so they could be taken care of. Lia didn't give up on living beings. Not until they forced her to. Clearing my throat, I said, "Look, I've been pretty hard on you, but the truth is, you seem like a good guy. You didn't have to go into the school to look for Lia, but you did. You didn't have to help take down that Ripper, but you did. I don't know what the future holds for any of us, but I do know that together, three people have a better chance at survival than two. And in a place like this, survival is all that matters. Let's find Lia."

I swallowed hard before speaking again. "Let's find her together."

He glanced from the fire to me and back again. After a while, he nodded. I wondered how much of the dried blood remaining on him had belonged to the Ripper . . . and how much had belonged to his family.

I cleared my throat. "Hey, about what happened last night with that Ripper, before I got there—"

"I screwed up. I know. Just froze and hid like a goddamn baby." His shoulders sank in disappointment, but he didn't tear his focus from the fire. "You don't have to point it out. I get it."

When a person's pride was wounded, sometimes they just couldn't engage. I knew that feeling well. "The first time I saw a Ripper, I almost peed my pants."

He shook his head. "Quinn, you don't have to do this."

"What am I doing?"

"Trying to make me feel better."

Staring into the flames, I let my mind wander back to a time that I wished I could forget. Maybe it would help to talk about it, though. Trying to ignore the existence of difficult truths only encouraged them to grow within you—to grow and grow until they consumed your whole world. "I was out with my brother, Kai. Our mom hated nights, hated darkness. So Kai and I . . . we wanted to catch a bunch of fireflies and put them in a jar for her, so she'd at least have light for her birthday. Maybe it was a little strange for two teenagers to do, but we wanted to see her smile again, y'know?"

He'd turned his head toward me. "That's really sweet."

"Stupid is what it was. That little adventure almost got us both killed." My throat felt drier than it had been. I attributed it to the fire, pushing down the guilt that was haunting the corners of my mind—guilt that threatened to release a dam of tears if I didn't keep myself in check. "We were in the park. The sun had only just gone down, so Kai was certain we could capture a few and get to safety before we'd have anything to worry about. We didn't yet know about Rippers being nocturnal, so we had no idea how much danger we were putting ourselves in."

Caleb's eyes were locked on me.

"Kai had the jar in his hands. I'd cup my hands around the fireflies to capture them, and when I had one, he'd open the lid and I'd put it inside. I was mesmerized by the soft blinking of tiny stars surrounding us, and I got caught up watching them. It was nice, seeing something so beautiful in a time when the fog wall had just surrounded Brume and gloom seemed to hang over everything."

Caleb spoke softly, empathy dripping from his every pore. "What happened?"

"The jar Kai had been holding smashed into the tree to my left. I remember Kai shouting for me to run, but when I turned, I was face-to-face with a Ripper." In my mind's eye, I saw the monster's snarling mouth, the muscles that moved fluidly beneath its see-through skin. I forced myself to relax my hands, as I'd balled them into fists without noticing, pressing my nails into my palms. "Kai had thrown the jar at it but missed."

Caleb was leaning toward me now, entranced by the story. I could only hope hearing it would put him at ease some—the way I'd wished someone had put me at ease back then. Wished someone had told me I'd done nothing wrong—that some things were just the fault of the world. "How did you get out of that?"

"Lucky for us, our dad had noticed we were gone, so he tracked us there. He and Kai managed to kill the thing. I just stood there watching, frozen and scared. The look on my dad's face as we headed back to safety still haunts me. I'd never seen him more disappointed. After that, he made sure that neither Kai nor I ever went outside alone at night." I met his eyes. "Like I said. Everybody makes mistakes."

Caleb pursed his lips. His eyes shone in sympathy. "You said it yourself. You were just trying to make your mom smile."

The wind outside picked up, slapping a tree branch against the outer wall in a steady, repetitive motion—almost as if it was drumming its fingers, waiting for the next night, the next bout of chaos to begin.

"Yeah." I met his gaze and held it so I could be sure my point came through loud and clear. "And you're just a guy who got a little freaked out because a monster was about to rip him to pieces. It's okay. It happens. We can't live in the past, because if we do, we won't have a future. We have to live in the now."

As I uttered the last word, I swore I heard muffled voices in the distance barking orders that reminded me of soldiers. But there were no soldiers in Brume. No heroes—only horrors. The sound soon faded, and I wondered if I'd heard it at all.

14

"How do you know if you love somebody?"

Dr. Hillard leaned forward, giving me a look that exuded empathy. An hour into our session, I was growing tired. But not tired enough to just agree that I was ill without further self-exploration. "God will tell you," he said.

I mulled that over for a moment. Caleb had said before that God is love. Lloyd had said that God wasn't here. It made me wonder, if both were right, if that meant that there was no love to be found here. I hadn't felt much love since I'd come to Camp Redemption. The only love I really felt was for Lia back home. "What if he's wrong?"

The image of Lloyd being carried off last night played over and over again in my mind. His eyes had been full of terror. He'd struggled to no end.

"God is infallible. He's never wrong. He wants you to get well, and the first step is embracing that he made you to be attracted to males, just as he made Eve to be Adam's counterpart."

Two men had gripped Lloyd and dragged him away. Randall had said the Serenity Hut wouldn't be as bad as Deliverance, but it would be close. I didn't want that—not for any of us here. What was happening to him now? Was he in pain?

"But I'm not attracted to boys. I mean, I've tried to think of them that way. It just feels wrong."

"That's the demon speaking. Humans were designed to procreate, and women were designed to give birth. The demon wants you to give in to your compulsion to lust for the same sex in order to curtail God's work and prevent child-bearing."

I took in what he'd said for a moment, rolling it over in my mind and looking for the bits of logic that I was sure he could see in what he'd said. It was a long, hard, fruitless search. "So basically, what you're saying is, if I get rid of the demon and have a baby, I'll save the future of mankind?"

"In the simplest of terms, yes." He blinked, and I could

tell that he was trying to figure out if I was mocking him or not. The truth was, I wasn't trying to, but it was difficult not to poke fun at the ridiculous.

"I'm sorry, Dr. Hillard, but that just sounds crazy to me. It sounds like the plot of a Syfy original movie." My mind refused to stay in the present. I saw Lloyd's eyes, full of terror. I saw the orderlies' hands gripping his arms. Either Lloyd had been scared, or the demon inside him was.

"It's normal to be resistant to treatment early on in the process. I assure you, Quinn, God has a plan for you, and we are here to help you understand and embrace that plan." He scribbled something in his notebook and responded to me without meeting my eyes. Maybe I'd embarrassed him. "I'm afraid our time is up for today, but I look forward to continuing this discussion tomorrow."

Would I be here tomorrow? Or would I be in the Serenity Hut next? At what point did they decide that the only thing left to be done with you was to lock you away?

The hall was empty when I stepped into it, but before I could head up to my room, Alice appeared with that sickly-sweet smile on her face. I wondered once again what sins she'd committed, and what made her an authority on what God approved of and what he didn't. Maybe she had a BS in BS. "Hello, Quinn. How was your session with Dr. Hillard?"

"Enlightening." It wasn't a lie. Not exactly.

"Just so you know, Reckoning is beginning earlier today. The others are waiting for us now. I just wanted to make sure you found your way." Once we entered the soft blue room, Alice settled onto one of the pillows on the floor and smiled. "Shall we begin?"

I glanced around and did a quick head count. "Shouldn't we wait for Susan?"

"Susan required more intensive therapy. As a result of that, she'll no longer be joining us for meals or Reckoning for a while." She spoke as if it were the most normal thing in the world. But then, "normal" was a relative term. What was normal outside of Camp Redemption may not be normal here. "Now, who would like to go first?"

Silence filled the room. Nobody wanted to go first. After what had happened to Lloyd the day before, the mood over the whole camp had been chilly, to put it mildly.

Caleb seemed ready to change that, though.

"Since my last Reckoning, I've snuck out of the house and kissed a guy." Caleb spoke fast, as if he had to pour the words out before they retreated inside him forever.

Randall gasped. "Lloyd?"

I shot Randall a look to tell him not to give Alice any more ammo against her favorite target, and he shrank back. We all knew how she felt about Lloyd, and we all knew that Lloyd was the boy Caleb had been tempted by. Alice looked at each of us, her skin flushing pink, her brow furrowed in concern. Concern that we all knew what she hadn't. That we were more out of her control than she'd realized.

Her eyes lit up with flames. "I must say, Caleb, I am very disappointed and troubled by this sinful act. You were doing so well to resist the temptations of Satan. I'm afraid you may have stained your soul with this action."

Caleb's shoulders sank. He stared at the floor, a look of shame on his face. All I wanted to do in that moment was hug him and tell him that he didn't do anything wrong.

Clearly, Alice disagreed. "Such an affront to the Lord. How did you feel afterward, Caleb? Repentant?"

"Real." Caleb's expression was flat, but he met Alice's gaze with conviction. "I felt real. Like I've been living in an imaginary world constructed for me by society, my parents, and myself, and all that crumbled away when our lips touched."

"God save you, child. Do you want to burn in hell?"

"No. Of course not. You asked how I felt. I told you the truth. God hates liars, and I'm not one." But the strength in his tone soon faded, clouded by doubt and fear. His shoulders slumped, his gaze dropping to the floor. "Only now I just feel confused and ashamed."

A cold smile curled her lips. She sure got some sick pleasure out of being right—even when she wasn't. "Maybe there's hope for you yet. After Reckoning, you'll come with me for further treatment. Don't give up on your journey to wellness, Caleb. You don't have to let the demon of lust within you win."

"What kind of treatment?" I couldn't help but ask. Would it be the kind of treatment that had marred Lloyd's skin? Or whatever Susan was experiencing now? I doubted it was just an hour-long chat with the good doctor.

"A lady doesn't speak out of turn, Quinn. Besides, that's not your concern. That's between Caleb and God." Annoyance filled me. I'd speak when I felt it was warranted, and I'd decide for myself what a lady did or didn't do—and what I'd do or not.

Brushing my curiosity to the side, she turned to her favorite camper. "Collins, why don't you share with us now?"

Collins sat up straight, beaming with pride. If I didn't know better, I'd have said he'd recently gotten laid. "Since my last Reckoning, I haven't had a single compulsion to act on any homosexual urges. I've kept up my prayers, and I think I might be ready to return home. I feel stronger."

"Praise be! That's wonderful, Collins. You've done so well here. Your dedication to healing serves as an inspiration to all who are afflicted. Dr. Hillard and I will discuss releasing you." Alice swept her eyes across the room, a smug look on her face. "Collins is a perfect example of what can happen with dedication to the treatment program."

Caleb crumbled and began to sob, his face buried in his hands. "I'm sorry. I'm so sorry. I screwed up."

My heart shattered for him. "Caleb, you don't have to—"

"Bless you, Caleb. You're right to admit your sin and embrace your guilt." Alice flashed me a look of admonishment before addressing the group. "We're going to have to pick this up tomorrow. Caleb is in need of prayers and further treatment. Keep him in your hearts while he struggles to find his way back into God's good graces."

She hurried Caleb from the room, leaving Randall, Collins, and me behind. Randall said, "I wonder where she's taking him."

The look in his eyes mirrored the worry in my heart.

The rec room was empty when I arrived later that night. At least, I thought it was, until I spotted Caleb sitting all alone on one of the stools in the back corner, at the table where we'd played poker the night before. He was staring at the tabletop, his eyes shimmering. I was about to leave when he said, "I just want to get better, Quinn. I don't want to be sick anymore."

I took a seat next to him. "I know what you mean. But what if the real sickness is people trying to convince us that being queer is wrong?"

"Isn't it? Wrong, I mean?" He met my eyes at last, his tears spilling over onto his cheeks. He was quick to brush them away and looked angry after he did so. If his parents had raised him to view being queer as an abomination, they'd probably also given him the false impression that real men didn't cry.

"Can I ask you something? About the kiss."

"If you're going to ask who—"

"I don't have to ask who. I saw the way you and Lloyd looked at each other two nights ago. Before you went to bed."

His eyes widened, his face flushed red in embarrassment. "We didn't sleep together, if that's what you're implying. I just . . . He's . . . he's really something, Quinn. I like him."

It took him a moment to speak again. The truth had a way of shining through to the surface, no matter what we did. "What do you want to know?"

It felt intrusive to ask, but I had to. I needed to know if I was alone in my feelings, or if maybe what I felt was normal. "When you were kissing him, did it feel like you were sick? Did it feel wrong?"

He didn't answer right away. I was thankful for that. It wasn't a question I wanted a quick response to. I wanted him to give it some thought, which he did. When he spoke, he kept his voice hushed, as if he thought someone else might hear. "No. What about when you kiss . . ."

"Lia?" I shook my head, the memory of her lips on mine, her tongue flicking between them. "Not once."

"Now can I ask you something?"

"Of course."

He bit his bottom lip in contemplation, then said, "Do you ever feel . . . different? Like maybe you don't fit in anywhere?"

"Yes. But not just because I'm almost certain I'm into girls." I'd said it. Out loud. Where even God couldn't deny my admission. "But . . . well . . . there's another reason, and I've never told anyone before."

"What is it?" Reacting to my hesitation, he said, "You don't have to say if you don't want to."

"Just between us?" He nodded. I inhaled. My head felt shaky and dizzy, like that feeling I got whenever I looked down from a really tall height. My words were whispers. "Sometimes—oftentimes, to be honest—I'm not so sure I belong in a girl's body."

He took in what I was saying, and looked as if he were trying to wrap his head around it. He wasn't the only one. "You mean you feel like you should've been born a guy?"

"Not exactly. Sometimes a girl, sometimes a guy. Sometimes both. Sometimes neither." It sounded strange when I spoke it aloud, but maybe that was because I wasn't used to saying it, let alone sharing it with another person. "But you can't tell anyone."

My heart hurt when I thought about Lia and the crack she'd made about transitioning before I left for camp.

"Your secret's safe with me." His smile was kind. "Just so you know. I really believe that God loves us all. No matter what."

He leaned forward and gave me a friendly, supportive pat on the knee. As he sat back in his seat, he winced, as if he were in pain.

I furrowed my brow. "Are you okay?"

He refused to meet my eyes. His lips became a thin line. I couldn't shake the feeling that I'd caught on to something that he'd been hoping I wouldn't notice. "It just stings is all. I'll be fine."

Images of Lloyd's scars filled my head. Had that been Alice's way of assisting Caleb with penance for his so called sins? "Show me."

He hemmed and hawed for a bit, and when he lifted his shirt, he kept his eyes down. His back had three long gashes slashed across it. My fingers flew to my mouth in horror. "Caleb . . . that's awful. Did Alice do this to you?"

"No, it was one of the staff members. Big guy. Alice just stood there, praying over me, demanding that the demon of lust leave me and free my soul." If we were anywhere else, the very concept would have been laughable. But here at Camp Redemption, demons were believed to be real, and whether that was true or not, our parents had given our caretakers the power to be demons themselves.

"Stay here." I hurried upstairs, keeping my footfalls as soft as I could manage. The house was silent as I moved through it. Everyone else must have gone back to their rooms already. The clock on the wall said it was 8:45. Almost lights out.

Retrieving a small medical kit from the upstairs bathroom, I snuck back downstairs. I was sure I'd be punished if I got caught helping Caleb tend to his wounds, but I didn't care. My friend was hurting, and if I could lessen that pain, I would, despite any risk.

Caleb was still shirtless when I returned to him with the medical kit. He sat, stoic and silent, as I cleaned his wounds with care and applied Neosporin. I covered the larger gashes with bandages, and as I pressed them onto his skin, he grimaced. "Quinn?"

"Yeah?"

"What do you think is going to happen to you, after this?"

I shrugged as I put the rest of the medical supplies back inside the kit. That was the million-dollar question.

He wore a far-off look. "My parents told me to come home 'right' or not to come home at all."

At least I wasn't alone. "Mine pretty much told me the same thing. Do you ever think they might just be scared for us?"

"No." He spoke with such conviction, it gave me pause. What if it wasn't fear? What if I was just making up an excuse so that I'd feel less resentment toward my parents? "I don't have to think it. I know it. They're scared for us and *of* us. Scared of change, of the unknown, of accepting someone who represents something they view as harmful."

A creak in the ceiling drew our attention. Someone was up and walking around on the floor above us. Probably Alice, making sure everyone was in bed by curfew.

"Yeah," I said. "I really do think they're scared that something bad might happen to us if we're queer. And they have reason to fear that, to wish for an easier life for us. Look at the violence against LGBTQIA-plus people. Look at all the hatred and discrimination. Nobody would want their kid to face all of that. It'd be so much easier to have a kid who would be easily accepted by society. Cisgender and heterosexual. That's what society wants." My chest was tight with anger at the injustice of it all. The word "cisgender" balanced on my tongue in a bitter dance. My parents already had a hard time accepting me as a lesbian. How much more would they struggle to accept that their daughter identified as something other than female? Maybe that was why I'd avoided exploring gender too deeply for so long. Because I was afraid to hurt them any more than I already had. Their fear had been pushing all these layers down deep inside of me. There were times when I felt like I didn't recognize the person looking back at me when I gazed into a mirror. My reflection felt smaller than who I really was inside. At least I had Lia to accept my sexuality. But I had no one to accept my gender identity. I didn't even have anyone to discuss it with. Until now. "Society is fucked up."

Caleb nodded. "My parents are more afraid they'll be embarrassed in front of our congregation. They don't have to say it. I've seen it in the way they act when I'm with them at church. The looks that tell me not to do anything remotely 'feminine.' The way they rush me home the moment any gossip starts." He clenched his fists as he talked. "My dad actually told me he'd rather be dead than have a fag for a son."

"Oh, Caleb. I'm so sorry. That's awful." My mom and dad hadn't gone that far. They hadn't resorted to any slurs that I could recall. They'd sent me here, but they'd always basically been nice about it. It gave me hope that maybe one day their minds could be opened. But that day might not come for a very long time—if at all. "My parents haven't said anything like that yet. They just don't want me talking to Lia ever again. So even though she's my best friend, I'm supposed to kick her out of my life, even if I did realize I'm not a lesbian."

"So, are you? A lesbian, I mean."

The shape of Lia's body filled my mind. Her laughter filled my ears. My heart raced at the memory of her eyes. I didn't mean to whisper, but I did. "I think so. I mean, yeah, maybe."

"Have you ever kissed a guy?"

"No. What about you? I mean, before Lloyd?"

His face flushed as he shook his head. The hint of a smile danced on his lips. "Nah. He was the first. But I've had girlfriends before, and I liked kissing them."

"Hey, Caleb? Can I ask you something weird? I mean, it's okay to say no."

"What is it?"

I cleared my throat. "Would you . . . would you mind kissing me? I just . . . I don't know."

He smiled in understanding. "You wanna know if you'll feel the same as you do when you kiss girls?"

"Yeah." I winced. "Stupid, right?"

"Not even a little." He smiled, but there was an awkwardness about it that I shared. "So . . . how do you want to . . . ?"

"This is weird, isn't it? I shouldn't have asked. It's so stupid."

Caleb shook his head. "No. No, it's a good idea. And if it helps you, I'm all in."

The expression he wore was so sincere, so supportive. I said, "You sure?"

With a nod, he leaned forward slowly. The air was warm between us, and his lips were so close to mine. I closed my eyes . . .

. . . but then immediately opened them again. What was I doing? Kissing Caleb wasn't going to unveil my inner truth. I already knew what I wanted and who I was.

Caleb met my eyes. We shared a pause that lasted the span of a heartbeat before he said, "Something wrong?"

"No. I just . . ." I shook my head. "No offense, but you're not the person I want to kiss."

With a smile, he pulled his shirt over his head and covered his freshly tended-to wounds with care. "I totally understand."

I owed Caleb. Because the almost kiss *had* made me feel something. It made me feel longing to be reunited with Lia once again. It made me miss her. "You're a good friend, Caleb."

"So are you, Quinn."

My truth filled me with confidence and conviction. I had my answer at last. I didn't belong here. I wasn't sick. And I was going home.

“We’re dropping like flies around here.” Valerie sat on the swing next to me on the small porch at the back of the house. Alice had suggested we share some reflection for the next hour about how heaven would greet us if we were to die today. It was a morbid proposal, I thought, and brought to mind that terrified look in Lloyd’s eyes when they’d carried him away. I wondered where exactly the Serenity Hut was, and what he’d have to say in response to Alice’s question.

Valerie and I pushed with our toes and swung with ease. Each of us had a glass of fresh-squeezed lemonade in hand. Flowers hung in baskets from the porch roof. If it had been anywhere else, it might have been a happy moment. An ideal afternoon.

But we were at Camp Redemption. Nothing here was ideal.

I said, "What makes you say that?"

She sighed and drew her slender legs up underneath her, sitting cross-legged. "Lloyd's in the so-called Serenity Hut, Susan is who-knows-where, and Collins is officially going home. It's just you, Caleb, Randall, and me now."

I didn't know what to say to that. If everything went according to plan, I wouldn't be here much longer myself.

"We haven't had the chance to talk much since you've been here," Valerie continued. I was grateful for the change of subject.

"Yeah, they keep us pretty busy, don't they?"

She paused, eyeing me, as if she was privy to a secret that we shared.

"I probably should've asked you already, but what are your pronouns? I try not to make assumptions about a person's gender. Besides, it's not what you look like that matters. It's what you feel like." She took a sip of lemonade. Condensation ran down the side of her glass, and a drop of water clung to the bottom, glistening there. "It's okay if you'd rather not say. I just want to show you respect."

"Oh. She and her are fine. I mean, I guess." I'd never

considered using a different pronoun. Even though the ones I did use had never quite landed for me.

"I prefer she and her, but they and them are just as comfortable for me. I never much cared for labels or limitations."

They. It wasn't a pronoun I'd ever heard a person use to refer to themself before. Something about it felt comforting to me.

She flashed me an authentic smile that gave me the impression that she'd enjoyed my company so far. "You have a girlfriend at home, right?"

"Yeah. What about you? Are you seeing anybody?"

She took another sip of lemonade and shrugged, seeming not to notice that I was distracted. "There are a couple guys I like, but I'm focusing on school right now. I'm going to be a therapist."

"That's awesome." Reflecting on my conversation with Caleb, I said, "Hey, can I ask you a personal question?"

"Sure."

It was a difficult question to ask. I didn't know if I'd offend her or hurt her feelings or make her feel awkward at all, and I wanted none of those things. I was just curious. But at the same time, it was none of my damn business, and she had every right to tell me off and refuse to answer. "Is it hard being trans?"

She didn't answer at first, and worry filled me that

I'd damaged our new friendship with five words that had seemed so very simple but weren't in the big scheme of things. I opened my mouth to apologize, but she cut me off before I could.

"Sometimes. It was really difficult coming to terms with it and coming out to everyone I know, and it was hard to look at myself in the mirror before I began physically transitioning. It's easier now." She flashed me a smile, which told me we were okay. More importantly, she was. "The parts of it that are still hard are mostly caused by ignorant people."

It had to be painful to be born into skin that didn't feel like your own.

I thought about that for a while. It sank into my pores, down through muscle tissue, into my bones. My voice caught in my throat for a moment. "If you could change who you are, go back and make yourself cisgender, would you?"

With that same warm smile, she reached over and gave my hand a reassuring squeeze. "Oh, honey, we can't change who we are. We can only embrace it and celebrate it."

She spoke with wisdom beyond her years. Just hearing it put a small lump in my throat. "You don't belong here, Valerie. You seem so sure of yourself. So in touch with your feelings and who you are. I wish I were so confident."

"I wasn't always this way, Quinn. Sometimes it takes us a while to become the people we really are." She shrugged.

"I mean, look at me. I had a choice of hiding who I was until I was eighteen, or being who I really am, even if that meant fighting against my parents. And here I am, eighteen years old, and being myself out loud."

Her voice hadn't dropped in tone, which told me she wasn't afraid who overheard our conversation. I said, "If you're eighteen, how are your parents able to make you come here? I mean, you're technically an adult."

"When I was fifteen, my aunt got custody of me. She was so supportive. The best person I've ever known. Without her, I don't know that I ever would've come to fully accept myself, and I know damn sure I wouldn't have gotten on hormones so young." The smile on her face wavered. "She got sick last year. Cancer. She died about four months ago."

It was hard for anyone to lose a family member, but I had a feeling it would be even more excruciating to lose a parent figure. "I'm so sorry."

The sun was still shining, but the sky seemed dimmer somehow. Less vibrant.

"Anyway, I turned eighteen shortly after that, but not before my parents were granted a court order that said I wasn't within my own faculties enough to make my own decisions. Basically, they told a judge I was crazy and the judge agreed that they should be in charge of me from a legal perspective." The sorrowful look in her eyes turned quickly to anger, though you couldn't tell so by her voice. She remained calm and poised. "And now I'm here. Until I'm 'well.' So they say."

I shook my head. "I'll never understand how people can be so shitty to other people."

"Some people are. But you can't let what they do affect what you do or how you behave."

"Wise words."

"My aunt." Her eyes, moist with the threat of tears, met mine. My heart broke for her.

A light breeze picked up, carrying on it the scent of roses. After a period of silence, I said, "Hey, do you know where the Serenity Hut is?"

"No. Thankfully, I've never been there." She looked around to make sure we didn't have any unwanted company. "But I can keep Alice distracted long enough for you to find out."

I flashed her a surprised glance, and she responded with "I miss Lloyd too. I'm worried about him. We all are, I'm sure."

I hadn't expected to find friends at Camp Redemption, which just proved that even at our lowest points, life was still capable of pleasant surprises. "Thanks. I'm taking Caleb with me tonight. It just wouldn't feel right to go without him, y'know?"

"I get it. He needs to see Lloyd. Even if he doesn't realize it."

I said, "What are you going to do to distract Alice?"

"I'll think of something." Her ears perked, and she placed her feet down on the wooden slats of the porch again. "Do you hear that?"

From somewhere in the distance—it sounded like the driveway in the front of the main house—came a voice I'd have recognized anywhere. Kai. "Quinn!"

My glass fell to the porch with a clink, splashing lemonade all over. As I rounded the corner on the side of the house, an orderly appeared, blocking my way. He looked more than a little bit winded, as if he'd hurried to stop me. I shouted, "Kai!"

The orderly said, "Miss, I'm afraid you're not allowed up front at the moment."

I took off like a shot, dodging the orderly, my heart hammering in my chest. I had to reach him, had to see him.

Sounds of a scuffle filled my ears. My feet flew over the grass. By the time I reached the front of the house, Kai was sitting in the driver's seat of his car, and the engine was running. What on earth had Alice threatened him with in order to get him to decide to cooperate all of a sudden?

Me. She must have threatened me. It was the only thing that would have made him change his mind like that.

Standing beside the car was Alice, her cheeks flushed, her posture confident and strong. "Your sister isn't available right now. Call the camp tomorrow and we'll see what, if anything, can be arranged."

My lungs burned and I could barely call out his name again, but that didn't mean I wasn't going to try. "Kai!"

By the time I reached the driveway, his car was pulling away with a start, sending up a cloud of dust. Drawing in a lungful, I resisted the urge to cough and called out to him one last time as I chased after him. "Kai!"

He slammed on the brakes, the back end of the car fishtailing as he brought the vehicle to a stop. I reached the car as he opened the door and climbed out. He pulled me into his arms with a tight hug. Comfortable. Familiar. Reliable. "Are you all right, kiddo? I've been so worried since our phone call."

Words spilled out of me like blood from a wound. "I'm *not* okay. I need you to get me out of here. This place is awful. And I can't go home, because I have my answer now, and Mom and Dad aren't going to like it. I'm gay, Kai. And I have to live with you now. Please!"

In the side mirror, I saw two of the large male staff members approaching. Kai noticed them too. "Get in the car, Quinn. We'll figure out what to do with you once we get you out of here."

Alice's voice was tinged with an air of superiority hidden behind a glaze of concern. "I'm afraid you're not Quinn's legal guardian. Therefore, I can't allow you to remove her from the property. We can wait until the police arrive and sort it out then, if that's how you want to handle this."

The look in Kai's eyes said that he was mulling over our options. After a moment, he clenched his jaw. "There's no need for that. I'm going."

He was leaving. Anger welled up inside of me—anger at him, for refusing to help, and anger at everyone who thought it was better to shut up than own out loud who you are.

Pulling me closer, he placed a small peck on my forehead and met my gaze. "We'll figure this out, kiddo. I know you can't live with me in the dorms, but I'll come up with something. Don't worry."

I could feel a small hairline fracture spiderweb through my heart. I had no words.

With an apologetic frown, Kai slipped a folded piece of paper into my hand just as the staff members' hands grabbed my shoulders, pulling me back. I gripped the piece of paper tight, hoping no one saw that he had given it to me.

As the men escorted me to the house, I could hear Alice call out to my brother. "You should know that such dramatic intrusions will only serve to harm your sister and lengthen her healing process. I advise you to think twice before visiting again unannounced and without permission."

Once I was in the house, one of the men shut the door behind me and stood guard outside—fitting, because this place was like a prison. I couldn't leave Camp Redemption. Not until I drank the Kool-Aid. And I wasn't thirsty.

Besides, where would I go if I did leave?

I unfolded the paper Kai had slipped into my pocket. It was a note. From the one person other than my brother who I desperately needed to hear from.

Dear Quinn,

I miss you. I know you have your reasons for going to that place, and I want you to know that while I may not support your decision, I do support you. Even if you can only come back to me as a friend, please come back to me soon. My world is gray without you. I love you so much.

Yours,

Lia

Outside, the sun was shining bright as ever—almost Stepford perfect. But that didn't outshine the truth. The truth was, my world was gray without Lia as well. I missed her. I loved her. And nothing—not fear of my parents kicking me out, not a gay conversion camp, not self-doubt—would ever erase the fact that she was the person who set my heart on fire.

That night after dinner, Valerie pulled Alice aside for a private conversation. I didn't know what they talked about, only that Valerie looked pained and Alice looked sympathetic. It was my cue.

Caleb and I headed outside. We kept our movements casual, like we were just going for a stroll—not something the staff would discourage, being that we were opposite genders in their view. What's the worst we could do? Create a baby and save the world, just to spite the demons within us? I was sure nothing would please Dr. Hillard more.

What we were really doing was reconnaissance. Locate where they were keeping Lloyd and Susan and check out the perimeter of the property. That was our goal. It felt kind of like a military operation.

"We need you, Quinn. You're our inspiration to go on fighting."

Lloyd's words whispered through my mind—words I'd never heard him speak. Or had I?

Yes. I could see him clearly in my mind's eye. He was wearing fatigues. Rubbing his brow, as if in an attempt to stave off a headache. I was—

"That's comforting." Caleb jabbed his chin at the large chain-link fence that seemed to surround the camp. Barbed wire ran along the top, as well as a security camera—for our protection, I was willing to bet Alice would offer as an explanation. A creek snaked its way across our path.

I watched the water flow under the fence, wishing that we could all leave so easily. Then it hit me. We could. "Caleb, look at the fence over the creek."

He slowed his steps to a stop and reached out, twirling a lock of my hair around one of his fingers and offering an endearing smile for the camera. Pretending to look at me but really taking stock of the fence over the water, he said, "This part of the creek is much deeper than what I can see of the rest. Can you swim?"

My chest tightened with the sensation of drowning. Remnants of years-gone-but-never-forgotten childhood experiences. "No, but I can hold my breath."

"Good enough. But one problem." He nodded toward the camera.

"How far back is the house? It took us twenty minutes to walk this far. Which means it'd take somebody at least that long to reach us from the house." Plastering a charmed smile on my face, I took his hand in mine. "We could leave. We could get out."

Caleb pressed his lips to the back of my hand in a soft kiss. Whoever might be watching was getting quite a show. "Lloyd's somewhere north of here, I think. It was dumb luck that I found him before. The night I . . . we . . .”

He was blushing. I smiled. “Let’s get everyone on board and go. The sooner, the better.”

We continued north, which led us deep into a wooded area. It seemed like we’d been walking forever when I finally spied a small shamble of a shack with a large padlock on its door. It couldn’t have been more than a twelve-foot square. A rusted tin roof lay flat on top of walls made from what looked like old barn wood. There were substantial spaces between the boards, but not enough to escape through. Could this be the infamous Serenity Hut? If so, it was definitely an ironic name. Nothing about it inspired anything close to serenity.

“If you’re looking for a threesome, I need a shower first.” Despite his unrelentingly bawdy sense of humor, Lloyd’s voice sounded smaller, more subdued. Just hearing it made the tiny hairs on the back of my neck stand on end.

We rushed over to the ramshackle building. Seeing his face through the small openings sent a wave of relief through me. “Lloyd! Are you okay?”

“I’m hangin’ in there.” His dry lips rose in a smile as he met my partner in crime’s eyes. “Hey, Caleb.”

“Hey.” Caleb rested his hand between two of the widely spaced boards. It didn’t take long for Lloyd to place his hand on Caleb’s. A heartbeat passed before their fingers were laced together.

Feeling very much like an intruder on their moment, I said, "We found a way out of here."

"The creek, under the fence?" Lloyd turned his attention to me. It had only been two days, but he looked thinner. "I discovered that about a month ago."

"Then why haven't you left before now?"

"Because there's someone I need to be here for. Whether or not he realizes it or however he feels about me, I can't just leave him behind, hating himself because of other people's opinions." Lloyd was no longer looking at me. His gaze was locked on Caleb. "How could I leave someone behind like that? Especially someone so ashamed of himself, so beaten down by his family that he'd subject himself to torture?"

"I'm coming with you." Even Caleb looked surprised to hear the words leave his lips. But he meant them. That much was clear.

Lloyd said, "Are you sure you're ready to be back out there?"

Caleb shook his head. "Not entirely, no. But I'm not going to stay here. I don't belong. I think God will understand. After all, if he made me and he's never wrong, then he made me how I am."

I glanced around, my nerves on edge. Someone had to be coming soon to check on Lloyd's well-being, or at least to ensure he hadn't managed to escape. "When do you think we should go?"

"The moment you can get me out of this personal hell-hole. Talk to Valerie and Randall, see if they're in. I don't think Collins—"

"He's going home tomorrow." Resentment colored my tone. Well-deserved resentment. Collins had drunk the Kool-Aid.

"Figures. Not everyone can just . . ." Lloyd shook his head warily but didn't have the strength for one of his usual rants. "It doesn't matter. We have to leave everything but our IDs and any cash behind. Travel light."

"Caleb and Quinn, I can see that you two are going to require some correction." Dr. Hillard's voice echoed through the trees as he approached, flanked by two large men. My heart hammered in my chest.

We were caught.

"I'm prescribing aversion therapy, effective immediately."

Lloyd gripped one of the boards and pulled with all his strength but accomplished nothing. "Hillard, you bastard! Don't you hurt them! Don't fucking do it!"

The man on the right, the one with the scraggly beard, grabbed me by the shoulders and began leading me back toward the house. The other man grabbed Caleb and all but carried him, shouting and struggling, out of sight. I squirmed beneath the orderly's rough hands. "What are you doing? Where are you taking me?"

The walk was brief and silent. Not far from the back of the guesthouse where Lloyd usually slept was a small building made of cinder blocks. A large steel door was its only entrance. My stomach clenched in concern. "What is this place?"

My captor was silent. He pulled open the door and gave me a little shove into the room. What I saw within looked like something a mad scientist might have in an old movie. A vinyl-covered gurney sat at the center of the room, surrounded by six television monitors. A single light hung from the ceiling, illuminating the strange setup. The walls were bare, and the corners of the room were dark. Goose bumps crawled up my arms. I shouldn't be here. I should be anywhere but here.

I took a step back but bumped into the man who'd brought me to this place. Gripping my wrist, he directed me toward the gurney. I pulled hard but couldn't break free. Panic began closing my airways.

With one swift movement, he picked me up and placed me on the vinyl. I kicked and clawed, but he managed to subdue me long enough to strap down each of my limbs. With a grunt, he tightened a fifth strap across my torso and left the room. Another man, one with stringy hair who looked too much like the gardener I'd encountered before to not be him, placed a rubber tube between my teeth and secured it there at the back of my head. He pressed a long, nicotine-stained finger against his lips. "Shh."

The light above me went dark, and I heard the only door open and close again. I was left to struggle against my binds with nothing but darkness and terror for company.

After several minutes, images began flashing on the screens. Most were of no consequence. A child taking communion. A man planting a seedling. But after several such images, a picture of two women kissing appeared. As it did, a shock of electricity shot through my body. Pain lit up every inch of me. Just as I felt relief that it had ceased, another image appeared—this one of two men and pornographic—and I was shocked again. It continued like that for what felt like an eternity, and eventually, my muffled screams began to sound like they were coming from someone other than myself.

Every inch of my skin ached, every muscle throbbed. My jaw hurt so much, I wasn't sure I could take any more. More images flashed on the screens. A meadow of wildflowers. A church steeple. But then something different. Large words, crisp white on a black background, flashed on the screens one at a time. Unlike the images before, they didn't feel random. They felt like a warning.

YOU
CAN'T
RUN
FROM
THE
MONSTER.
THE
MONSTER
IS
YOU.

Confusion filled me, but it was zapped away by the lightning that shot through my body. It felt like it would never end.

Maybe it never would.

12

Falling forward, I felt Caleb tug his blade free from my gut. The blood pouring from my wound, soaking my tactical vest, felt warm on my skin. Slick. There was no pain, just an intense rush of warmth over every inch of my body. The sensation didn't last long, though. My fingers and toes soon felt cold, even in the temperate night air. My lips were tingling. Trembling. I'd read somewhere once that a person would feel hazy and dizzy after getting stabbed in the stomach and losing a lot of blood, but my vision was crystal clear.

For a while.

Oh.

Caleb's face blurred before my eyes. I tried to hold on to him to keep myself on my feet, but I could feel my body slipping lower and lower to the ground.

Bleeding to death—that's what I was doing. What was the word for it? Lia had taught it to me several months ago, when she'd been stitching up a soldier who'd caught the brunt of shrapnel from a grenade.

Exsanguination. That was it. I was exsanguinating to death. And there ain't no party like an exsanguination party, 'cuz an exsanguination party stops when the heart does.

Hysterical laughter bubbled up out of me. Lia would have glared at me for laughing over such a serious issue. She was a problem solver who wasted no time. In fact, she sometimes—

My heart felt heavy as it slowed. I couldn't remember crumbling to the ground, but there I was, on all fours, hearing my breath rushing in and out of my lungs. I couldn't focus on the fact that I was dying. All I could think about was Lia. I would never see Lia again. Never kiss her lips. Never dry her tears. Never hold her all night until the sound of gunfire and explosions quieted. I would never see her again. Ever.

The sound of Kai's gun firing seemed muffled and far away. Someone was crying. Someone else was pleading for it all to stop, just stop. Then the pain began, gnawing through my abdomen. The feel of it sharpened my senses some, but not much. Mostly it sharpened my fury toward Caleb. That asshole had actually stabbed me in the stomach like a witless coward. He didn't face me in battle as an equal. He didn't pit his combat skills against mine. He waited until I was unarmed and outnumbered and buried a blade in my gut as my brother methodically went down the line and killed my friends on his order.

So much for resolving this peacefully.

My head felt like it was filled with concrete, but I managed to lift it and look up at my killer. Caleb watched me, his head tilted slightly. By the look on his face, I wondered whether or not he'd ever seen a person bleed to death before his eyes.

His expression shifted from curious observation to alarm the moment a knife blade pressed against his throat.

Lloyd.

My number one was taking charge, protecting me and the remaining members of our squad. I wanted to thank him. I wanted to apologize for not sharing everything about myself with him. But it was too late. I was at death's door.

I could just make out Lloyd's face as he spoke into Caleb's ear, though I couldn't hear what he said. He must've broken free of his bonds somehow. Caleb grimaced, but when Lloyd pressed the blade into his skin, Caleb broke. He shouted to his men, "Stand down!"

Kai appeared to my left. I hadn't seen him step up, but I

could see the gun in his hand, pointed right at Lloyd's head. "One bullet, Lloyd. That's all it takes. Think about it. Let him go."

A strange sensation washed over me, and I realized to my shock that I was concerned not just for Lloyd's life, but for Caleb's. The whisper of a voice—my voice—passed through my mind.

"We'd better get going. They hunt in twos. One attacks, and if the attacker dies, the other is ready to go in for the kill on the weakened prey."

They were words I'd spoken to Caleb. But when? Why?

Lloyd turned, revealing a gleam of metal in his right hand. In addition to the knife, he was pressing the barrel of a gun into Caleb's back. His glare hardened. "Like you said, Kai. One bullet. That's all it takes."

Kai seemed to weigh his options. On one hand, he'd never been a person to give up something without a fight. On the other, he had to calculate if he could plant a bullet in Lloyd's brain before Lloyd planted one in Caleb's spine.

Caleb didn't appear to be a fan of insubordination. "I said to stand down."

Shame washed over Kai's features, and he stepped back, holstering his weapon.

I recalled Caleb and me sharing a bonding moment—we'd just done something brave and terrible together. But I couldn't put my finger on when. It had happened. But where? My head swam.

Lloyd kept his weapons trained on Caleb, but he looked over at the few Resistance fighters who had escaped murder thanks to his bravery. "Stevens, Garret. Help Quinn walk. Be careful. He's bleeding pretty bad."

For a strange, surreal moment, I felt bad for whoever that Quinn person was. Then the burning pain at my center reminded me it was me.

Lloyd barked into Caleb's ear, "Order your people to disperse. Now."

When Caleb spoke, it sounded like he had to choke the words out. "Kai. Take the men and return to base."

It took a few lingering seconds for Kai to obey. His gaze swept over me as he turned to leave, and when he met my eyes, the corner of his mouth tugged downward. Disappointment? Regret? Maybe he felt a pang of guilt over following the orders of a man who'd just gutted his only sibling. Maybe not. I'd never know.

He rounded up the troops. As quickly as I'd become a thought in his head, I was dismissed as an afterthought.

As Lloyd had ordered, Garret knelt beside me, looking more than a little concerned about the still-spreading blood at my center. He said, "Sir? Stevens and I are going to help you stand up. We'll carry you back to base after that."

"I can walk." I'd intended to come off sounding determined, but my voice betrayed my weakness. I was bleeding. I was dying.

He and Stevens exchanged glances of disbelief. Then Stevens said to me, "Sir, please. Let us help you."

Truth be told, I wasn't certain that I could get to my feet on my own, let alone get back to base. But I couldn't appear weak—not in front of Caleb, not in front of Kai. "Then help me walk. I don't want those bastards to see me getting carried out of here."

"You got it."

Stevens and Garret each put an arm around me, and with a look of trepidation in his eyes, Garret said, "You ready for this? Because it's gonna hurt like a mother. On three."

I wasn't ready—that much I knew. But I also knew I couldn't stay where I was, or I'd die for certain. I gave a nod, even though my entire body was screaming no.

"One. Two. Three." They lifted me, and a hot white pain shot through me. It was the last thing I could recall before the world crumbled inward and I was left with patches of memory—a damaged filmstrip that had been taped together again with clumsy, shaking fingers.

The night sky, full of stars. Sounds of far-off voices and the coolness of the air lapping at my hot skin like an animal trying to help me heal.

Black. A darkness so deep and all-encompassing that it filled me with delirious fear. In a strange panic, I searched the black for comfort, but found none.

I stretched my memory as far as I was able, trying to recall the exchange with Caleb that I was certain I'd experienced. We'd been on the same side for a time. Fighting . . . someone. No. Some*thing*.

The image of razor-sharp teeth and sinewy muscles moving beneath translucent skin flashed through my mind.

The Rippers. How had I forgotten the Rippers?

Brume was different there. I was different too. I stretched my mind outwardly, trying to grasp more details of the memory, but couldn't. I had to be hallucinating again, losing my grip. The price of waging this war was losing my mind.

A swirl of people and antiseptic smells. Voices surrounded me, but none really permeated the strange, invisible veil in my brain. It was as if I existed on another plane, and no one and nothing could break through. What was it medieval philosophers had believed? That the world was made of five elements—earth, air, fire, water . . . and something.

Aether. That was it. I was in the aether. The purest element that permeated the celestial sphere. Where war, bigotry, gender constructs, and weapons didn't exist. Part of me wanted very much to stay there forever.

"Will he live?" A familiar voice, deep and assertive.

"Of course he'll live." Even though my eyes were closed, I knew the second speaker to be Lia. Which meant that I was back at the school. The hospital. And suddenly, the veil was gone. "He's lucky. The blade seems to have punctured his stomach but missed any other vital organs."

The familiar voice that had spoken first sighed. "Sounds like we're all lucky. The Resistance wouldn't be the same without Quinn."

Lia's voice dropped to a hushed tone. She sounded worried, despite her assurances. "Nothing would."

Forcing my eyes open, at first I saw rectangles drawn in the sky. Blinking, I recognized the ceiling tiles of the school and relaxed some. I was definitely back at base, and I was going to be okay. Lia had said so.

Lia.

My head began to clear. When I looked at Lia, I found her double-checking the saline bag that was attached to the tube in my left arm. I croaked, "Don't be so dramatic."

Her eyes snapped to mine, and she bent over me, kissing my forehead, hugging me to her chest. "Oh, Quinn. I'm so glad you're okay. I was worried."

"We all were. You lost a lot of blood. Lucky for you, I'm your type." Lloyd sat in a chair beside the gurney I was lying on, a tube running from his left arm to my right. A blood transfusion. No one could say he'd never given me anything.

"You are definitely not my type, Lloyd." I laughed, but the pain in my abdomen cut my humor short. "Where's Caleb?"

Lia wrinkled her nose in disgust and removed the tube from Lloyd's arm, pressing a cotton ball into the small hole left behind. Lloyd held the cotton in place and Lia removed the needle from my arm as well, but left the one attached to the saline bag in my other arm. She tossed the needles and tube into a red trash bin and stepped into the doorway closest to us, where the medicines were stored. Lloyd said, "He's chained up downstairs. Seemed like a good place to keep him. I have two guards on him now. Think we should double it?"

When I shook my head, my vision went soft and a sort of giddiness washed over me. It had to be from pain medication. I thought of the soldiers we lost and felt giddiness give way to remorse. But knowing that the sacrifice my men had paid—that my orders had led to a good result at the end—filled me with hope. "Caleb won't be a problem. It's his people we have to worry about. Get as many soldiers as you can to guard this building. Kai won't abandon his leader. Especially not after the conversation you two had back there."

"Understood. I'll get Stevens on it right away." Lloyd shook his head, releasing a sigh that spoke volumes. With his free hand, he reached up and scratched his scarred cheek. "Your brother never was my biggest fan."

For a moment, Lloyd's voice echoed through my memory. But it wasn't this Lloyd. It was some other Lloyd. From some other place. *"Welcome to the family, Quinn."*

Clearing my throat, I said, "Where'd you get that scar?"

"Not surprised your memory's foggy, with all you've been through." He ran a finger over the X shape on his cheek. "A gift from Kai last year, remember? As he was questioning my loyalty to our cause."

A scar. A question of loyalty.

Here my brother had done that to Lloyd. But somewhere else, another time—maybe another Brume, as crazy as that sounded—it was Lloyd himself. I didn't know how I knew that, but I did.

Trying to determine how those things could both be true made my head ache. It felt like a puzzle that was too far beyond my abilities to comprehend. Shaking my head, I said, "I guess you never really know a person."

Lloyd shrugged. "I guess not."

The realization that I'd never given Lloyd a chance to know me, to really know me, and I had a second chance to do so now, hit me hard. How was I to know how he'd react to my truth? It felt like I'd been lying to him all this time. After all, the intentional omission of the truth is just that—a lie.

"Listen . . ." I swallowed hard, wanting to continue the conversation I'd attempted with him about the hypocrisy of the Resistance—about how I was feeling more and more like I didn't fit into the male role that society had dictated. Wanting to lay my soul bare to my best friend and trust that he'd have my back once again, as always.

But then Lia returned with a vial in her hand and filled a syringe with its contents. As she moved to inject the medication into a port on my IV, I grabbed her arm. "Supplies are low. Save it for someone else."

She said, "Don't be ridiculous. You need this."

Certain that Kai would be planning a counterattack, I shook my head, wanting to keep my mind clear. "Don't give me anything to make me sleep."

Taking my concern for stubbornness, she sighed and pushed the plunger. My arm burned for just a second but righted itself. She said, "This is for pain. A side effect is that you may get sleepy, but it's that or hurt like hell. And I'll be damned if you're suffering under my care. Got it?"

A false smile touched my lips. She'd patched me up a hundred times. It felt so safe to be in her care. Like coming home. But I wasn't in the mood to smile. I was feeling remorseful and angry and confused and so many other things that my head was spinning. Relaxing back into my pillow, I said, "Yes, ma'am."

The smile didn't last long. The moment Lia turned away to move on to assist one of the doctors with their next patient, it faded. There was too much to share with her. My truth, yes, but also the strange impression that I existed on another plane of being.

Lloyd noticed my shift in mood right away. "You look troubled, sir."

The last word made me wince. "Drop the 'sir,' Lloyd."

He leaned forward with his elbows on his knees and kept his voice low, so that only I could hear it. "What's on your mind, Quinn? You seem a million miles away."

My head felt strange from the medication, but the pain in my stomach receded. It was embarrassing to talk about my recent hallucinations, but if I could confide in anyone about it, it was Lloyd. I said, "Do you ever have memories of situations that couldn't have happened?"

"You mean déjà vu?"

"No, more than that. Like . . . actual memories and a nagging feeling that you really experienced those moments."

An image flashed in the forefront of my mind. Dead, lidless eyes. Sharp teeth. Clawed hands. Rippers. Fucking Rippers.

He chuckled and sat up again. "What did she put in that IV anyway?"

I barked, "I'm dead serious."

He gauged my reaction—and perhaps my sanity—for a moment, before leaning close again. "So . . . what? Are you experiencing some kind of personality break or something?"

"I don't think so. It's almost like I've experienced other lives. The same people are there, but . . . life is different." I still wasn't sure exactly how different. There were several pieces to this multilevel puzzle, and I only held a few of them. "If I'm actually living them, that is, and not losing my damn mind to PTSD."

"Am I in these other lives?" I couldn't determine whether or not he was pandering to me.

"I believe so." I hadn't counted on it making me feel weak to discuss what I thought was happening. Was this just another one of those times when I was supposed to "man up"? "I have a feeling we don't like each other in one of them."

"That alone should show it can't be real." He forced a smile, but he couldn't hide the concern in his eyes. He probably thought I was going crazy. He wasn't the only one. "You should get some rest."

As Lloyd stood and made his way down the hall, I caught a flash of movement in my peripheral vision. When I turned my head, I saw the Stranger standing there, now wearing filthy scrubs and a pleased expression. "You're waking up."

People moved about the ward I was in without giving him so much as a glance. It was enough to make me wonder if they could even see him.

"I've seen you before. Here, but there too." I was growing more certain about my memories. In one life I was trying to get back to Lia. She and I—

The memory hit me fast and hard. The bracelet on my wrist that had been a gift from Kai. The love letter from Lia. Leaning in to kiss Caleb. Quietly, I said, "There, I'm . . . different."

He blew out a mouthful of smoke as he spoke. I hadn't noticed he'd been clutching a cigarette between two fingers until just then. "Almost fully awake. You're full of surprises. None I can't see coming, but still."

I met his eyes. They were dark—so dark they appeared black. For a moment they looked like snakeskin, but it had to be a trick of the light. "You're a gardener there."

The corners of his mouth curled upward. The simplest gesture—a smile, a nod—looked unnatural and devious on him. "Am I, now? Are you so sure of that? Or is that just your interpretation?"

I strained to grasp the threads of my memory. "You may not be a gardener, but you are a man."

He met my eyes with a sinister grin. "Am I, now?"

My chest tightened. Just like it had that day in the

school with Caleb. The day I saw black spindly arms dragging a creature's large body through a doorway. The day I finally saw—

I swallowed hard, sitting up as much as I was able. My breaths were coming fast; I was panicking at my realization. The answers, they were all there. How had I forgotten? It was real. It was all real. "I know you. Your name is Coe. You turned Lia's mother into a monster. You put that rubber hose between my teeth before I was electrocuted. You broke my life into thirds, and changed things. I know you, Coe."

A satisfied smile settled on his lips.

"And I know me," I continued. "I'm not male at all where the Rippers roam. Or female. I'm . . . I'm . . ." A nurse approached, syringe in hand. She didn't even look at the Stranger, which made me wonder if he was invisible to all but me. Was he all in my head? After checking my chart, she filled a syringe and injected something into my IV. For a moment, I recalled the story of Alice falling down the rabbit hole. My world began to fade fast, but not before I heard Coe speak.

"Sweet dreams, shattered Quinn."

The chuckle that followed his words echoed down into the deep hole of sleep I fell into, the soundtrack to my nightmares.

11

When I opened my eyes again, the Stranger was gone. A single word clung to the cobwebs of my mind.

Genderqueer.

My IV was still attached, but my head was feeling clearer, so the medication must have worn off some. My center was sore but had downgraded from painful to tender. Not at all the blinding pain that it had been before I'd been brought back to the school. I strained to recall every detail of the conversation I'd had with the Stranger, but it was fuzzy.

Carefully, I sat up, then placed my feet on the floor, gauging my pain level before attempting to stand. There was no way I was going to ask any of the medical staff if I could get up and move around. Medical folks always wanted patients to rest, and that was something I just couldn't afford at the moment. The leader of the Allegiance was in my base of operations, and I'd be damned if I was going to lie around in bed when the path to peace was finally in our custody.

The tape and needle stung as I ripped out my IV, but I wasn't about to carry the damn bag with me downstairs. Bad enough that so many had seen the face of the Resistance lying wounded on a gurney. What they needed was to see me strong and steady. They needed hope. They needed confidence in my ability to lead. Especially now.

"Oh, but wait. I owe you *something, don't I?"*

Ignoring the echo of Lloyd's voice in my head, I slipped out the front and repeated to myself that the Lloyd in this Brume was my trusted friend. Not like the jackass he was there, in that place where bloodthirsty creatures roamed free.

It was real, that place. I was certain of it, which meant that the mirror was also real. And Coe was real too. What did that say about me?

I arrived at the door to the base unseen by anyone with the authority to stop me. Stewart was on guard duty. We exchanged greetings as I punched the code and let myself in. Just inside stood two guards—Ames and Drew, exactly who I'd have chosen to watch over our guest.

Caleb was sitting on a metal chair in the center of the room. He looked relatively well, which meant that whoever had brought him back to base had resisted the understandable urge to beat the crap out of him for good measure. His wrists were handcuffed. His ankles were shackled to the table in front of him.

As I approached, Ames and Drew straightened. We'd worked together against the tyranny of the Allegiance long before I'd become the face of the Resistance. Back when I was just Quinn, a person ready to do anything for our freedom, but who had no idea how to load a gun, let alone fire one. I'd been against weaponry of any kind when I was younger. But once an Allegiance soldier had pinned me to the ground with his boot and aimed his rifle at my head, my views on violence shifted. I still hated guns. But sometimes, when the world is full of monsters trying to take you down, you have to become a monster yourself just to survive.

It was Ames who spoke first, and he did so with a modicum of suspicion. "Sir, I thought you were injured."

My left hand went instinctively to the thick bandages on my midsection. "I'm fine. Give me a moment alone with the prisoner."

"Sir?" Drew looked hesitant to follow my order.

Straightening my shoulders, I managed to resist the

urge to wince at the pain. "I need privacy to discuss the situation with our guest, soldiers. You're dismissed for the time being."

"Yes, sir. Of course, sir." Amoo unlocked the door, and the two of them stepped outside.

The moment the door's lock was engaged, Caleb flashed me an arrogant smile, but it was too thin to hold weight. His eyes betrayed him with a subtle flash of fear. "I'm glad you came to kill me personally. I would've been insulted otherwise."

"I didn't come to kill you." I spoke the truth. After all, I wouldn't give him the satisfaction of becoming a martyr. "Don't get me wrong. We'll see how things go, but I didn't drag my happy ass all the way down here with the intent to end your life."

He nodded slowly, as if he almost believed me. I thought about the way he'd laced his fingers with Lloyd's through the bars of the Serenity Hut, the way he'd handed me the knife when it was time to kill the Ripper. Caleb was my ally—maybe even my friend—in the other Brumes. Surely that meant he could be my ally here, too.

Stop it, Quinn. One life at a time.

With a sigh, he said, "So why are you here?"

"I'm here because I'm trying to figure out what to do with you." With only a small wince of pain, I threw one leg over the seat of the empty chair facing him and sat, squaring off against my worst enemy. Worst. But not only. "Thanks for pointing out the first option, by the way."

He weighed my words for a moment in an attempt to decode what it was that I wanted from him if not his death. "I'm not intimidated by you, so I'm not sure what you hope to accomplish during this little visit. If you want information, you should know I'd rather die than betray the Allegiance."

I was sick of his bullshit already and I hadn't been in the room for a full minute. If we were going to get anywhere, it was going to be because I could find a way to reach through the fog of our feud. "You seem fixated on me killing you, Caleb. Let's move on from that for a moment and focus on something that I'm very keen to know."

"What's that?"

"Was killing your father worth it, just to take his place as leader of the Allegiance?"

The corner of his mouth tugged up in a smile. "I like you, Quinn. You don't fuck around."

That I didn't. Not when it came to asking questions that no one else seemed bold enough to ask. "I'd be lying if I said the feeling was mutual."

"It's true, I killed him. Old bastard put up quite a fight too. But yes . . . it was worth it." A disturbing look of pride washed over him, filling me with disgust. He gauged me in silence for a moment. "How'd you know?"

I shrugged. "Just a theory I had. Do the other Allegiance high-ups know?"

"As far as I can tell, only three people do. Me, you, and the departed general." Resting his cuffed hands on the table, he said, "So why *haven't* you killed me yet? Isn't taking down the Allegiance your little group's main goal?"

I met his steely gaze and softened my expression as much as I was able. "Have my parents spoken of me? Has my brother?"

Silence fell between us. I'd surprised him. But he soon gathered himself.

"Many times. In the past few years, your parents have proven themselves to be quite dedicated to the Allegiance. In fact, they've been invaluable supporters of our cause. They just hosted a fundraising dinner at my home in Charleston last week." His tone was casual, as if we were old friends catching up. In a way, if I thought about the Caleb I knew in the other Brumes, we were. "And Kai, as I'm sure you know, serves me well. I couldn't have chosen a more loyal second-in-command. I'm sure they would welcome you with open arms if you came to your senses and joined the Allegiance."

It was hard to imagine my family missing me. Intel over the past two years had given me the impression that I was no better than an unfortunate memory to them. But even so,

I couldn't deny my curiosity. My family may not have been my biggest fans, but they were still my family, and for that, I yearned. But not enough to betray all that I'd fought for.

"I miss them, you know," I said. "This war. It's cost all of us so much. Friends, family. Lives . . ." Locked in the forefront of my mind was the image of Kai moving from one person to another, pulling the trigger without remorse. Each shot reverberated through my memory. So many lives taken, and for what? Vengeance? Stolen goods? Ego? Genuine tears threatened to well in my eyes, but I swallowed them down. "I hate Kai for following your orders back there and killing my people. But I hate you more for ordering him to do it."

"You would have done the same thing if the situation had been reversed." His tone wasn't a defensive one. It just . . . was.

"Never."

He cocked a sharp, disbelieving eyebrow. "You're telling me that if my troops and I invaded this building, stole supplies, and set off fiery explosions that murdered people you know and worked with—fought alongside for your mutual cause—you wouldn't have hunted us down? You would have let us go, or if you did manage to catch up with us, you would've simply rapped us on the knuckles? That's some bullshit right there, Quinn, and we both know it."

He was right. It was bullshit. But looking at it from his

point of view didn't silence the sound of gunshots that was still ringing in my memory. "I want this war to stop."

"Then surrender." The corners of his mouth lifted in a derisive smile.

"Good one." I sighed, moving on to the next phase of my plan. It was now or never. Caleb would either be interested in talking of a road to peace, or he wouldn't. My throat felt dry. "Neither of us is willing to surrender, but maybe we can find somewhere in the middle that would satisfy both sides. I can't make the final call for the Resistance—after all, I'm only in charge of our base here in Brume—but I can try to convince my people to trust that your cooperation is sincere. If it is, of course. Don't try to deceive me, Caleb. I'll know it. I've been betrayed enough in my life to know a lie from truth."

He leaned forward. "I'm listening."

"We both know that the Allegiance isn't doing as well as you'd have people think. Ending this war would save lives—your people and mine." I flashed him a pointed glance. "Correct me if I'm mistaken, but my understanding is that the Allegiance wants all people to fall under one rule. The Resistance wants people to be ruled by no one. I propose that we make a deal and draw a line on the map. Those who want to be ruled by the Allegiance can move to whatever land we agree is yours, and those who want to be free move to our side."

"Are you actually suggesting we give you land to call your own?"

"I'm suggesting a compromise that will save lives on both sides. Because if we don't end this war soon, you and I both know that you will die—and you can trust that it will be by my hand—and your cause will suffer because of it. Your father established the Allegiance to act like a shepherd leading sheep—a doctrine we both know you believe—and with their shepherd gone, the sheep will scatter." I was appealing to his sense of reason now. The truth of my next words was so heavy that it weighed on them until they cracked. "If an agreement that leads to peace is not achieved, eventually, we will all die—every one of us—and have nothing to show for it but bloodshed."

Caleb cleared his throat without meeting my eyes. "What you're suggesting is . . . it's . . . interesting. Impossible, some might say, but intriguing nonetheless. Where exactly are you proposing we draw this literal line in the sand?"

My heart beat once. Twice. It wasn't disbelief that filled me, but a strange sense of relief that, even after all that he'd done, Caleb might actually still retain a small shred of humanity. Maybe no one was a lost cause. "To begin with, I want the Allegiance to immediately hand over all of Brume to the Resistance as a show of good faith. The rest can be determined later."

He offered only a nod in response. I didn't know if he was agreeing to my terms or merely acknowledging them.

Standing, I said, "I'm going to grab some paper and a pen from my office. When I get back, we can discuss possibilities and hammer out details of an agreement. At least something to end the fighting here in Brume."

"I've agreed to nothing yet. And even if I did, you know I'd have to take your proposal back to Allegiance headquarters. So, I suppose the question that remains is whether or not that's something you'll allow." His focus was locked on a spot on the floor. I wondered if he felt coerced, or maybe a sense of shame for even considering my proposition. He was the head of the Allegiance. Did the idea of compromise fill him with shame?

As I stood, I dared to think about the possibilities that could come from my conversation with him. Maybe it had taken kidnapping the leader of the Allegiance and locking him in a room with me to get him to listen to reason, but if that was the price of peace, it was a small one. By the time I stepped inside my office, I was feeling fairly confident. Maybe that was my first mistake.

A loud, familiar sound ricocheted through base. A single gunshot. Screams followed it from the floor above, along with shouted words and frightened children crying out. Instinctively. I reached for my holster, which was hanging over the back of my desk chair, but found it empty.

My stomach shriveled. My lungs seized inside my chest, and I bolted back to where Caleb was chained. It couldn't be. I was wrong. I was still medicated and not thinking clearly. There was no way—

Lia stood in front of Caleb, her shoulders slumped. Tears lined her face, and I wondered if they were tears of remorse or relief. She held my pistol in her hand. The guards were nowhere to be seen. How had she managed to evade the sniper and get by the door guard? How'd she get through the door without the code? Questions raced through my mind, but their answers would have to wait. What mattered was what she had done.

The weapon dangled from her fingers, threatening to tumble to the floor. But she didn't seem to care about that. She'd already accomplished what she'd set out to do.

Caleb's lifeless body lay crumpled on the floor. Blood pooled around his head in a crimson halo. If there was a heaven, he was entering its gates well equipped.

My voice shook with anger and disgust as I ripped my still-warm gun from Lia's hand. "What have you done?"

At first, she didn't even seem to be aware of my presence. Gripping her by the shoulders, I shook her and shouted, "What the hell have you done?!"

Words left her lips in a whisper: ethereal, intangible,

but nonetheless very much real. “I’ve saved lives.”

“You’ve damned us all! We were there, Lia. Peace was within reach. And now . . . now Kai will take Caleb’s place, and no amount of talking will convince him to end this war.”

It was over. Everything we’d all fought for. Lia had sentenced us all to death with the single pull of a trigger. A sudden wave of nausca hit me hard. I released my grip on her and stepped back. “The guard?”

“We had an understanding. But it’s not important how I got the code. All that matters is that I did what had to be done.” She looked at Caleb’s body in a way that could only be described as wonder.

“Families, Lia. Friends. Everyone. You’ve just killed us all.” I stormed back to my office. Lia had once described to me the human instinct of fight or flight, and I was in pure flight mode. Because there was no one to fight. At least, no one I’d feel good about hurting. I grabbed my tactical vest, holster, and knife, and put them on as fast as I could. As I was snapping my pistol into my holster, my hands slowed. Scribbled in my handwriting, tacked to the wall beside the map, was a note that read “You can’t run from the monster. The monster is you.”

Only I couldn’t recall having written it.

Furrowing my brow, I shook my head, stowing my questions about when I’d written it and why. I’d have to think about it more later. Right now I had a mess to deal with.

I wished I could scrub what I'd seen out of my brain. But I could never unsee it—so much of Caleb, spilled out all around his lifeless body. How could Lia be so reckless? So . . . violent?

The irony of my questions hit me hard. If anyone should be able to comprehend those things, it was me. But I didn't. I didn't understand at all. The only thing I did understand was that I never believed, in any existence, that Lia would've done what this Lia had just done.

"What are you doing? You should be lying down. You're still injured." I hadn't noticed Lia enter my office. Her voice was steadier now. She sounded like her old self. But she was different. She'd never be the same to me again.

I snapped, but my voice was shakier than I'd intended. "You murdered him."

Her face paled. "Where are you going?"

My response came out in a growl. "Outside for a cigarette."

Her words followed me out the door. "I won't apologize for doing the right thing, Quinn. You know I made the right choice!"

But I didn't know that. What's more, I didn't know her anymore. It broke my heart to doubt Lia, to feel my absolute trust in her wash away like it was nothing. My trust in her had been a thread that had kept my heart together through war and stress and pain. Who was I when that thread was broken? Would I fall apart completely?

I punched in the security code, stepped outside, and locked the door behind me. Shift change had occurred, so it was Mika I barked at. "Lia is inside. Take her into custody immediately."

"Sir?"

"*Now*, soldier."

I wasn't sure where I was going, just that I needed to be away. Away from Lia. Away from Caleb's corpse. Away from the people of the Resistance who would be looking to me for answers.

Answers that I didn't have.

"Surely, you have one or two." I jolted at the words—words that suggested the speaker somehow knew what I'd been thinking. To my left, having appeared from nowhere and matching my stride away from base, was the Stranger, once more donning his black snakeskin trench coat. He looked at me through the wet curtain of his dark hair and smiled. "Everyone has at least a single answer to a single question at some point in time."

The image of him in every existence, every Brume, was clearer than ever in my memory. It was as if I'd always known him. As if he had been following me around with his insufferable riddles my whole life. “There was a time not so long ago when I thought I had answers. At least some of them. Like who understood me and who didn’t. If anybody had asked me who I knew I could count on, the answer was Lia. It’s always been Lia. But now . . . I don’t know. Lia would never do something like that.”

“Considering that she just did, it seems that she would.” His steps slowed, and I felt compelled to match his pace. He lit a cigarette, and with the filter clenched between his teeth, said, “Do I detect a smidgeon of trouble in paradise?”

My insides felt hollow. “It’s like I don’t know her.”

“Have you ever?” He sucked in a lungful of nicotine and tar, and as he did so, the corners of his mouth seemed to crack. Two crooked, fine lines spiderwebbed up each of his cheeks as if his flesh were made of glass. The lines stopped at each ear, but I swore I heard the crackling sound of the glass threatening to shatter. When he exhaled, the cracks were gone. If they’d ever been there in the first place.

We’d come to a stop just in front of the small cave in the park. I hadn’t realized we’d walked so far.

“I may not know everything, but I thought I knew Lia.”

“Then why does she continue to surprise you?” The last two words drew out of him in a hiss. “No one ever fully knows anyone—not even themselves.”

He was right about that. No one knew who was good or

who was evil, because we were all a little of both. More of one or another, depending on whose point of view was doing the judging. But both, nonetheless. "You're saying Lia is a stranger to me?"

"No stranger than I." He smirked, and for a moment, I wondered if he knew that I thought of him as the Stranger, the way he seemed to know other things without my uttering a word. Could he really read my thoughts? Was that even possible?

Maybe I was clinging to denial. But I refused to let him think he knew better than I did when it came to my relationship with Lia . . . in any life. I shook my head. "I don't buy it. I know Lia. The real Lia."

His voice took on a Puckish tone that I despised immediately. "How can you know which Lia is real? You can't even determine which *you* is real."

I swallowed hard. "What are you talking about?"

"You can see it now. Oh yes, here you can see it. Here you're wide awake." He tapped ashes from his cigarette and drew in another lungful of tar.

My heart thumped hard against my ribs. "I don't know what you mean."

"Sure you do. Certain things are immutable. Your feelings for Lia, for instance. Whether you recognize it or not, it's the same in each existence. But other things are . . .

fluid." He wore a small smile, as if he'd just uttered an inside joke—one that I didn't understand.

"What is happening to me?" The question was directed as much to myself as it was to him. It was unbearable.

"Right now, you are attempting to seek even an ounce of forgiveness for the girl that you love for maybe undoing all that you've worked for. At the same time, you are running from monsters and feeling trapped by the wall of fog. All the while, you are also attempting to escape a group of people you thought could help you determine who it is within your capacity to love, when really you need no help at all." He took a drag and released it with his words in gray puffs. "That is what is happening to you. That is what you are allowing to happen to you."

I raked my hair back from my face with my free hand. "Which . . . which is real?"

He pointed his cigarette at me, and ashes fell from the end. "They all are. That's the beauty of it. They're all as real as real can get. But only one can be yours."

My throat dried. "You mean I have a choice?"

"Only in which monsters you'll live with. Some things may seem like variables, when in fact they are unchangeable."

"What things?"

His smile curled. "The fact that you are genderqueer,

or Other, as you've thought of it here. You must decide in which world you would prefer to exist. A world where you are female and your family is alive and well, but your parents will never accept a queer child as their own. A world where you are male and command the respect of many, but risk living under the rule of a group that wishes to snuff out the queer of society. Or a world full of monsters and mayhem, where your family is dead, but gender doesn't matter. Only you can choose your path. Only you can decide if the price of a closet is worth it."

"That can't be true. This is all a trick. Only one world is real. One life. It has to be." My hand found my pistol, but somehow, I knew that a bullet would mean nothing to the man—the creature—standing in front of me. Nevertheless, I pulled it from the holster and aimed the weapon at his head. "Which life is mine?"

"None of them." He leaned forward, pressing his forehead against the barrel. A childlike glint reflected in his eyes. He was daring me.

"You're lying."

"All of them." He closed his eyes, and for a moment, a look of absolute serenity washed over him. I wondered if this man, this . . . thing . . . was capable of death. If not, was he daydreaming about what it might be like now?

"They can't all be real. That would be . . ." Realization

filled me like a splash of frigid water on my face. I lowered my gun. ". . . a paradox."

"Putting it in the most scientific of terms . . . you'd be fucked."

Kai's voice entered my mind, but not the Kai I knew here—and not the Kai I'd known in the life fraught with Rippers. A different Kai. One who was still alive and still the brother I knew and loved, who loved me as well. No matter what.

The corners of the Stranger's mouth twitched into something resembling a smile. On his forehead was a small circle impression of my gun's barrel. "An interesting theory."

My head was spinning. "That's what this is, isn't it? Three Brumes. Three versions of myself. Three lives. All real. Something that cannot possibly exist."

"But they do exist. You exist." He raised an eyebrow. His impish smile remained. "Don't you?"

"How can I resolve a paradox?" The question was more to myself than him. In my memory floated Kai's response. *"That's the essence of a paradox—it cannot be solved. It essentially asks a question that cannot be answered."*

There was only one question that existed in each of the three Brumes, and Coe had laid it out for me. But even if the question lying at the heart of my situation was my gender identity, I had no clue what resolving the paradox would look like.

"You're going to be surprised when all is said and done." The Stranger spoke as if he'd already experienced this moment—all these moments combined. He spoke as if this were the past and he was well aware of what the future would bring.

I snapped my eyes to his with an eagerness I couldn't deny. "Then I do it? At some point, I choose which life to live?"

"You have. You haven't. You will. And you won't. But the key is . . . you can . . . and you must." He took a long, slow drag on his cigarette before dropping it to the ground and crushing it with the toe of his boot. As he returned his eyes to mine, with a casual tone, he said, "Watch your head."

Confusion filled me. I opened my mouth to question him—

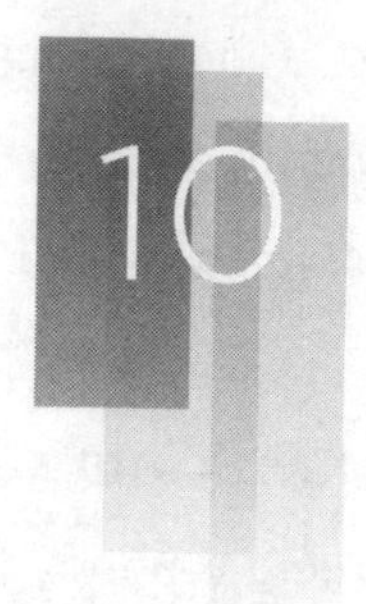

—the bright pain brought with it the sensation of lightning crackling through my skull. I jolted awake and scrambled to get my bearings. I didn't have long to recognize that Lloyd and two of his followers had managed to track Caleb and me down before Lloyd drew his foot back and kicked me in the head again, the steel toe of his boot slamming against my temple this time. The world tilted on its edge for a moment but righted itself before I could lose consciousness. The vignette that darkened my field of vision faded out after a moment. My hair was wet with what could only be blood.

Standing over me, in a circle, were Lloyd and his brutes.

It took a moment to recall the house we were in. Caleb and I had found it late last night and fallen asleep. The ceiling above the gang members was as gray as the fog around town. I pictured myself floating up and through it, higher and higher until I was among the stars. Free.

But freedom always came with a price.

"For freedom."

A voice so familiar to me that it might have been my own. The words felt as if I'd spoken them before. To Lloyd. But how could that be?

Because we're friends, I thought. *Not here, but in that other Brume. The one I remember when I'm sleeping but forget upon waking. The Brume where I present as male and Lloyd is my most trusted ally.*

Crouching down beside me, Lloyd said, "Rise and shine, asshole."

I rolled my head to the right, looking for Caleb. My vision was wonky, but I could make out the two people holding Caleb at bay. Susan, I thought. Collins too. Caleb's body hung limply, as if he'd been beaten pretty badly. I wondered how long they'd been at him before waking me. It felt like my brain was sloshing around freely inside my skull. Caleb winced when Collins gave his hair a tug.

Lloyd's eyes flashed with delirious fury. "Ten of my people, ten of my *family*, died because of you. Maybe it was the

Unseen Hands that did the killing, but you put them in that position, Quinn. And I don't forgive easily. No one messes with family."

Sliding my hand down my side, I reached for my gun. But it was gone. My holster was missing as well. Panic began to rise up within me until I remembered which Brume I was in. Here I had a bat for a weapon. A bat that was who-knows-where at the moment. I needed another method of defense, and I needed it now.

Glancing around, I saw nothing in reach to hit him with. All I had were words. "Listen, you insufferable prick. It wasn't my fault they died, and you know it. Now let us go. No harm, no foul."

His face turned red with hatred. The whites of his eyes were bloodshot. He had the look of a man unhinged. I wondered if he'd been dipping into more of that bathtub gin. He screamed, "But there is harm! There was foul! You have to pay for what you did. I don't make the rules here in Brume, Quinn. I just enforce them."

There *were* rules in Brume. Unspoken ones. The most important being that Brume was scary enough without violence against other people. If you were going to hurt someone, they damn well better have it coming. It was the Unseen Hands that had killed his people, not me. So Lloyd had already broken that rule, and the look on his face said he was about to break it again.

He drew his foot back to kick me again, and I squirmed as much as I could across the floor to escape him. His jaw was clenched, his eyes ablaze, and I knew in that moment that Lloyd intended to kill me.

An eye for an eye. A tooth for a tooth. A life for a life.

His boots made solid thumps on the floor as he approached, sliding his knife from its holster. He crouched down beside me and put the tip of it to my throat. "Even after I kill you, you owe me nine times over, Quinn. Nine lives. Well . . . eight, once I take care of Lia. When I'm done with you, I'm going back to where I've put her to finish the job. That is, if she's still alive when I get to her."

My heart shot into my throat. A mixture of fear and relief washed over me. Lia wasn't dead. Not yet. She'd been taken by Lloyd. Which meant that Caleb and I could save her. If we got out of here alive. "Where is she?"

"I don't have to tell you that. Just know that I'm going to take my time hurting her." He climbed on top of me, his weight cementing me to the floor, and pressed the blade in, breaking skin.

From the corner of my eye, I noticed that Susan had a crossbow slung over her shoulder. Lia's crossbow. On her thigh, she wore Lia's quiver. There was only one arrow left. "I didn't kill anyone, Lloyd. I was just trying to get free.

It's not my fault the Unseen Hands attacked. I don't control them. I'm sorry your friends died, but killing me and Lia won't bring them back."

"Maybe not. But I'll sleep better knowing I avenged their deaths."

My face grew hot with anger. I shouted at him, not caring that his knife sank deeper into my flesh as I did so. "Where is she, you fuck?!"

The corners of his mouth curled up in a sadistic smile. "She's in the one place you'll never be able to reach her. In fact, the only ones besides us who can reach her . . . are the Unseen Hands."

The window behind Susan shattered as gray talons smashed through it. An enormous creature, still hovering above the ground, seized her by the shoulders, puncturing its claws through her flesh, beneath her collarbones. Gripping her tight, the beast flapped its ashen, skin-covered wings. Susan screamed, dropping the crossbow. As she wriggled, the thing opened its mouth and emitted a sound—one exactly like the scream that had just come from Susan's mouth. It yanked her out the window and flew off, their matching screams comingling into one terrified cry.

Before I could wrap my head around what had happened—*a Screamer! Oh God, that was a Screamer!*—a terrible popping sound ripped through the air and speckles of wet heat spattered the side of my face. It was only when I looked at Lloyd that I realized it was blood. We both froze and turned our heads to see where it had come from. Where Collins had once stood was now just a puddle of blood, and small bits of meat and bone. From the darkness of the fireplace, the Unseen Hands had snatched Collins's life away.

In the center of a pool of Susan's blood lay a single arrow. It must've fallen out of Lia's quiver as the Screamer had taken Susan for its next meal.

Caleb hurried to his feet, flashing me a look of terror and surprise. I threw a nod to the door and he bolted. Balling up my fist, I punched Lloyd hard in his Adam's apple. He made an inhuman sound, clutching his throat, but still didn't budge from on top of me. Thrusting my hands forward, I dug my thumbs into his eyes. With a string of obscenities dripping from his lips, he backed away. Scrambling to my feet, I snatched up Lia's blood-covered crossbow and arrow, and then took off in the direction Caleb had run. Across the room, through the house, and out the door.

Behind me, Lloyd cursed my name. "Run and hide for now, Quinn! I'm going to kill you and your friends, and you'll never see it coming!"

His words gave me pause. It wasn't an empty threat. So long as Lloyd was alive, our lives were in danger.

Caleb saw that I had stopped in my tracks, and he turned

back to grab me, tugging on my arm. "Quinn, come on! We have to find somewhere to hide!"

From inside the house, I heard the creaking of Lloyd's feet on the stairs. He was coming for us. "You can't hide forever, Quinn! Sooner or later, I'll find you. I'll gut you and your little boyfriend and then finish off Lia too."

He was laughing, and the tinny sound of it felt like a rusty nail dragging across something metal.

Loading the crossbow, I locked eyes on the door. My jaw was tight with determination.

From behind me, in a shaky voice, Caleb said, "My God, Quinn. What are you doing?"

Lloyd exited the front door, a grin on his face, his Adam's apple already swollen. He stared me down, hardly seeming to care that I had an arrow cocked and ready. Maybe he didn't think I had the guts. Maybe I wondered if he was right. "I could skin Lia. Use her hide for leather. What do you think, Quinn? I could use a new bag."

I knew Lloyd's gang meant a lot to him. I knew he didn't take betrayal lightly. I even knew how much he'd wanted me to join his group. But I'd had no idea how fragile his grip on sanity and human decency was until now. I'd be doing the world a favor. I could save all our lives with a pull of the trigger.

I could do it. I could kill him.

I raised the crossbow and aimed, then fired. The arrow whipped through the air and hit my mark, piercing Lloyd's shoulder, pinning him to the front door.

Maybe Lloyd would've killed me if our roles had been reversed. But I wasn't Lloyd. I was better than him.

After a brief cry, he erupted in laughter. "You think a little shoulder wound is going to stop me? I'll never stop. Not until you get what's coming to you."

My jaw felt tense. "Tell me where you're keeping her."

"Hmm." He cocked his head to one side in mock consideration. "No."

I tried to muster the patience and empathy I remembered having in another Brume—the one where my parents sent me to that awful camp, and I just kept forgiving them, kept wanting to understand things from their point of view. But something in me snapped, and the warrior fury I'd felt when storming Allegiance HQ took over. I remembered it, remembered it all. I was neither of those Quinns. Neither . . . and both.

My steps were sure as I headed straight for Lloyd. I dropped the crossbow on the porch before gripping his shirt collar in one hand and the arrow in the other. I pulled him hard to me, twisting the arrow some. He winced at the pain but did not scream. Fresh blood moistened his shirt. I said, "Last chance, Lloyd. Tell me where Lia is."

"Last chance before you'll do what exactly? You bore me, Quinn."

I looked at him—really looked—and tried to see the ally he'd been to me at Camp Redemption, the friend he'd been to me throughout the war. I wondered if the man in front of me could recall any of the other Lloyds, the way I recalled the other Quinns. But even if he did, that was his journey. Not mine. If he ever uncovered the existence of all three Brumes, maybe he'd grow as a person. Maybe not. That wasn't for me to figure out. I had my own life to live, and he had his. Hopefully he'd live it better from here on out.

I gave him a hard shove and stepped off the porch, moving toward Caleb. The concern in Caleb's expression was washed quickly away by fear, paling his skin. I turned back to the house just in time to see Lloyd wrenching his shoulder free. He shouted and cupped the wound with a shaking hand, but the pain didn't register in his eyes—only the thirst for vengeance. Behind him, still embedded in the door, was the arrow. Liquid dripped from the feathers like horrific raindrops.

Panic welled in my chest. "Caleb! Run!"

It happened so fast it barely registered in my mind. One moment, Lloyd was ripping the arrow from the door and loading the crossbow. The next, he was pointing the weapon at my head. He pulled the trigger. Tiny droplets of blood dabbed my ear as the arrow flew by, just missing me. Lloyd moved at me fast, a wild, unhinged look in his eyes. Maybe I should have run, but all I could think about was getting Caleb to a safe distance. "Lloyd, stop! We can talk about this!"

"We're done talking." He lunged at me, grabbing me by the throat. "And you're done breathing."

He gripped me tight and squeezed until my head swam. The urge to cough filled me, but I couldn't. I could draw no breath in, and had no breath to blow out. He tightened his hand, choking me. There was nothing human lurking in his expression now. Only animalistic want to take down his prey. I clawed at his fingers in a desperate attempt to free myself, but to no avail. Black dots filled my vision. I was losing consciousness.

Suddenly, he relaxed his grip, but only enough for me to wriggle free. Fresh blood dripped from his hairline to his cheek. As I scrambled away, I noticed a bloody rock on the ground. Lloyd stared across the yard at Caleb, who was looking more scared, I thought, than he had the night we'd killed that Ripper. Scared or not, Caleb plucked another rock from the ground. "Let them go, asshole!"

My throat burned. Several coughs ripped through me. I had to fight to keep my breathing deep and steady so I wouldn't pass out. My legs felt like jelly. Standing wasn't an option, so I crawled away as fast as I could.

A hand, hot and firm, grabbed my ankle and pulled. Lloyd had me. And he was going to kill me.

In the grass ahead of me lay a rusted hammer, and I grabbed it instinctively, with no thought or plan.

Lloyd gripped the back of my hoodie and yanked me from the ground, his voice an inhuman growl. "Good afternoon, Quinn. You're going to die today."

I didn't know how it happened, exactly. One moment, the hammer was high above my head. The next, its claw was buried in Lloyd's neck. In a moment that might have been comical if it weren't so horrible, Lloyd and I exchanged a look of surprise, as if neither of us could believe what I'd done. Lloyd gripped the handle in desperation and pulled the hammer free. His chest was instantly covered in deep crimson. There was no saving him now. Not even if I wanted to.

His face paling fast, he opened his mouth to speak, but only a terrible gurgling sound came out. I couldn't tear my horrified gaze away from his face. I'd just killed a man. I'd tried so hard not to let the monstrousness of this Brume pull me under—I tried so hard to escape—but in the end, I really was a monster after all.

I plucked the gore-covered hammer from the ground and stared at it in a petrified daze. From somewhere nearby that sounded far away, a voice said, "Come on, Quinn. It's over. Let's get out of here. It'll be okay. I promise. It'll be okay."

I could only assume that the voice belonged to Caleb. Everything but the slow sound of Lloyd's blood as it dripped from his neck to the puddle on the ground beneath him was white noise. His eyes glazed over with the absence of a soul. Lloyd was dead. I'd killed him.

And I was certain that the Stranger, Coe, whoever, whatever he was, had seen everything.

He'd seen me. He'd seen everything I'd done.

By the time the last electric shock ceased ripping through my body, the words that had been on the screen had been replaced with a picture of a butterfly perched delicately on a red rose.

The screens went black, and I was left in a pitch-dark room. I must have twisted and strained against my straps more than I'd thought, because my wrists and ankles felt rug-burned. My head hurt worst of all—even more than my jaw. My face was dripping with sweat and tears. No sound came from the darkness. No light. No hope. There was only me and my thoughts. I supposed they wanted me to consider what had just transpired—that every time an image that was remotely queer had flashed on the screen, I'd experienced intense pain. But I barely gave that a thought. Mostly, I thought about the words on the screen. *You can't run from the monster. The monster is you.*

Was I a monster? Did Dr. Hillard have a point?

I could've really used a cigarette to steady my nerves.

Only . . . I didn't smoke. Where had that urge come from?

"Oh, that's right. Not here you don't."

The gardener. He'd offered me a cigarette and spoke as if he knew another version of me from somewhere else. He'd been here recently too. Placing that rubber thing between my teeth. I could still smell the nicotine wafting off him.

Lying there in the dark with no sound, I sank into a place of near sensory deprivation. I thought about the gardener and how familiar he'd seemed to me, though I hadn't recognized him at the time. He was a stranger to me. The Stranger. And I *had* seen him before. In a white lab coat. In a black snakeskin trench coat. But where?

Eerie fog coated my thoughts, with the sounds of war echoing in my ears. At first, I thought maybe they were things I'd heard during the treatment; there'd been so many images, flashing across the screens. But no. They were memories. They had to be. They were too real not to be.

The door opened and fluorescent lights buzzed on,

hurting my eyes. Hands undid my straps and removed the rubber hose from my mouth. Hands carried me all the way to my room and laid me on my bed. Darkness fell over me like a heavy blanket. When I opened my eyes again, I was standing just inside the small cave across from my school. But the cave was a half mile away from Camp Redemption, so how could that be?

My bare feet moved over cool stone and dirt as I walked deeper into the cave, stepping over dozens of empty liquor bottles—maybe from bored teenagers, I couldn't be sure. There, at the very back of the cave, a large mirror hung in midair. Its frame was black and twisted. Several sharp points jabbed outward, giving it a menacing appearance. I could see no strings or wires holding it in place. It just floated there. Within it, I saw my reflection. I had the strangest feeling the mirror had been waiting for me.

I looked over my shoulder, toward the entrance. The air felt dense, making it hard to breathe.

A face appeared in front of me as I turned back, just inches from my own. It was smooth and had the gleam of polished porcelain. A mask. Only I couldn't discern the eyes of the wearer through the eyeholes. "Wh-who are you?"

The wearer of the mask didn't speak.

In the darkness, I couldn't quite make out their body, but it looked like they were wearing a costume of some kind.

A huge form, wrapped in black snakeskin.

The texture sent a shiver up my spine. Before I could stop myself, I stretched out my hand toward it. I had to see who it was, lurking within this elaborate costume. After a moment's hesitation, I held my breath and gripped the mask—noting how warm it was, like flesh—and pulled.

But it wasn't a mask after all. It was a face. It was the true face of Coe.

Coe, the man in the trench coat. Coe, the creature at the school. Coe, the gardener. Coe. Memories of him filled me so quickly, I thought I might burst.

A tiny sliver toward the bottom of the masklike face opened, spreading wider and wider until it was an infinite black cavern. All along Coe's throat were toothlike thorns that looked capable of tearing through flesh like it was tissue. I could see that far and even deeper, into Coe's belly—where I swore I saw a mess of bones and flesh. Atop the stomach contents sat an eyeball that had been ripped from its socket. As I stared, horrified and speechless, the eye turned up to me, looking at me, as if its owner were still experiencing the endless hell of being digested by Coe.

I scrambled away from him, and Coe's mouth closed into a small slit once again. I could see the large snakeskin body and long, spindly legs clearly now. But I couldn't see the cave entrance anymore. I was trapped.

My foot came down on what felt like a beer bottle, and I fell back, hitting the ground with a thud. Another broken bottle sliced through my left palm. Pain shot through my body, but I barely had time to register it. Coe was inching closer now, pulling that immense body deeper into the cave, closer to me, with those impossibly thin legs. Hunger was in the air—a hunger that I suspected could never be satiated. Coe was coming for me.

I half expected him to lunge forward, to snap at me or grab me with his clawed hands. But Coe moved with the confident patience of a predator who'd never lost a meal. He inched closer, and the slit opened wide, revealing a long, black tongue that snaked its way out of his mouth and caressed my cheek. A scream tore from my throat, and the next thing I saw was a bloody, broken bottle in my hand stabbing forward, piercing his cheek. I expected the porcelain-looking surface to crack, but it cut and bled like flesh—black, glistening blood. An inhuman sound rumbled from within him—one that spoke of pain and suffering and vengeance and death without his even uttering a word.

My hair blew back from my face as I ran. I didn't know how I'd managed to stand or get out of the cave. I just knew that I'd instinctively chosen fight before following it up with flight. I just knew that Coe was behind me, and I wasn't going to live much longer if I didn't get out.

I knew I couldn't run away, couldn't escape the nightmare, but I ran anyway. I didn't stop running until I closed my bedroom door behind me. I was home. I shoved my dresser in front of the door and locked my window, knowing full well that it wouldn't help.

Coe was coming for me. And he was hungry.

I snapped my eyes open into wakefulness and shot up in the bed at Camp Redemption.

A dream.

It was just a dream.

Wasn't it?

As I rubbed the ache from my left hand, I noticed the sun was setting outside. I must have slept for hours after the shock therapy. I lay still, steadying my breathing, trying to loosen the knot that had formed in my chest. *Caleb.* I had to help Caleb. And Lloyd. And the others. We had to get out of here.

Emergency lights flashed in through my window, splashing the walls with color. Blue and red. Over and over again. A warning of some kind.

I sat up with a jerk and rushed to the window. An ambulance was parked in front of the house. Two ENTs were loading a gurney into the back. The person on it was too far away for me to make out. I hurried downstairs and burst out the front door. Several staff members were standing outside, along with Alice, Randall, Collins, Caleb, and Valerie.

Caleb looked more than a little exhausted. Alice fidgeted nervously. Several other staff members had haunted, worried looks about them. There was no sign of the gardener. The Stranger. Coe.

Dr. Hillard was talking to one of the ENTs, who scribbled something down on a clipboard before climbing into the driver's side of the ambulance. The other ENT closed the back doors and hurried to the passenger door. As they were pulling away, I grabbed Valerie by the shoulder. "What happened? Who—"

Valerie burst into tears and hugged me. "Susan. It was Susan. They . . . they performed an exorcism on her. She's . . . hurt. She's hurt bad, Quinn."

My heart sank like a stone. I gripped Valeric tight. Though I couldn't seem to find any tears to shed, I let her cry enough for the both of us, soaking the front of my shirt with her anguish. One of us was hurt badly enough to warrant a hospital visit. She'd been sent here to become worthy of heaven and instead had experienced hell.

As if holding court, Dr. Hillard turned to face us all, holding up his hands. "Please be comforted, children. Pray for Susan. She is in God's hands."

"What happened to her?" Caleb's voice sounded smaller than it had before they'd dragged him away from Lloyd and me. I wondered what they'd done to him, and if it was as bad as or worse than what they'd done to me. My wrists still ached from the straps digging into them.

In the calmest tone, Dr. Hillard replied, "Susan had an accident. She fell down some stairs. She'll be fine."

He was lying. It wasn't even a convincing lie, which made it all the more upsetting. As the heat of anger spread up my body, I reached instinctively for the pistol on my hip, but when I felt nothing there, I paused in confusion. I hated guns. I didn't ever carry a gun.

Not here, anyway.

Alice stepped forward. "But even as we witness a loss, we have an opportunity to witness a tremendous win, as one of our own shall emerge from the Serenity Hut renewed."

The last time I'd seen Lloyd, he hadn't exactly looked "renewed," in any sense of the word. He'd looked hungry. He'd looked tired. But he hadn't looked defeated, which was the most important thing.

As if he were taking us all out for ice cream, Dr. Hillard spoke in the kindest-sounding voice. "If you'll all please follow me."

We walked around the house, and at the sight of the building where I'd been electrocuted—sorry, I mean "treated"—my stomach turned at the memory of the experience. That feeling stayed with me all the way to the Serenity Hut.

When we reached the prison shed, Dr. Hillard withdrew a set of keys from his vest pocket and unlocked the padlock that had been keeping Lloyd inside. The door swung open, and Dr. Hillard gestured for Lloyd to exit. Valerie gasped at the sight of our friend.

In his trademark calm tone, Dr. Hillard addressed Lloyd, but as he did, he looked at the rest of us, like he wanted to make sure we were seeing what happens to someone who rebels against Camp Redemption. "Lloyd, please share with us what enlightenment you received from our Lord after your time in solitude. How do feel after your treatment?"

"I feel . . . good, to be honest. I thought about you the entire time, Doc." Lloyd's expression sent a worried chill through me. Had they broken him at last? Was the Lloyd I'd been so charmed by now forever changed into whatever they'd deemed appropriate? I glanced at Caleb, who looked as concerned as I felt.

Alice straightened her shoulders in triumph. A look of pride washed over Dr. Hillard's face. They'd won. They'd always win.

Then the corner of Lloyd's mouth lifted in an impish smirk. Offering the good doctor a wink, he said, "Incidentally, you might wanna mop the floor. It's pretty sticky in there."

Alice took a sharp step toward Lloyd. Only a stern glance

from Dr. Hillard stopped her. After all, they couldn't risk an injury so grave that another ambulance had to be called. She spat at Lloyd, "You're disgusting. And a poor example of what any human being here on God's green earth should strive to be."

Dr. Hillard's jaw tensed. I couldn't help noticing his hands had clenched into fists. "Obviously, we'll have to resort to more aggressive treatment. As Saul was shown the light on the road to Damascus, you will be cleansed, boy."

"When are you gonna understand, old man, the more you do to me, the more you hurt me, the more I come to enjoy it." The fire in Lloyd's eyes had returned. "You're not curing me of anything, 'Doctor.' You're just getting me interested in leather bars and BDSM."

Dr. Hillard's lips pursed in revulsion. His eyes were locked on Lloyd's, but Lloyd wasn't backing down. "Perhaps your humility will emerge once you've spent an additional three days in the Serenity Hut. With daily flagellation to tame the demons within you."

Lloyd swallowed hard. He didn't say a word, but he did struggle some when two men forced him back inside the shack and placed the lock back on the door. Once the door was closed, I swore I heard soft sobbing coming from within. My heart cracked into pieces at the sound of it.

Alice's eyes filled with fear, which tightened my chest

in panic. If she was worried about Lloyd spending a full five days locked away, it had to mean that Dr. Hillard had snapped.

His calm, confident demeanor returning, Dr. Hillard spoke through a crack between the boards—the same crack Caleb and Lloyd had laced their fingers through. He said, "Some demons can be resisted, some forced out, but the demons infesting your soul, my dear boy . . . I fear they must be starved and beaten from you."

Turning on his heel, Dr. Hillard led us back to the house. None of us spoke during the walk. Once we'd stepped inside, before she retired for the night, Alice reminded us that it was almost curfew and that we should pray for Susan, Lloyd, and ourselves before bed. Her demeanor was subdued.

When she was gone, I looked into the eyes of each of my friends and said, "We're getting out of here. Tomorrow. And we're taking Lloyd with us. Before any of the rest of us end up in the back of an ambulance."

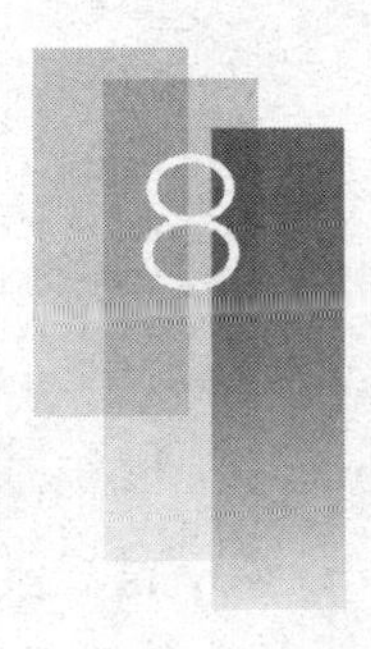

Behind me, I heard the telltale flick of a lighter, followed by Coe's voice. "I told you to watch your head."

I turned to face him, my thoughts swirling as I tried to figure out how he'd moved in a blink from my side to the tree he was leaning against, but came up empty.

I said, "How did you . . ." But I stopped, knowing better than to ask the riddle master for useful information.

With his nicotine-stained fingers, he offered me a salute. Then his body sank into the tree, through the bark. Not becoming one with it or encased by it, just through it, like a corpse sinking into a scummy pond. He faded away, swallowed by bark and moss. Just like that, once again, Coe was gone.

"Hey, Quinn." I hadn't noticed Lloyd approach, so when he spoke, it startled me. Not just because I wasn't expecting to hear his voice. But because the last time I'd seen him, he was being dragged away by homophobic zealots, and the time before that he'd died by my hand in a world fraught with actual monsters.

He had no idea that Caleb was dead. Or that Lia had killed him. Or that I had just stabbed him through the jugular with a rusty claw hammer in an alternate life.

My hand was trembling as I brushed hair back from my face. I tried to appear calm, but my eyes kept darting from Lloyd to the tree where Coe had disappeared and back again. Lloyd raised an eyebrow in concern. "You all right?"

I was about as far from all right as a person can get, but how the hell was I supposed to explain that to him? I was having a hard time looking into his eyes now without seeing the horrified realization in them once the hammer had pierced his skin in the other Brume. Overwhelming guilt filled me at having caused him pain, but I'd have been lying if I'd said I didn't feel a sense of justice as well.

He said, "Does Lia know you're out here?"

"Do I look like I care at the moment?" I took a pack of cigarettes from my pocket and tapped it against my palm.

My thoughts swirled around the question of how to solve this paradox. Coe said that I had to choose which life I wanted to live. Even if I could decide, how could I possibly implement that choice?

With the filter of a smoke pressed between my lips, I accepted a light from Lloyd, closing my eyes as I inhaled. The burning intake of breath that would normally have brought me an instant sense of relief and calm simply burned without purpose, filling my mouth with an acrid, empty taste. Unsatisfied, I dropped the butt to the ground and crushed it with my boot.

The Stranger was nowhere to be found, but it was becoming clear that his hints at other lives weren't without merit. Those lives were very real—as real as this one. The Stranger had told me that I had a choice in which life to live. If that was true, I needed to remember everything I could about those other existences.

"What's going on with you? You're a world away."

Three worlds, actually. "Nothing. I just have a lot on my mind."

"Care to share?"

Across the street, life was carrying on like business as usual. A mother was holding her daughter's hand as they climbed the steps to the front door of the high school. Two men in civilian clothes greeted a third as he approached. A light breeze rustled the park's trees. I wondered, if the Allegiance and Resistance destroyed one another, how different the world would look. Maybe it would be as savage and broken as the Brume where monsters roamed free. Maybe our worlds weren't so different. But at least in that Brume, that Quinn could live their truth openly. At least that Quinn had some semblance of what it was like to live free . . . even if they did seem lonely.

I brought my thoughts to Lia. I'd done the right thing by ordering Mika to take her into custody. But that didn't mean I felt good about it. "Caleb's dead."

Lloyd's face went white with shock, but soon reddened in anger. "What?! How?"

"Lia." Her name felt foreign on my tongue. "She shot him."

The question of why hung on his lips, but he didn't give voice to it. Maybe he understood that now wasn't the time for whys. "Shit! We're . . . we're . . ."

"The word you're looking for is 'fucked.'"

"When did she do it?"

"About twenty minutes ago."

He frowned. "The moment they catch wind of the news, the Allegiance is going to start killing civilians. So what are we going to do?"

"I don't know. But for now I'm going to stand here and

consider lighting another cigarette."

Lloyd shook his head, his mouth a thin line. "Come on, Quinn. A real man doesn't run from his problems."

I thought about the Allegiance's creed. *As God intended.* I wondered if God's real intent was that we all end up dead so the world could be cleared away for some new form of life. Intent or not, like it or not, we were headed in that direction now. All because of Lia. Without meeting his gaze, I said, "What if I'm not a 'real man'?"

There was a distinct pause before he replied. As he did, he took a small step back. "What are you talking about? You're not . . . gay or anything. Are you?"

Sadness filled me. Lloyd was the one person I knew who I thought would accept me no matter what I was, no matter how I felt. I was supposed to be able to count on him. Too many of the people I trusted were showing their true colors—colors I had never seen in them before. "Would it matter if I was?"

"Well, you're not, so it isn't even an issue. Right?" He fidgeted some. Seeing it made my heart sink.

"Right." It pained me to let the word slip from my mouth, but I could think of no other response to offer my best friend, my closest confidant . . . the man who'd just behaved as though being queer were a communicable disease. "I never wanted this, y'know. I never wanted to fight or to be in the Resistance, let alone be the face of it. I never told anyone. But that's the truth."

He offered only silence, understanding that now wasn't the time for his input or opinion. He knew I wouldn't hear either. I couldn't at the moment. All I could hear were my own thoughts and the soft cracking of my heart. "I've been betrayed, Lloyd. Again. How can I support the Resistance when I can't even tell friend from foe within our own ranks?"

Lloyd stood there, seeming to wrestle with something. After a moment, he withdrew a folded piece of paper from his inside vest pocket. "I came to find you because this message just came in from the Allegiance. It came through on channel nineteen, broadcast wide in hopes we'd hear it."

Of course it had. I knew what it said. That, at least, I had a good grasp on. "From Kai, I assume?"

Lloyd gave me a single, telling nod. "He says that you and he need to talk. As soon as possible."

"And?"

"What makes you think there's more?"

There was no keeping the curtness out of my tone. "You wear your lies all over your face, Lloyd. Even the unspoken ones."

He sighed. "He wants you to come to Allegiance headquarters."

"What choice do I have given our current situation? If I

don't go, he could send another assassin after me." My mouth felt dry. How many Allegiance loyalists might be lurking in our midst, disguised as freedom fighters? Who could I trust at my side in a skirmish now? "If he confirms at that meeting that he knows of Caleb's assassination, it means there's still a spy among us, Lloyd. And a damn good one, too."

"Meeting with Kai won't go well. You can't trust him. You know that."

"I know I can't trust him. But I have to meet with him anyway. It's our only chance to negotiate a truce." A truce. Something that felt impossible now. But I had to try.

"Permission to speak freely?"

I nodded.

"I don't think you're being rational at the moment."

I raised an eyebrow. "You'd better have a point to make, Lloyd."

"How will a single discussion with Kai—the brother who, last I knew, wouldn't piss on you to douse the flames if you were on fire—change anything between the Allegiance and the Resistance?"

"I refuse to give up hope. Caleb was willing to discuss the possibility of a truce. Right up until . . ."

Understanding passed over Lloyd's expression then. "I had no idea Caleb had opened up to talks about ending the war."

Across the street, foot traffic had picked up. Hospital workers moving inside and out due to shift change. Families making their way up and down the thoroughfare. Life.

"You're right. I can't trust Kai. But with Caleb dead, he's now the leader of the Allegiance. He's also my family, for what it's worth. If there's anything at all about that that means something to him, then maybe we can somehow reach an accord and put an end to this madness." My chest ached as I sighed. "I'm tired, Lloyd. I'm tired of the fighting and the hunger and the fear. I just want it to end."

"We all do, sir."

"Gotta say, I'm not entirely convinced of that." Through my memory flipped a hundred pictures. Kai, Caleb, and so many others in both the Allegiance and the Resistance. All faces I knew or had known. All people who could never seem to find a reason to stop fighting. "I think there are some people who are used to the chaos and thrive on the argument. I think some people would rather battle till the end just because they have too much pride to lower their weapons, stow their ambitions, and reach middle ground with the other side."

His voice quieted some. "I'm sure you're right. But it takes two to stop a fight."

I took a drag on my cigarette, drawing heat and smoke and death into my lungs. As I put the butt out with the bottom of my boot, I said, "Fair point. But one can start the conversation that might end it."

I began my return with a less-than-confident step. Once I'd rounded the building and let myself in the back door, I tried not to look at the body or the pool of blood on the floor. Three soldiers were tending to the scene, and as I entered, they each greeted me in numb silence. The air smelled like copper.

I entered my office, noting that the thin linen square, embroidered with an *L*, still lay on the corner of my desk. I knew it was much more than a simple piece of cloth. It was more than a gift, even. It was a part of Lia that could be with me when she couldn't. It was her way of accompanying me into battle when she knew I wouldn't let her. It was a symbol of the love that she felt for me, despite what I may do or say.

Placing my palm over the cloth, I closed my fist, squeezing the handkerchief in my hand. With my eyes closed, I took in a long, slow, deep breath and released it. Then I picked up the handkerchief and tucked it inside my vest.

Because in the end, anger—no matter how seemingly all-encompassing—was so much smaller than love would ever be.

For what felt like the last time, I looked around my office at the desk, the maps, the trophies brought back from each triumphant battle. But I didn't really *see* any of those things.

All I could see was Lloyd and me laughing after pulling off a damn-near-impossible supply raid; Lia perching on the corner of my desk, a knowing smile on her face, the day I finally gathered the courage to tell her that I loved her. Memories filled the room, and I was about to leave them all behind. Because I knew that this would be the last time I'd ever stand in my office. Brother or not, Kai intended to kill me.

From a small box in my top desk drawer, I withdrew my grandfather's watch and clasped it around my wrist. My grandfather had been a war hero in his time. But he'd insisted until the day he died that his more important accomplishment was the way he'd treated his family, including his own brother. To him, there was no relationship more important than that of two brothers. *Hellfire can't split a brotherhood, Quinn*, he'd told me on many occasions. *It can singe it a bit, but burns can heal. Brotherhood is forever.*

Despite my grandfather's words floating through my mind, I removed the box of ammunition from the same drawer and loaded two bullets into the clip of my gun. One for my brother if things got out of hand, and one for anybody who got in Lloyd's way when he was booking it out of there on my orders. I didn't need any more than that. I didn't want any more than that. I never liked shooting the damn thing anyway.

Reaching into my pocket, I withdrew the only gift I could think to leave for Lia—something she'd wanted for as long as I'd known her; something that would tell her that in the end, I loved her more than the blood in my veins. The pack of cigarettes crinkled when it hit the desktop. I was done. For Lia, for myself. No amount of nicotine could calm my nerves or bring me any sense of peace now. I was about to kill the only brother I had, or he was about to kill me.

It was a long trek to the other side of town, where Allegiance headquarters stood. Lloyd walked at my side, his expression stoic, but I knew better. He'd been pissed when I'd refused to bring any additional support, and he, like all of us, was afraid of this building and all the people in it. He'd never say so, but we were both shaking on the inside as we moved up the front steps of what once had been city hall.

One of the guards opened the door and gestured for us to go inside. "Wait in there. The general will be with you momentarily."

General. I supposed he had Lia to thank for the promotion. Before the death of Caleb, Kai had been merely a colonel. It also meant that Kai knew that Caleb was dead.

Lloyd and I exchanged brief glances. It was strange that no one was patting us down or demanding we remove our weapons. Maybe they weren't worried about us, even if we were armed. Maybe they were just playing mind games to convince us we weren't a threat. All I knew was that there was no way they'd overlooked it.

Before even stepping through the arched doorframe, I could see the baroque wallpaper, torn and faded over the years. The room was completely empty of furniture or anything that would indicate it was still in use, even as a storage facility. Above the empty space hung a large crystal chandelier. Its crystals, once reflecting every glimmer of light in a declaration of beauty, were now caked in years of dust. It had a different kind of beauty now.

The room was empty of people, too. No guards on the inside. No cameras that I could see. The door behind us closed, but I didn't hear a lock click. Still, a trapped-animal feeling built up inside of me. Where was Kai? What was this? I exchanged another glance with Lloyd. We didn't need to speak out loud to hold a conversation.

"A setup maybe?"

"I'm not sure. Let's give it a minute before we head back out that door."

"It'll be a fight to get out of here."

"I know."

He nodded with the understanding that the only way we'd make it out of here alive was with Kai's blessing. This was a do-or-die mission. Either we reached an accord with the new leader of the Allegiance . . . or we would die fighting for our cause. There was no in-between.

A door at the far end of the room opened, and in stepped Kai and a single soldier. If I were a trusting person, I would've viewed the arrangement as a show of equality and respect. But I'd had my trust taken advantage of before.

I could see a pistol on the soldier's left hip, and by the bulge in his vest, I could tell he was carrying at least one more. On his right hip, in a leather sheath hanging from his belt, was a sixteen-inch kukri blade. The sheath was unsnapped for ease of access.

Kai appeared to be unarmed, but that didn't mean much. I'd once watched as my brother choked a man to death with his bare hands. I still woke on occasion with the image locked in my mind. Kai didn't need to carry any weapons. Kai was a weapon.

Lloyd and I moved forward, and when the four of us met at the center of the room, the air thickened with tension. Kai was the first to speak. "I'm surprised you came, little brother."

"I'm surprised I've been here this long without being attacked." I did a quick sweep of the windows with my eyes. No explosive devices. No guards posted outside. "The world is full of wonders, it seems."

"My operatives have informed me of Caleb's execution.

Will you verify it?" As expected, he was all business.

"Yes. Caleb is dead." I wasn't about to expand on the details. Especially knowing who'd done the deed.

Kai nodded with the calm demeanor of a man who'd been privy to this information since the moment it had occurred. "He was a good man."

Resisting the urge to roll my eyes, I said, "On that, we disagree. Now can we move past pleasantries to discuss why we're really here?"

"If you insist." Once he'd cleared his throat, he said, "Unlike my predecessor, I'm not above staging negotiations between our factions. The Allegiance has certain ideas about how we can reach common ground here in Brume, at least, and I'd like to share them with you. With luck, and patience, maybe we can set the example that brings an end to the fighting on a national level."

Something dark and foreboding prickled at the base of my skull. My eyes moved to the silent soldier at Kai's side. He was standing at parade rest, hands clasped behind his back. "If you truly mean what you say about wanting peace, perhaps we should be holding this negotiation without armed mediators watching over us."

Kai paused, as if debating his next move. Then he gave the soldier a nod, dismissing him. The room felt somewhat lighter when the door closed, leaving just Kai, Lloyd, and me inside.

"Look. Caleb made things more difficult than they needed to be. I'm running things now, and the truth is, I don't want the fighting to continue. It's gotten out of hand." He met and held my gaze. In my mind's eye, I saw his finger on the trigger of his gun as he walked from one member of my team to the next. I could still hear the shots ring through the air, still see their lifeless bodies crumpling to the ground. Even if I wanted to, I couldn't trust any semblance of sincerity coming from him. He was full of shit. I'd bet my life on it. "Let's end this, Quinn. Together. We'll be remembered as heroes."

I didn't want to be a hero. I just wanted people to be able to live life as they chose, so long as it didn't hurt anyone else. I said, "Before he died, Caleb expressed interest in eventually dividing the land so the Allegiance could have their territory and the Resistance could have theirs. Is that something you might consider?"

Clasping his hands behind his back, Kai looked to the ceiling in thought. I wondered if he could see the beauty in the chandelier. "It's not a terrible plan, and we may reach that stage eventually, but for now, the Allegiance would be interested in dividing Brume, setting up barriers, and seeing how that arrangement plays out."

"No." I could feel Lloyd stiffen in surprise beside me. But I wasn't going to budge on Brume's freedom. I owed it to my people there to do all I could to achieve peace. "The

Allegiance leaves Brume as a show of good faith. Then we can discuss dividing up the rest of the country."

After a quiet moment, Kai sighed. "I can take it to the table for discussion, but I make no promises. However, if we do get that far, I think that some sort of barrier between our territories would be best, and once a citizen aligns with the Resistance, they can never cross that border. If we make a split, it's a permanent one. Agreed?"

"You run your world however you want. My people just want to live free."

Freedom. Peace. Without and within. It was all I ever wanted.

Stop it, Quinn.

Kai said, "There are a lot of details we need to discuss, a lot of questions that we both need answers to. I'm sure you understand that I can't agree to anything officially without discussing with my people. That being said, I'm glad you've come around."

I shook my head. "I haven't come around to anything, Kai. This isn't about the Allegiance winning."

The hint of an amused smile touched his lips, but just as I noticed it, it was gone again. I wondered if it had been a figment of my imagination. He was good. Very good. "Regardless . . . I like what I'm hearing. I think we can find some common ground in this."

Lloyd glanced my way. I didn't have to meet his gaze to know what he was thinking. *This is too easy. Dangerously easy.*

He was right. "What do Mom and Dad think about your willingness to find 'common ground'? Did you coerce them into thinking it was a good idea like you coerced them into leaving the Resistance in the first place?"

"I didn't coerce anyone, little brother. Our parents realized they'd made a huge mistake and joined the Allegiance in an effort to correct that mistake. If you had any family loyalty at all, you would've come with them. But no. You chose to stay. All so you could reap the fame and fortune of becoming the so-called face of the Resistance. Well done, Quinn. Well done." He clapped his hands together slowly in mock applause. He clenched his jaw. Finally, an honest emotional response.

The idea that he could reduce the destruction of our family to a single moment in time set my insides on fire with anger. "You think that's why I stayed? I stayed because I wanted a better life for everyone. Including them. Including you. I stayed because I wasn't arrogant enough to think that I matter more than anyone else."

Kai shook his head. "That's not what it means to be part of the Allegiance."

"Isn't it, though?" I could feel Lloyd's eyes on me,

pleading with me to stop, but I didn't care what happened to me anymore. If I was going to die here, I wasn't going to die with my feelings bottled up inside of me. "Would a person of color's voice be heard in the Allegiance? Would a queer person be regarded with respect? Don't piss on my leg and tell me it's raining, Kai. We both know that your so-called Allegiance is a machine created to control people and force society to conform to your fucked-up ideals. You feed on bigotry. And fascism is just a way of life for you all. *That's* why I stayed behind, *brother.* That's why it sickens me to see you standing there, a general of a goddamn dictatorial regime."

Small droplets of sweat glistened on his brow. I was getting to him. He snapped, "You don't get to decide what anyone else's life should be like."

The general of the Allegiance was preaching against his own doctrine. Who was the hypocrite now? "Neither do you."

He was refusing to look me in the eye. From his inside jacket pocket, he retrieved a handkerchief. White linen. Lace edges. An embroidered letter on one corner. As he dabbed the sweat from his bow, I saw it was the letter *L*.

Noticing where my attention was directed, Kai straightened and placed a kiss on the piece of cloth before tucking it back inside his jacket. "A gift from the woman I love."

My chest grew so tight that it hurt. I wondered if a person

could actually feel their heart breaking. "I had one of those once."

"But did you really?" A smirk settled on Kai's lips. "Lia sends her regards, by the way."

Lia? My Lia? But how? She was back at base, in handcuffs and well guarded, I was certain. "What are you talking about?"

"It was a shame when Collins went rogue and tried to kill you before our plan was carried out. But I must say, I've been delighted with Lia's work."

Lia.

Lia was the spy.

My heart shattered, its splinters scraping at my insides until I thought I might go mad from the pain of heartbreak.

"She and I went to a lot of work to get Caleb here in Brume, and after all that, it seemed like you weren't going to kill him. Who were we supposed to pin his death on, if not the Resistance? With him dead, murdered while in the Resistance's custody, by one of yours, according to Lia's eyewitness account, I can run the Allegiance with Lia at my side, with no questions from my followers about my involvement in Caleb's demise. The perfect life. Once we dispose of you and your pitiful militia, of course."

I wanted to ask him how long they'd been together, if my relationship with her had just been part of the con. But wanting to ask something and desiring an answer are two very different things. Any answers he gave wouldn't change the facts or lessen the pain I felt.

He wore a smug smile that reminded me of Caleb. "Oh, one piece of advice? You should be more careful who you trust. At last count, the Allegiance had six spies within your ranks here in Brume. And they are very loyal. Fast too, considering how quickly Lia was returned to me after killing Caleb."

It had all been a setup. Lia had urged me again and again to kill Caleb, and when I didn't, she took matters into her own hands. All so she and Kai could run the Allegiance untethered.

I said, "The talk of peace before? It was bullshit, wasn't it?"

"Yes, but it got you here. In a place where you're surrounded by hundreds of armed soldiers at my beck and call, and no one to help you, but the sad excuse of a first officer who accompanied you here." A chuckle escaped him. "Besides, I wanted to see the look on your face when I revealed the truth. And it is delightful, little brother."

Kai could never be a brother to me in this reality. He chose over and over again not to be.

Carefully, so he knew I wasn't drawing my weapon, I removed the watch from my wrist and handed it to him without a word.

A look of genuine surprise washed over his features. "Grandfather's watch."

He strapped the watch to his wrist and examined its face. "I thought you'd never let me have it."

"That's the difference between you and me, Kai. I can change." He was so wrapped up in getting what he wanted that he didn't bother asking why I'd given it to him now. Typical. "Are we done here?"

He didn't respond, too focused on his newest possession. My jaw tightened. I turned back toward the door through which we'd entered the room. I was about to step outside, suspecting that his guards would be waiting for Lloyd and me with their rifles at the ready. But an uneasy feeling crawled up my spine, slowing my steps before I could open the door.

A loud bang rang through the empty room, dragging time to a crawl. In a matter of seconds that felt like ages, I turned back to face Kai. His right arm was outstretched. He gripped a pistol in his hand. A small line of smoke curled from its muzzle. His finger was on the trigger, and his hand was steady with intent. Lloyd tumbled to the floor in that slow-motion moment, his chest covered in blood. It took the span of a breath for me to comprehend what had happened. Kai had taken a shot at my back, intending to kill me in a coward's fashion. Lloyd had seen what he was about to do and dived forward, taking the bullet in my stead.

Without another thought, I brought my arm across my body and pulled the 9 mm from the holster under my arm. Time inched forward, still moving as if it had forgotten how. I ran at Kai, my feet moving soundlessly across the floor. When I squeezed the trigger of my gun, the shot sounded as if it was coming from some far-off place—another world, maybe. Kai shifted before the bullet reached him, and it grazed his arm, ripping through the fabric of his jacket. The second shot blew through his shoulder.

Damn.

Kai aimed his gun at me, and I watched, expecting to die, as he pulled the trigger.

But I didn't die.

Kai's face dropped. He pounded the side of the barrel with the heel of his hand. His gun must have jammed. After another solid hit, his action seemed to knock loose whatever had been slowing time. A symphony of chaos filled my ears. Lloyd's shallow breathing. The echoes from our gunfire. Raised voices outside. At once, I was on Kai, pointing my empty gun at my brother's forehead, my finger on the trigger.

Kai pressed his head against the muzzle, his eyes aflame with anger, hatred, venom—everything but fear. Briefly, the image of Coe doing the same thing flashed through my mind. He growled, "Do it. Do it, you fucking coward."

Whoever this man was, he was no brother of mine. He was a murderer. He was a monster.

A familiar feeling slipped over the edges of my being. One I'd had upon killing Lloyd in that other life. That I was a monster.

Shaking it away, I drew my arm back and brought it forward, pistol-whipping him. He hit the ground, a look of pain in his eyes. Pain, but not surprise. It troubled me that nothing I did seemed to surprise Kai.

I snatched the walkie clipped to his belt and pressed the button on the side. "All clear. Repeat. All clear."

Time slowed again as I waited for a response. My heartbeat pounded in my ears. If they doubted the all clear I'd given, this room would fill up with well-trained, well-armed soldiers faster than I could blink.

A crackling sound came over the walkie, followed by "Roger that."

Hurrying back to Lloyd, I knelt at his side and watched his chest rise and fall. He was still alive. I pressed my fingers to his neck. His pulse was weak, but steady. If I could just get him back to base, he might have a chance.

Kai chuckled as he moved to stand once again. A thin line of blood trailed from his hairline to his left eyebrow. He had no weapon, but that didn't weaken his resolve. "You really think you're leaving, don't you? You actually believe I had any intention of letting you live. So naive, Quinn, and so wrong."

Outside, chaos had erupted at the sound of gunfire. I weighed my options. The easiest choice—one that I discounted the moment it occurred to me—was to abandon Lloyd and run. A second possibility was to locate a med kit containing a shot of adrenaline and get Lloyd on his feet well enough that he could run with me, but that would require running *into* the heart of HQ first. The only idea that actually seemed viable was the third. I could carry Lloyd on one shoulder and get the hell out the front door. It was the shortest point between us and freedom, a straight line. And if I managed to pull it off, whispers of my escape would spiderweb their way through the Allegiance, inspiring fear and awe.

Whatever I was going to do, I had to act fast. If everything went according to plan, I had less than five minutes to get us both to cover.

Lloyd's eyes were closed, but moving slightly beneath his eyelids, as if he were dreaming deep. I hoped it was a good one.

"You'll die whimpering, little brother. You'll die begging for your life to be spared. You'll die yearning for the life I have, the girl I love, and our parents' unending respect and affection." The corner of his mouth twitched. To my surprise, he didn't take a single step toward me. He also didn't call for help. Maybe he was confident that we'd never get out of HQ alive. Maybe his arrogance had convinced him the Allegiance was unbeatable. "I almost feel sorry for you."

As I pulled air into my lungs and released it, I found my center—that place of calm where I wasn't a slave to my fear. As I took in another breath, I slipped the knife from my boot and threw it hard at Kai. He tried to dodge it, but the blade plunged deep into his stomach. Not enough of a wound to kill him outright. Just enough to keep him occupied.

I wondered if he felt like someone had just punched him. I wondered if his vision had begun to fade.

With the sound of Kai stumbling, then falling to his knees behind me, I pushed the door open a crack and spied the guard standing just outside. Swinging around the door, I cracked him at the base of his skull with my gun. He crumpled to the ground, unconscious. I exchanged my weapon for the loaded pistol from his holster, and then I kept my steps as fast and as light as I could as I moved back inside. I didn't want to use the damn thing, but I would if I had to.

It took some effort to hoist Lloyd's unconscious body up over one shoulder. Lucky for me, he was all lean muscle, no bulk. But that didn't mean that his deadweight was easy to bear. After one last look at the man who'd been my brother at one point in time—was still my brother in another existence—I checked the time, said a silent goodbye to Kai, and stepped out the door.

My boots sank into the earth as I rounded the corner of the building and kept close to the wall. The courtyard was occupied by about twenty soldiers policing the base and fifteen civilians. When we'd approached HQ initially, there had been a large platoon outside the gate, guarding the entrance. I hadn't thought I'd be leaving. Just Lloyd, if we were lucky. But plans change.

Lloyd was heavy on my shoulder, so I shifted his weight and kept an eye on my six as best as I could. So far, so good. Just another fifty yards and we were home free.

"Stop! Halt!"

Damn.

I looked over my shoulder to see an older man raising his rifle to aim. The gun dropped out of his hands when my bullet ripped through his shoulder. He'd live, but he might never shoot again.

Soldiers turned their heads toward me, aiming their weapons. I was going to die. After all this, I was going to die anyway. I bolted for the tree line, the only sound my heart thundering in my ears.

Then the air clapped hard with a thunderous explosion, nearly knocking the wind from my lungs. I stumbled, and Lloyd and I both fell to the grass. Bits of debris fell all around the courtyard, the ground sprinkled with ash that was falling like snow. The smell of burning building filled the air. I watched in sad triumph as the fire spread from the main building we'd just left to the smaller one next to it. The soldiers had forgotten about me for the time being—their focus was on the mayhem. People were running. Panicking. But I had done what I'd come here to do.

Maybe part of me actually thought I might be able to reason with Kai. But if that were true, I wouldn't have pressed the timed trigger on the side as I'd handed the watch over to him, starting a countdown to the dangerous explosive material that had been carefully placed inside the watch. Randall, one of our munitions experts, had said that the new incendiary he and his team had been working on was both terrifying and effective, and he'd delivered on that statement. Allegiance headquarters was burning to the ground.

"Come on, Lloyd. Let's get you home." I wished I felt like, though I was leaving a brother behind, I was rescuing the one in my arms, but that would have been a lie. The truth was, care for Lloyd as I did, I was saving him out of a sense of obligation. The Resistance didn't leave anyone behind—not if they could help it. But I wasn't driven by the bond of friendship. Not anymore. Not since he'd shown me that he could never accept my truth. Between his response to my hint at queerness and learning of Lia's betrayal, I was feeling more alone than I ever had before. Unless I thought of the other Quinn that I was, in the other Brume where Rippers were the norm. We were both lonely. Maybe we were doomed to be lonely forever.

After what felt like hours, I sat in the front hall of the school, on a chair not ten feet from the room in which Lloyd was being operated on. My face was in my hands, covered with Lloyd's blood and my tears. Both of which dripped to the tile floor below. My head felt too heavy to lift. He had to live. They had to save him. In spite of everything, I couldn't lose—

A loud tone rang through the halls. My heart didn't just sink—it chewed its way deep inside of me.

Lloyd had just flatlined.

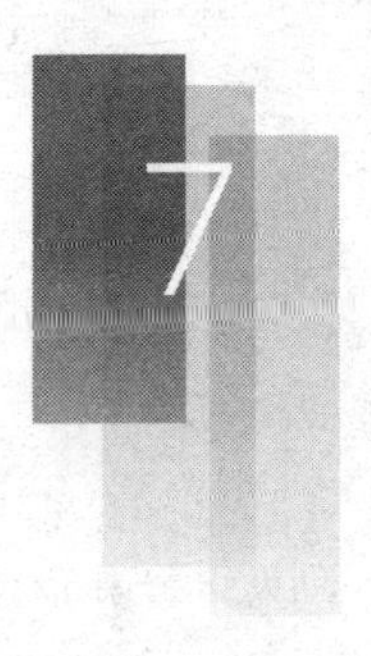

I sat up, but I refused to wipe my tear-streaked face dry. On the floor of the cave across from me lay Caleb, fast asleep. His head rested on his folded arms. His legs were drawn up close to him, as if he were cold . . . or frightened. As the war-torn Brume fell away from me, memories from this one came flooding back. I'd killed Lloyd, and then we'd run. We'd hidden in the cave in the park because it was close.

Lloyd . . .

My clothes were covered in blood. Was it the blood of Lloyd my enemy, or Lloyd my friend? Against my will, I pictured the hammer jutting out of Lloyd's neck—the wild, confused look on his face. His blood as it poured forth, bubbling out of his jugular like a low-pressure fountain of horror.

It was only then that I realized I was still clutching the hammer in my hand.

My stomach lurched with a dry heave, drawing me to my feet. I gagged as I moved away from where Caleb slept, convinced I was going to vomit, but only acidic-tasting saliva filled my mouth. Resting my free hand on the wall of the cave, I spat on the floor and took a few calming breaths.

"Are you okay?" Caleb sat up, rubbing his eyes into wakefulness.

"I've been better." My voice sounded hoarse. I wanted to let go of the hammer, or to throw it as far away from me as I could, but something within me insisted on keeping it in my hand. By the look of the light on the cave walls, the sun was up. "We've gotta find Lia."

He stood, brushing dirt from his pants, which struck me as strange, considering how filthy his shirt was. "I think we should take a little time. Don't you?"

"No." My voice was deadpan.

Caleb looked like he was debating something, but whatever it was, he laid it aside and said, "Any ideas on where to start?"

My lungs were burning. It almost felt like I'd been

smoking. "Lloyd said he put her in the only place I couldn't get to."

"Maybe he meant the other side of the wall of fog. If there is another side. Or maybe *in* the fog."

"No. For all his bravado, Lloyd is . . ." I trailed off, swallowing the lump that had formed in my throat. It went down hard. My grip tightened on the hammer. I couldn't let go of it. In a strange, sick way, it felt like releasing it from my grip would somehow defend my actions. ". . . *was* . . . a real coward when it came to that wall. Most people are. He wouldn't put her there. He'd put her somewhere I had no chance of reaching her."

"Maybe a well?"

"Or a cellar." Realization hit me like a slap across the face. "Caleb, I think I know where Lia is."

"Where?"

I thought of the last time I'd seen the wine cellar. The *POP* sounds that had chased me down the street, ripping Lloyd's followers to bits. The cloud of blood that had reached out for me. "Right where Lloyd said—somewhere I can't get to. Not without three or four people to help lift a hunk of marble."

Caleb said, "Why lift it?"

I cocked an eyebrow at him.

"Marble's surprisingly easy to break apart with the right tool," he explained. "All we need is a sledge . . . or a hammer."

Caleb's face paled. His eyes flitted to the thing in my hand and back. "I'm sorry."

"Why? He wasn't my friend." A hollowness filled me as I watched Lloyd in my mind's eye take a bullet in the chest—one that my brother had meant for me. A ringing sound filled my ears. No. Not ringing. A high-pitched tone. One that told me Lloyd was dead.

Here too, I thought.

Caleb took a cautious step toward me. "Quinn, you've just experienced something really fucking traumatic. It's okay to not be okay."

I picked up my bat and looked toward the cave entrance—anywhere but at Caleb's face. I didn't think I could bear seeing empathy in his expression. Monsters like me didn't deserve empathy. "We'd better hurry. We don't know how long she's been down there, Caleb—if she's down there at all. We don't know how much food she has, if any. We don't know if he gave her a lantern to keep the darkness at bay. We don't know if she's still alive. So let's go."

Our walk back to the house with the wine cellar was stoic. The streets were empty and the sun was brighter than usual. As we wove our way through the streets, I listened for telltale sounds of Screamers, but heard nothing. But for the sound of our feet moving across the pavement, Brume was silent.

The house came into view down the street to our right,

with its loose shutters and sagging porch. I stopped and turned my head to the left. Toward the house where Lloyd's dead body now lay. Because of me.

Lloyd. The boy who'd made me smile at Camp Redemption.

Lloyd. The man who'd saved me from Caleb's wrath at the rendezvous point.

Not just the violent gang leader who'd threatened my life, my friends' lives.

But *Lloyd*.

The hammer's surface had become tacky from Lloyd's blood dried, as had my palm and fingers. His blood was on my hands in every sense.

"There's nothing you can do, you know." Caleb stuck to my side, his gaze following mine. "His death is on him. You were defending yourself. He was going to kill you, Quinn."

He was right. I knew he was right. But that couldn't wash away the murderous grime that had darkened my soul the moment I brought that hammer down, piercing Lloyd's flesh. I wondered if anything could.

Caleb put a hand on my shoulder, his words gentle and coaxing. "Come on, Quinn. Let's go get Lia."

In silence, we turned right and headed to the large house where Lloyd's wine cellar was located. No gang members that we could see were in the yard or on the streets, and the house was empty—small blessings. I led Caleb through the living room and into the kitchen, where the marble slab blocked the entrance to the cellar. As we examined it, Caleb said, "What do we do if she's not in there?"

"We keep looking for her. We don't stop until we find her."

A muffled voice came from below. "Help! Is someone there? Please help me!"

Lia.

I raised the hammer, and as I slammed it down on the marble, I saw myself swing hard, the claw end of it biting deep into Lloyd's neck. It was bad enough to relive that moment once, but it repeated with every hit on the marble. BOOM. Lia was almost free. BOOM. Lloyd was almost dead. BOOM. I couldn't run from the monster. The monster was me.

"Please hurry!" Lia cried out. "The lantern is dying!"

Chunks of marble flew. Several small bits hit my cheeks, my forehead. I could feel beads of blood well up on my face, but I kept pounding. Had to keep going. So that Lia would be free.

The slab cracked in two and Caleb grabbed one half, dragging it off the entrance. I watched as he moved the next, and then I called down to Lia, "Give me your hand!"

The lantern flickered and then died. The cellar was pitch-dark.

Waking from my nightmarish daze, I dropped to my

knees and reached for her, seeing that Lloyd had destroyed the shelves so that she wouldn't be able to climb. Caleb and I each grabbed a hand and pulled. Lia was shaking as we held her, bringing her up to safety. Just as she was high enough to climb up on her own, a scream tore from her throat. I gripped her tight and yanked her from the opening. Fresh blood drew crooked lines on her calves. The Unseen Hands had only just missed her.

We sat there on the floor, the three of us—survivors all. Lia was safe. We were all safe. For now.

No more than an hour later, my back was against a rocky surface, and I was seated on the ground. Before me sat a single lantern. Its fuel was burning out, and once that happened, we'd be encased in darkness and subject to the wrath of the Unseen Hands. My bat rested beside me, its surface covered with the blood of a Ripper we'd killed just outside of the park before fleeing the horrors of this Brume and heading here. Houses were close but the cave was closer, so it became our sanctuary for the time being. Outside, I could hear tortured voices tearing through the night, crying out for help—Screamers, I was certain. The scent of our last remaining sage was all around us. When the light was gone and the sage had burned away, we were dead.

Caleb and Lia lay huddled closely together near the wall

of the cave opposite me, passed out from exhaustion. I couldn't sleep, couldn't bear another dreamless night, couldn't face the darkness when plagued with so much pain and too many questions. I watched the lantern's light dim and squeezed my eyes shut, trying to close out the world—*to close out three worlds, actually*—for a heartbeat or two. Standing, I trailed my fingers along the wall and around a series of bends. At the deepest part of the cave, I found it. The mirror that I'd seen in the war-torn Brume. Its frame resembled vines, flames, and snakes, twisting upward, reaching outward. The tips of each spike looked incredibly sharp. As I stared at it, I let the memories of the soldier Quinn fill my head. We had a choice to make—which life to live. It was a paradox, the three of us in these three Brumes. But how could we solve a paradox? How could I? And could I possibly manage such an insurmountable task before the light and sage were gone?

I stepped closer, wondering if Lia and Caleb would see it too if they were awake and standing at my side. Something within me told me to smash it, destroy it, send it back to hell. If there was a hell. If hell wasn't here.

Plucking a rock from the ground, I whipped it at my reflection. The stone flew forward and was enveloped by the glass, as if the surface of the mirror weren't solid at all. I reached my hand out toward my reflection. We touched palms. Glass. The mirror was glass. So how did the rock . . . ?

Maybe the mirror wasn't just a mirror . . . or maybe I'd gone crazy. It was easier to believe that I'd lost my mind. Maybe it had happened the moment I'd seen Coe back at the school, just like it had happened with Lia's mom. Maybe it had happened when I'd killed Lloyd.

To my left, someone clucked their tongue. "That's a bit presumptuous, don't you think?"

I was startled, but I forced myself not to look at the speaker. I knew his voice, even if not from here. Here he was a monster with claws for hands. Here he'd made me see my dead brother rot before my very eyes after torturing Caleb with images of his dead sister.

I'd been in this cave before. And I hadn't been alone. Something had been with me. The same something that had dragged its large body through the door inside the school with the use of its long, spindly arms. Two voices—voices that felt so familiar to me that they felt like my own—whispered inside my mind.

"Coe."

Nightmarish images filled my head. The mask that hadn't been a mask at all. The long, black tongue caressing my cheek, warm and wet. The teeth . . . the teeth.

My hands were trembling. I hadn't noticed I'd been clenching my fists until I felt my nails digging deep into my palms, almost breaking the skin. I'd seen Coe's true face before. Right here in this cave. I didn't know if I could bear it again.

A sound, more like a growl than a laugh, but somewhere in between, bubbled up from within him. "That's also presumptuous of you. To think you've seen my *true* face."

With a shaking breath, I turned to see a man standing beside me. His stringy hair hung over much of his face. He wore a black snakeskin trench coat that conjured goose bumps on my skin, and he held a cigarette between two fingers. I recognized him, but not from this Brume.

"Shall I give you a hint?" A fiendish smile curled on his lips. His eyes looked strange. It took me a moment to see what was wrong. The irises weren't just dark—they were black as night. But more than that, they looked to be the texture of snakeskin—and the snake was writhing within. Then, as quick as it had begun, his eyes went back to normal. "More? Or is that enough to jog your memory?"

"That's . . . that's enough."

He took a drag on his cigarette. His fingernails were filthy, as if he hadn't cleaned up in a good long while. As he blew out the smoke, he said, "Beauty is in the eye of the beholder. Just as horrors are in the mind of the realist."

The scent of roses filled my nostrils as I recalled him standing in a garden, offering me a smoke. The taste of nicotine covered my tongue as I remembered him leaning up against the school, asking for a light. Focusing on the man instead of the monster, I said, "I feel like we're beyond this cryptic bullshit, Coe."

The corner of his mouth lifted in a smirk. "Do you, now?"

I cleared my throat. "We both know that I'm living three lives, in three different Brumes."

"Do we, now?"

With my mind's eye, I saw my hand, feminine, brushing hair from my eyes so I could get a better look at him. I saw my hand, masculine, holding out the lighter, shuddering when my skin had touched his. They were me. I was them. He was the Stranger. He was Coe. And now he was here. My tone grew bitter. "You've ruined my life."

"Have I, now?"

I glared, but all it did was inspire him to raise an eyebrow. He said, "I don't ruin lives. I touch them. There is a difference."

I snapped, "You touched mine enough to break it into three. Whether or not you think so, you ruin lives."

His eyes met mine, his playful tone gone, leaving behind crisp, biting words. "I unearth truth."

Not wanting to provoke him, I quieted my voice. "So what's the truth about me?"

"We've discussed this, genderless—at times, gender*more*—Quinn. Don't you recall?" He dropped his cigarette butt to the ground and crushed it with the toe of his boot. "A precious commodity, life. It's traded, given away, wasted, spent."

I snorted with disdain. "Seems pretty pointless to me. Like trying to hold sand. No matter what you do, it'll slip away."

He pointed a long, nicotine-stained finger at me and said, "You miss the point. It's not how much sand you lose, it's how long you hold the beach in your hand."

I didn't care about the symbolism of the beach. I was done. I was just done. With all of this. "I can't do this anymore, Coe. I just . . . can't. Whatever it is that you want from me, just take it already."

He chuckled. "Another point that you miss. This isn't about what *I* want. It's about what *you* need."

"I need . . ." My heart swelled until I was certain it was on the verge of shattering. I looked at the mirror and wondered: If I went through it, would I disappear, like the rock? "I need peace."

Coe's voice, for the first time, softened in what could've been mistaken for empathy. "You do."

My eyes filled with tears—tears I didn't bother holding in or blinking away. My reflection's cheeks remained dry. "How do I find it?"

His attention turned to the mirror in front of us. "I like mirrors. They reveal the truth of things, and there is peace in speaking one's truth. But then . . . what would you know about truth?"

What was he getting at? "I know the truth. My truth. I know who I am. And I know I'm going to keep waking up in these three different realities until I figure out the paradox and decide which life I want. I just don't know how to choose."

He held a single finger up as if to pause my words. "That is one truth. But the bigger truth is hidden in the lies you've told yourself again and again."

"What exactly have I lied to myself about?" The question was as much to me as it was to him.

"The wall of fog surrounding Brume is quite thick, don't you think? It's been there for years." He cocked an eyebrow at me. "Hasn't it?"

Of course it had. One day the town had been filled with sunshine. The next it had been closed off, or maybe even removed, from the rest of the world. If anyone knew that, it had to be Coe. He was responsible for it, after all. The fog, the monsters, the fracture of my existence into three. Everything. "What's your point?"

He withdrew a fresh pack of cigarettes from the pocket of his trench coat and tapped the end of it against the heel of his free hand before opening it. As he placed an unlit cigarette between his lips and put the pack away, he closed his eyes long enough to light it. His movements were ritualistic. He was worshipping at the altar of nicotine and tar—the filth of which suited him well. Satisfied, he exhaled a cloud of smoke. "If you'd see your lies for what they are, you'd know when the wall of fog appeared. When and why."

I hated to give a second thought to his enigmatic statement, but I didn't have a choice if I wanted answers. "Are you insinuating that I have any inkling why the fog came?"

His eyes flashed with something resembling irritation as he made a point of order. "The day your father piled you all into that boat . . . was he really attempting an escape from the horrors of Brume?"

Of course he was. We were all on the boat, and Dad was paddling with determination. Somehow, we'd gotten turned around in the fog. Brume wouldn't let us go. Coe wouldn't let us leave.

The corner of the Stranger's mouth twitched. He pointed his cigarette toward the mirror and tapped ash from its tip. The mirror's surface swirled, looking like mercury and molten steel, and when it settled, it felt as if ice were moving through my veins. Then the cave was gone. I was still there physically—could still feel the rock beneath my feet. But my consciousness moved through time and memory, until I was standing on the bank beside the lake four years before. It seemed impossible, but it felt so real. I tried to call out, but could make no sound. I tried to move, but couldn't. Because I wasn't really there. I wasn't a participant of this moment, merely an observer.

I watched as my dad piled my mom, Kai, and me into a small rowboat with him, a picnic basket, a cooler, and fishing gear. He paddled us as far as he could, the whole time without a word to my brother or me. It wasn't an unusual event. Dad was the type of man who worked hard all day and came home to eat dinner while watching whatever game was on the television. We'd learned to keep quiet around him—especially after he'd had a few drinks.

My mom dug a beer out of the cooler and handed it to Dad. The two of them managed a conversation about the weather and what a great day it was for a family outing. Dad talked about filleting whatever fish we caught, and Mom asked him how he wanted them cooked. Things felt light that day. It had seemed like the perfect moment to share with them something I'd been feeling for a long while. "Mom? Dad? I need to tell you something."

My father's eyes were focused on the horizon, and my eyes locked on his expression. A determined, maybe angry, crease lined his brow. He didn't speak a word. Neither did Mom or Kai. Maybe they knew what I was about to say. Maybe not. I clung to the hope that maybe they'd understand. We were family, after all.

"The thing is . . . I'm genderqueer."

"You're what?" A chuckle escaped Mom as she spoke. I couldn't tell if her question had been rhetorical or not, but either way, I answered.

"Genderqueer. Sometimes I don't feel male or female. Sometimes I feel both. Sometimes I feel like I'm something else entirely."

"Goddammit! You're queer? Are you fucking kidding me?" Dad had yelled, his reaction immediately more horrible than I'd imagined in my worst fears. Gripping the paddles, he maneuvered the boat around again and headed back to the dock. Determination drove each stroke. Mom didn't seem to notice how tightly she was clutching the handle of the picnic basket in her hands. Kai stared at the lake, as if wishing he were anywhere but here. Water splashed at every lunge of the paddles. Drops of it dotted my skin. The paddles hitting the water were the only sound besides my father's angry breathing. The boat inched forward until we'd reached the dock. "All of you, get in the goddamn car. We're going home."

"Mom?" My voice sounded hushed. She refused to meet my eyes, just shook her head in utter disappointment. The small shred of hope that I'd been clinging to evaporated like fog.

Everything that our family had been changed forever that day.

The visual memory melted away, returning my consciousness to the cave. I shook my head in horror and denial. "No. That can't be. I remember the fog. He was trying to save us from Brume."

The Stranger gauged me for a moment as he took another drag. "Was he, now? And the night you and your brother valiantly fought off the Ripper in the park? Was he trying to save you then as well?"

He stretched out his hand once again, pointing his cigarette at the mirror. As he tapped ash from its end, I said, "Don't."

Once more the mirror's surface swirled, but this time I was transported to my house, just after we'd returned home from our failed family excursion.

Dad got drunk and screamed harsh words at me. Mom put her head in her hands and cried. She went on and on about how I was just saying I was genderqueer to hurt her. Kai had gone out with friends, so I was alone in the tornado of emotions that filled our home. Eight beers later, Dad passed out, and Mom fell asleep on the couch watching reruns of *The Twilight Zone*. I went to the park to think, but more so to be alone. I'd always liked it there. There was no yelling there. No parental judgment. No cloud of dissatisfaction like the one that hung over our house. I was leaning against a tree, looking at the entrance to the cave, when a beer bottle smashed against the tree's trunk. It shattered in an explosion of brown glass and stale beer. When I turned to see who'd thrown it, my stomach had shriveled.

Kai's eyes were glazed—the way Dad's got after he'd had a couple of drinks. But more than that, the angry expression he wore made him look a little too much like our father—a man he'd sworn he would never become. "You think you're doing anybody any good, stirring up shit like that, Quinn? You think Mom and Dad are gonna feel bad for you because you're some oppressed queerbait? It's not gonna change a fucking thing!"

Once more, the memory melted away. My cheeks were wet with tears. I wanted to deny the memories. I wanted to blame them on Coe . . . but I couldn't. It was true. I'd finally come out to my family, and they'd lashed out against me. Every one of them. Even Kai. "The Ripper . . . the fireflies . . . I . . . It had all felt so real. But Kai didn't save me that night. There was nothing in the park to save me from . . . except for him."

Coe's tone softened. This time I was certain it was in pity. "And your parents. How did they die again?"

My gaze locked on the mirror. "Show me."

With one last flick of ash, the surface swirled and disappeared again, leaving me with nothing but the painful truth.

My parents, Kai, and I had been driving to my

grandmother's house two towns over. It wasn't a trip we made often—Grandma was a smoker with a heavy hand. I was pretty sure both Dad and Mom hated her, but felt some sort of familial obligation to visit. As Dad navigated the streets, he barked at me, "I don't wanna hear any of that bullshit about you being a queer in front of your grandmother, you hear me? Buncha bullshit, if you ask me."

I shook my head. "But it's not. I'm—"

"For Christ's sake, Quinn. You're only a teenager! You don't know what you are." Mom rolled her eyes dismissively.

"It's a fad now. Everybody her age is saying something similar." Kai snorted from the seat beside me. "Gay is the new cool."

"I'm not gay." I all but whispered the words, fearing my dad's reaction, but trying desperately to cling to my truth.

Dad erupted again. "Yer damn right yer not! None of my kids are gonna be faggots!"

Mom said, "She isn't a faggot, Harold. She's just confused."

"Don't tell me what she is! Maybe if you spent more time watching her and less—"

The car had picked up speed, and I wondered if Dad had been drinking before we'd left the house. Kai and I exchanged looks as the vehicle wavered from one lane to the other, but neither of us spoke. Maybe we were too afraid to interrupt our parents. Maybe we knew that something terrible was about to happen. Whatever it was, something terrible did happen. One moment, Mom and Dad were speaking heatedly in the front seat. The next, the car rolled and the interior exploded into a cloud of blood. It took just a second for Kai and me to become orphans.

The pain in my chest was unbearable as my mind returned to the cave. I slid down the cave wall until I was kneeling on its floor, my tears flowing freely now. "But I saw the Unseen Hands kill them. I swear . . ."

"Have you ever stopped to consider why those hands are unseen?" He crouched beside me, the bottom edge of his trench coat looking like a broad, thin snake resting on the cool stone. Maybe I should have been afraid of him still, but I wasn't. Not just then. I was more afraid of myself. "It seems to me that it wasn't the hands you were trying not to see that day. It was the truth. A truth you've hidden under a blanket of lies you've told yourself again and again. A truth you've smeared onto the canvas of your memories beneath layers and layers of painted falsehoods."

"It can't be." I looked at Coe, knowing the truth, but refusing to accept it. "Can it?"

"Just how supportive was your brother, oh fractured Quinn?"

"Stop it! Kai loved me. He always supported me. He

alwa—" Without the aid of Coe and the mirror, the memory returned to me. Kai and I had been standing beside his car, the sun baking down on us. The back seat was filled with his belongings. As he slid into the front seat and put the key in the ignition, he looked at me with venom in his eyes and repeated the words the vision of him had said to me that day in the school. "It's your fault they're gone, you know. It's all your fault."

My chest felt hollow. And I knew the memories—all that Coe had revealed to me—to be real. "Kai left me. Our parents died and he just . . . left me."

As I spoke, my words sounded as if they were coming from someone else. They were too painful for me to say. Too painful for me to admit. I disassociated for a time and let the truth drip from my lips. "That's when the fog rolled in. That's when the monsters appeared. The Rippers, the Screamers, the Unseen Hands—none of them existed before that moment. Before I'd lost everything but the truth of who I am."

Standing, Coe clapped his hands together slowly. "And so, we come to the center of the shrubbery maze."

"How could I have convinced myself that my family was so supportive, so loving? How is it that I can still recall so clearly the fog, the monsters, the world falling down around us all, if it hadn't until they were gone?" I pressed my back against the wall and stood. My legs trembled. My knees felt weak.

"It seems to me that *the* world collapsed when *your* world collapsed. But it was easier to imagine a mystery that you couldn't comprehend than to face what really happened." He took another drag and blew it out. The stench of the smoke almost made me choke. "Lies are often cushions against a hurtful truth."

The horror of my situation filled me until I thought I might burst. I'd created the wall of fog the day that Kai had left me behind, shutting out the light of the world. Only I couldn't bear the torture of my reality, of my family's utter rejection. So I'd built a new truth—one so vivid that I made it reality. "It was me. This whole time I blamed you for what Brume has become. But . . . it was me. I made it this way."

I was certain now. I was also certain that the responsibility didn't fall on my shoulders alone. I hadn't done everything—not on purpose. But I'd created the fog, the monsters . . . it was me. Lia's mom, Caleb's sister. Everyone had been made to suffer because I somehow turned our world into the nightmare that it was. Wondering if there even was an answer to my question, I said, "How do I fix it?"

For a moment, Coe stood silent. I wondered if he was sympathizing with me or relishing in the pain of my realization. He lit a second cigarette and took a drag. His words were puffs of cloud in the air between us. Like fog. "You solve the puzzle."

I stared into the mirror for a long time, considering Coe's words. What puzzle was there to solve?

My reflection glanced down at their body before locking eyes with me again. We were one, they and I. Same face. Same hoodie. Same expression. But we were separate entities as well. Just like me and the other Quinns. But what had they meant by the gesture? Were they hinting at an answer to what the puzzle might be? Was it related to my—*our*—body somehow? My reflection's lips drew a thin line in frustration. They waved a hand across their face, and revealed something new. A face I knew well—pretty and feminine. It was me, but the female me. Under my breath, I whispered to the mirror, "I don't understand."

Their hand waved across their face again, this time revealing scruff and the hardened gaze of the masculine me. A third wave revealed my reflection's original face—though I was certain we weren't sharing the same expression. They looked like they had the answers.

Sudden realization tore my eyes from the mirror and focused them on Coe. "The puzzle of why I'm shifting between realities. The paradox. It's me."

Coe the Stranger said nothing.

"I caused the split . . . just like I caused the fog. I couldn't face the possibility that Lia might not want me as more than a friend because I'm genderqueer. So I broke my existence into thirds. I created the paradox—three worlds, but with different relationships, different gender identities, different experiences . . . but one singular problem. In each reality, I've been looking for people outside myself to accept me for who, for what, I am."

His smile grew twisted as he tilted his chin down. His eyes lit up with an unnerving, excited glow.

"It's my fault the split happened. But if I created it, I can fix it. I just need to find a common thread. Something that will tell me which Brume is the real one." I looked at the mirror again. Could it somehow be the solution to my problem? I pictured the rock as it flew into the mirror, to parts unknown. I thought of the other two Brumes and the impossible task that lay before me. Only . . . maybe I was making it seem more impossible than it really was. "Wait. You're wrong—no. No, I'm wrong."

The Stranger stood silent.

With an air of wonder, I said, "All three Brumes are real. My life hasn't been split. It's . . . more."

As I moved past Coe toward the front of the cave, where Caleb and Lia were sleeping, he chuckled. The sound of it echoed low off the cave walls, his fading words trailing it. "Don't forget. You get one life, fractured Quinn. Make it count."

When I glanced back, he was gone. Just as I'd expected him to be.

After shaking Caleb and Lia awake and directing them back to the mirror, I tried hard to explain what I'd been experiencing—how my life had become three lives, and all that was facing each one of me, the paradox that I'd created. I wasn't surprised to see the doubt in their eyes, or the quiet glances they exchanged as they questioned my sanity. I said, "I know how this sounds. But it's happening, I swear."

Lia took a moment before she spoke, as if choosing her words carefully. "Do you hear what you're asking us to believe, Quinn? Three different Brumes? Escaping some psycho camp? Fighting some war? It's . . . it's just a lot to take in without doubt."

"Look. We live in a place where monsters kill people indiscriminately. Where the town is surrounded by an inescapable wall of fog. Where a woman can walk into the high school and come out a bloodthirsty banshee." Sharp pain sliced through Lia's expression, but I had to say it. Like slapping someone to relieve their shock, sometimes pain helped anchor us to reality. I didn't mention that I had a hand in her mom's transformation. Hadn't I hurt her enough already? "If you can believe all of that to be real, what makes what I'm saying seem so farfetched?"

"I suppose it's possible," Caleb said, his tone soft, but

not indulgent, which I appreciated.

Lia looked up at the ceiling of the cave, as if the answers might be written there. Finding none, she sighed and met my eyes. "So what if it is real? What if you haven't lost your mind? What then?"

Straightening my shoulders in determination, I said, "I caused the paradox. So I have to resolve it. And I have to do it now, before the lantern dies and we're all reduced to nothing but blood and bits of bone. If the Rippers don't get us first, that is."

Caleb cocked an eyebrow. "But you can't—"

"I know. A paradox can't be resolved. But I have to try."

"Just how do you propose to do that?" Lia had drawn her arms up around herself, as if searching for warmth . . . or comfort.

I gestured to the back of the cave with a nod. "I'm going to enter the mirror and choose which life I want to live."

An invisible emotional wall went up in front of Lia. She shook her head. "You can't do that, Quinn. Even if it were possible to pass through a mirror's surface, even if some realm existed within it or beyond it, you can't just go into that thing and expect to survive. You have no idea what it really is."

Caleb said, "It's no ordinary mirror. We know that much."

Lia flashed Caleb a look that said he should stop trying

to help. “Are you really willing to risk your life based on wild guesses and Coe’s guidance?”

As calmly as I could, I said, “It’s more than that. It’s . . . this feeling I get.”

Throwing her arms up, she scoffed. “Seriously? A monster like Coe stalks you, and then, because your exhausted, confused, frightened brain tells you it’s a good idea, you’ve decided to throw yourself into a weird-ass floating mirror?”

Deciding to help me again, Caleb said, “Didn’t you say that Coe does both good and bad? What if this is one of the good things?”

Ignoring him, Lia met and held my gaze. I knew what she was thinking. If anyone could talk some sense into me, it was her. “My point is, I think we should maybe investigate this whole thing a bit before you trust it with your life, Quinn.”

“Which life, Lia? What’s there to investigate? Can you possibly tell me any more about the mirror than I already know? Can you come up with a better solution? Because that lantern is dying, Lia. And we will be too soon, if I don’t do something fast.” Aggravation pulsed through my veins.

“What if you’re wrong about creating the paradox? What if going through that mirror is the sort of thing that changed my mother into that shrieking banshee monster she became? What if . . .” Tears welled in her eyes. I struggled to recall if I'd ever seen Lia cry before in this Brume and came up empty. "What if I lose you too, Quinn? I don't think I have the strength to take the loss of your life as well."

"I'll be okay." I wasn't sure if I was lying. Even if I was, it'd be worth it just to quench her tears before they fell.

But fall they did.

My hands shaking in frustration, I ran my fingers through my hair, combing it away from my eyes. My chest felt tight, like my lungs weren't getting enough air. "Look. Coe said that the choice was mine, and that I have to choose. I can live whatever life I want. They're all real. If the mirror is a portal, somehow, to whatever life I pick, what choice do I have but to step through it?"

Lia folded her arms in front of her, shaking her head, her cheeks still wet. "This is crazy. Even if it works, even if you come out on the other side okay . . . how do you choose which life you want?"

"I have no idea." A sigh escaped me. "In the Brume where I present as a girl, I have to hide the most important parts of myself, or my parents will shut me out of their life. My whole world will come crashing down if I don't keep the fact that I'm genderqueer a secret from them. But my family is alive."

"And in the other Brume, where you present as a guy?" Caleb glanced from me to Lia and back, checking on her while he spoke.

"There I'm respected and confident, and changing the world for the better. But I have to hide who I am inside because too many people might lose that respect for me, and the Resistance could suffer, the entire country could fall under the control of a fascist regime." The light coming from the beginning of the cave, from our lantern, was fading fast. I could no longer smell burning sage. "Neither of them is great, but they each have their advantages."

Caleb began pacing slowly back and forth, his lips drawn in against his teeth, as if he were deep in thought.

"What about here?" Lia said. "What about this Brume? There's gloom and death all around us. There are Rippers and Screamers, violent gangs and the Unseen Hands. Your family's been taken from you. What could this life possibly offer you?" Lia had been raising her voice with every word, and by the time she finished speaking, she was practically shouting. Her skin had flushed pink. Her chest rose and fell in panicked breaths. She thought I was leaving her. Like her mother had left her. And the truth was, I didn't know if she was wrong to think it.

"True. It's ugly here. Downright terrifying at times. But at least here, I'm free to be myself out loud without judgment."

"I guess I just don't get it." She sounded hurt.

Caleb stopped pacing. His eyes lit up with something

resembling excitement. "Wait. Why not do what you can to change things in those lives? Find your people who'll stand by you, and come out? That way you can finally leave this Brume behind, but still have the freedom that comes with being out."

I imagined what it would be like to live a life without my parents accepting me for who I am. To live with friends—maybe those I'd made at Camp Redemption. What it would be like to be out and in charge of the Resistance. Maybe with enough resolve, I could change perceptions there. I didn't know. But even if I did reveal my true self to people in those other Brumes, there would always be that other thing.

"The problem is that monsters exist in every world." They both snapped their eyes to mine in horror. I knew what they were thinking, that I'd left out the part about the Unseen Hands being everywhere. But, in a way, what I'd meant was much worse. "Sometimes those monsters are Rippers. Sometimes they're people who'd hurt a person for being different. Sometimes they're turncoats and bloody acts of war. But there are monsters in every life. At least here I know how to fight them."

Lia and Caleb grew quiet for a long time. They both just stared at me, as if they'd discovered a new species and were desperately trying to understand its inner workings. It was Lia who broke the silence at last. Her voice was barely louder than a whisper. "But is that enough?"

Caleb furrowed his brow. "What about us? When you choose which life you want to live, what happens to Lia and me?"

The two of them exchanged looks of intermingled wonder and horror, but I could offer no words to comfort them. The truth was, I had no idea.

I thought about the mirror in each of the Brumes and wondered why it was the same in each world. If stepping through was the answer, then what was the question exactly? What question lay at the heart of the paradox?

Opening my eyes, I looked at my reflection and mused how three people could look into the same mirror and see the same person. How could we all be me? I didn't know the answer to that, but I had a feeling that if we each looked into the mirror at the same time, we might find it.

I leaned back against the cave wall and closed my eyes. "I don't know, Lia. But it's getting dark in here."

Outside, I heard a Ripper growl.

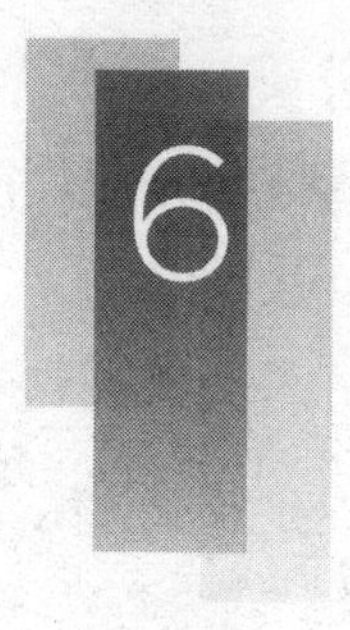

6

Breakfast was filled with laughter and smiles the next morning. Therapy with Dr. Hillard was fruitful. Reckoning was revealing. Prayers were said. Blessings were offered. All of us even managed hugs and well-wishes to Collins when his parents came to whisk away their newly healed son. There was growth spreading through Camp Redemption, despite—or perhaps because of—the darkness that had shrouded the evening before.

It was all bullshit.

Once postdinner duties had been finished, the remaining few of us retired to the rec room. Valerie made certain we were alone and in the clear, and then Randall set a pair of wire cutters on the spool table. "I nabbed these from the toolshed after lunch. Think they'll be enough to cut through the fence, if we need them to?"

I nodded. "The fence stops at the surface of the water, so we hopefully won't need them."

Valerie said, "I think we should bring them just in case. What if there's some other fencing material blocking our way? Better to be prepared, right?"

I pictured Dr. Hillard's hands on the padlock that held the door shut, keeping Lloyd inside. "What about bolt cutters? For the lock on the shed where they're keeping Lloyd?"

Randall held up a pair. "Gotcha covered."

Caleb placed some bills on the table. "I have fifty bucks. That should be enough to get us away from here. Not by much, but . . ."

"Here's my last twenty." Valerie added her money to his small pile.

Caleb said, "What about the security cameras?"

I said, "If we trip the breakers, it should knock out the power for a bit—maybe long enough to get us close."

"What about after we get out? Where do we go?" Randall's voice cracked in fear—fear that I was willing to bet we were all feeling.

It was all I could do to ignore the nightmare I'd had about

the cave and the mirror—about Coe—as I replied. "There's a pay phone outside the high school. I'll call my girlfriend to come pick us up."

We had a plan. Now we just needed to take action without getting caught.

It was a long, slow trek to Lloyd's prison. We stuck to the shadows, hiding the best we could. Randall managed to cut the wires to the camera by the opening in the fence over the creek. Maybe it would buy us time. When we reached the shack, Randall whispered, "Shit."

One of the larger staff members was sitting on a chair just outside the door. His arms were folded across his chest, and though at first glance he looked as if he might be slipping into a nap at any moment, further examination proved that he was squinting but alert, scanning the darkness for any sign of trouble.

Valerie's shoulders sank. "There's a guard? Since when?"

I sighed. "My guess? Since Lloyd wasn't miraculously obedient when they opened the door last night."

"What do we do now?" Randall shook his head slowly. Doubt clouded over us all.

With his jaw set, Caleb yanked the bolt cutters from Randall's hands and crept up behind the guard. He raised the tool high in the air and brought it down with a hard thwack. The man fell to the ground, unconscious.

Valerie gasped. "Jesus, Caleb! I thought we could throw a rock into the woods and draw him away or something. That was—"

"Effective, but scary?" Randall was looking at Caleb with what seemed like newfound respect, and maybe a healthy dose of fear.

But Caleb wasn't listening anymore. He'd come here to set Lloyd free, and that was what he was going to do, guard or no guard.

From within the shack came a small voice, peppered with coughs. "I hope you guys brought a rubber hose, a tub of Vaseline, and a live chicken, because I've had a lot of time to think in here, and I've got a few extracurricular ideas."

Caleb snapped the lock off and dropped the bolt cutters to the ground. As the door swung open, Lloyd collapsed out of his prison and into Caleb's arms. Caleb cradled him. "Come on, Lloyd. I've got you."

Lloyd looked into Caleb's eyes, unable to hold back the tears in his. "And here I thought I'd be saving you."

After a silent exchange between the two of them—one that was none of our business—we made our way to the creek. The water smelled fresh and clean. The earth was soft beneath my feet. Valerie went first, dipping into the water before holding her breath and swimming beneath the fence.

Randall followed. Caleb and Lloyd went together, but Caleb made certain that Lloyd got through to freedom before he did. They were all free, with just a fence, thick bushes, and water between us.

I stood on the bank, taking deep breaths, preparing myself. I couldn't swim, as I'd told Caleb before, but what I hadn't mentioned was how terrified of the water I was. Gathering all my strength and will, I jumped into the creek. After a moment, I dunked my head under the surface to get a feel for it, ready to be free of this damned place forever.

Damned. Like the staff here thought all queer people were. If we were, then so be it. Better to be damned for being honest than praised for telling lies.

The moment I came up for a big breath of air, a hand gripped the hair on the top of my head and pulled me from the water. The owner of that hand dragged me onto the creek bank. A large orderly stood over me with a scowl. Beside him were Alice and Dr. Hillard, looking as calm and certain and superior as ever. There was no way they'd missed seeing the others escape. Dr. Hillard said, "And on her forehead was written a name of mystery: 'Babylon the great, mother of prostitutes and of earth's abominations.'"

But I wasn't a mother. And I wasn't female. Not entirely.

"Quinn's not a girl. Not a guy either, really. They're kind of both. Or neither, depending on the day. Depending on a lot of

things, I guess." Lia's voice came through in my thoughts, bringing with it the sudden vivid memory of that world, that life. I was supposed to do something. Something the Quinn of that world was doing now. So that we could stop the . . . shifting.

"If you would please escort Quinn to her room, Roderick." Dr. Hillard began to turn away just as Roderick was dragging me to my feet, but turned back again with a light in his eyes—a light that scared the hell out of me. "On second thought, take the young lady to the Serenity Hut. It would seem she has much healing to accomplish."

There was something to be said for the strength of an oppressor, but quite something else for the strength of a person's resolve when they've been attacked. I planted my foot in Roderick's balls and shoved with all my might. He cried out, crumbling backward. The moment I was free, I dived back into the creek. A strong hand grabbed my arm and pulled. I looked up at Dr. Hillard. His eyes flashed with vile, unhinged hatred. "You will be cleansed, whore! If not through the will of God that has been stowed upon me, then by baptism in his holy name!"

With his free hand, he pushed my head into the water, holding me there, his fingers tangled in my hair. My lungs burned. I tried to scream, but only bubbles emerged. I wriggled free enough to take a breath, and before I was plunged back under, I heard his babble of insanity—the final sound to reach my ears before I would die, I just knew it. "We ask forgiveness for this child, oh Lord, that she may be welcomed into your heavenly arms this very night!"

Under I went again, gulping in mouthfuls of water. My head swam. I was drowning. I was dying.

From within me, I felt the two other Quinns urging me on. Fight. Fight, they said.

Turning my head, I sank my teeth deep into Dr. Hillard's arm. In shock and pain, he released his grip. I grabbed a quick breath of air and dived under once more, pushing my fear of the water away long enough to get under the fence and come up on the other side. Once I was there, my friends pulled me to safety.

Dripping wet and shaking, we hurried to the center of town. Once at the school, the six of us went to the pay phone right outside. There was strength in numbers, after all, and we weren't guaranteed safety just yet.

I dialed zero for the operator and placed a collect call to Lia. Every second that passed as the phone rang stretched out into eternity. We were almost safe. I had no idea what was ahead of us, but at least we weren't at Camp Redemption anymore.

"Hello?" Her voice filled me with joy. Lia. At long last.

"Lia! Can you come get me? I mean us. My friends and I

broke out of Camp Redemption. We're at the school."

Her tone reminded me of the sunrise—bright and promising. "Oh my God, Quinn! I'm so glad you're okay! Of course I'll come."

Flashing a grin at Valerie, I said, "She's coming."

"Oh good!" Valerie was grinning too. It was refreshing to see true happiness on her face. I hadn't realized how muted her smile had been back at the camp. There was joy in freedom.

Lia broke in. "Who's that?"

"That was Valerie. You'll like her, I promise." My cheeks hurt, I was smiling so much.

"Did you break out with a bunch of lesbians? That's phenomenal. Like some kind of lesbian prison gang." Lia laughed and so did I.

I said, "Not exactly. There are six of us here and we're all over the LGBTQIA spectrum. So we're more like a renegade queer squad."

The phone went silent. Worry filled me that the call had been dropped. "Lia? Are you still there?"

The silence stretched on, and just when I was about to hang up and call again, Lia said, "Yeah. I just . . . y'know, you're clearly shaken up after your time in there with all those confused people. Once I get there and get you safely away from all of them, we can talk about this again."

My chest tightened sharply. My voice came out hushed—probably because I couldn't fill my lungs with air. Shock was suffocating me. "None of us are confused. I know more about myself now than before I went to that awful place."

"It's just . . ." Her tone was careful, almost like she was speaking with someone who was on the verge of a mental breakdown. "Those people are really delusional, Quinn. I hope you know that."

Those people. Meaning my new friends. Meaning . . . me.

"Lia . . ." Words froze on my tongue and dissolved. It took me a while to speak again. The silence hung heavy between us. When I spoke, I turned away from Valerie so that maybe she wouldn't hear the conversation. "How can you be so closed-minded? There's nothing wrong with *anyone* under the queer umbrella."

There was a distinct pause before she said, "What did they do to you at that place?"

"What do you mean?"

She sighed, and when she spoke again, her words were painted with what sounded like frustration. "I mean it sounds like your new friends filled your head with a bunch of crap. I worried you'd change while you were there, but I never expected this."

"Neither did I. Not from you."

"Listen, I want to be here for you, but I refuse to be there for the people who messed with your head. You said they were all over the 'LGBTQIA spectrum.' Do you even hear yourself right now? You do know that all these people who are trying to jump on the gay and lesbian bandwagon because it's cool are just moving the fight for our rights backward, don't you?"

My fingers tightened around the receiver. "What are you talking about? It's the same fight."

"Puh-lease. We were finally gaining some ground and then all this bathroom law bullshit came up and now our rights are being threatened all over again."

I couldn't believe what I was hearing. Lia had always been outspoken and opinionated, but I'd always thought when she was speaking about "our" rights, she meant everyone on the queer spectrum. "Were they ever not threatened? It's a day-to-day fight for acceptance, Lia. I don't understand why you're placing the blame on trans people. We're in this fight together."

Suddenly her tone wasn't the sunrise. It was bleak and empty, like darkness in the desert. "Look. I'm not going to argue with you about the effect trans people are having on the rights of gays and lesbians. I'm just not. We both know the *T* in that initialism never should've been added in the first place."

So that's what the love of my life thought of me. She

didn't know I was genderqueer—how could she? But whether or not she knew, how could anyone be such a closed-minded asshole? "Stop it. I don't even know who you are right now. How could you say those things?"

"Because it's the truth! Shit, Quinn, what is wrong with you? You're talking like some brainwashed idiot." Her words were venomous. It was like speaking with someone I'd never met before. "Y'know what? Call your brother. I just remembered I'm not in the mood to do you any favors."

"Lia—" The phone went dead. The tightness in my chest had given way to pain. After returning the receiver, I looked at my friends, hoping they hadn't heard—especially Valerie—but knowing they'd probably heard enough. "She's not coming. We . . . we need a new plan."

Valerie wrapped her arms around me in a hug that I very much needed. She was probably the only person in my life who could truly understand what I was going through. As we parted, she said, "It's okay, Quinn. It's really okay. All of it."

It wasn't okay. It was so far from okay that it couldn't even see okay on the horizon. I was in shock, for sure. You think you know a person. But people could always manage to surprise you—both in good ways and bad.

Lloyd looked more solemn than ever. He squeezed my shoulder and said, "We'll think of something. Why don't we sit at one of the picnic tables in the park and talk it over?"

The park. The cave. The mirror. That's what the other Quinn was doing. That's what I was supposed to do now. Enter the cave. Look at my reflection. Search it for answers.

Meeting Lloyd's eyes, I said, "Let's go to the cave instead."

The walk across the street and through the park to the cave felt like it passed in slow motion. Valerie and I didn't talk. The others exchanged quiet conversation, but I couldn't hear what they were saying. I was too focused on two memories of the other Quinns filling my head. Lloyd ripping his shoulder free from the crossbow arrow. Kai moving methodically down a line of soldiers, killing them off one bullet at a time. On their heels was a question. The question that the other Quinn, the one facing the mirror now, had asked.

How could three people look into a mirror and see the same person? The answer, I determined, was within the mirror.

It had to be.

“Does it, now?”

I looked to my right to find the Stranger sitting next to me in the hall, once again wearing filthy scrubs. The loud, high tone that signaled that Lloyd was dying blared in my ears. My face was still slick with my tears and Lloyd’s blood. The mixture stung my eyes. At the moment, I didn’t give a damn about whatever riddle the Stranger had brought me. I just wanted to be alone. “What are you babbling about?”

“You, but not you, but still you, were about to enter the cave and musing whether or not they . . .” He clucked his tongue, admonishing himself. "You. Whether or not *you* would find the answer you seek in the mirror."

The image of a long, black tongue caressing my cheek filled my mind. It was so vivid, I could almost feel it now. I shuddered and considered how different each of my realities were.

"Not completely different." He lit a cigarette with what I recognized to be my lighter and then returned the lighter to his front shirt pocket. "As I told you before, certain things are immutable."

"Lia." My voice was gruff from crying.

"Not just Lia." He took a drag and exhaled it in words that gave me a chill. "And not just me."

My head was pounding, but not enough that I couldn't think clearly. I sat up straight with realization. "The mirror. The mirror is a constant. That has to mean something."

"Does anything?" Coe turned his eyes to the open door, to the room where Lloyd lay dying, perhaps dead already.

The shoulders of the people surrounding the operating table sagged in defeat. Machines were turned off. A nurse scribbled something on a clipboard. The time of death, I assumed.

Lloyd was dead. In two realities, Lloyd was dead.

In two realities, it was my fault.

* * *

The coin spun in circles, wobbled a bit, and then fell on my desktop with a clink. Pinching it between my forefinger and thumb, I spun it again and watched the silver blur. It wasn't *something* to do while people readied a grave for Lloyd's body outside, not fifty yards from where I was sitting. It was more that it was *nothing* to do. That was all I wanted at the moment. Just a little nothing amid all the painful something.

I couldn't go outside and watch them dig the grave. Not this grave. I couldn't watch them lower the sheet-wrapped body down into it and cover it with dirt. Not Lloyd's body. And I damn sure couldn't listen to the proud, loving words that people would say about him. The sensation in my chest was an unbearable fullness, as if I were ready to burst from sorrow. If I attended his funeral, I might just lose my mind.

I could feel the other Quinns urging me to go to the mirror, to gaze at my—our—reflection. Go, they said. The answer is there.

But I didn't much give a fuck about finding how to stop the shifts from one reality to the next. What was the point? In every life, I'd feel alone. In every life, I'd have horrors to face. And what made me so worthy of being rescued from this endless maze? I was a monster.

Still pinned to the map on my wall was that small piece of paper on which I had, at some point that I couldn't recall, written "You can't run from the monster. The monster is you." I looked at it for a good, long time, reading it over and over again, trying hard to absorb its meaning. Had I been running from myself? Had I been struggling with facing the reality of who and what I was? If I was honest with myself, the answer was a resounding yes. Fear had held me back for so long—fear of judgment, fear of rejection. But I'd kept on running, stayed quiet about being genderqueer, fell in line, kept my secret. But sooner or later, the monster was going to catch up with me. Because I couldn't run from myself no matter how hard I tried. I had to face my truth. It was the only path to truly being free.

My thoughts drifted to the mirror. Why were the other Quinns so certain I needed to enter the cave, to gaze into the mirror's surface? Did the truth of my shifting realities lie within my reflection? Or was it something more?

Inside my heart I felt a tug of understanding. How could three people each look into a mirror and see the same person?

They couldn't . . . could they? Could we?

With a timid step, Susan entered my office, a mug in her hand. Steam wafted up from its contents. She eyed me warily, and when she spoke, her voice shook. I wasn't the only one mourning. She said, "I brought you some coffee."

"Thank you." I kept my tone calm and kind, even though I was feeling anything but. The coffee smelled wonderful—perhaps more so because I hadn't eaten or drank anything since the day before. The day that Lloyd had died. "Is . . . is everything going okay out there?"

"The service is over. It was beautiful."

She didn't say "You should've been there," or anything else that would have made me feel like shit. She understood why I hadn't gone. Without me even explaining it, she understood.

Approaching with careful steps, she placed the mug on the desk in front of me and took a seat. "I'm so sorry, Quinn. About Lloyd, about Kai, about Caleb . . . about Lia. I wish—"

"Stop." Susan knew about Lia. Which meant that everyone did. I closed my eyes, and, in a whisper, I said, "Just be here. Just be here with me right now. I need a friend."

"Of course." The words came out without hesitation.

"I was wrong about you." I didn't meet her eyes. Like a coward, I couldn't meet them. "You're fully capable of going into battle. You're capable of so much more than so many in Brume think. The fact that you're a woman doesn't matter, and I should have voiced that before."

Susan hesitated. "I . . . I appreciate you saying so, sir."

"Quinn."

Taken aback, her tone softened. "Pardon me, sir?"

I looked her in the eye. "We're friends, right? Call me Quinn."

"Quinn . . ." She rolled the name off her tongue as if feeling it out. Then she said, "Intel's come back that the Allegiance is making plans to double down their efforts here in Brume. More soldiers. More weapons. And they're moving fast. With Caleb and Kai dead, they're out for blood. They want revenge. Resistance members are afraid. Everyone is. They're losing hope of ever achieving peace."

Peace. All I ever wanted was peace.

I was done running. I'd never be able to stop the fighting here. Could never bring the peace to my people that they so richly deserved. Not until I found peace on my own. Hard as it was, I had to admit to myself that I knew how to achieve my own peace. And if I accomplished that, maybe they could all feel at peace as well.

"Quinn?" Susan's words were a concerned whisper. "You went pale just then. Are you okay?"

At last, I raised my eyes to meet her gaze, a weary smile on my face. "I'm fine. I just wanted to apologize for not treating you right when I had the chance."

"I . . . Yes. Of course, sir." Sir. Some habits were hard to break.

I stared for a moment at my reflection in the coffee mug. Then, with a decisive nod, I stood and moved out the door without another word. On guard duty was Gregg—a soldier in his fifties who had never failed me in the past, despite his initial reluctance at following such a young leader. On my way out, I told him, "Whatever you do, don't let anyone follow me."

"Sir?"

I barked over my shoulder, "Don't question my orders, soldier. Just do it."

It wasn't a time for explanations or discussion. It was a time for action. With determined steps, I moved across the street, toward the entrance of the cave.

Caleb was looking at me like I'd stopped speaking midsentence. Behind him and Lia was the mirror.

Blinking, I said, "I think the other Quinns are on their way to the mirror. The soldier Quinn definitely remembers us. The other is starting to. It's working."

Lia's jaw dropped. "You're going to risk your life on what could be a delusion?"

But her fears were baseless. They had to be. This was it. I had my answer. Only by entering the mirror could my life be my own. Or it would end . . . but I was betting on my gut feeling—on my keen instincts—that I was right and my chosen life lay waiting on the other side of chaos. "I'm going in, Lia. With or without your approval."

As I stepped forward, Lia grabbed my arm, but Caleb pulled her away from me and met my eyes, nodding his support. Maybe Lia couldn't trust what I was about to try, but Caleb had my back—something I never would've guessed when we first met. It didn't matter if he believed me about Coe and the reality shifts or not. This was my journey, my decision, my risk. Caleb got that. And though I wished Lia understood, I was beyond that now. I'd made my decision. I was ready.

Stepping forward, and ignoring Lia's cries, I took a deep breath, hoping like hell I'd made the right choice in which life I wanted to live.

Randall and Valerie stood close together to stay warm in the surprisingly cool cave. Caleb had a smile on his face and Lloyd's arms around him. As they chatted, debating where we should go and what to do once we got there, I made my way to the back of the cave alone. The moment I laid eyes on the mirror, every moment of my other lives, my other existences, came into crystal-clear focus.

"It's about time. Forgive me, the other Quinns are a tad keener than you." Coe, disguised as the Stranger, with his snakeskin trench coat and nicotine-stained fingers, sucked on his cigarette as he leaned with his back against the cave wall. "I was beginning to wonder if you'd ever make the connections."

My voice was hushed. "I know you. You're a . . . a . . ."

"God? In a manner of speaking, I suppose." If I wasn't mistaken, the ghost of a smile had appeared on his face.

I snapped, "I was going to say 'a monster.'"

Coe shrugged. "Gods and monsters. There's such little difference, really. Mostly a matter of opinion."

Shaking my head, I said, "This whole time. And you're not even a person."

A low chuckle rattled out of him. "Who is? All the world's a graveyard and the people merely corpses."

I swallowed hard. "As I understand it, I have a choice to make. Survivor, soldier, or myself as I am now. But we're all the same. We're . . . I'm . . . genderqueer, and have a choice to make about which life I choose to live."

Sweeping his arm across in a grand gesture, he said, "Never let it be said that a late essay doesn't deserve the highest merit."

It made total sense to me now that I'd felt an immediate connection with Valerie. She was transgender, as was I. She was MTF, or male-to-female; I was genderqueer. We shared an umbrella. We shared a cause.

The other Quinns and I shared a cause as well. We wanted peace. They were at the mirror now, waiting for me.

No, I thought. *We aren't a plural they. I'm a singular they. And that means I contain multitudes.*

I looked down at my bracelet and thought of Kai—of how he loved me, but couldn't help me the way he wanted to, the way I needed him to. I had a choice in front of me. Which life to live, despite the pitfalls. More than anything, I wanted to live a life where I was loved and happiness was worth the fight for it.

When I raised my eyes again, Coe was gone. Of course.

Smiling, I said, "It's time, Coe. I'm ready."

The mirror looked so much bigger than it had before. Or maybe it was just a trick of my eyes. Its surface gleamed. Its frame appeared sharper at the edges. If I hadn't felt so unsettled by the sight of it, it might have been a beautiful thing to behold.

I was so tired. So very, very tired. Maybe it was exhaustion from fighting the war against the Allegiance, or maybe it was something else.

Coe spoke from behind me, "You're finally facing the mirror."

"As you knew I would, I'm sure."

"Have you determined what it is yet?"

"It's a puzzle piece."

He stepped up beside me, so that I could see him in my peripheral vision. It looked like he was smiling. "But where's the puzzle?"

"I'm the puzzle." Jesus. I was beginning to sound like Coe. "And the picture is starting to come into focus."

Coe took a long drag off a cigarette that I hadn't noticed until now. "Picture?"

"Of course. It's always easier to complete a puzzle when you know what the final picture will be." Biting my bottom lip, I traced the frame of the mirror with my eyes before finally setting my gaze on my reflection. "The only question is, how do I tell which of the three pictures is the real one?"

He paused, as if waiting for me to continue. When I didn't, he said, "That would be a very good question, if . . ."

My chest grew tight. It took me the span of two heartbeats to realize I'd been holding my breath. "If I were looking for three different pieces. But I'm not, am I?"

Coe didn't speak.

"All three mirrors are the same piece of the puzzle, aren't they?" I had it then, I was sure of it. The answer to the question of which life I wanted to live, and how to choose it. I had to enter the mirror. It sounded absurd, but so did the notion of living three different lives. "It's not about the mirrors at all, is it? It's about the person reflected in them. In all of them. Because we're all the same person."

The corners of his mouth curled into an approving smile. "That could be a dangerous assumption."

Within the mirror was the reflection of all three versions of myself. Three Quinns stood together, looking back at me. All three Quinns that I knew I was. The Quinn I was here. The one who presented as female. The Quinn who openly presented as genderqueer. There were people I cared about in each life, but only one life could be mine.

"You're right. It could." I turned to face him and held his gaze, hoping he'd see the sincerity in mine. "But danger's never stopped me before."

Backing into the mirror, I kept my eyes on the Stranger until I could see him no more.

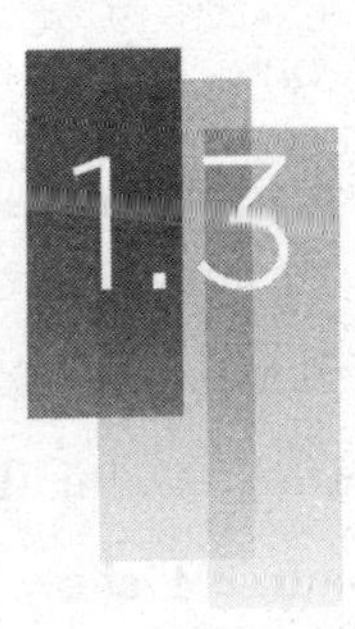

Blocking out Lia's cries, I approached the mirror, but paused to look at my reflection. Reflections. Three Quinns now looked back at me. All three Quinns that I knew that I was. The Quinn I was here. The one who presented as male. The Quinn who presented as female. There were people I cared about in each life, but only one life could be mine.

None of us looked like monsters, even though we'd each felt that way at times. But maybe we were—at least parts of us. Maybe everyone had something monstrous about them, and survival sometimes depended on tapping into our monstrous side. Maybe the key to happiness was to learn to love every aspect of yourself, monster or not.

Nervous at what to expect—and not knowing if I could trust a single word that Coe had uttered in all this time—I stepped through the shimmering surface to the other side.

Colors bled all around me as I moved forward, leaving Caleb and Lia behind in the cave. The silver of the glass melted away, while purples, greens, and white swirled all around me in an indefinable space. There was a distinct absence of sound—even my breath was eerily silent. Everything that wasn't me churned into a metallic rainbow. It looked as if I were standing in a torrent of wind, but I felt no breeze on my skin, no rustling of my hair. For a moment, I froze, uncertain of what to do next.

Was this it? Was this oblivion? Had I stepped from the realm of existence to one of nonexistence? Had I died?

My chest rose and fell in quick, worried breaths. My heart thumped against my rib cage. I was alive. I had to be. So what did this mean? Where was I?

Where the hell was I?

I crept close to the mirror, my eyes fixed on it. When I stretched out my hand toward it, the tips of my fingers caused a ripple effect on its surface, as if the glass were liquid. A terrifying thought occupied my mind. What if I drowned? What if this was the end of me, rather than the beginning? I very nearly backed away from it, but then I thought about the decision I had made, and I stepped forward, ready to enter.

Within it was the reflection of all three versions of myself. Three Quinns stood together, looking back at me. All three Quinns that I knew that I was. The Quinn I was here. The one who presented as male. The one who presented openly as genderqueer. There were people I cared about in each life, but only one life could be mine—and I was ready to live it. I wasn't running from the monster anymore. I was facing it head-on. Facing my fears. Facing my truth. Even though it scared me.

The mirror surface churned, looking too much like water. Dr. Hillard's words flitted through my mind. *"We ask forgiveness for this child, oh Lord, that she may be welcomed into your heavenly arms this very night!"*

My heart rate had picked up as I moved forward. It felt as if I were falling rather than walking. Tumbling through the cave toward the surface of the mirror. My body rolled and I saw Coe standing in the cave, a smile on his face. For a brief flash, I locked eyes with him. He said something—I could see his lips moving—but I couldn't hear him. My body broke the surface of the mirror, but the glass didn't break. I plunged into it and the silvery liquid enveloped me. It felt more like knives on my skin than fluid. I tried to gulp in air, but there was nothing to breathe in but water and more water, filling my lungs with a heaviness that sent a wave of panic through me.

I was drowning.

Colors swirled around me, encircling my limbs, my torso. They entered my nose, my mouth, my ears. Soon there would be no more Quinn. There would be only the mirror.

And I would be the mirror too.

The surface of the water was ahead of me, and I willed my body toward it. My lungs felt as if they were being crushed. But freedom was there—my choice had been made. There was only living ahead of me now. I wasn't dying. I was choosing to live.

I stretched out my hand, so close to touching the air I so desperately needed, the life that I wanted.

Sound left me as I backed into the mirror. Touch, taste—all but sight. Colors swirled around my uniformed body. My senses were a calm blur. The sensation reminded me of the quiet moments after a battle had ended, when all that's left to do is count your blessings. But this was no war. This was a choice. And I knew that I was choosing the right life for me.

Peace. All I ever wanted was peace. Who knew that it had been waiting within the surface of a strange mirror the entire time?

Coe had. But this wasn't about him.

It wasn't about Lia. Or Caleb. Or Kai. Or anyone else.

This was about me.

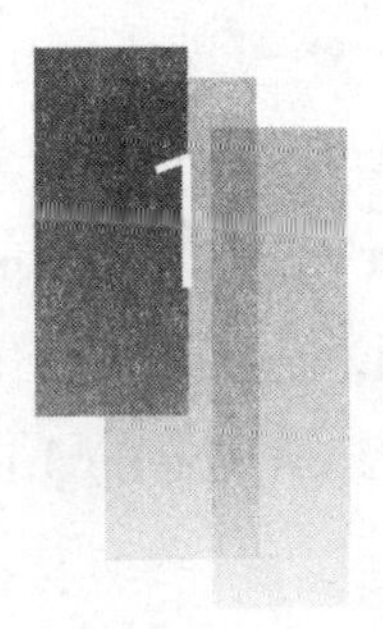

The area above my head solidified in a brief, impossible image—a whirlpool of colored water. A girl fell through the liquid to the ground in front of me, coughing and gasping for air. The water was washed away again by the chaos of the place. Her hair was dry, as were her clothes, and when our eyes met, the terror that I'd seen in hers dissolved in an instant. Familiarity washed over us both.

She was me, and I was her. Of that, there could be no doubt. Her very presence made me feel somewhat more solid.

As she stood, I stretched out my hand, and she mirrored my movement with her own. We were so close to touching,

I could feel the heat of her on my skin. Just an inch apart, we each hesitated. She smiled, her lips lush and pink, and offered an understanding nod. This was it. This was real. I wasn't dead. I was more alive than I had ever been.

We intertwined our fingers, holding hands as we gazed into each other's eyes. I loved her, this girl. I'd always loved her—I knew that now.

Her body began to dissolve into nebulous specks of lavender. It started with her feet and moved upward, toward the hand I held. Instinct made me tighten my grip on her, but I knew it wouldn't make a difference. As she disappeared, a tear escaped my eye and rolled down my cheek. It wasn't sadness that brought the tear, but a strange sense of joy. Her smile never ceased—even as she vanished into nothing . . . into everything.

There was movement just to my right, and when I turned, I saw a man in a tattered uniform, backing into this place between places. I knew him. Of course I knew him. And loved him. Like the girl, he was a part of me . . . and real.

When he turned to examine the mirror he'd entered, he noticed me too. For a moment, he seemed stunned, but then an understanding smile touched his lips. He gave a salute, which I returned. Much like the girl, he began to dissolve into flecks of color from the feet up. As his undoing reached his face, he offered me a reassuring wink. Then he was gone.

I was the only one left. Just me. But it had been that way the entire time. I knew that now. There was only me. There had only ever been me. No matter what body I had occupied. No matter what life I had lived.

The swirling space around me ceased its movement at once, solidifying into walls that cracked and fell away, revealing coarse rock. I was back in the cave, and the mirror was gone. A single shard of it lay on the cave floor. Caleb and Lia were nowhere to be seen.

I didn't need to be told that I wasn't alone. Turning to face Coe, I said, "You're a sadistic son of a bitch, ya know that?"

"I'm no one's son." Coe the Stranger grinned. Something black and quivering crawled across his upper teeth. It was the first time I'd seen him without a cigarette. I wondered if his need for it had been satiated by something else.

A mixture of anger and relief filled me, but there was something else too. I was grateful. For the journey, for the experience. But mostly, for my life—flaws and all. "Why? Why all of this only to bring me here?"

"I didn't bring you anywhere. You did." He cocked his head slightly, holding my gaze. "That is, if you went somewhere in the first place."

I pressed my lips into a thin, hard line. "What about Lia's mom? Did you change her into that . . . that thing? Did you send her after Lia?"

His response crawled from his throat in a low rumble. "Everything that she had been in the past was her doing—just as everything she did after she'd transformed."

"And the transformation itself? Were you responsible for that?"

"I was, and I take great pride in my work. I pull out of a person that which plagues, haunts, rots them from the inside, and make them face it head-on. Look how well it's turned out for you."

Bristling, I glanced past him to a familiar shape on the ground just yards away. My bat. It was as if it were welcoming me home and offering a potential solution to the problem standing in front of me. "Name one way that you've helped me, Coe. You made my life a living hell for your personal amusement."

"Make no mistake, mended Quinn. I am not amused." His dark eyes were fire as insult built up inside of him. "Because of my work, it's become clear to you that this Brume, this life, for all its challenges, is your home. You learned that you are strong enough to continue on without your family or their approval. But most importantly, you've finally realized that as painful as it might be, it's better to be alone than to chase affection from someone who doesn't love you that way."

"I could have come to all of that without questioning my sanity."

"No. You couldn't. Or else you would have." He cocked a knowing eyebrow. "I don't play the game. I merely set the board when the player is in need of it and help them to discover their truest nature."

I shook my head. "You're a monster."

He spoke with a biting tone. "Am I, now?"

"If you're not a monster, then what are you?"

His calm demeanor returned at once. "I am you."

I furrowed my brow in confusion. "Then who am I?"

"You are me." A hint of a knowing smile crossed his lips, but it didn't last for long. I had a feeling he wasn't screwing with me. "We are Coe. In the end, we are all Coe."

"I don't understand, you self-indulgent psychopath!" I gripped him by the lapels and shook, but he didn't budge.

Coe had only brief silence to offer me as a response.

Releasing the lapels of his coat, I took in an angry, shaking breath. "How long have I been shifting between realities?"

"Twenty-four hours precisely."

Stunned silence filled me. "That can't be right. It's been weeks, at least."

"Perception is everything. For instance, you perceive me to be a monster, but which of us murdered their own brother? Which of us severed Lloyd's jugular vein and watched him bleed to death?" His words slipped out in a tone that bordered on gleeful. "You perceive that we are nothing alike, yet we both felt the joy of Lia's lips pressed against yours. You also perceive that you didn't choose this journey. That it chose you."

I held his gaze, my words crisp. "How am I supposed to trust what's real and what isn't?"

"What is the concept of real, but another perception?"

My chest heaved. My face flushed with the heat of anger. "I hate you."

"I know." It didn't seem to bother or delight him. He reacted as if hatred was just another state of being.

A shimmer caught my attention briefly. The single shard of the mirror that lay on the cave floor. It was like a message from my other selves, to end this forever. "I'm not walking out of here while you're still alive, Coe. I can't. I won't."

"Do your worst. Do your best. They are, after all, one and the same." He spread his arms wide and bowed, tilting his face up so he could offer me a reassuring smile. He knew what was coming, what I was about to do. For Coe, there were no surprises.

Plucking the shard of glass from the cave floor, I ignored the way the edges cut into my palm and whipped my hand forward, stabbing it into Coe's chest. He howled—the sound of his pain was metallic and echoed off the walls of the cave—but he didn't retaliate. The Stranger's skin morphed from human to black snakeskin and back again. His face contorted in pain, and then that too changed. The featureless mask appeared. His arms stretched out until they were spindly. I stared in horrified fascination as he fell back against the wall of the cave, the weapon still in my hand, dripping with his blood.

As his shape settled back into the person I called the Stranger, I noticed black liquid pouring out from between his fingers as he clutched the wound. His breathing was labored. When he looked at me, a strange sense of pride settled on his features. "Ask for me tomorrow, and you shall find me a grave man."

"What?"

"Oh, that's right. You don't know Shakespeare. Not here you don't." Wincing at the pain, he stumbled forward and fell to the ground.

"I'm sorry." It was a lie and we both knew it. Kneeling at his side, I said, "I just can't let you hurt anyone anymore. It has to end."

Coe chuckled, sending bubbles of black fluid down his chin. When he smiled, I could see his teeth were coated in the stuff. "There is no end. There is only understanding."

The whites of his eyes filled with black until they were all unseeing darkness. He said, "Goodbye, Coe. For now."

My voice caught in my throat for a moment. "You're Coe. I'm Quinn, remember?"

"They are one and the same. And we are a monster."

"No. That's not right." The words left my mouth in a

whisper. I thought back to when this all had begun, and the feelings that those events had stirred up within me. But one feeling stood out among all the rest. "You and I are not interchangeable—you represent the darkest part of me, a part we all have inside, but you only came out of me and into existence because of what my parents did."

I'd altered my reality. First, by changing this Brume. Then, when it wasn't enough to keep my pain at bay, I'd broken my life into three. I'd created the wall of fog, the monsters, the camp, the war . . . but I must have done so to shield myself from the monstrous acts of my family. But then the new worlds I'd created grew to be more than I could handle, and the dangers I was forced to face at the jaws of a Ripper and the like were far worse than what I'd been running from—my memories. I hadn't done any of it on purpose, or with intent to harm anyone. I was just trying to protect myself from pain. It was instinctual. And Coe . . . Coe had been feeding on that pain. But his meal was done now. I'd faced my truth. I realized that my family's reaction to my truth wasn't a reflection of who I was. It simply *was*. I couldn't change it. I couldn't run from it forever. But I could acknowledge the trauma of that rejection and move forward with newfound wisdom.

A small, warm tear rolled down my cheek at my realization. "I'm not a monster, Coe. Even if sometimes I might worry that I am."

"It's been a pleasure, wise Quinn." He went still, eyes open, and I knew that he was gone. I'd killed him. I'd killed Coe.

My heart ached. My being ached. Even though relief had flooded my every cell.

Vindicated. Justified. Right. Those were all things that I had expected to feel upon Coe's death, but I felt none of them. Strange enough, what I felt was . . . pity.

With gentle fingers, I closed the lids over his eyes. His body liquefied then—black, shiny ooze painting the cave floor. Then it suddenly dissolved, filling the small space with a haze that dissipated just as quickly.

With newfound strength, I stood and exited the cave into the morning gray. Waiting for me were Lia and Caleb. As I approached, Caleb reached over and took Lia's hand in his, giving it a gentle squeeze that she returned with a smile. Lia's voice filled with wonder. "Do you see that?"

Caleb's jaw dropped in disbelief. "My God. The wall of fog. It's . . . it's clearing."

I watched the gloom with fragile hope. It looked as if it *was* clearing—just as Coe's haze had a moment ago. But I didn't trust it. That is, not until I saw the street signs on top of the stop sign, which read Taylor Drive and Oaks Avenue . . . and the buildings beyond.

We were free.

I was free.

ACKNOWLEDGMENTS

After publishing so many books, you'd think it'd be easier for me to name and thank all the many wonderful people who helped me out along the way, but the truth is, it never gets any easier—which is a blessing, really. I'm surrounded by so many supportive people. Family, friends, business acquaintances, librarians in the trenches, teachers . . . how am I supposed to thank them—you—all in a couple of paragraphs? The answer is . . . I can't. But I'm damn sure going to try.

Unending thanks to my brilliant and ever-so-patient editor, Andrew Eliopulos, who guided me through every inch of making this book work. Without you, Andrew, Quinn simply would not be Quinn, and I'd probably be lost in the wall of fog. You've been a wonderful friend and your unfailing belief in me is a beacon in my life. Here's to new worlds that we'll build together, and all the good that will come of our collective hard work.

To my fabulous agent, Michael Bourret: MB, you've been an enormous part of my career—and better, my life—for over fourteen years as of the first publication of this book. You've cheered with me during the good times and given me a shoulder to cry on during the bad times. In short, you've always been there for me, and I hope you know that I'll always be there for you too. Keep up the good work, Jiminy. Because I need you in my life.

No worries, Minion Horde, I haven't forgotten about you. Whether you're a first-gen Minion or new to our weird little family, you inspire me every day to keep going, keep fighting, keep trying, keep living. I owe you so much. From my li'l black heart to yours, every word I write is for you. Thanks for having my back, as always. I'm hugging you all with my squishy, squishy brain.

To all my friends—and it fills my heart with astonished glee to know that I have so many . . . too many, in fact, to list you all here—you've supported me in ways that I did not realize one could be supported. Thank you, from both current me and that teen me who didn't have any friends. Each one of you is a positive ripple in the pond of life.

And finally, I owe unfailing gratitude to my family, the Brewer clan. Alex, you inspire me every day to keep laughing no matter what I'm dealing with and remind me when it's time for swearing and when it's time for hugs. Jacob, you inspire me to be strong in the wake of any storm and to know my truth and embrace it fully. And my dearest Paul . . . life is full of roses and thorns, my love, and though it's not always easy to walk through the garden, I'm so glad to be walking through it with you. You've all been there for me even when I couldn't be there for myself. I'm alive because of me, but I enjoy living because of you. Thank you. For both your love . . . and the many, many cups of Starbucks you provided during the creation of this tale. What's all we got, fam? Because that's all we need.